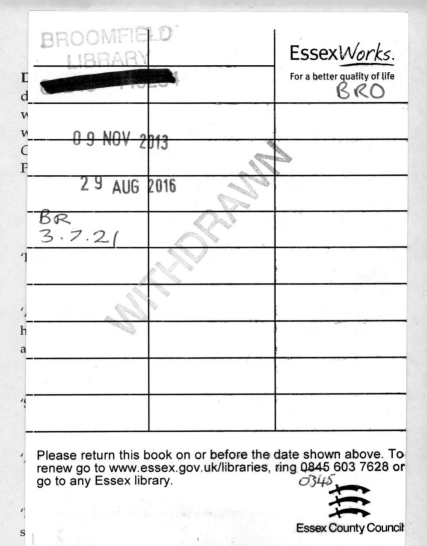

'Lovers of British mysteries will enjoy Powerscourt's latest
adventure.'

ist

D1339882

Titles in the series
(listed in order of publication)

Death at the
Jesus Hospital

DAVID DICKINSON

CRIME

CONSTABLE
&ROBINSON

Constable & Robinson Ltd
55–56 Russell Square
London WC1B 4HP
www.constablerobinson.com

First published in the UK by Constable,
an imprint of Constable & Robinson, 2012

This paperback edition published by Robinson, 2013

A copy of the British Library Cataloguing in Publication
Data is available from the British Library

ISBN 978-1-78033-031-0 (paperback)
ISBN 978-1-78033-030-3 (ebook)

Printed and bound in the UK

1 3 5 7 9 10 8 6 4 2

For Sheila and Helen, and in memory of Alan

PART ONE

THE ROSE AND CROWN

1

When there is no moon in January the dawn creeps in very slowly like the second hand on a clock that is running slow. By the River Thames at Marlow in Buckinghamshire, some twenty miles from London, the trees reveal themselves gradually. The water in the river begins to show its patterns and its ripples. The screeches of the owls, strident and imperious, fall away. In the great houses by the water's edge the housemaids are awake early, cleaning out last night's fires and preparing new ones. The kitchen staff are beginning work on the servants' breakfast, always served before the master and his family in the servants' hall. A couple of early risers could be seen striding towards the railway station to catch the first train to the capital.

Some in the Jesus Hospital on the outskirts of the little town were also awake early on this morning, the twenty-second of the month. It is neither a church nor a chapel, nor are the sick healed within its red brick walls. Jesus Hospital is an almshouse, founded in the early seventeenth century by a rich London merchant called Thomas Gresham whose portrait hangs in state in the dining hall,

all black cloak and feathered hat. In shape, the hospital resembles the court of many a Cambridge college, also built around this time, a rectangular structure of two storeys whose walls are now covered in red ivy. Twenty male persons over the age of sixty are resident here, each man with a small apartment of his own, consisting of a living room and primitive kitchen on the ground floor and a bedroom and bathroom above. There is a simple entrance examination: to gain admission candidates have to be able to recite the Lord's Prayer and the Apostles' Creed from memory. Some of the inmates pay no rent at all for the privilege of living in the Jesus Hospital and receive a weekly allowance; others who are better off make a small contribution. The founder, Mr Gresham, was not only one of the wealthiest men in the City of London, but also Prime Warden of the Ancient Mistery of Silkworkers, one of the oldest livery companies in the City, founded in the fourteenth century. The Jesus Hospital was run and administered by the Silkworkers Company. Their officers selected the future inmates and the Warden who ran it.

In Number Four, Bill Smith, known to all as Smithy, who had spent his working life on a farm near Marlow, was reading his Bible. He began every day in this fashion. This was the third time Bill had gone through the good book. Rather like the people who painted the Forth Bridge, a task that took so long that the workers had to go back to the beginning once they had reached the end, Smithy had discovered that once he finished the Book of Revelation at the end of the New Testament, he had totally forgotten the Book of Genesis. So he went back to the beginning, thinking very occasionally that he might, just might, have read this section before.

In Number Seventeen, Josiah Collins was saying his prayers, kneeling on the threadbare carpet in his room. On his last visit to the doctor – it was one of the rules of the hospital that every man had to go for a check-up every six months – Josiah had been told that he had not very long to live. He might make it to the spring, he might not, the doctor had said in the special voice he used for the very old and the very nearly dead. Every morning now Josiah, who had found God late in life during a hellfire sermon in Hackney, said the Lord's Prayer and the collect for the day and read aloud from the Prayers for the Sick. This usually left him feeling better until the middle of the morning when despair returned. Sometimes Johnny Johnston would take him to the Rose and Crown when it opened just after twelve o'clock to ease his sorrows; sometimes he walked down Ferry Lane and stared at the passing river. By two-thirty in the afternoon Josiah was always sleep.

The repose of those still sleeping in the other numbers between one and twenty in the Jesus Hospital was shattered by a scream. Or rather, by a whole series of screams that sounded as though they would never end. Nellie the kitchen maid was just beginning to lay the tables for breakfast – tea, porridge, two sausages and toast on this occasion – when she saw the body lying across the table nearest the kitchen in the dining hall. At first she thought the body might have fallen asleep. That would have been unusual but not impossible, for several of the old gentlemen were known for falling asleep in the most unlikely places. It was only when she saw the blood dripping very slowly from the body's neck to make red marks on the floor that she realized the man was dead. It was Abel Meredith from Number Twenty. He had been an inmate of the hospital for less than six months. Meredith was leaving it in the most dramatic possible style, lying dead across one of the hall tables, his throat cut from ear to ear. The less squeamish among the residents realized that he must have been murdered elsewhere and the body brought here, for there was not very much blood. If the knife had passed across his throat in this room the floor would have been awash with dark red liquid, running down the slight slope of the floorboards.

The screams alerted all those who were already dressed to head for the hall. The others peered out of their upstairs windows and got themselves ready as fast as they could. In their blue coats with white buttons down the centre, the official uniform of the silkmen, as they were known, the old gentlemen gathered inside the main door of the hall and stared at their late colleague. Those who had served in the military were the least shocked. A few of them gazed at the corpse and were suddenly transported back to the battlefields where they had fought as young men and seen the bodies of their fallen comrades. For the silkmen whose lives had been more prosaic, spent in field or counting house, this was the first murdered man they had ever encountered. The Catholics among the inmates crossed themselves and began saying Hail Marys. There was a low murmur from the watchers as they exchanged views in whispers. One or two of them looked suspiciously at their colleagues as if they knew they had a murderer in their midst.

One of the last to arrive should have been the first. Thomas Monk, Warden of the Hospital, sprinted across the grass and blew loudly on his whistle to break the stifled screams and the sighs of the newcomers as they peered into the hall. He always found a whistle useful

6

when communicating with the very old and the very deaf among his flock. Thomas had spent most of the previous evening playing cards for money in the snug of his local pub and his winnings had almost been wiped out by the number of rounds of drinks he had to buy for the losers. Monk acted fast when he saw the body and checked that Meredith was dead.

'Silkmen,' he began, 'we should leave this terrible sight at once. Come with me now to the chapel where we may rest in peace and say our prayers while we wait for the authorities to arrive.'

Monk escorted his charges to the chapel on the opposite side of the little court, and then walked as fast as he could to his office on the right-hand side of the entrance. He was of average height with black curly hair and a piratical beard. He was full of nervous energy, so restless that some of the silkmen complained that they felt tired even looking at him. Of all the inmates of the Jesus Hospital, Thomas Monk had the most to fear. He had lied about his past when he applied for this job three years ago. Had he told the truth he would never have obtained the position. Now, as Thomas Monk reminded himself of his activities since he arrived, he shuddered at the thought of policemen crawling all over the hospital, checking everything, asking questions, digging into people's pasts. He wondered if, as Warden, he could be above suspicion, but he doubted it. He checked the coast was clear with a guilty smile and locked his door. He poured himself a very large glass of whisky and downed about a third of it in one gulp. That was better. Monk picked up his telephone and began shouting into it as loudly as he could. The instrument had only recently arrived at the hospital. Monk had never believed anybody would be able to hear at the other end if he spoke in a normal voice. Regular recipients of his calls used to hold the receiver at arm's length. He would, they told themselves, get used to the telephone in time. The doctor and the policeman he asked to come at once. He left a message at the Silkworkers Hall in London, saying there was a crisis at the Jesus Hospital and requesting a senior officer of the company to come as soon as possible.

The first to arrive was Dr Theophilus Ragg, medical adviser to the hospital. Dr Ragg, with his white hair and pronounced stoop, looked far older than his fifty-five years. The cynics among the silkmen said that he should be an inmate rather than their medical adviser. The doctor had originally come to Buckinghamshire as a contrast to his years in the slums of the East End of London where too much of his time was spent healing the wounds of street fighting and domestic violence. Buckinghamshire, he had told himself, would be different. Buckinghamshire was different. Dr Ragg was now as tired of the varicose veins and the neurotic headaches and the depressions and the inability to sleep of his wealthy patients as he had been with the very different characteristics of the poor of Shadwell. Murder – he resolved not to tell anybody this, not even his wife – murder was a welcome break from his normal fare. He inspected the dead body and resolved to make a closer examination when the corpse was in the morgue. It was, he reflected sadly, just like being back in the East End. Dr Ragg went to comfort the old men in the chapel while he waited for the officers of the law.

Thomas Monk had long prided himself on the old-fashioned nature of his neckwear. Not for him the prosaic necktie now worn by clerks and officials all over Britain. Monk sported a wide variety of cravats in the manner of Lord Byron. Blue cravats, red cravats, green cravats, multicoloured cravats were all part of his flamboyant collection. This morning he switched to a black one, tied in sober fashion, and stood outside the hospital to wait for the police to arrive from Maidenhead, Marlow being too small and too law-abiding to merit a full station of its own. Attack, he reasoned, might prove to be the best form of defence.

It was not long before the local police Inspector arrived on his bicycle. Inspector Albert Fletcher, resident of Buckinghamshire for all the thirty-five years of his life, was widely tipped as a coming man, though his critics pointed out that there was little sign so far of Albert actually arriving anywhere. He had hoped for a transfer to a London station for many years but so far all his efforts had been in vain. The Inspector had one characteristic which was in itself commendable but led in certain quarters to doubts about his competence. From the days when he first talked, Albert Fletcher had always paused briefly before he spoke. There were usually slight gaps in the flow of conversation. Albert would have told his critics that he was weighing up his options, making sure that he did not commit himself or his force to the wrong response or the wrong course of action. But to those who did not know him, or those impatient to press on with the business in hand, it seemed as though he was slow or stupid or both.

'Good morning, Inspector,' said Monk, drawing him inside the gates of the Jesus Hospital as fast as he could. 'This is a terrible business. I presume you will want to see the body first. The residents are at their prayers in the chapel. Heaven knows, we all need prayers at a time like this.'

Here came that tiny pause, just long enough to leave the other person wondering if the Inspector had heard properly, or was going deaf.

'Yes,' Inspector Fletcher said, 'yes. I would like to see the body, if I may.' There was another slight gap in the conversation. 'Has the doctor come yet?'

'He's in the chapel with the rest of them.'

Inspector Fletcher peered at the corpse. He thought the man had died from a knife to his throat but he didn't want to commit himself just yet. Better to let the doctor examine Abel Meredith and pronounce the official verdict.

'Dreadful business,' he said at last. 'Quite dreadful. Some more of my officers are on their way with a wagon. They can take him off to the morgue for a full examination. I'd better start questioning the silkmen.'

For the next few hours a slow round of interviews began in Monk's little office. Monk made himself available as helper and general adviser to the old men, thus keeping himself abreast of the police knowledge. Monk was not to know it but the veteran, the man with the deep knowledge of strange and sudden deaths, was the doctor. For the Inspector, although he did not say so, Abel Meredith was the only corpse he had seen on duty. This was his first murder investigation.

And it was the doctor who made the strange discovery about the death of Abel Meredith. As he examined the body in the Maidenhead Hospital he knew from long experience that rigor usually became apparent two to four hours after death and he therefore concluded that the murder must have been carried out earlier that morning. But it was not the time of day that struck him there in the morgue with the trolleys and the antiseptic smell and the green overalls and the blood on the floor. There was no doubt about what had caused the death: a knife or other sharp instrument drawn across the victim's neck with great force. But he noticed a strange mark just above the dead man's heart. It looked as if somebody had pressed a thistle hard into Abel Meredith's flesh and the imprint of the spikes was there for all to see. But the thistle, the doctor thought, must have been made of wood or some other hard substance – an ordinary thistle picked up in a field would be incapable of leaving the deep imprint on the dead man's skin.

Sergeant Donaldson arrived shortly after eleven o'clock as reinforcement for the Inspector. Fletcher asked Monk to show him the dead man's quarters.

Once they were up the stairs and into the upper floor, it was clear where Abel Meredith had been killed. His bedroom was a charnel house. Thick seams of blood had run down from the pillow, which had turned a dull, dark red, the colour of dried blood. There was little sign of a struggle.

'My God, Inspector,' said Thomas Monk, 'do you think he was still asleep when he was killed?'

'He might have been,' said the Inspector finally, after an extra long pause. 'The doctor should be able to tell us.'

Inspector Fletcher carried out a long and slow examination of the room but he found little to help him. There was a cupboard with Meredith's clothes, and his best and only civilian suit was hanging on a hook at the back of the door. There was a reproduction of a painting of Queen Victoria on the wall, staring out at some bleak Scottish landscape with Balmoral in the background and a couple of distant stags. There was nothing luxurious about the little apartments inside the hospital.

'We'll take this stuff away later,' Fletcher remarked, waving at the tiny desk and the few books on the shelf.

11

'I know it looks bad,' said the Warden. 'I mean, the men seem to have so few possessions. We insist on them bringing as little as possible when they come to us. It's part of the arrangement.'

'Quite so, quite so,' said Fletcher absent-mindedly. 'Tell me, if you would, Warden, what are the arrangements and the timings of the gates in the hospital? The murderer must have been in here by the early hours of the morning.'

'The doors are closed at eleven-fifteen every evening and opened at six-thirty the following morning. Some of the old men wake up early and like to take a short walk.'

'And who is responsible for the opening and closing?'

'Usually it is the porter. Last night he was off duty so I did it at the usual times.'

'And you saw nothing unusual on either occasion?'

'No, I did not.'

'Could the killer have come in yesterday evening,' said Inspector Fletcher, 'and spent the night in the hall or the chapel?'

'Well, he could, but I don't think we'd find any trace of him. The hall is locked overnight, the chapel left open in case religion overcomes the old men in the night. The chapel was cleaned early this morning at seven o'clock before the body was discovered. And the old men have been tramping all over both hall and chapel since then.'

Inspector Fletcher paused. Another line of inquiry seemed to have been blocked off. Before he had a chance to say any more, there was a shout from a constable on the grass outside.

'Inspector, sir! You're to come at once, sir! We've got a visitor!'

Fletcher groaned. Visitors on occasions like this at the

very start of an investigation usually meant trouble. Sometimes they were superior officers, keen to carp and criticize. On this occasion, as he told his wife that evening, it was much worse than that.

The third visitor to the Jesus Hospital that morning arrived just before twelve o'clock. Those residents comforting themselves from the shock of murder in the morning and, what was worse in their book, murder before breakfast, looked out of their windows and saw an enormous motor car arrive and a tall portly gentleman with white hair and a black walking stick climb out and knock imperiously on Thomas Monk's door. This was Sir Peregrine Fishborne, Prime Warden of the Silkworkers, come to inspect the crisis in his kingdom. He was well known in the City of London, Sir Peregrine, for his speed in the despatch of business and his position as head of one of the foremost insurance companies in the country.

'Monk,' he said to the Warden when he had regained his office, 'what the hell is going on here? What's this crisis you mentioned on the phone? Damn inconvenient having to trundle out into the back of beyond for some mess in this bloody hospital!'

'There's been a murder, sir,' said Monk, standing to attention as he always did when talking to the Prime Warden.

'Murder? Here? In Buckinghamshire? In the Jesus Hospital? Don't be ridiculous.' He turned to stare at the policeman. 'And who the hell are you?' he said, eyeing Inspector Fletcher as if he had just delivered the week's coal.

'Ah, hm, ah, I am the policeman assigned to the case.' He paused as if he might have temporarily forgotten his name. 'Albert Fletcher, hm, Inspector Albert Fletcher, at your service, sir.'

Sir Peregrine threw him another of his turn-a-man-to-stone-at-fifty-paces looks. 'And what can you tell us about the dead man?'

There was another pause while the Inspector searched in his pockets for the vital notebook.

'Well,' he began, inspecting his handwriting carefully, 'the dead man was called Meredith, Abel Meredith. Ah, hm, he died of a knife wound to the area between the pharynx and the larynx.'

'Somebody cut his throat, you mean,' snarled Sir Peregrine. 'We're in a bloody almshouse here, not a medical school, for Christ's sake. What age was this unfortunate Meredith?'

'Hm, ah,' said the Inspector, 'over sixty at least or he wouldn't be here. Do you know how old he was, Warden?'

The Warden intervened immediately in case there was another salvo from Sir Peregrine.

'Sixty-four, sir, that's how old he was. Last birthday six weeks ago. He paid for a very fine drinking session in the back room of the Rose and Crown, Abel Meredith, I'll give him that. One of the very few occasions he was known to pay for a round.'

'I see,' said Sir Peregrine in his most glacial voice. 'Tell us if you would, Inspector, if you have identified any of the dead man's enemies, maybe even arrested them. He's been dead for some time, after all.'

Inspector Fletcher looked at Sir Peregrine more in sorrow than in anger. There was another of those pauses. 'The old men aren't making much sense at the moment, Sir Peregrine,' he said at last. 'It's impossible to say at this stage if he had any enemies or who they might be.'

'Course the man had enemies, you fool; he's dead, isn't

he? One of his enemies must have killed him. I'd have thought even one of the swans on the bloody river could have worked that out by now. Christ Almighty!'

Inspector Fletcher was saved further thrusts from Sir Peregrine by the reappearance of Dr Ragg. Even before he was introduced, the doctor took a violent dislike to Sir Peregrine. There were many of his sort living in and around Marlow, often in sub-Palladian villas by the Thames. The doctor thought them arrogant, self-satisfied and smug, with little regard for their fellow men. He had even changed his golf club to escape their pomposity and their braying self-regard.

'I'll give you my report, gentlemen,' Dr Ragg began, 'and then I must be off on my rounds. In my judgement Abel Meredith was killed by a sharp knife being forced across his throat sometime between four and six o'clock this morning. The knife may have had an irregular and uneven blade like the kris knife often brought home by travellers and military men from Ceylon and the Malay Peninsula. Death will have been instantaneous. I fear he was probably awake at the time of the incident. That is all.'

'Surely you must know something more than that, Doctor?' Sir Peregrine felt he, too, would be in need of medical attention soon if the natives continued to infuriate him. 'You've been poking about in the corpse's innards for some time now, haven't you? You must have found something out.'

'Are you experienced in the examination of dead bodies, Sir Peregrine? I rather doubt it. We doctors are not obliged to reveal the secrets of our patients' medical history, even the dead ones. So why don't you write the insurance policies and I'll write the medical reports.'

With that Dr Ragg closed his bag and headed off towards the nervous headaches and the insomnia of his morning rounds. He had not told the people in the Jesus Hospital anything about the strange mark on the dead man's chest. It was such an unusual piece of information that gossip would start circulating along the river and through the City of London. Soon Abel Meredith would have been found dead with the imprint of fifty pineapples all over his body. He would tell Inspector Fletcher, of course, but only in the privacy of the police station. Dr Ragg had no idea what had caused the strange mark and even less idea what it might mean.

Sir Peregrine, meanwhile, was metaphorically pawing the ground as one of his potential victims fled the field. He made mental notes on the key players he had met this morning who were involved in the bizarre death of Abel Meredith. The doctor? Barely competent, in his view, but he had tangled too often with the medical profession in the past and failed to get his way. Better to leave Theophilus Ragg in peace. Thomas Monk, the Warden? Another incompetent, in Sir Peregrine's opinion. Why was it so difficult to get hold of sensible men once you were out of London? It was as if there was a whole world of inefficiency clogging up the nation beyond the City walls, a world stretching west to Bristol and north to the people Sir Peregrine had always referred to as the Caledonians in the wilder parts of Scotland. His fiercest wrath, however, was reserved for Inspector Albert Fletcher. That officer of the law had marked Sir Peregrine down from the beginning as a man to beware of, a man who could damage your career through his contacts in high places, and who would take pleasure in doing so. As a result the pauses were slightly longer than usual, the mental reservations sounded like incompetence, the gaps before speech the mark of an idiot. Something would have to be done. Sir Peregrine looked at his watch. Already he had spent far too much time down here among this human dross.

'Telephone!' he barked.

'That's a telephone over there on the table,' said the Warden, pointing helpfully to the instrument.

'I know what a telephone looks like, you fool. There are hundreds of them in my offices in London. Now get out while I use it.'

Sir Peregrine could not raise the person he sought, which added fuel to his fury. Listening at the keyhole, Thomas Monk smiled. Anything that irritated the Prime Warden of the Silkworkers Company was music to his ears. Sir Peregrine was leaving a message for his personal assistant, a young man called Arthur Onslow, with a distinguished career at Eton, a first-class honours degree in Classics from King's College, Cambridge, and three years in the Blues and Royals, now in his second year as guard dog to Sir Peregrine, as he described it to his friends. It was a pity that he was a younger son for his father was widely believed to own half of Leicestershire.

'Onslow. See me in my office. One hour from now. Don't be late,' barked Sir Peregrine, leaving Monk's cramped quarters and heading back to his enormous motor car. It was the Inspector's pauses, his hesitations, that raised Sir Peregrine's heart rate to what Dr Ragg would have regarded as dangerous levels.

'Damn Fletcher, damn him to hell!' Sir Peregrine muttered as his vast car rumbled back into the suburbs of London. 'I'll break that man if it's the last thing I do. Inspector Fletcher indeed!' All through his career in finance Sir Peregrine had preached the benefits of private enterprise, of individuals looking after themselves rather than expecting the state to do it for them. Old age pensions, public money for the unemployed, schools funded by the taxpayer, all of these, in his view, were unnecessary intrusions by government into areas where people should look after themselves. Private enterprise, his private enterprise, was looking after those old men in the Jesus Hospital. Maybe even the police could be done away with, Sir Peregrine reflected as his limousine passed St Paul's Cathedral, and replaced by a force of citizen constabulary. Inspector Fletcher and all the other Inspector Fletchers, thousands of them, in the Prime Warden's view, could be thrown out like old pairs of sheets. The money saved could be given to the wealth-creators of the nation, the deserving rich as he had called them to great applause at a City dinner the week before. At any event, he resolved to find himself an investigator of his own, the finest man in London to look into the death of Abel Meredith. That was the commission he had in mind for young Onslow at his desk in the temple of finance back in Bishopsgate. A detective of his own. The finest available in the capital.

Inspector Fletcher sighed as he returned to his interviews with the old men. He found to his horror that the first person he had talked to, Albert Jardine, the oldest resident of the Jesus Hospital, aged eighty-four years, born a decade before Victoria came to the throne, had forgotten that he had ever spoken to the Inspector. This Albert was generally known as Number One, as he lived in almshouse Number One. Abel Meredith was Number Twenty. For some reason the old men found it easier to remember numbers than names. Number One had no memory at all of a conversation that had taken place only two or three hours before. The Inspector made a note in his book. This was one resident who would never make it to the courtroom if the case came to trial. Jack Miller, Number Three, and Gareth Williams, Number Eight, had both arrived too late in the hall to see anything useful to his inquiries. Freddie Butcher, Number Two, who had spent most of his life working on the railways, had been one of the first on the scene but his eyesight had virtually gone and he had no testimony to give except that it was a crying shame and wouldn't have happened under the administration of the previous Warden. Number Eleven, Archie Dunne, had slept through the whole affair and complained bitterly about the lack of breakfast. Wondering if he would ever collect any useful evidence at all and fearful of another visit from Sir Peregrine, Inspector Fletcher made his way across the courtyard to Number Six, temporary home of one Colin Baker, who had a wooden leg from his time in the army.

Arthur Onslow had received his instructions from the Falcon, as he referred to his boss. He regarded this search for a detective as rather a lark that would take him out of the office and away from his master for a whole afternoon. He spent his time in a variety of different places, confirming in a way Sir Peregrine's original assessment of him that he was an enterprising young man. The early part of the afternoon he spent in the offices of *The Times* where he had a Cambridge friend on the staff and where he believed all sorts of arcane wisdom were to be found. Then he made his way to Grays Inn, to the chambers of a barrister called Charles Augustus Pugh. This Pugh was a friend of his mother and had been a popular guest at a party in the Onslows' grand house some years before where the talk was of a recent court case where Pugh had saved a man from the gallows, thanks to the work of a London detective whose name Arthur could not recall. Pugh was in court but the clerk gave him some useful information. Finally he visited a Salvation Army charity near Charing Cross where they cared for reformed convicts. They might have reformed from crime, Arthur muttered to himself, as he made a slightly unsteady return journey to his office, but they had certainly not reformed from drinking. His information had cost him many pints in the Rat and Compass.

Sir Peregrine had gone out on Silkworkers Company business. Arthur had long suspected that there was something suspicious going on in the world of silk. His master was more shifty and more devious than usual, if that were possible, about his activities in those quarters.

Arthur Onslow left a note on Sir Peregrine's desk. 'He has served in Army Intelligence in India,' he wrote, 'and led that branch of arms in the Boer War. He has been employed by the royal family and by a previous Prime Minister and by the Foreign Office. The man you want is Lord Francis Powerscourt, and he lives in Markham Square, Chelsea.'

2

'Do you think I should tell him?' Number Nineteen, a tall, very thin man called James Osborne, with a few white hairs left on the side of his head, was talking to his friend from Number Eleven. Number Nineteen was next door to the apartment of Abel Meredith, still interred in the hospital morgue. Inspector Fletcher was working his way round the almshouse, questioning each old gentleman in turn. Number Eleven, from the other side of the quad-rangle, was, in contrast to his friend, short and rather fat with a full head of curly brown hair. His name was Archie Dunne and his last job had been as a car mechanic.

'For the fifth time, James,' Number Eleven said, 'I think you should tell the Inspector. It can't do any harm.'

'I'm not sure, I'm not sure at all. It might get me into trouble. What would happen if they threw me out of here? I've got nowhere else to go.'

'Don't be ridiculous. They're not going to throw you out. If you don't tell him, you'll just worry about it for days.'

'Oh dear.' James Osborne, Number Nineteen, began rubbing his hands together, as if he were a reincarna-tion of Lady Macbeth, a sure sign that he wasn't happy.

'What am I going to do? That policeman will be here in a minute. Oh dear.'

'Well, he won't want me here when he does come,' said Number Eleven. 'You should tell him, James. It's the right thing to do. It's the only thing to do, for God's sake. What would Mabel say if she was here? You know perfectly well what Mabel would say. Tell him, that's my last word on the matter.'

Even as he said it, Archie Dunne, Number Eleven, realized that mention of Mabel was probably a mistake. Mabel's passing, after all, just over a year before, was the reason Number Nineteen was in the Jesus Hospital, unable to cope on his own.

'Don't mention Mabel, please. Don't set me off again. I couldn't bear it.'

There was a light knock on the door. Inspector Fletcher said a polite good morning and sat down in the second chair. Deprived of a place to sit, Archie Dunne from Number Eleven made his excuses and left.

The Inspector was learning fast about the memories and afflictions of old men. They were, he thought, the most unreliable collection of witnesses he had ever come across. They weren't lying, or if they were, they weren't aware of it. They weren't lying deliberately. They were also, although he didn't know it, well suited to his temperament, the pauses, the hesitations. A more vigorous officer might have flustered the silkmen so much they would have said anything at all to be rid of him.

'How kind of you to give up your time to see me this morning. I'm sure all you old gentlemen are still shocked by the events of yesterday.'

Number Nineteen did not feel it necessary to tell the policeman that his next fixed appointment was the weekly game of shove ha'penny at eight o'clock in the evening at the Rose and Crown in five days' time.

'It's all very upsetting,' he said, and gave a pause the policeman would have been proud of, 'most unexpected.'

'Now then.' Inspector Fletcher opened his notebook and wrote Number Nineteen in large letters at the top of a clean page. 'I have to write things down too, you see. Otherwise I forget them. They go clean out of my mind.' The Inspector managed a little smile at this point. 'What I would like you to do is just tell me in your own words everything you did yesterday morning, from the time you woke up until the body was found.'

Number Nineteen looked alarmed, as if this was an awful lot to remember in one go.

'Well,' he began, 'I must have woken up some time around seven, half past maybe. I don't have a watch, you see, so I take my bearings from the light and the people moving around outside. I got dressed as usual. Thursday is my day for a clean shirt so I put that on. I'd polished my shoes the night before; I don't know why, I usually do them after breakfast. Then I went downstairs and out into the court. Most of the men were talking over by the hall. Number Fifteen, he's not been right in the head for weeks now, that Number Fifteen, he was crying like a baby. I'd seen plenty of dead bodies in my time in the army so I wasn't that bothered. Shocked, mind you, shocked that such a thing should happen in a place like this.'

By this stage in his career Inspector Fletcher had mastered the art of looking at his interviewee and writing his notes at the same time.

'That all sounds very normal, Mr Osborne,' he said. 'Can you remember anything unusual?'

This was the moment Number Nineteen had been

23

dreading. This had been the subject of his discussion with Number Eleven and the unfortunate invocation of the dead Mabel. What was he to do? He waited for so long before he spoke that the Inspector knew his man had heard something in the night. It would have been too dark to see anything at the time of the murder. The Inspector thought there was only one thing it could have been but he might be wrong. He leant forward in his chair.

'There was something,' he said very gently, 'something in the night, wasn't there? I wonder if it was something you heard.'

'I won't get into any trouble, will I?' The old man looked very frightened now.

'No, no, there won't be any trouble. Not unless you killed him and I don't think you did that!'

They both managed a laugh of sorts. Gallows humour, said the Inspector to himself, making a mental note to tell his wife about it that evening.

'I'm sorry, I'm so sorry.' For a brief moment the Inspector thought James Osborne, Number Nineteen, was going to confess all. 'For not having a watch, you see. I can't tell you what time it was. When I heard the noises, I mean.'

He had said it now. It hadn't been that bad. He began to feel a little better after the start of his confession.

'Can you be any more specific about the time? Was it nearer the dawn than the middle of the night?'

Number Nineteen paused for thought. 'Forgive me for bringing in personal details, Inspector, but I usually have to go to the bathroom two or three times during the night. The last time, I think would be about six o'clock. I'd only been twice when I heard the noises. Four o'clock? Something like that? Is that helpful?'

'Very helpful,' said the Inspector, wondering what a

brutal QC at the Old Bailey, would make of this strange method of timekeeping. 'And now perhaps you could tell me what you heard.'

'I heard somebody coming down the stairs,' Number Nineteen began. 'And there was a bump as if he was bringing something heavy down with him. It wasn't very loud. The walls here are pretty thick so you don't hear very much from next door.'

'Did you look out of the window? To see where the person went, I mean?'

'Well, I did take a little peep out of the window, but I couldn't see anything much. It was too dark.' Number Nineteen leant back in his chair and sighed, as if he had just come through a long ordeal.

'And that was all? There wasn't anything else?' Inspector Fletcher thought his man had said all he was going to say, but he had to be sure.

'That's all I can remember.'

The Inspector felt that the information was useful but hardly sensational. Somebody in the little community was likely to have been aware of something, the man who lived next door more likely to have heard it than most. What was interesting, as he said to his Sergeant that evening over a pint at the Marquis of Granby near the Maidenhead police station, was that the unorthodox timekeeping of James Osborne, Number Nineteen, placed the murder somewhere between four and six in the morning, which was exactly the same as Dr Ragg's conclusion, who had at his disposal all the latest scientific expertise.

Lord Francis Powerscourt received his commission and his instructions in the morning post. He had a head of unruly black hair and a pair of blue eyes inspected the world with detachment and irony. He thought that Sir Peregrine did not waste much time on pleasantries. There was no mention of whether he would wish to take the case or not. There was no thank you for helping out at the end. He was told in no uncertain terms that the doctor was a milksop, the Warden a crook and the policeman one of the most useless specimens ever to put on a uniform. Lady Lucy was intrigued by the idea of the almshouse. She had heard of them, of course, but she had never actually seen inside one. Would Francis be able to arrange that? she wondered aloud, passing him another slice of toast. Her husband muttered darkly about such places maybe having it written in the rules and regulations that women were not allowed on the premises, being too likely to provoke excess excitement in the old gentlemen and thus be harmful to their health. Lady Lucy was tall and slim with blonde hair and a pretty little nose. Her eyes were a deep blue, deeper than her husband's, and quite disconcerting when they were wide open.

Powerscourt thought about his children as he drove off down to Marlow in his Rolls-Royce Silver Ghost, freshly polished by Rhys the butler and chauffeur. Lady Lucy's son by her first marriage, Robert, was now in the Royal Navy, believed at that moment to be on manoeuvres in the Pacific. Thomas, eldest son of Powerscourt and Lady Lucy, with his mother's mouth and his mother's eyes, was seventeen years old with a flair for languages and mathematics. The boy attended Westminster School and was virtually fluent in German, Russian and French. Powerscourt felt Thomas could have picked up Hottentot at record speed if required. Olivia, the eldest daughter, was at St Paul's School for Girls, eager to be an art historian and continually dragging one or both of her parents to exhibitions of people they had never heard of in obscure parts of London. On one occasion Olivia had persuaded her parents to take her to Paris where the entire city seemed to Powerscourt to be filled with blotches of paint on canvas masquerading as modern masterpieces. The twins, eight years old, were tormenting the teachers at a nearby school. Powerscourt was certain that a successful career in international crime awaited them if all else failed.

But it was Thomas he worried about. He had told Lady Lucy of his deepest concerns two days before, and she had confessed that her fears were exactly the same. Powerscourt was fairly sure there was going to be a war with Germany. This wasn't unusual – some of the newspapers had been prophesying such a conflict for years. And, unlike some commentators who predicted a quick war, Powerscourt felt it would be long. And very bloody, with a great many deaths. Maybe it would be like the American Civil War all those years ago. All the young men would want to go and fight for their country. Many of those would go and die for the cause. Including one Thomas Powerscourt, who could be called up if there was a war that started as early as next year. What were they to do? For the moment neither of his parents had any idea.

Inspector Fletcher had not been told he was coming. Neither had Monk the Warden. Neither had the old men. So Powerscourt's first moments in the Jesus Hospital were spent showing parts of his letter of commission and generally persuading them that he was a bona fide investigator.

'I'm not surprised you're here, mind you,' said the Inspector after a call to his superiors at Maidenhead had convinced him Powerscourt was genuine, 'I don't think Sir Peregrine cared for me at all.'

'Never mind,' said Powerscourt cheerfully. 'He'll think differently when you've solved the murder.'

Fletcher told Powerscourt all he knew about the case over a hasty lunch at the Rose and Crown. It was an old coaching inn, the Rose and Crown. The front was festooned with red and white roses, appropriate to the origins of the name, in spring and summer. The back room with its eight small tables was the destination of choice for the old men of the Jesus Hospital, its walls and faded curtains stained with centuries of smoke. Powerscourt wanted to know if he could see the body and the room where Abel Meredith had lived.

'What do you know of livery companies, my lord?' asked Fletcher. 'We don't have any of those things in Maidenhead or Taplow or Pinkneys Green. One or two of the old men drone on about them and I don't understand it.'

'I doubt if I know much more than you do, Inspector. They're very old, going back to the fourteenth century, those sort of times. To start with they were guilds, defensive guilds, if you like, formed to look after the common concerns of brewers or bakers or fishmongers, or silkworkers, who banded together to look after their own particular interests. They had special uniforms and great halls where they held their feasts and so on. Most important,' he paused to digest a portion of the local steak and kidney pie, 'they are now rich, very rich. Many of the members left property to their company in their wills. Number Sixteen Lombard Street might have been worth five or six pounds in thirteen ninety; it's worth a lot more now. Hundreds and hundreds of times more, I should think.'

Powerscourt took himself to the Maidenhead Hospital immediately after lunch. The Inspector had telephoned before they went to the Rose and Crown to ensure that the body was not moved yet. Powerscourt introduced himself and his mission to the old attendant. He thought, as he often did when looking at corpses, how quickly life moved out of people. A moment before they had been alive with fluent features and eyes and faces that expressed their emotions. Then they were transformed into something you could have found on a butcher's slab.

He looked for a long time at the marks above the heart. 'Have you seen anything like these before?' he asked the elderly attendant who looked as though he had been a curator of corpses since the Crimean War, if not before.

'Nope, I have not, my lord. Neither has any doctor in this hospital. You know what they're like, doctors, with the new and the unexpected; they've flocked down here, peering at the mark and prodding at it like they've never seen a dead body before. One of them said it was the sign of some African witch doctor, stamped on the bodies of the dead to improve their passage to the next world. I ask you. We don't have no Africans or no witch doctors in Marlow, not even over in Reading, if you ask me.'

Powerscourt stared again at the thistle-like marks on the body.

'Were you here when they undressed him?' he asked.

'I was indeed,' said the attendant, casting a quick glance at the corpse.

'I was wondering,' said Powerscourt, 'not that it's any use for the investigation, but I was wondering if the mark above the heart was put there before or after he was killed. Was it knife first? Or the other way round?'

'The shirt wasn't buttoned up, my lord. Not when they brought him here, anyway. Dr Ragg noticed that, I remember. I'm not sure what the order was, my lord. It would be easier to kill him first, pull back the shirt and then put the mark on him. He couldn't put up a fight if he was dead.'

Powerscourt started work on a drawing of the mark in his notebook.

'Hold on, my lord, this might be helpful. One of our young doctors is going to send an article to the medical journals to see if anybody can identify the mark. He was very good with his pencil, so he was.' The old man opened a drawer in the table and pulled out a bundle of three or four drawings of the strange marks. 'Perhaps you would like to have one or two of these, my lord. It might be useful.'

'That's so much better than my effort. I'm more than grateful to you.' Powerscourt gave the old man half a crown and hurried on his way.

Inspector Fletcher was looking forward to Powerscourt's return. As he continued his interviews with the old men of the Jesus Hospital, he had encountered a pair who were so confused they left his head spinning. Numbers Nine and Ten insisted on being interviewed together. Otherwise, they said, they would get in a muddle. They brought a whole new line of evidence into the investigation. Johnny Johnston, Number Nine, had spent his working life in the post office. Peter Baker, Number Ten, had been a clerk in the City.

'Of course it must have to do with the Silkworkers Company, the death,' said Number Nine.

'Stands to reason,' said Number Ten.

'Improved terms and conditions of residence, that's what they said. They'd paint my place from top to bottom and it hasn't had a lick of paint in years. You've got to look behind the picture to see all the walls were white to start with. Everything else is dirty grey now.'

'That's one way of looking at it,' said Peter Baker, Number Ten. 'The other people say there won't be any money left to keep up the hospital. We'll be thrown out and the place will be sold for rich people's houses.' He paused and peered out of the window. 'Thrown out,' he repeated, 'thrown out. Where would we go?'

'But there's them that say they can't do that. Throw us out, I mean. The statues – no, they're not statues, are they? What's the word?'

'Statutes?' offered Numbered Ten.

'Statutes, that sounds right,' Johnny Johnston, Number Nine, went on. 'They say they can't throw us out. If they sell this place they have to build us another, that's what that man in the grey suit told us.'

'Hold on a moment,' said the Inspector. 'Could we just take this from the beginning. You're not saying that the hospital is going to be closed, are you? It's been going for nearly four hundred years.'

'Sold,' said Number Ten. 'Turned into luxury houses. People like living in luxury houses in Marlow, people with plenty of money, I mean. We're not meant to talk about this, Inspector, we've all been sworn to secrecy. But it's a great worry and that's a fact.'

'It only gets sold if one lot of Silkworkers have their way.' Johnny Johnston, Number Nine, was scowling at the very idea that the hospital might be sold. 'That man with the big moustache didn't think it could happen.'

'But the other fellow, the thin lawyer man with the long

face and the monocle from Chancery Lane, he said it was going to happen anyway.'

'Didn't moustache man say there had to be a vote? The vote that Warden Monk is so keen on?'

'Gentlemen, please.' Inspector Fletcher put down his notebook. 'Am I right in saying that there is a discussion going on in the Silkworkers Company about the future of the Jesus Hospital? And that one group wants to sell it and the other doesn't? And somehow or other there is to be a vote on the matter, here in the hospital?'

'Not just in the hospital, Inspector,' said Peter Baker, Number Ten, who felt that his experience working in the City gave him more authority than most on this subject. 'That's where you're wrong. All the members of the Silkworkers Company are to have a vote. We're all members. We wouldn't be admitted to the almshouse if we weren't, you see.'

Inspector Fletcher sighed. He couldn't see how these transactions could lead to Abel Meredith having his throat cut. He returned to the more prosaic details of the murder. Had either Number Nine or Number Ten heard or seen anything unusual on the night of the death? No, they had not. Did Abel Meredith have any enemies, as far as they knew? There was a pause.

'Yes,' said Johnny Johnston, Number Nine, 'yes, he did.'

'He cheated,' said Number Ten, 'he cheated at cards and he cheated at shove ha'penny over at the Rose and Crown.'

Inspector Fletcher did not have the strength to ask how a man could cheat at shove ha'penny.

'He was very unpopular,' Peter Baker, Number Ten, added, 'probably the most unpopular man in the hospital.'

'Come, come now, ah, hm,' said Johnny Johnston,

Number Nine, 'you're not supposed to speak ill of the dead. Somebody or something is meant to come and strike you down if you do.'

This may have been the Inspector's first murder investigation but he did not lack imagination. His horizons had been broadened by regular readings of the many novels of E. Phillips Oppenheim. They kept the latest volume for him in the Maidenhead Public Library. He knew from experience how bitter relations could become in closed societies like police stations or almshouses. With little to occupy the inmates' minds, cheating could be magnified out of all proportion. Could it, he wondered, be magnified enough to become a motive for murder? He wasn't sure.

'He was always borrowing money, that Meredith man,' Number Nine went on.

'And he never paid any of it back,' added Number Ten. The corpse was beginning to assume pariah status in Inspector Fletcher's mind. He paused for a moment.

'Maybe he simply forgot,' he said, 'forgot to pay it back, I mean.'

'Don't think so,' said Number Ten. 'And there's another thing. I don't think he ever took a bath.'

'For God's sake,' said his friend, 'he wasn't the only one in this place who never takes a bath.'

The Inspector had had enough. For once he managed not to pause, even for a second.

'Thank you very much for your assistance, gentlemen. If you remember anything else that you think may be useful, please get in touch.'

He walked back to Monk's office, thinking of a man with stinking clothes making his way to the Rose and Crown to cheat with borrowed money at the shove ha'penny table. But he couldn't connect that figure with the corpse with its throat cut and a strange mark on its chest stretched out in the morgue at the Maidenhead Hospital.

Among his many responsibilities at the almshouse, Thomas Monk, still wearing his black cravat, was the custodian of the old gentlemen's wills. They were stored in a little safe in the corner of his office. This practice was not included in the ordinances of the Silkworkers Company for the inhabitants of the Jesus Hospital. The custom had begun with Thomas's reign as Warden and he had not bothered to tell any of his masters from the Silkworkers Hall in London about it. If the old men had not made a will – and Thomas was sure to discover this if they failed to hand it over on arrival – then he was prepared to help them for a small fee. He had, he assured the intestate newcomers, a draft will prepared by the finest solicitors in the capital which he could make available for them. Indeed he would help them fill it in. It just happened that the draft will ran to two pages. The second page merely repeated that this was the last will of the testator and left room for the signatures.

Since the murder Thomas had not had the time, or been alone in his office long enough, to check what the status of Abel Meredith's will was. He suspected Meredith had had his will already prepared on arrival. He didn't like to check in case Powerscourt or one of the policemen should barge into his office at the wrong time and start making inquiries.

The Inspector took Powerscourt for a walk down to the river on his return from the Maidenhead morgue. He felt there was a network of old men trying to listen in to any of his conversations in the hospital. He told Powerscourt about the possible changes at the almshouse and the unpopularity of the victim.

'I'll speak to my brother-in-law about the Silkworkers Company,' Powerscourt said to the Inspector as they neared the bottom of Ferry Lane. 'He knows about these things, or if he doesn't, he knows people who do. What did you think of all the rest of it, the cheating at shove ha'penny and so on? I know these are old men and that feelings can run high in places like this, but they're not going to lead to murder, are they?'

Inspector Fletcher agreed. 'Damn it,' he said, staring at a pair of swans making a regal progress down the Thames, 'I knew there was something I forgot to ask the doctor. I'll have to find him this evening.'

'What was it that you forgot to ask?'

'Well, it's this, my lord. You just have to look at the old men walking out of the hall. Do any of them have the strength to commit the crime? It's hard to imagine any of them being able to summon up enough force to draw a knife across the dead man's throat like that.'

'You could well be right,' said Powerscourt thoughtfully. 'I wonder if you could devise some sort of test to work out who would have had the strength to do it, like drawing the bow at the end of the *Odyssey*.'

There was a pause. A small flock of black river birds flew past, close to the water's edge.

'The killer, if the killer comes from inside, would surely fail any test to deflect suspicion,' said the Inspector gloomily.

Half an hour later Powerscourt went to look at Abel Meredith's room before the police took the contents away.

35

He remembered suddenly the instructions given to new entrants to the Royal Hospital Chelsea, that men could bring precious little with them for there was precious little room in their quarters, and that earthly possessions were not needed whether they were going on to heaven or to hell. Here Powerscourt found the clothes and the few books Abel Meredith had brought with him to what he must have thought would be his last resting place on earth. The inhabitants of these almshouses came here to live out their last days and their hosts would not welcome the prospect of wading through a mountain of personal belongings when the residents went to the cemetery and the grave. One thing did strike him. Most people, he thought, would have brought some mementoes of their past life with them, family photographs if they had any, letters from relatives or from a workplace, some keepsake left them in a relative's will. There was none of that. Abel Meredith had arrived with a few spare shirts and trousers and a jacket and a few books and personal knick-knacks, but nothing else. It was as if he had deliberately obliterated most of his sixty-four years on earth. Had he something to hide? There were no official documents of any kind. There was, he noticed, no will to be found among his few papers. He wondered again about the strange marks on the dead man's chest. One of the doctors in the hospital had talked of witchcraft, of strange African practices come to an unsuspecting Buckinghamshire. Powerscourt didn't think that could be true; Africa was too far away. But if they weren't African, where in God's name had they come from? The mountains of Peru? The Gobi desert? The high passes of the Hindu Kush? He was lost.

Inspector Fletcher came to join him, clutching a telegram. It was another missive from Sir Peregrine and told him of another murder at a property linked to the Silkworkers Company, in Norfolk this time, another murder marked by the mysterious imprint of the thistle deeply embossed on the dead man's chest. Powerscourt was ordered to go to the scene as soon as possible.

Allison's School in Fakenham had been founded in the sixteenth century by Sir George Allison to replace a priory that had been abolished in the dissolution of the monasteries. Sir George endowed the school handsomely with a number of parishes in Norfolk and further properties in the City of London. The entire endowment was placed in the hands of the Silkworkers Company of London where it has remained to this day. There were over a hundred and fifty boys in the school, with the normal range of teaching and ancillary staff. The victim was the bursar. He was found in his office – pen in hand over a set of accounts on his table, strangled, with great purple weals on his neck – shortly after ten o'clock in the morning when he was due to attend a meeting with the headmaster concerning action against those parents who were late with their fees. His shirt had been ripped open to receive the imprint of the thistle that had disfigured the body of Abel Meredith at the Jesus Hospital in Marlow.

Roderick Gill, the bursar, was nearing retirement in his fifty-fifth year, with fifteen years' service at the school. His office was on a long corridor that everybody in the school used, from the teachers to the most junior boy to the cleaning staff.

Powerscourt reflected on his train to Norfolk that the killer must have travelled this line yesterday, on his way

37

to his second murder. Surely someone would have seen him. Or had the killer access to a large and powerful motor car which could have taken him to East Anglia with less chance of being spotted? He wondered if these two dates at the end of January carried any particular significance.

Another murder, another Inspector of police. Not for the first time Powerscourt wondered about the wisdom of having so many different police forces in the country. Surely these two cases must be linked. Yet two separate forces would conduct their own investigations, with the possibility of much information falling into the cracks between the two inquiries.

Allison's School was in a state close to chaos. The porter at the front gate blamed the telephone. Mothers from near and far had heard of the murder and had come in person to seek assurances from the headmaster that their child was safe and should not be taken home immediately. Only a timely directive from the policeman on the case, Inspector William Grime, that all the boys were to remain in school until they had been questioned by members of his force, prevented a mass exodus. The queue to speak to the headmaster stretched for fifteen yards outside his office and out into the quadrangle. Powerscourt saw as his cab dropped him off that the mothers were growing more rather than less distraught. 'There he was, that poor bursar man,' he heard one of them say to her neighbour in the line, 'sitting at his desk, and then, whoosh, he's gone! Who's to say the killer couldn't do the same to my Georgie or any of the other boys? They still haven't caught the murderer, you know. The brute's still at large, waiting to kill again. He's probably hiding in the grounds.'

Some of the boys were in lessons, though Powerscourt

doubted if they would learn very much on this day. Others were talking to the policemen in a geography classroom made over to the constabulary. Some of the younger boys, Powerscourt was told later, reported sightings of a bearded man climbing over the chapel roof early that morning; others mentioned a tramp who looked remarkably like the headmaster, who had taken to hiding round the back of the cricket pavilion. The boys had not yet learnt, Powerscourt was glad to discover, of the strange mark left imprinted over the dead man's heart.

It was late that afternoon before some sort of order was restored to the headmaster's quarters. John Davies, the headmaster, had agreed to brief a group of mothers every morning in the main hotel in the town. He had secured, he told Powerscourt, an undertaking that no boys would be withdrawn until the police were satisfied with their collection of evidence. Inspector Grime had apparently indicated that that day might be some way away. The police had no wish for potential witnesses to be dispersed across central and southern England. Leaning back in his chair, Davies told Powerscourt that the affair could close the school down unless the murder was solved quickly. One mother taking her son away, he reckoned, could be dismissed as eccentric, two could probably be finessed as over-cautious, but let three go and the trickle could become a flood. Headmaster Davies was in his early fifties, brown hair beginning to turn grey above his ears. Years of power over classrooms and colleagues had left him with authority stamped on his face, a Roman consul in the glory years of the Republic perhaps, or a viceroy of some far-flung outpost of Empire.

'This is every headmaster's nightmare, Lord Powerscourt, some out-of-the-way event like an outbreak of an infectious disease or a murder that makes the parents wonder if their child is safe. Stopping them taking their children away becomes like Canute trying to halt the incoming tide. I've just about managed it so far, but the water is lapping round my ankles and swirling round my calves at the back. God, I'll be glad when all this is over and we can get back to serious problems like Form Three's appalling French and the lack of a decent goalkeeper for the football team. You and I know perfectly well, Lord Powerscourt, that seventeen-year-old boys are quite capable of looking after themselves. But devoted mothers would not see the matter in those terms. Once the drip turned into a stream, Allison's School could be empty in a matter of days. And think,' he said finally, rising from his desk to prowl around his office, 'think of the effect it's going to have on recruitment for future years. Send your child to Allison's where members of staff are throttled in their offices. Send your son to a school where the bursar is killed in broad daylight. Welcome to the murder class.'

The headmaster sent Powerscourt on his way, saying that he had called an emergency meeting of the governors, some of whom were on the evening train from London. He recommended him to the bursar's closest friend in the school, a maths teacher called Joshua Peabody.

The maths teacher wore some of the strongest glasses Powerscourt had ever seen. The poor man, he thought, must be nearly blind. Receding hair, shirt buttons fastened out of line and a general air of absent-mindedness gave Peabody the appearance of a professor of some abstract subject like linguistics or Indo-Arabic languages, whose wife has recently left him. Powerscourt wondered what the boys thought of him.

Peabody led Powerscourt out of the school on to a path that circled the football pitches and took them some distance away from the main buildings. Only when they were well out of earshot did he speak.

'This is a terrible business,' he began, kicking a punctured football into the long grass, 'terrible. I can scarcely believe it, even now. It's so unfair that it should happen to Roderick.'

'Perhaps you could tell me about him. It always helps.'

'Well, I don't know anything at all about his early life, where he was born, where he went to school, that sort of thing. He never talked about growing up, not to me, at any rate. I only got to know him when I joined the staff here nine years ago. He was never the heart and soul of the staffroom, Roderick, if you know what I mean. Maybe we teachers are always a little uneasy in the company of bursars, I don't know. I do know that he took his job very seriously. The headmaster was fond of saying that if all the teachers kept their books as well as the bursar, his life would be much easier.'

'So how did you become friends?' asked Powerscourt, noting that the net at the back of the football pitch needed mending, another item of expenditure to be recorded in the bursar's ledgers.

'He loved the mountains,' Joshua Peabody said. 'When I was younger and my eyes were better I was always climbing whenever I could. Roderick, too, had been a fine mountaineer in his youth. Now we're not so young we used to go on walking holidays in Scotland or in the Alps. He always used to say that he wanted to see the Himalayas before he died, though I don't think he ever

41

did anything about it. He and I were planning a trip to the Dolomites in the Easter holidays.'

None of this, Powerscourt reflected, was likely to draw a killer to Allison's School and murder its bursar at his desk. 'Did he have any enemies? Do you have any suspicions about something in his past perhaps that could have led to his terrible end?'

'As I said,' Peabody had taken his glasses off and was rubbing them carefully on a large and rather dirty handkerchief, 'I don't know very much about his past. There is one thing I should tell you, Lord Powerscourt. It only started about two weeks ago, maybe less.' There was a pause while the handkerchief was restored to its pocket and the glasses replaced. Peabody looked more than ever the absent-minded professor, wondering where he has left his books. 'Over the last week or two,' he went on, 'Roderick Gill changed. He became a frightened man. He would stare anxiously at strangers when the two of us were walking into the town for a drink. I think, but I'm not sure, that he had been burning a lot of documents in the school incinerator and in the grate in his own rooms. Whether those were papers relating to his past or to the school or something else altogether I do not know.'

Two small boys kicking a football dashed past them on their way to the goal with the broken netting.

'Roderick would wait for the post in the morning with a look almost of terror on his face. One of the English teachers said he knew the cooked breakfast in the staff dining room was bad, but that was no reason to be afraid of it. I know that Roderick had asked for, and been granted, the option of two weeks of compassionate leave to begin the Monday after next. He had refused to tell anybody, not the headmaster, not even me, his closest friend in Allison's, where he proposed to go. And now this.' Peabody waved his hand back in the general direction of the school. 'All this fuss. Policemen. Anxious mothers. Special investigators from London. The headmaster fretting about the future of the school. All of this Roderick Gill would have found very hard to bear. Whatever it was he was afraid of,' Peabody stopped and looked Powerscourt in the eye for the first time during their talk, 'he never told me. He never told me what it was. Roderick Gill was a very frightened man in the last days of his life. Whatever or whoever it was he was frightened of, he was quite right to be terrified. They've got him in the end.'

3

Powerscourt found Inspector Grime staring wearily at a large map of North America on the wall of the geography classroom. Grime was grey haired now, with lines etched on his face and on his forehead. He had the air of a man who had seen as much as he wanted of crime and most other human activities. He was one of those unfortunate people who give the impression that they really enjoy being miserable.

Powerscourt told him of his conversation with Peabody and the fear that had gripped Roderick Gill in his last days.

'Peabody?' he said. 'That the one who teaches maths and wears those strong glasses? It's a wonder he can read his own equations when he writes them on the blackboard.'

'The same,' said Powerscourt. 'I'm sure some schools wouldn't employ him because he looks so scruffy. Bad example to the pupils, that sort of thing. Shoes polished, blazer middle button fastened, tie straight, that's what they like.'

'That's as may be,' said the Inspector, 'but the boys say

he's a brilliant teacher, especially with the ones who don't like mathematics. Anyway, he's told you more about the dead man than I've learnt from these boys all afternoon. Only thing we're sure of is that Bursar Gill died somewhere between eight and nine-thirty in the morning. I don't know if you've noticed that corridor where his office was. It's the main thoroughfare of the school, with classrooms and offices off it, including the dining hall at one end and the chapel off a side corridor at the other.'

'Would there be lots of boys moving about between those times?' Powerscourt asked.

'Breakfast is at eight o'clock, my lord. By about twenty past lots of them are going back to their dayrooms or their studies to get the books they need for morning lessons. By a quarter to nine they all charge up the corridor again for morning prayers. By nine o'clock they're back in it again en route to the first lesson. Somebody must have seen something.' The Inspector gave an aged globe a vigorous shove and the continents of the world whizzed round on their axis. 'They're so young, these boys, and so innocent most of them, even the older ones, they leave you feeling quite exhausted and very old, very old indeed.'

'What did they tell you?' asked Powerscourt.

'Well, I don't know if somebody told them to say as little as possible or not. It certainly sounded like it. I've heard burglars in Norwich in my time who were more forthcoming than some of these lads. Basically, they didn't know the bursar at all. He didn't teach them; he didn't do any coaching at games. They hardly ever saw him. The only thing they knew about him was that he had dismissed the previous head cook for overspending his budget and fiddling the figures. The new man, apparently, is terrible. One cheeky monkey suggested one of the boys might have killed him because the food is now so bad they're hungry all the time. A couple of them said he looked worried. One of the senior years said Gill had been spotted in the town drowning his sorrows in The Poacher's Catch with the maths teacher Peabody. He didn't say how he came by this information, mind you. The rogue must have been skulking in the public bar – the staff here use the lounge, always have.' The Inspector gave the globe another spin. 'I'll have to interview the rest of them tomorrow and maybe the next day, though I don't have much hope of anything very useful. The headmaster insisted I interview every single pupil, probably so they can tell their parents. You'll be wanting to see the body, my lord, down at the hospital in the town.'

Powerscourt wondered how many years these maps had been on the walls. The colours were going. Central Canada, he observed, had faded to a dull pink while the two coastlines at opposite ends of the country were still red. 'Have you ever seen anything like that mark on his chest before, Inspector?'

'I've never seen anything like it in my life,' replied Inspector Grime, 'not even up here in the wilds of Norfolk.'

Later that evening Powerscourt met the headmaster in his study. Davies had his feet on his desk and was nursing a very large glass of whisky.

'I don't normally drink in the term time at all, but that governors' meeting was terrible,' he said, grimacing at the memory. 'They virtually accused me of having carried out the murder. There's one very old governor who was at the school about the beginning of the last century, and he's been on the governing body for years, certainly far longer than I've been headmaster here. Discipline, he always goes on about discipline. In his day, I expect, a boy was flogged for anything at all, shoelaces not properly tied, running in the corridor, that sort of thing. He claimed lack of discipline caused the bursar's death, though he couldn't explain how.'

Powerscourt saw that the headmaster's study was more or less what you would expect in a place like this. There was an enormous desk, virtually guaranteed to intimidate nervous new teachers or schoolboy criminals. The walls were lined with school photographs. There was an oar from the First Trinity Boat Club, the rowing arm of Trinity College, Cambridge, behind the headmaster's desk. Powerscourt noticed that a recently appointed bishop of the Church of England and a junior member of the cabinet had rowed on the Cam with the headmaster. There were bookshelves, one shelf full of a volume called *The Future of the Public Schools*, written by the headmaster himself. A selection of vicious-looking canes were prominently displayed next to the oar to strike fear into the hearts of malefactors.

'Peabody says Gill was frightened in the last few weeks of his life. Did you notice that too, Headmaster?'

It was just like being in the army, Powerscourt remembered. You called a man by his title, not by his name, as if function was the sole criterion in addressing your fellow man.

'I thought he looked a bit under the weather. But remember, Powerscourt, there are a lot of people to look after here. I'm not the matron or the father confessor to the staff or anybody else.'

'May I ask you a difficult question, Headmaster? I

apologize for troubling you but time is important in murder cases. What precisely was the link between the school and the Silkworkers Company down in London?'

'I wish they'd stay in London, those people, and not come up here and give me a hard time during governors' meetings,' the headmaster said wearily. 'The Silkworkers look after the endowments of the school. Always have, always will, I expect. The chairman of the board of governors is always one of theirs, as are four of the other school governors. It's like one of those cabinets packed with the Prime Minister's relations in Lord Salisbury's time. The family, or in our case the Silkworkers, call the shots. It would be very difficult to push through a policy they didn't approve of. Silkworkers appointed me; they'll probably appoint my successor.'

'I have heard that there may be changes afoot in the world of the Silkworkers,' said Powerscourt. He had told the Inspector about the death of Abel Meredith but nobody else. Sometimes he wondered if this policy of closed boxes was the right one. 'Have they affected you here, Headmaster?'

'You're damned well-informed about our livery company, Powerscourt, if I may say so. I would ask you to treat what I'm about to say in confidence. We're not meant to talk to anybody about it.' Powerscourt thought Davies must sound like this when talking to junior members of staff, slightly superior, slightly supercilious. 'The changes relate to the increase in value of the endowments since they were first bequeathed. Some land near the Mansion House, for instance, would be worth infinitely more now than it was back in the fourteenth century. There's talk about having a vote among the membership about what to do. Oddly enough, that was part of Roderick Gill's responsibilities.

He was preparing a report for me on the implications of the changes for the school and whether we should support them. It was due next week as a matter of fact.'

'Do you know if he had written it? If it was finished and ready to go?' Powerscourt wondered if one of Grime's constables would have appreciated the significance of such a document, stacked away in his office with the annual reports and the quarterly financial projections.

'I don't, as a matter of fact. I rather suspect Roderick would have been against any change in the current arrangements. He was that sort of man. I think it's all very clever and rather cunning myself.'

'In what way?'

'Well,' said the headmaster, finally restoring his legs to ground level from the vast expanse of his desk, 'suppose you're the Prime Warden of the Silkworkers. You've got these almshouses to keep up, and these schools and the pension payments to the old boys. You've got this vast property portfolio all over the City of London and the richer counties of southern England. And you think there's going to be a war. First thing to go when the guns go off will be the value of property. Your little empire will be worth far less than it was, the rents will tumble, it will be difficult to sell places. So liquidate it all now and come back to the market when the prices are depressed later on. Stash it all away for the time being in America or Canada or somewhere your bankers tell you it's safe.' The headmaster refilled his glass with a very small helping of whisky. 'Clever, don't you think? Of course you can't say what you're about; you can't say why you're really doing it. People would say you were mad or unpatriotic, or greedy or something like that. This is only my theory, you understand.'

For the second time in less than a week Powerscourt resolved to talk to his banker brother-in-law William Burke as soon as possible.

Silence fell in the headmaster's study. Some night bird was calling urgently outside the windows. A very modern clock, there to keep the headmaster punctual, was ticking at the corner of the desk. Powerscourt could just make out the inscription: 'To John Davies with thanks for five years of excellent work, from the headmaster and staff of Rugby School.'

'There is one thing I should tell you about Roderick Gill.' The headmaster gathered the ends of his gown behind him and began pacing up and down his command post. 'I don't suppose Peabody told you anything about the women, did he?' he asked with the air of one who expects the answer no.

'Not a word,' replied Powerscourt.

The headmaster stopped by his curtains and drew them back a couple of feet. Outside it was very dark, with a few lights burning over in the masters' quarters.

'This isn't easy for me,' Davies continued. 'The thing is, Roderick Gill was notorious for having affairs with married women. They were always over forty, for some reason. Maybe he liked them older or more experienced, who knows. Maybe the younger ones wouldn't have him. Maybe their husbands would be less violent. He never carried on with the few wives we have here; it was always with women in the town. Roderick was a church warden and later treasurer of Saint Peter and Paul in Fakenham. It's got a bloody great tower and they say they stored gunpowder in there during the Civil War. Anyway, Gill's position at the church was his base camp for getting to know the women of the parish. Some of the more cynical members of the congregation used to refer to him as the Groper in the Vestry, I gather. I don't know if he launched any assaults in the precincts of the church itself – I rather doubt it. But there it is, or rather was. It had been going on for years now.'

'Thank you for telling me,' said Powerscourt, as the headmaster strode back to his desk. 'It can't have been easy for you. And forgive me for asking, but do you know the names of any of his conquests in the last few years?'

'I do know there was somebody on the books fairly recently. They were seen coming out of a hotel in Brandon last summer, I think it was. Mrs Mitchell, the lady was called, Hilda Mitchell. Early forties, very pretty, I was told, her husband away a lot on business. He was a mason, specializing in restoring old buildings like churches or manor houses, so he was away a lot. I don't know if it's still going on.'

Powerscourt suddenly wondered if he should match the headmaster's confidence about the private life of Roderick Gill with an account of the strange marks on his chest. But he preferred not to. He didn't think it would help. He wondered if he was right in his reticence.

'Could I ask you a final question, Lord Powerscourt?' The headmaster was bringing the meeting to a close. Perhaps there are a couple more meetings scheduled after I go, Powerscourt thought – head of Classics asking for two more hours a week for Latin classes, head of woodwork complaining that the boys kept stealing the screwdrivers. 'I know it must be very difficult to know, but can you give me any idea how long it will be before you find the murderer and the case is closed down? It's going to be rather like a siege here, you see. It will be difficult for people to concentrate on what they're at

Allison's for, teaching and learning, with the police on the prowl and so on.'

Powerscourt was quite relieved to have been relegated to 'and so on'.

'I wish I could help you there, Headmaster, but I would not wish to give you false comfort. It could take a week. We could still be here by Easter. The timetables of murderers and of those who would catch them are outside your control as they are outside mine. If you can steel yourself to prepare for a long haul, that would be for the best. I'm sorry I can't be more hopeful. You have been very frank with me and I'm most grateful.'

That night Powerscourt had a strange dream. He thought when he awoke that it might have had something to do with the globes and the maps in the geography classroom. He was standing on top of a great sand dune in the middle of a vast desert. Down below him was an enormous plain of sand, completely empty, not even a small oasis or a solitary palm tree to be seen. To his left and right the landscape was the same, sand, hills of sand, plains of sand, seas of sand, nothing but sand. He suspected he might be in Saudi Arabia or one of those Middle Eastern countries. When he looked more closely at the plain below he saw to his horror that the sand had been blown into a particular pattern. It was exactly the same as the strange patterns on the dead men's chests, as if a giant thistle of Brobdingnagian proportions had been pressed into the sand. It seemed to go on for miles in all directions. When he looked closer, shading his eyes from the pitiless sun above, he saw a small figure marching resolutely towards the centre of the thistle. He was not dressed in white robes as you might have expected in this landscape, but in a three-piece suit and bowler hat that looked as though they might have come from a fashionable tailor in London's Jermyn Street. As he stared down, Powerscourt realized something stranger yet. It was if the sands were shifting under the man's feet. For march on as he might, he was making no progress towards the centre, no progress at all. The centre of the thistle remained as far away as ever. He was never going to reach it.

Shortly after eight o'clock the next morning Powerscourt met Inspector Grime outside the main entrance to the school. Over from their left came the enormous racket of one hundred and fifty boys eating their breakfasts at the same time. In front of the buildings a severe frost had turned the playing fields almost white.

'No more murders in the night anyway,' said the Inspector morosely. 'I suppose our man's got clean away by now, damn his eyes. Hospital first for you, my lord. Ask for Dr Pike, as in fish, he's expecting you. Then we've left the bursar's quarters exactly as they were before he died for you, before we start taking things away. The headmaster wants his office papers and the ones in his room left where they are now. Count yourself lucky, my lord. I've got the three youngest classes to talk to this morning. One at a time, for God's sake. Might as well listen to the birds on the marshes as this lot. All those maps and globes in that room get me down. I always hated geography when I was at school; the teacher used to steal our pencils when he thought we weren't looking. Never mind. I'll see you later this morning. Out of the mouths of babes and sucklings. God help us all.'

The boys were being released from breakfast, charging down the corridors to find their books for early lessons. A tall boy of about eighteen in a striped blazer, who Powerscourt thought must be a prefect, was shouting at them. 'How many times do I have to tell you! Walk, don't run in the corridor!'

The hospital was new, the paint still fresh, the walls not marked by the passage of too many trolleys. Dr Pike was a young man of about thirty who told Powerscourt cheerfully that he had no idea about the marks on the chest, that death must have been almost instantaneous, and that the murderer must have had very strong arms. Death, he said, must have happened between the hours of eight and nine-thirty. To Powerscourt's surprise he inquired about Inspector Grime.

'How is the good Inspector these days? Is he still as miserable and morose as ever? He came here last year to investigate some nasty thefts from the dispensary and we almost kept him in he was so gloomy. Might have cheered him up, a week or so on the mental ward with people even more disturbed than he is.'

'Since you ask,' Powerscourt replied with a smile, 'I'd have to report that there appears to be little change in the patient's condition. Barometer permanently set to miserable, as far as I can see. He seems a capable officer, mind you.'

'Oh, he is. He cleared up our burglary very quickly. Send him my regards anyway. Tell him we often think of him up here at the hospital.'

The late bursar's rooms were on the top floor of the new building. He had a large sitting room and a tiny bedroom at the back. Powerscourt saw that one long wall was entirely covered with files. Bursar Gill, it appeared, had been a careful man. Looking closer, Powerscourt discovered that Gill had been one of those people who never threw anything away, the years marching across the wall to end in the year 1909. In this universe of files, 1910 had not yet begun. Not for him the annual cull of useless papers, sorted into the good and the useless between Christmas and the New Year. The earliest file went back to 1855 when Gill was seven years old. There were papers relating to his early schooling, even a report or two from a well-known prep school near Oxford, 'very quiet in class', 'shows promise in mathematics', 'poor grasp of Greek grammar'. But then there was a gap in the files. From 1865 to 1880 there was nothing at all. Powerscourt wondered if these were the files that Gill had been burning in his last days, some in the college incinerator, some in his own grate. Perhaps he had simply changed his mind about filing, a young man with better and more interesting things to do with his time than pushing pieces of paper into folders. Perhaps he had spent his entire life in those years pursuing women over forty.

In the years that followed there was a file a year, sometimes two. They showed that Gill had worked for years for a firm of accountants in London before coming to Norfolk. His years at Allison's were thoroughly covered, though Powerscourt noticed that the subject matter was always in the public sphere, details of the estimates for the new buildings put up around the turn of the century, records of the annual financial performance of the school, separate sections for his role as the treasurer at the church. But of correspondence with ladies, under or over forty, there was no trace at all. Of anything that might have made him fearful in his last days there was no sign either. Powerscourt looked closely at the bottom of the grate in case the remains of any documents were still to be found among the ash but there was nothing. He wondered if Gill had a secret hiding place somewhere in this room where compromising or frightening letters might be found. He decided to ask Inspector Grime's men to test the room for such a place. Grime could authorize that in a murder hunt. He, Powerscourt, could not.

When he discussed it with the Inspector at break time that morning he found the policeman in unusually cheerful mood. 'It might be nothing, it probably is,' he said to Powerscourt, walking slowly along the front of the dormitory block, 'but one of those young hooligans said something very interesting to me this morning. I've heard all sorts of rubbish. You'd think they had better things to do with their time than read the works of Sexton Blake, but no. Most of the boys had theories that were wildly improbable. But just this one lad, fourteen years old, looking exactly like the choirboy he is, gave me a very interesting snippet. It was the postman, he said. What was the postman doing there that early in the corridor where Roderick Gill's office was? Postmen don't usually arrive till mid-morning break. And he thought, but he wasn't sure, that this wasn't the usual postman. Now here, my lord, here is where he becomes a credible witness, young Ewart Jenkins. When I asked him how the postman was different, taller, shorter, fatter, that sort of thing, he said he couldn't answer, he couldn't be sure. If I went on making suggestions, he said, he would get confused. He was sure about what he had told me, but no more. I'm going to talk to the postal people once I've finished with the lower forms. One of their senior men lives a couple of doors from me.'

Shortly before lunch it began to snow. It fell quickly, settling on the roofs of the red brick buildings, obliterating the grass on the playing fields. Out in the Wild West beyond the football pitches a junior gardener reported that the lake was frozen. If the weather went on like this for a day or two, he said, the ice might be firm enough for skating. With the snow came a bitter wind that blew the snow into drifts up against the school windows and rendered the headmaster's car virtually invisible just outside the front door. One of the younger science teachers brought out a series of sticks he had used in years gone by. He got the boys to place them in different places around the school and to write down in their notebooks the height of the snow on all the days it remained. The teacher believed this would teach his pupils the value of experiments and the proper collection of data.

The weather put the headmaster in a remarkably good mood. He observed with glee to his deputy, a very boring man who had been teaching the same history syllabus for over thirty years – at this point in the school year, towards the end of January, it was time to kill Cromwell off for the senior forms and move on to the Restoration – that at least those wretched mothers would not be turning out to complain in the same numbers. He so hoped, he said, with a singular lack of Christian charity, that they would be bloody well snowed in for days, if not weeks.

In the lunch break smaller boys began construction of a vast snowman which Powerscourt thought was going to be on the same scale as the Statue of Liberty on

Ellis Island in New York. Elder boys organized snowball fights. The prefects in their striped blazers tried to look superior, gazing with lofty indifference on the activities of their younger brothers and schoolfellows as if they, the prefects, had put away these childish things years before.

Powerscourt wondered if the snow made the business of detection easier or more difficult and decided it made no difference at all. That afternoon, while the Inspector departed to talk to the Royal Mail, he proposed to call on the late Roderick Gill's mistress. The Inspector was delighted Powerscourt had taken on this particular assignment.

'Fact is, my lord,' he said, neatly dodging a long-distance snowball sent his way by the finest fielder in the First Eleven, 'I think you'll do that much better than I would. I'm actually not sure I could bring myself to start asking questions about her affair with Gill, if that's the right way to put it. I'd be too embarrassed.'

'I'm afraid I've had these kinds of conversations before,' said Powerscourt. 'They're not too bad as long as you keep the whole thing as matter-of-fact as possible. Don't even think of mentioning the word love. It would only set them off.'

'Good God! How absolutely frightful for you. I'll be much happier with the postmen.'

Twenty minutes later Powerscourt was walking up the Cromer Road to Mrs Mitchell's house just beyond the postbox. The snow was still falling, the countryside almost obliterated by its thick white coat. The house was a two-storey cottage with a thatched roof and ancient windows. Mrs Mitchell, when she answered the door, was not ancient at all. Powerscourt thought she looked much younger than the forty years assigned to her by the headmaster. She was blonde with soft blue eyes, her figure almost totally concealed behind a large blue apron dotted with bunny rabbits.

'Please forgive me,' she said, pointing to her apron, when Powerscourt had made his introductions. 'I was just making a cake for the children's tea. They'll be so excited about the snow.'

Powerscourt had timed his arrival for the gap after lunch before any children might be home from their lessons. Mrs Mitchell showed him into a small chair by the fire.

'I expect you've come about Roddy,' she began. 'The vicar told me about his death yesterday. It's terrible, just terrible. He was such a kind man.'

'Please forgive me, Mrs Mitchell, if I have to ask some difficult questions. I'm afraid death and murder have no respect for people's history or their emotional lives. Could I ask when you first became friends?' asked Powerscourt. 'Not the particular day, just the time of year.' Avoid the 'l' word at all costs, he reminded himself again. Friendship was a much duller word, but useful on occasions.

'It must have been two years ago,' she replied, 'round about the time of the Harvest Festival. I always help out in St Peter and Paul round about then and Roddy was in the church a lot, working on the accounts. He had to present them to the parish council the week after.'

'So the friendship developed in the weeks and months after that service?' said Powerscourt, wondering what would happen if he had asked when they became close.

'Well, yes,' Mrs Mitchell said, blushing slightly. 'It would have been about the middle of December. Jude, my husband, was away a lot around then, working at York Minster.'

'Quite so,' said Powerscourt. 'I'm not concerned with the nature of your relationship with the bursar, Mrs Mitchell, but I would like to know about Mr Gill's state of mind in the weeks before he died.'

'It's so strange hearing you call him Mr Gill,' she said. 'He was always Roddy to me.'

'What did the vicar say about the manner of his death, may I ask?'

She gazed into the fire. Outside on the window sill an angry robin was staring at them, as if it blamed them for the snow. 'He told me Roddy had been murdered,' she said finally, 'by a person or persons unknown, as he put it. What a terrible phrase. So impersonal.'

Powerscourt supposed the information must have reached the vicar via the headmaster.

'Well, I'm afraid he was, murdered, I mean. That's why it's important we know about his state of mind.' Powerscourt was speaking as gently as he knew how. He suspected Mrs Mitchell might burst into tears at any minute and he would have to leave. 'One of his colleagues told me he was worried about something in the last weeks,' he went on.

'I couldn't say,' she said 'All the time I knew him he was a very calm person. He was like a sailing ship that never had to adjust the sails, if you know what I mean. Things might change around him but he stayed the same, calm and quiet and matter-of-fact.'

'Just what you would expect from somebody who trained as an accountant,' said Powerscourt. 'But you didn't notice any changes in the weeks before he died?'

Mrs Mitchell looked into the fire once more. 'I don't know,' she said at last. 'He didn't tell me. And I hadn't been seeing as much of Roddy as I used to, these last three or four months. He was so busy on the history of the relations between the Silkworkers and the school and trying to work out if the changes were going to help Allison's or not. But I do remember him saying that the past never leaves you alone, never.'

Powerscourt wondered about the missing years in the filing system on the shelves of Gill's room. 'Did he talk to you about his earlier life at all, about growing up, being a young man, that sort of thing?'

'No, he didn't, Lord Powerscourt. Oh dear, you must think I'm a terrible witness, unable to answer so many of your questions. He never talked to me about any previous women in his time either. It was as if,' she paused for a moment, 'as if I was the first woman in his life. That's how it seemed to me at the time, anyway. Thinking about it now, I'm sure I wasn't the first one, not by a long chalk. But I'm not complaining. I can't make a fuss about the times when I didn't know him.'

'How very sensible,' said Powerscourt. 'Did he ever tell you if he had been married before? Before he knew you, I mean?'

'No he didn't, he didn't tell me. He could have been married fifty times for all I knew about it.'

'Forgive me, Mrs Mitchell, I suspect you may have had this thought yourself since you heard of his death. Do you think some relationship in his past may have had something to do with his murder?'

'Some jealous husband, do you mean, who had just learnt about an earlier affair, risen out of the past like the avenging angel? I have wondered about that, Lord Powerscourt, of course I have. Yet again I don't have an answer for you.'

Powerscourt thought she was on the brink of tears.

'You have been very honest with me, Mrs Mitchell, and I am grateful. I doubt if many people could have been as frank in your circumstances. One last question, if I could, and then I'll leave you alone. How would you describe Roderick Gill, Mrs Mitchell? What was his character?'

'My Roddy?' She smiled across at him. 'Well, he was calm. He was gentle. He was the same on a Thursday as he was on the Monday. I don't think you could say that about many people. Like many men concerned with money, so the bank manager told me when Jude and I were in danger of falling into debt, he was very good with other people's money and no good at all with his own. He was always complaining about being about to run out of cash, his salary for that month all gone and so forth. He was very generous to me, always buying me presents. He was always careful only to come when the children would be out or at school, in case they said something to their father.' She paused. 'I don't think that's all there was to him,' she said sadly. 'He wasn't eloquent, he wasn't funny, but he was very gentle and very kind.'

She stopped once more and Powerscourt felt she was very close to tears now.

'Thank you so much,' he said, rising out of his chair by the other side of the fire. 'I've taken up enough of your time. You've been most helpful. Could I just ask, if you think of anything else that might help, please get in touch. The school will know where to find me.'

Hilda Mitchell showed him to the door. 'Even if I do,' she said very softly, 'think of something, I mean, it's not going to bring him back. Nothing's going to bring him back now, is it, Lord Powerscourt? I shall never see Roddy again.'

4

It was the largest force Inspector Fletcher had ever commanded. It wasn't a regiment or a battalion or even a company. His unit this January morning, he thought, remembering the books on military history he loved as a boy, was somewhere between a squad and a platoon. Apart from himself and his Sergeant, he had eighteen men on parade outside the Jesus Hospital in Marlow. Three police stations in Maidenhead had been denuded of some of their officers to provide the manpower. Manoeuvres were to start shortly after eight o'clock when the last silkman had left his quarters and reported for breakfast in the dining hall.

As the clock above the little tower reached eight o'clock, the Sergeant, on duty by the dining hall, waved an unobtrusive arm to his superior officer. The old men were all sitting down. The eighteen policemen marched into the almshouse. Each one had been assigned a particular room and the Sergeant had one of his own. All had been briefed half an hour before at a specially convened assembly in the Maidenhead police station. They were searching, the Inspector informed them, for the murder weapon which had cut the dead man's throat, and the strange instrument which might have made the marks on his chest. Inspector Fletcher had wondered long and hard about whether he should tell his little force about the stigmata, as he now referred to them. Eventually he decided that he had no choice. If his men didn't know what they were looking for, how could they possibly find it? He swore the police constables to secrecy on this matter, assuring them that whoever mentioned a word about it, even to their own families, would have all his holiday entitlement cancelled for the foreseeable future. And they were also looking for papers, any private papers they could find. These, he told them, might be letters from family or friends, papers relating to their previous lives, wills, any memorabilia that might say where they had been and what they had done in earlier times. Each officer had a folder with the number of the room he was assigned to inscribed in large black letters. Inspector Fletcher had had enough of the confused memories of the over-seventies. Evidence, hard evidence was what he needed.

The old men were having a treat this morning. Fried eggs and bacon happened to be on the menu, a rare combination. This always improved morale. As they tucked into their portions, sauce bottles at the ready, the policemen slipped into their rooms and began the search. They pulled open the drawers, they checked the small cupboards, they emptied the pockets of any jackets left on a hanger, they knocked on the walls in the quest for hidden compartments and they checked underneath the threadbare carpets for any loose floorboards that might mask a treasure trove of hidden weaponry. They shook any books they could find to see if any documents were being concealed in the pages. They inspected the pictures on the walls and any photographs they could find, just as the Inspector had told them, taking the pictures out of the frames to see what might be lurking behind. They checked the stairs that led to the upper floors. Some of the folders filled up quickly. Others were less profitable, with only a couple of items being removed.

The Inspector reckoned that the time required to eat breakfast, even with the luxury of fried eggs and bacon, might not be enough for his purpose. The chaplain, also the curate of St Michael and All Angels in Marlow, had been pressed into the police service for the day. All the old men were to make their way to the chapel immediately after breakfast. Going back to their rooms was not allowed. They were to attend a special service for the feast day of St Thomas Aquinas, which fell on the following day. The curate had preached on this subject before, having made a special study of the late St Thomas Aquinas and his theology at university. He was to preach until the Sergeant opened the main door and nodded to him. At that point the silkmen were to sing a final hymn, 'For all the saints who from their labours rest'. This, the chaplain assured the Inspector, had no fewer than eleven verses and if sung at a funereal pace as dictated by the organist of St Luke's on the hospital piano, should last between five and ten minutes, ample time for his policemen to pick up their belongings and beat an orderly retreat.

The Inspector paced anxiously round the quadrangle. His Sergeant conducted spot checks on the officers, ensuring that they were obeying orders. Eventually the Sergeant blew on his whistle after the third verse and the eighteen policemen from Maidenhead were marched out of the hospital to carry their booty back to the station. It was just before half past nine. The Inspector had told nobody, not Monk, not any of the old men, about this morning's exercise. He stayed behind to reassure the silk-men that their sacrifice was only temporary and that their possessions would be returned to them in due course. He did not specify, and the men did not think to ask, how long that might be. As recompense, he assured them, the police would be buying drinks for everybody at the Rose and Crown that evening between the hours of eight and nine. By eleven that morning Inspector Fletcher was back in his office. The spoils of war were laid out on his floor in numerical order from Number One to Number Twenty. Albert Fletcher hung his jacket behind his chair and set to work.

One hundred and fifty miles to the north-east the other Inspector in Powerscourt's life was really rather pleased with himself. The two men were standing on the edge of the playing fields where the snowman was being erected. Grime refused to go back to the geography classroom if he could avoid it. He refused to talk anywhere in the school where small boys who ran as if in training for the next Olympic Games in Stockholm in two years' time might appear round a corner at any minute and hear things they were not meant to know. The snowman, Powerscourt observed, was now higher than most of the junior members of the school. They had built small towers in the manner of building workers with their scaffolding and were adding to the figure with a selec-tion of stolen shovels. The lake, one small boy had told Powerscourt solemnly, was not yet ready for skating. Pemberton Minor of the Upper Fourth had ventured across its frozen surface only for the ice to open and swallow him up. But for the timely intervention of a couple of gardeners, there would have been a great sadness in the Pemberton household. The soaked victim was now wrapped up in bed in the infirmary with a couple of hot water bottles for company.

'How was your witness?' inquired the Inspector.

Powerscourt took some time to reply. He had been thinking about his interview with Mrs Mitchell on his way to the school that morning and was surprised at how little she had told him. He wondered why she had not mentioned Gill's anxieties in his last days.

'Well,' he said, 'I rather think she had the better of the encounter.'

'What do you mean?' asked the Inspector.

'I don't think she told me any actual lies,' Powerscourt replied, staring out at the relays of Allison's youth, totally focused on the task in hand, beginning to put a face on the snowman. They appeared to have laid their hands on a pipe and an ancient muffler of indeterminate colour to decorate their creation.

'I think she left out quite a lot. I'm sure there are things she's not telling me about. God knows what they are. Looking back on it, I may have been too gentle with her. It's amazing what you can get away with if you look on the verge of tears all the time.'

'Did she actually break down and cry all over you?' asked Grime with horror.

'No, she didn't. But she did manage to convey the impression that it might happen at any time. I'd back women to be more devious than men in those circumstances any day of the week, wouldn't you, Inspector?'

There was a mighty wail from the snowman party. Pipe and muffler had fallen out, pulling a great deal of snow that might have been the nose, forehead and mouth behind them. The snowman looked as though he had been shot in the face, white snow falling to the ground in place of the blood that might have come from a human.

'Will you go and see Mrs Mitchell again, my lord? Do you think you might do better a second time?'

'I did think of writing to her, but I suspect that would meet with even less success. She'd have all the time she wanted to compose her replies. I shall think about it. Now then, how were the postmen?'

'Ah, my lord, I think there is progress in that direction. Only limited progress, mind you, but it's something. You see, it would seem that my angelic choirboy may have been telling the truth. There may have been a postman in the corridor that morning, but he wasn't a real one. It must have been somebody dressed up as a postman, but probably a bringer of death rather than the morning mail. The real postman who comes to the school on his rounds, Matthew Cameron, did visit the school as usual that morning. But he came at half past ten and was able to observe the confusion brought by Gill's death. He's sure there was no proper postman up here at the earlier time. He's busy at the moment but he's promised to come and see us on his way home.'

Inspector Fletcher and Sergeant Donaldson were nearly halfway through their folders with the paperwork from the Jesus Hospital. Fletcher had not been sure exactly what he would find – in some ways the early-morning raid had been a shot in the dark – but one aspect of the paperwork he found absolutely astonishing. They had looked through a lot of material they had expected to find, letters from family members in distant parts, some as far away as New Zealand and Nebraska. The old gentleman in Number Fourteen, Stephen Potter, was a great reader who seemed to belong to three public libraries. He had Conrad's *Lord Jim* by his bedside, and recent volumes by Conan Doyle and Kipling on his shelf. Fletcher noted with interest that all these books were now overdue and Number Fourteen was going to have to pay a hefty fine when he returned the books to their libraries of origin. It was his Sergeant, Peter Donaldson, a tall young man of about thirty with the largest moustache in the Maidenhead force, who first drew the startling fact to his attention.

'Could I make a comment, sir?' said Donaldson, whose parents had always pressed on him from the earliest age the virtues of politeness and cleanliness. One or two of the older Inspectors had been known to complain that Donaldson always smelt like a bar of soap first thing in the morning.

'Of course,' replied Fletcher, turning an ancient Bible upside down and shaking it vigorously. Three old pieces of paper fell to the floor.

'Well, sir, we've been through eight or nine of these folders so far. And four of them have quite a lot of money tucked away in banks or building societies, nearly four thousand pounds in one case, with the account books hidden in the man's atlas between the maps of Paraguay and Brazil. But there aren't any wills. You'd have thought that if they were that careful with money they'd have been bound to make a will, wouldn't you?'

'Ah, hm, well, you would, that's quite right. How very odd. Maybe their last wills and testaments are with their solicitors.' Inspector Fletcher paused again. Sergeant

Donaldson had worked out long before how his superior officer's mind worked. He knew what was coming.

'When we've finished with this lot, Sergeant, perhaps you could call on the relevant offices, banks, solicitors and so on, and make inquiries. You'd better try Reading after you're through with Maidenhead.'

'Of course, sir.'

It was dark when the real postman arrived at Allison's School. The snowman seemed to glow slightly in the reflected light from the great windows. Pemberton Minor in the infirmary was making a quick recovery, pleading with matron for more pieces of cake after his tea. Cake in the school was a luxury only offered to recovering invalids. The postman, a cheerful Cockney called William Cameron, long exiled to East Anglia, showed them his normal rounds.

'We do a rough sort-out of the post beforehand, sir. Headmaster's mail gets delivered to his secretary's office, masters' mail to the common room, boys' mail to the porter's lodge, registrar and bursar's mail to their offices in that long corridor. Bursar Gill, sir, he always had a lot of post, parents paying their bills, that sort of thing, I suppose.'

'Did our phantom postman actually deliver any letters anywhere?' asked Powerscourt. 'Or was he just dressed in the uniform so people assumed he was a postman? I've always thought uniforms make people almost invisible. People notice the uniform rather the person inside it.'

'Well, sir,' said the real postman, 'there's a thing and no mistake. I checked in the headmaster's office as they were locking up on my way here. Their mail arrived with me, not with the other bloke. I don't think he can have delivered a thing.'

'How would he have known where the bursar's office was?' Inspector Grime was writing busily in his notebook.

'Well, sir, or sirs, that's your department, not mine, I reckon. Maybe he was a part-time member of staff. Maybe he had worked here in the past and had a grudge against the bursar. Some grudge, mind you. Maybe he just rang them up and said he had a parcel to deliver and exactly where was the bursar's office.'

'You'd have made a good policeman, Mr Cameron,' said Powerscourt. 'I suppose we'll have to interview everybody all over again to see if anybody else remembers noticing something. Those are all very intelligent questions, my friend. You'd have been a credit to the force.'

'I was a policeman once, sir. It was some time ago now, mind you.'

'What happened?' said Grime, laying his pencil aside for a moment. 'Did the force not agree with you?'

'I think it was more that I didn't agree with the force, sir. I had a truly terrible Sergeant, you see. He was so horrible to his constables that two of us knocked him down, right in front of Kensington Town Hall. He was out cold, but I was out of the police.'

'Do you miss it, police work?' asked Powerscourt.

'No, I don't, sir. I don't miss it at all. I felt sorry for the criminals most of the time. If I'd been as poor as some of them, I'd have gone round burgling rich people's houses in Chelsea or Mayfair. Those people could afford to lose a thing or two. The poor bugger burglar, forgive my language, gentlemen, didn't have enough money to feed his family most of the time.'

Inspector Grime had not smiled at all during the story

71

of the Sergeant felled in front of Kensington Town Hall. He looked as though he disapproved strongly of such behaviour.

'Quite,' he said, 'quite. Now is there anything more you have to tell us? We mustn't keep you from home too long.'

'Don't you worry about me, sir. Wife's gone to her mother's, thank God. Miserable cow.' Powerscourt wondered which one the epithet belonged to, but thought it better not to ask. 'I'm meeting a few friends at the Green Dragon the other side of Fakenham. But there is one thing, sir. I asked down the office if anybody had lost a uniform or had one stolen. Nobody has. So wherever our imposter got his kit from, it wasn't from our place.'

'We've kept you long enough,' said Inspector Grime, frowning slightly. 'Thank you so much for your information, it's been most helpful.'

'Bright chap, our postman,' said Powerscourt. 'Maybe he should have stayed in the police force after all.'

'Didn't care for the fellow very much myself,' said Inspector Grime. 'Bloody man might have knocked me down, too.'

Joseph the manciple was making his final tour of the tables laid out for 'The Silkworkers' dinner that evening. A wine glass was out of position. A fish fork was aligned five per cent out of true. A salt cellar was too far away from its partner the pepper pot. These minutiae were meat and drink to Joseph, who had been in charge of catering at Silkworkers Hall for over twenty years. He came originally from Ephesus but nobody could pronounce his surname. Simple Joseph he became and he was now as widely known in the City as the Prime Warden himself. He had taken one very important decision in his early years. He had watched as other, less scrupulous manciples in other livery companies helped themselves to their employers' funds and their employers' food and their employers' drink. Most of these organizations, as Joseph well knew, were heavily stocked with account-ants and bankers among their membership, well able to sniff out corruption at a couple of hundred paces. So Joseph confined himself to very small, some might have called them minute, helpings. By now he was a rich man, probably richer than some of the members. He asked prominent people for investment tips on a regular basis. This regular flow of inside information, he would tell anybody who queried his house and his lifestyle, was the basis of his fortune.

Joseph made a final check on the menus with their sketch of a chorus line from the Folies Bergère on the front page. Nine courses were displayed on the two inside pages, and the Silkworkers' emblem, an enormous bale of bright red silk, festooned with pictures of the sailing ships and dhows and junks and steamships that brought the material to London's docks from the East. A previous Prime Warden in the fifteenth century had once worked in the trade in Venice and a pretty gondola with a red-shirted gondolier plied his craft along the bottom of the emblem as if he was making his way down the Grand Canal itself, past the gothic palazzos towards the basin of St Mark.

Joseph had borrowed a young French chef from the Savoy for the evening, and the smells of his cooking were already creeping out from the kitchens. Twenty-four members of the honourable company, twelve at the top table and six each at the two sides, were to take their places for the evening banquet. There were a dozen

Santenay sous la Roche to accompany the fish course and six bottles of Chateau d'Yquem from the company cellars to adorn the sweet. With duck at the heart of the meal, two dozen of the finest Haut Brion had been presented for the feast as a thank-you to his fellow silkmen from a newly elected member who had made a killing in Latin American railway shares.

Sir Peregrine Fishborne, Prime Warden of the Company, was the first to arrive. He liked to look at the freshly laid table with its crisp white linen and the tall candles and the priceless cutlery from the early eighteenth century. He liked looking at his distinguished predecessors who lined the walls. He liked thanking God that he had arrived at his present station with a lot more money than he had had when he started out as a clerk in an insurance office. He liked savouring in his mind the plan that he hoped would make him richer yet. Most of all, and this evening was no exception, he liked going down to the lower floor with a glass of white wine and standing by the great pillars, staring out at the dark waters of the Thames swirling and gurgling on its way to the sea, ready to ferry yet more wealth to the capital. If Sir Peregrine had been Italian in earlier times, his supporters club liked to say, he wouldn't have been a merchant in bloody Venice, he'd have been the Doge himself, sailing out once a year to wed the sea with a ring in his golden barge. His companion on this occasion was his predecessor as Prime Warden, Sir Rufus Walcott, a former Lord Mayor of London, elected with Silkworker support, now Lord Lieutenant of Norfolk and a man who collected directorships as other people might collect Wedgwood china or old paintings.

When the pair returned, the members had all arrived. There was a lot of gossip about the Stock Exchange. A man in metals had been hammered that morning, unable to pay his debts. There had been a great deal of activity in North American stocks. The first course was carried in and Sir Peregrine said the customary grace in Latin. Sir Peregrine liked people to think he was virtually fluent in Latin.

Benedic nobis, Domine, et omnibus tuis donis, quae ex larga liberalitate tua sumpturi sumus, per Jesum Christum Dominum nostrum. Deus est caritas. Qui manet in caritate manet in Deo et Deus in illo. Sit Deus in nobis, et nos maneamus in illo. Bless us, O Lord, and all your gifts, which through your great generosity we are about to receive, through Jesus Christ our Lord. God is love. He who abides in love abides in God and God in him. May God be in us and may we dwell in him.

They started with Beluga caviar and native and rock oysters, always a favourite in the City, followed by Pot au feu Henry IV – the shoulder, shank, rib and tail of beef braised all day and served in their broth with a blob of Béarnaise.

Joseph had wondered for a long time about whether he should serve a red wine with the Pot au feu but thought that too rapid a change from white to red and back to white at this early stage of the evening might bring inebriation on even earlier than usual. Some of the senior members had waistlines virtually the same size as the King's, and carrying them out of the building late in the evening to their cabs outside was a difficult process.

One of the new waiters stumbled and almost fell before recovering himself as he carried in the next course on its enormous silver salver, sole cardinale and whitebait, which was meant to be a choice of dishes but the younger members helped themselves cheerfully to both. Three courses down, only six to go, Joseph said to himself, as he supervised proceedings unobtrusively by the door into the kitchens. Sir Peregrine was boring his neighbours with a long lecture on the early history of the company. This was a regular feature of these occasions. Some men maintained that these great feasts were only held to give Sir Peregrine a captive audience for the longest possible time. He had reached the end of the fourteenth century when the next course arrived, chicken d'Albufera, in which the roasted bird is served in a sauce of boiled cream, triply reduced, with mushrooms and black truffles and quenelles of veal tongue and chicken.

A spirited debate had started at the end of the main table about the likely winners of the Eton and Harrow cricket match that year. Two of the members had children at the schools, who were likely to play for their respective elevens, and each man was claiming that his son's team would be easy winners. A wager of twenty pounds was placed on the result. Joseph and his waiters were now bringing the bottles of Haut Brion to the table. There was a toast to the man who had provided it. Sir Rufus was holding forth to anyone who would listen about the size and beauty of the wool churches in Norfolk. Saddle of lamb with spring vegetables and parsley potatoes was one of the chef's more conventional offerings that evening. Ordinary families in ordinary homes in ordinary parts of the capital might, just might, have been having the same thing. They would not, however, have been enjoying the course that followed, the chef's signature dish.

Pressed Rouen ducklings, in which six birds, killed specially for the occasion in France, were roasted and their bones and organs crushed in a solid silver duck press, the resultant juice then reduced at the boil in a silver dish to produce a sauce for the meat, which the waiters irreverently called 'bloody duck's blood'. Sir Peregrine, his face growing redder as the room grew warmer, had reached the early stages of the Silkworkers in the Civil War. One of his victims wondered if he could feign a heart attack in order to escape. Sir Rufus, who had heard the history of the Silkworkers many times before, moved on from the churches to the beauty of the Broads.

The food grew quieter after the duck. Joseph could see the end in sight now. Sir Peregrine's neighbours could not. Asparagus hollandaise, murderous for those afflicted by gout, who were well represented here, was followed by peach melba served in a hand-carved ice swan as big as a ten-year-old child. Canapés à la Diane, last but by no means least among the chef's masterpieces, brought up the rear.

Joseph wondered, not for the first time, how their constitutions and their figures could stand it; then he remembered that in the summer many of these people went as a matter of course to Homburg or Marienbad to get rid of the accumulated excess, and then returned to start on another year's course of rich living. Really, he thought, there was very little difference between Marienbad and the vomitorium of the Romans.

Sir Peregrine rose rather unsteadily to his feet and proposed the loyal toast. A selection of cigars was brought round the table. Men pushed their chairs back and stretched out their legs. It was just after half past ten. Joseph brought some more bottles of the Haut Brion to the table. It seemed to be more popular than the Chateau d'Yquem. Sir Peregrine had just sailed past the Glorious Revolution and was carrying the history of the Silkworkers into the reigns of the Georges. An argument had developed at the bottom of one of the side tables about whether there should be another election that year over the veto powers of the House of Lords.

The bells of the City churches rang for eleven. The more domesticated of the Silkworkers collected their coats and hats and headed for home, keen to return to their families while they were still in control of their faculties. By twelve only the two knights were left, still replenishing their glasses with Haut Brion. At one Sir Rufus decided on a farewell visit to the river one floor below. He declared that it was so peaceful that he wanted to spend a little time down there alone with his thoughts. Sir Peregrine, with over two hundred years of Silkworker history still to go, staggered off into the night.

Sir Rufus's corpse, stabbed through the heart with the familiar stigmata on his chest, was found there early the next morning.

Inspector Grime brought Powerscourt news of the latest death over bacon and eggs that morning. Police messages were despatched earlier than ones from the Silkworkers Hall after a feast. Powerscourt told the Inspector that he would have to return to London for this, the third body inside a very short time. This latest victim, Grime eyed his telegram suspiciously, was a rather grander personage than the first two: Sir Rufus Walcott, Lord Lieutenant of Norfolk, a prominent figure in the boards and director-ships of the City of London and the predecessor of Sir Peregrine as Prime Warden of the Silkworkers Company. The cleaners, tidying up after the dinner the night before, had found Sir Rufus, a great stab wound in his chest, with the familiar marks of the thistle on his chest, at the top of the steps leading down to the water as if he was waiting for a boat to take him home. There was no sign of the murder weapon. Twenty-four people had attended the dinner the night before. Those that had been contacted so far recalled nothing unusual about the feast, apart from the rueful admission from two of the guests that they, and Sir Rufus, had partaken rather too freely of the Haut Brion during and after the food. 'And that, my lord,' said Grime, folding away his telegram, 'is all I can tell you for the present.'

That afternoon Powerscourt introduced himself to his third Inspector on the case. Miles Devereux was in his early thirties with a languid air and the remains of one of those cherubic faces that convinced people he must have been a choirboy in his youth. It was, he told Powerscourt sadly, his second murder of the year, with only a month gone. He took Powerscourt round the Silkworkers Hall and the place where the body had been found.

'We think the killer probably came by boat,' he said. 'So many bloody boats go up and down this river, nobody would have taken any notice if another one went by with a murderer at the oars.'

'How would they have known he would be here at that time of day?' said Powerscourt. 'In the other two cases with the strange marks, Inspector, the killer would have known where to find his victim. The man in the almshouse would have been in his place, the bursar at Allison's School would have been in his office. How did they know this old boy was going to be here at one o'clock in the morning?'

'Perhaps they sent him a message,' said the Inspector thoughtfully.

'Meet me by the water at one in the morning,' suggested Powerscourt. 'You'll know who I am because I'll have a large knife in my hand, waiting to stab you through the heart.'

5

At seven o'clock that evening Lord Francis Powerscourt was watching a man change his shirt. Powerscourt's brother-in-law William Burke was a mighty power in the City of London, a banker who knew most of what was going on in his little kingdom. He was married to Powerscourt's sister Mary and he was due at a formal dinner of his own in half an hour.

'Damn it, Francis,' he said, wrestling with his white shirt and white collar, 'I can just about fit into this bloody thing. When Mary bought it for me last year it was never this tight.'

'Perhaps it's shrunk at the laundry,' said Powerscourt tactfully. Burke grunted and continued his sartorial struggles with the buttons on his waistcoat. It, too, seemed to have shrunk slightly in the wash.

'I shall just have to hold my breath half the bloody evening,' Burke announced sadly, sorting out his tie in the mirror above the marble mantelpiece in his enormous office. Burke's offices seemed to his brother-in-law to double in size about every four years. Powerscourt felt sure he would end up in a place about as large and as grand as Westminster Hall itself.

'Odd, isn't it,' Burke said, slipping into his tailcoat, 'your man from the Silkworkers goes to a formal dinner last night with the members and ends up a corpse. I'm off to a formal dinner tonight and I'm telling you what I know about livery companies. Shouldn't think,' he paused to look suspiciously at his black patent leather court shoes as if they might be short of polish, 'there'll be many murderers where I'm going; Tower of London too forbidding, I'd have thought. Now then, Francis, we haven't much time. Mary's coming to meet me downstairs in her latest evening gown in half an hour.'

Burke pulled his waistcoat and his jacket down and lowered himself carefully into an armchair by his fire. 'Don't want any damned buttons popping this early in the evening. Livery companies, Francis, you wrote to me asking about livery companies. Your victims in this case, you told me, all have connections with the Silkworkers Company. I presume you know about their history already. In general terms, I mean. You don't know yet if they were killed because they were members of the company or if they just happened to belong to it. Am I right so far, Francis?'

'You are,' said Powerscourt.

'I don't care for the bloody livery companies myself,' said Burke, giving his left shoe a firm rub with his handkerchief. 'God knows how many have asked me to join them over the years. I've always refused. You see, I'm as fond of tradition as the next man, but traditions need to have some purpose, in my view. Bloody monarchy – it may be old, but it's still useful. Same with the House of Lords, even now. Bank of England, bloody ancient institution, but it still has a function. But tell me this, Francis, what is the point of the Honourable Company of Basketworkers? Glove-makers? Honourable Company of Needlemakers, for God's sake? I doubt if any of the members has made a glove or a basket or a bloody needle in the last hundred years.'

'What is it about them that makes you so cross, William?'

Burke laughed. 'I'll tell you what a fellow told me a couple of years back. He belonged to these livery companies the way other people belong to clubs like the Garrick or the Carlton. He was a member of five or six of the things, maybe more, I can't remember exactly. Do you know what he told me about them? I've always thought it rather sharp. He said they reminded him of school. I don't know how many new public schools have opened in the last fifty years, the man went on. Heaps and heaps of them, all busy inventing ancient traditions as fast as they can to impress the parents. My man claimed each livery company was like a house in one of those new public schools. Wardens and so on are the prefects, fancy uniforms and so forth.'

Powerscourt had a sudden picture of one of the prefects at Allison's: 'Walk, don't run in the corridor.' At least, he thought, they had a couple of hundred years rather than a couple of decades to invent their past.

'All the different houses,' Burke went on, unaware that his brother-in-law had temporarily abandoned him in favour of school corridors, 'get together every now and then to elect the head boy, except he's now called the Lord Mayor of London. Most of the pupils going to these new public schools are first-generation buyers. If the fathers had been to one of the old foundations like Eton or Winchester, they'd probably have sent their sons there. Those places are stuffed out with the sons of old boys, for God's sake. Same thing when the men from the new schools come to the City. First-generation buyers again; most of their families have no tradition of working here. These damned livery companies are like a home from home. Welcome back to your house at school. Welcome back to the uniforms. Welcome back to the school food and the dreadful puddings. Welcome back to the prefects. This is England in nineteen hundred and ten.' William Burke looked at his watch.

'I'm going to have to go in a minute, Francis,' he said, standing up to check his clothes in the mirror. 'I've left the most important bit till the end. The first thing is that many of these companies are rich, very rich. Their members have been leaving them land and houses and baskets and gloves and silk and gold and God knows what else in the City and elsewhere for centuries. They're stuffed with money. What's more, your lot, Honourable Company of the Ancient Mistery of Silkworkers, to give them their full title, are one of the richest of the lot. And,' Burke brushed a speck of dust off his formal trousers with stripes down the sides, 'there's something very strange going on about the money and the Silkworkers. I can't be precise and I wouldn't want to give you wrong information, not with all these corpses with strange marks lying about the place, but I have feelers out. I may pick up some hard information at this dinner tonight. I haven't finished with them yet.'

There was a knock at the door. A porter in dark trousers and a blazer marked on the pocket with Burke's bank emblem of a flying eagle informed him that Mrs Burke was waiting for him downstairs.

'There you are, William,' said Powerscourt happily to his brother-in-law. 'Even your porter is in a kind of livery.

So are you, in a way, now I come to think about it. Can't get away from them.'

Burke laughed and took his wife away to sup with the ghosts of those executed or murdered in the Tower: Anne Boleyn and Sir Walter Raleigh, Lady Jane Grey and the Earl of Essex.

'Three corpses in ten days, Francis, that must be some sort of record, even for you.'

Powerscourt's closest friend Johnny Fitzgerald was draped across a sofa in the Powerscourt house in Markham Square, clutching a glass of red wine firmly in his left hand. He had just returned from a research trip to southern France, working on his latest book on the birds of the Midi and the Auvergne. Two earlier volumes on birds of the British Isles had sold well.

'Do you think that's the end of the road, or do you expect more strange bodies to turn up next week?'

'Johnny,' said Powerscourt, 'I'll be honest with you. I haven't a clue. I wish I knew. I really do. Part of the problem now is going to be travelling from here down to Marlow and then up to Norfolk all the time. You can't do a great deal of detecting on a train or in the Silver Ghost.'

'Let's hope there aren't any more murders, my love.' Powerscourt's wife, Lady Lucy, was making a close inspection of a catalogue in her lap that was filled with advertisements for antiquarian booksellers and their wares. She had been wondering if she should buy Francis a first edition of the works of John Donne as a birthday present.

'Those poor old boys down there in Marlow,' she went one, 'they must be terrified. Nobody goes into an almshouse expecting to be murdered, do they? Certainly

84

nobody we know. And the mothers of those boys at the school, they must be having a dreadful time, not sure if their children are alive or dead.'

'I expect, Francis, that you will have some particularly disagreeable task for me to perform in the usual fashion?' Johnny had been Powerscourt's companion in arms in all his detection cases. 'By the way,' he held his glass up to the light and peered happily at the dark red wine, 'this isn't your usual tipple. Where does it come from? I'd like to order a case or two from your wine merchant.'

Powerscourt's brain was far away, watching the waters swirl round the Silkworkers Hall. He wondered if the murderer had hidden in there all night. He wondered where the murderer was now and if he might have made his first mistake.

He smiled at his friend. 'It's Italian, that wine. You might be suspicious, I certainly was, about the lack of label but the new fellow at Berry Bros and Rudd said there was a reason for that. Printing press for the labels collapsed apparently; the Italians had forgotten to put any oil in it for months. Eyewitnesses said the noise of metal strangling metal was incredible, the sort of thing you might read about in H. G. Wells. And it went on and on until the machine was just a heap of bits of metal lying all over the floor and the dust so thick you could hardly see across the warehouse. Brunello di Montalcino, it's called, Johnny. Comes from a place called Montalcino, south of Florence.'

Johnny Fitzgerald looked at his friend suspiciously. 'That sounded like a rather long-winded way of avoiding telling me about some really horrible job you've got for me, something so distasteful that even you are scared of mentioning it.'

Powerscourt laughed. 'Not true, Johnny, not true. I

have, I must admit, been thinking for some time about where to deploy your talents to best advantage in this case. With the pupils of Allison's School perhaps? Or their mothers? Silkworkers here in London? Maybe. But all the evidence seems to me to point in another direction. It is a choice between the young and the old. The place for you, Johnny, is in the Rose and Crown, High Street, Marlow. Your mission – you can see it as well as I do – is to make friends with the old boys. "That new chap is always buying people drinks, especially if they come from the hospital." I've even booked you a room at the posh hotel, Johnny, just down the road.'

'How long for?' asked Johnny Fitzgerald, looking yet more suspicious.

'A week or so in the first instance,' said Powerscourt cheerfully. 'We can always review the position in a couple of days.'

'I see. Tell me this, Francis, do you want me to raise the subject of the murder straight away?'

'Absolutely not. I want you to talk about anything other than sudden death to begin with. I want you to encircle them from a distance, if you know what I mean.'

Johnny stomped off for a dinner with his publisher. Powerscourt looked over at Lady Lucy. She had closed her catalogue. Tomorrow, she had decided, she would go and buy this John Donne. It would give Francis so much pleasure. She had felt rather lost as the men had sat here and made their plans.

'My love,' said Powerscourt, who knew better than anybody the vital role his wife had played in so many of his investigations, 'you mustn't think you have been left out of this inquiry. Nothing could be further from the truth.' He stroked her hair.

86

'What do you want me to do, Francis?' she asked.

'For the moment I want you, like that Scottish regiment, to keep watch and to pray. You are what one great Commander described as the most important of his forces in the lead-up to a battle. Think of Napoleon's reserve, the Imperial Guard, who never lost a battle till they met their Waterloo. Just for now, Lucy, you are the reinforcements who will carry the day, like Napoleon's reserve.'

Sergeant Peter Donaldson of the Maidenhead force was feeling great sympathy with his counterpart from *The Pirates of Penzance* who complained that 'a policeman's lot is not a happy one'. The Sergeant had seen the Gilbert and Sullivan operetta at an amateur performance by the Buckinghamshire Police Drama Group and Choir the year before and some of the arias had stuck in his brain. At this moment the Sergeant was leaving the offices of Hook, Hawthorne and Brewster, Solicitors and Commissioners for Oaths, at the end of Reading High Street. This was the tenth firm of solicitors he had visited in the town that day, and he had learnt nothing to his advantage in any of them. Well might he produce his credentials, well might he stress the importance of this part of the murder inquiry, well might he kowtow as best he could to the arrogant solicitors who confronted him, but they repeatedly assured him that they could not help. None of the names of the men with no wills from the Jesus Hospital, Marlow, meant anything to them. 'It's not natural,' he remembered his Inspector saying to him. 'Twelve out of the twenty with no will? I simply don't believe it.'

There were different ways of saying no, the Sergeant said to himself, remembering the various members of the legal profession he had met that day. Some of them brought out their ledgers and showed him their lists of the clients they did have, the day they were taken on, the dates of any important transactions in their affairs. But most of them just took a cursory look in a file and said, 'No, we've never heard of any of these people. Good day to you, Sergeant. If anything happens, of course we'll be in touch.' And all of them treated him with disdain, as if he'd come to clean the windows, the Sergeant said to himself bitterly. He thought of the look he could expect on his Inspector's face when he reported that he had toiled all afternoon and caught nothing. The Inspector had a pained expression he put on at moments of difficulty and setback, a look that said you've let me down. How could you. I'm so disappointed.

But late this afternoon, as Sergeant Donaldson came back to Maidenhead to make his final inquiries, and the shopkeepers and businessmen began to shut up their stores and their offices, he was wrong. Inspector Fletcher was not disappointed when the Sergeant told him the news. He hardly took any notice. His eyes were bright and he began walking up and down his office, smacking one fist into another.

'There's another one, Sergeant! Another dead body with the strange markings! That makes three of them! It's the biggest case we may ever see. Three murders, one after another! And the most important one right here on our doorstep!'

Fletcher stopped suddenly and looked at his Sergeant. He might have a hangdog expression when he was being told bad news. Fletcher's own superior officer, Detective

Chief Inspector Galway, did not care for such niceties. He shouted at people. Some of his officers reported that they were sure he was on the verge of knocking them down.

'I do hope,' the Inspector said, with the elation draining slowly out of his face, as he realized what might happen next, 'that they don't take the case away from us. They might give it to somebody senior. Or they might bring somebody in from London. I do hope they don't. This may be the biggest case I'll ever see. If I don't get promotion after this, Sergeant, then I never will.'

The newspapers' reaction to the three murders was proof that the really important news is what happens closest to home. Distant earthquakes, plagues in countries with unpronounceable names, civil wars in far-off lands like Kurdistan, failed to make it into print in local organs of opinion like the *Reading Chronicle* or the *Norwich Evening News*. Both of these papers carried banner headlines, 'Murder in the Almshouse' for Marlow, and 'Public School Murder' in Fakenham. The last of the three, Sir Rufus by the Silkworkers' steps, merited a small article on an inside page of the local papers in London. None of the reporters who wrote the stories mentioned the strange marks on the dead men's chests. So far the police had managed to conceal that information in all three cases. Nobody knew how long the line would hold, or how many days it would be before a policeman would sell the information to a journalist who would have a scoop on his hands.

One of the very few people apart from Powerscourt and the forces of law and order to know of the stigmata was Sir Fitzroy Robinson Buller, Permanent Secretary at the Home Office, regularly described by insiders in the Civil Service as Whitehall's head prefect. Sir Fitzroy had been watching over the Home Office's wide powers, which included supervision of the police and the criminal justice system for many years. In that time he had developed, as he liked to confide in his fellow permanent secretaries over a regular lunch at the Athenaeum, a Nose For Trouble. In his long career he had divided his political masters, the Home Secretaries of the day, into four different types. There were those who listened to his advice and were too stupid to understand it. There were those who listened to his advice but were too frightened to do anything about it. There were those – 'Too many, alas, too many,' he would confide to his lunchtime companions over the port – who didn't even listen to his advice at all. And there was a rump party, far too small a body in Sir Fitzroy's view, who listened to his counsel and did something about it. The Permanent Secretary still had an open mind about the current incumbent of the great office he served, Herbert Gladstone, youngest son of the legendary Prime Minister. Once he had listened and acted decisively. Once he had listened and done nothing at all. Sir Fitzroy was too seasoned and too wily an operator to think that his advice on this current matter could be decisive in the formation of his judgement. Never or impossible were not words that should pass from a Permanent Secretary's lips. Salvation should surely be available to ministers as it was to the many sinners of London. Looking out at St James's Park, with the nannies wheeling their charges round the lake and the birds poised and ready for action in the bare trees, he composed his memorandum to his master.

'Dear Home Secretary,' he began, 'I do not need to remind you of the gravity of the current situation regarding the three very recent murders where the bodies have been disfigured in a particularly distasteful fashion.'

Sir Fitzroy was reluctant to mention the precise details of the disfigurement. One of the reasons for his long tenure at the Home Office was his refusal to trust anybody completely. Home Secretaries, he said to himself, have been known to leave their red boxes in the backs of London taxis. One particular box had managed to travel successfully all the way to Edinburgh in the luggage rack, its owner having left the train at Grantham. Like many public servants, Sir Fitzroy had a total horror of what might happen in his world if the public were to find out what was really going on. Secrecy, in his view, was the lubricating oil of government, a vital weapon in the long war against disorder and democracy.

The newspapers, as you well know, Sir Henry, have not yet heard of the disfigurements to the dead bodies. Coverage in the Press has been muted so far. I would, however, be failing in my duty if I did not draw your attention to the possibility, nay, in my opinion, the near certainty, that this intelligence will leak out into the public domain and will do so very soon. In my judgement there are a number of developments likely to follow from such a revelation.

One, there will be a massive hue and cry and general frenzy in the newspapers of every stripe. Nothing succeeds in terms of raising circulation and increasing advertising rates like scandal and sensation. Three dead bodies with stigmata of an unusual kind rate high in the ledgers of scandal and sensation. We are having a fairly quiet time at present in terms of major political developments. The public have grown tired of the rows between the Commons and the Lords. They are even more tired of the depressing number of strikes and the growing popularity of industrial action. They may even – would that it were so – be growing tired of rumours of foreign wars. There is, as you well know, Minister, nothing the newspapers like more than real murder mysteries. All the present one lacks is a female element, some suspicion of adultery or foreign adventuresses. If no such facts come to light, we may be sure that the newspapers will invent them.

Two, in the light of the eventualities referred to in the previous section, I should draw your attention to the likely reaction in the House of Commons. The only thing – and I know you share this view – worse than the baying of the newspaper columns is the hypocrisy and self-advertisement of various backbenchers who will attempt to get their names in the Press by asking ridiculous questions. Why is the Government not doing more to catch the culprits? How is it that the Home Secretary allowed this foreign criminal – in the minds of many, if not most newspapers, all murders are committed by foreigners – into our country and slaughter our fellow citizens?

Three, if the news emerges, as per section one, above, the most damaging charge that can be levelled at the Government is the accusation of waste and duplication. Why do we have three separate police forces investigating the murders, which are so clearly linked and the work of a foreign gang? Why should we, as taxpayers and ratepayers, have to bear the expenses of three senior detectives and their teams when one would do? Why does the Government not take control of the matter and put the investigation into the hands of one of the Metropolitan Police's most senior officers who will, by definition, have more experience of murder inquiries than the inexperienced of Marlow and the novices of Norfolk?

Four, I fear that the Department is about to face a most difficult decision. You are caught, Minister, to use a phrase too readily invoked, I fear, by my colleagues, caught between Scylla and Charybdis. Refuse the pleas for a single man and the newspapers will hound you for taking the wrong decision. Appoint a single man who fails to solve the mystery and the newspapers will hound you for taking the wrong decision. Consistency has never been a necessary feature of the behaviour of the Press. Opportunism is all.

Sir Fitzroy paused at this point and read his memorandum back to himself. There were, he knew, many of his colleagues who would give firm advice at this point to follow a particular course of action. It was known at the Athenaeum lunch club as making the minister's mind up for him. But that was not Sir Fitzroy's way. It was not for him to tell his minister what to do. Not this time anyway, with such a delicate issue. His job was to marshal the arguments for and against, to make sure that the minister was fully informed about the options involved. Anything more definite, as he used to say in his introductory lecture to new recruits to the Civil Service, would be a usurpation of the functions of government.

The man they called Eye Patch stood motionless behind his curtains and stared out to sea. It was half an hour short of midnight and nothing moved on the streets and the seafront of the little town. The moon was nearly full and if he looked closely he could see the small collection of yachts moored in the harbour. The largest and most mysterious was his own. He could, had he so fancied, have looked at her through the finest telescope money could buy, permanently sited up in the top floor of his huge house, but he couldn't be bothered to climb two flights of stairs. There were no lights on in the drawing room looking out over the waters. The man disliked the thought of being overlooked. He valued security above all else. Why else should he hide himself away like a reclusive millionaire or mad English lord who locks himself up in his hall or his grange to spend his waking hours on the collection of Lepidoptera or the stuffing of small furry animals?

Not many people alive had known the man before he acquired his eye patch and his nickname. Once he realized how useful it was to be known in this way he only used his real name when it was absolutely necessary. Friends, who were few, colleagues who were largely frightened, enemies who were numerous, all referred to him as Eye Patch because they did not know what he was christened. Some people wondered if his women or his mistresses addressed him as Eye Patch even in the most intimate of circumstances.

The wound that led to the patch had happened decades before. The circumstances also left him with a slight limp in his left leg. The man wondered often in the early years of his disfigurement if it wouldn't have been better to have lost a leg rather than an eye if he had to lose something. He would much rather have become Long John Silver than Eye Patch but there it was. The present version of his patch, handmade by the finest tailors, was of a dull grey, which its wearer thought the most unobtrusive in his small collection. He had a black one he wore when he wanted to frighten people. There was a dark red one he wore when he wanted to impress a lady. Eye patches, he had found, had a strange fascination for the opposite sex. They always wanted to know how he came by it, if there was any hope of sight ever returning. The man would smile, refuse to answer any questions, and maintain the veil of secrecy. Over the years he had decided that his red eye patch was blessed with considerable aphrodisiac qualities. He rarely failed to conquer. He resisted the many attempts by his valet to order him a new one.

Outside, the moon passed behind a cloud. There was a faint hint of silver on the water. Eye Patch had come to this place with a mission. He was pleased with his progress so far. Very few people knew he was here. Very few people knew who he was. Groceries were delivered to his staff. No local had crossed his door. He never went out, except at night to visit his yacht, and then he wrapped so many scarves round his face that he was unrecognizable. He took a long last look at the sleeping town which looked as though God himself might have tucked it up in bed. As he climbed the stairs to his bedroom above, the man smiled as he thought of his red eye patch. It seemed to him a very long time since he had worn it. When the business was finished he would see if its seductive charms still worked. He looked out at the sea once more before he closed his bedroom curtains. His yacht was still there, the easiest means of escape if that should become necessary. She was swaying slightly in a midnight breeze. The man could not see the name painted in bold letters on the side but he knew it was there. The yacht was called *Morning Glory*.

PART TWO

THE ELYSIAN FIELDS

6

All was not well in the Jesus Hospital in Marlow. The old gentlemen were restless and unsettled. The funeral of Abel Meredith had been delayed for some unaccountable reason. The residents of the almshouse liked funerals. Funerals reminded them that they at any rate were still alive. They liked singing the hymns like 'Rock of Ages' and 'The Day Thou Gavest Lord Is Ended'. They weren't quite so sure about the dead man being lowered into the ground but by that stage many of them were already thinking of the wake in the dining hall that the hospital organized for its own after a funeral, with special cakes and scones and homemade raspberry jam.

But what unsettled the old gentlemen even more, though they never mentioned it to anyone, not even their closest friends, was that they might be living with a murderer. And none of their rooms had locks. The authorities had decided long before that the ability to rush in and take a sick man to hospital without breaking doors down was essential. But here was the disadvantage of that policy. Number Nine or Number Fourteen or Number Eleven might rise in the night and kill once again, and nobody could stop them rushing in, knife or gun in hand. Freddie Butcher, Number Two, whose life had been spent on the railways rather than selling meat, had done considerable damage to his back trying to pull a sofa across his living room to a position right by the front door so that any intruder would have to push past it to get to him. The general amount of conversation, usually gossip of one sort of another, had dropped. The only bright spot on the silkmen's horizon was the arrival of a new regular at the Rose and Crown. This Johnny chap, they said to one another, had a fund of good stories and an inexhaustible supply of money for buying rounds of drinks. He didn't seem very interested in the hospital, not even in the murder. He was one of those people who give the impression of always being cheerful. And once you were sitting in the corner table of the Rose and Crown, with a pint of the landlord's best in your fist, you felt safe. Nobody was going to come and murder you there. So it was not surprising that some of the old gentlemen had taken to staying longer and longer in the pub, nor that they were so cheerful on their return that they might not have noticed whether they were being murdered or not.

Warden Monk was aware of these undercurrents swirling round his kingdom. He tried to reassure the old men that nobody was coming to kill them. In old days he might have asked Sir Peregrine to come down if he had a moment and give the old boys a pep talk. In these homilies Sir Peregrine always sounded like a house prefect instructing his charges to play up in the house football competition and get fit for the cross-country running championship. But Sir Peregrine did not have a moment and did not come. Those who did, and who came far too often for Monk's liking, were the officers of the Buckinghamshire Constabulary, who always lowered morale. Why do they keep coming, the old gentlemen would mutter to each other, unless they know that the murderer is here, is one of us, within these walls? One down, the old men muttered to themselves, nineteen to go.

Monk himself had other things on his mind. It was not surprising that Sergeant Peter Donaldson had been unable to find Abel Meredith's will in the lawyers' offices in Maidenhead or anywhere else. Monk had not one last will and testament of the late Abel Meredith, Number Twenty, but two. The Authorized Version, as Monk referred to it, was in a secret place inside a floorboard in Monk's bedroom. One of the many occupations he had had to leave in a hurry in an earlier life was that of carpenter, but his departure had not come before he had learnt a lot about the trade. People, especially the police, were great believers in the fact that criminals liked hiding things under the floorboards. Monk was a great believer in hiding things inside floorboards. His secret place could only be unlocked by pressing a whorl on the lower side of the board. Nobody looking at it, not even the most suspicious policeman, would have imagined that there was anything concealed inside. Like the wooden horse of Troy, Monk would say to himself, the most important parts are on the inside.

The other version of the will, the Revised Version, as Monk put it, was in the file marked Wills on a shelf on his office. This was one of those unusual wills, two pages long, where the second page only required a signature. Monk may have been a thief. But he was not greedy. He was, he would remind himself from time to time, a reasonable man. When engaged on will work he always took care to keep to the original intentions. Abel Meredith had left a large amount of money, well over two thousand pounds, a figure that would have sent Inspector Fletcher's instincts into overtime. All of it had been left to a brother in Saskatchewan in the original. In the new will Monk split the figure, half to the brother in Canada, half to 'my good friend and counsellor, Thomas Monk, with thanks for all the help and advice rendered to me'. This was not the most valuable will created in Monk's office. It was, in fact, the third most valuable. Once the funeral was over, he would take it to a rather grand solicitor in the West End who would launch it into the legal system.

'Don't think very much of this lot, actually,' said Powerscourt's third police officer. Detective Inspector Miles Devereux was wearing a cream shirt and a very old-fashioned suit that might have belonged to his father. 'You're not going to believe this,' he told Powerscourt, 'but I am the tenth of eleven sons. No jokes about cricket or football teams, please, absolutely not. Family may be numerous, family funds are not. By the time they got round to deciding what to do with me, I had, I still have, now I think of it, brothers in almost every conceivable occupation. I have brothers who can sell you a house, look after your money, train your racehorse, christen, marry and bury you though not all at the same time. There's one who farms in Argentina and one who runs enormous ranches in Canada. There's one who will buy your antique books and sell them on at an enormous profit, and another who claims to be opening the wines of

Italy up to new markets in Britain, though the family say he merely opens the bottles. There are, I fear, even more of them. So I decided to do something different and join the police force. It's quite fun, really, especially when you get a tasty one like this case here. But all this stuff here,' he waved a languid hand at the strange collection of objects on the table, 'contents of Sir Rufus's pockets, pretty dull, I'd say, wouldn't you? Why are we always so keen to have a look at these things? I've never known. It's not as though the murderer is going to pop his calling card into a waistcoat pocket, is it?'

Powerscourt smiled. Behind the slightly dreamy exterior he suspected Devereux had a sharp brain. He looked young to have risen to Detective Inspector. In one pile on the table in Cannon Row police station were the items he dismissed, a collection of keys, coins, currency notes, a wallet, a letter from his bank telling him he had two hundred and sixty-three pounds in his account, two tickets for the opera from three days before, a large unopened white handkerchief and a receipt from Simpsons in the Strand.

'Do you know, Powerscourt, they always put me on to these kinds of cases now. Rich people's murders, all that sort of stuff. Here am I, longing for some tasty gang violence in the East End and I end up yet again with death from Debrett's. It's really not fair. What do you think of this other lot?' He pointed to a rather larger heap of miscellaneous rubbish. 'This lot is the stuff found all over the Silkworkers Hall that day by the good Mrs Robinson, cleaning lady and occasional waitress. She kept it especially for us.' A long pianist's finger stirred up the random bits of paper. Powerscourt thought cigarette packets or cigarette stubs, tickets or parts of tickets seemed to be the most frequent objects in this display, bus tickets, underground tickets, train tickets.

'One section about football results from last week's *Times*,' said Devereux, stirring the mixture slowly, as if it were a sauce. 'Our man may have been a Tottenham fan as they won five–nil. Two empty beer bottles from Messrs Young's and Company of Wandsworth, a couple of unpaid bills, one return ticket from Hastings and one from somewhere ending in "be", two brown leaves and a menu from last night's dinner. They seem to have done themselves pretty well, don't you think, Lord Powerscourt? Any of these bits and pieces ring a bell with you?'

'Nothing unusual that I can see, nothing unusual at all.'

'Well, we'll keep them safe for now. Let me tell you what I have set in train so far,' said the Inspector. 'My men are calling on all those who attended the dinner last night. By this evening we should have a reasonable picture of what went on. The chef and the waiters should be here in an hour or so. I have an appointment this afternoon with a senior doctor at Barts round the corner. I am going to ask him about the strange marks on the body, or bodies I should say after what you told me earlier. I do have a theory about the marks though I'm sure it's probably wrong.'

'What is that?'

'I just wonder if they weren't all suffering from some strange disease that produces that pattern. A number of those tropical diseases can bring on some very unusual symptoms, people changing colour, or marks appearing all over their skin, that sort of thing.'

'It's certainly possible,' said Powerscourt tactfully. 'Perhaps the medical gentlemen will be able to help.' Privately he was less certain. The only thing all three corpses had in common, as far as he knew, apart from the strange marks, was membership or connection with the Silkworkers Company.

'I should like to be present when you talk to the chef and the waiters, if I may,' he continued, 'and I, too, have an appointment this afternoon, though with a man of finance rather than medicine.'

Powerscourt told the Inspector about his inquiries with William Burke about the livery company and the suspicion that something untoward might be going on.

Inspector Grime of the Norfolk Constabulary was not, by nature, a cheerful man. That was not his way. On this day he was, once more, not cheerful. But he would have said that affairs were moving in a not wholly unsatisfactory fashion in the case of the bursar. Grime had now finished his interviews with the pupils of Allison's School. No more would he have to stare at those maps in the geography classroom and the countries of the world ready to spin for him in their globes at the touch of a finger. He suspected that the headmaster would have some other form of torture ready for him to do with the boys. No woman had fallen for Inspector Grime's particular temperament since the death of his wife some years before. There was no Mrs Grime at home waiting for him at the end of the day with pots of tea and warm scones. There had been no little Grimes to delight a parent's life. As a result he eyed small boys, even larger boys, with the same suspicion he brought to the rest of the human race, the same lack of charity. It was, he had said to himself often enough, precisely that lack of charity that had brought him success in the business of detection and solving crimes. If you thought all the witnesses were lying and potential criminals, you were bound to be proved right some of the time.

The particular development that was lightening his burdens this afternoon was to do with the postman, or rather the one who had pretended to be a postman. He had arranged with the postal authorities and the headmaster for a real postman, dressed in the proper uniform, to visit the school the following morning at exactly the same time as the visit on the day of the murder. This mailman would retrace the steps of his criminal predecessor in every particular, ending up with a phoney delivery in the bursar's room. Only the headmaster knew about the plan. If word got out, Grime believed, the fevered imaginations of the younger children might get the better of them. Morning prayers would start the day's work at Allison's School shortly after the visit. The headmaster would ask if anybody remembered anything about the day of the murder and the visit of the postman. He, Inspector Grime, would have to attend the assembly, which he would have avoided at all costs under normal circumstances. The combination of boys and prayers and singing would have been too much for him. But on this occasion the prize might be great, another opening into the strange death of Roderick Gill.

There was another reason for the Inspector's mood. He had never been as excited as Powerscourt about the strange marks on the dead man's chest. Fancy stuff, he thought, but it might have nothing to do with the murder. Gill's affair with Mrs Hilda Mitchell, the Inspector felt sure, was a more promising field of inquiry than livery companies and unusual anatomical details. And that very morning he had received intelligence from York where

Mr Mitchell was believed to be carrying out restoration work on the minster, as he had on an earlier occasion two years before. A local Sergeant had called on the dean for confirmation of his presence. Jude Mitchell, master stonemason, the policeman was told, had indeed been employed at the minster for work on the statues in the crossing. But he had completed his part of the restoration a week ago and left. He was due to return in a week's time to begin a programme of repair in the chapter house. The landlady in his rooms confirmed his departure and his date of return. Nobody knew where Jude Mitchell, cuckolded husband of Roderick Gill's mistress, Hilda, had gone. But he had left the place where he was supposed to be three days before the murder.

Warden Monk had made a mistake. He knew it the minute he stopped talking. He did not know how damaging it might be. The old men were still restless, suspicious that one of their number might be a murderer, upset over the delay in the funeral arrangements, troubled by the visits of the Buckinghamshire Constabulary. Monk, resplend-ent today in a brand-new green cravat, had been having a conversation after lunch in the hall with Henry Wood, Number Twelve, about the dead man before the silkmen went off for their afternoon rest.

'I don't suppose, Warden, that we know if Number Twenty had any money to leave?'

Monk knew from long experience that wills, along with the weather and the looks and other physical attributes of the barmaid in the Rose and Crown, were among the most popular subjects of conversation in the Jesus Hospital.

'He left a lot more than you might think,' Monk replied.

'How much?' said Number Twelve.

'Well, if you thought of a figure round about two thousand pounds, you wouldn't be far out.' Monk always liked showing off about his knowledge of the hospital and its inmates.

'And where did the money go?'

'Half went to a brother to Canada.'

'And the rest?'

'Let me just say that the rest ended up nearer to home.'

'What does that mean?'

'I don't feel I can reveal any more at this stage,' said Monk, turning a pale shade of pink in the face. 'Poor man's not even in his grave yet.'

Henry Wood, Number Twelve, popular with his colleagues in the Jesus Hospital, had worked for most of his life in the fish business. He had long ago decided that human beings were much more slippery than the fish he traded in. A private game of his was to decide what kinds of fish other inmates resembled. Bill Smith, Number Four, known as Smithy, was a trout, John Watkins, Number Fifteen, was a lemon sole, Josiah Collins, Number Seventeen, was a perch. From the very first day he had met Monk, Number Twelve had him down as an eel.

'It's you, isn't it?' he said suddenly, staring at the changing colours in Monk's face. 'He's left the money to you. Or so you say.'

'I have no further comment to make,' said Monk stiffly. 'Now, if you'll excuse me, I have a report to prepare for the Prime Warden of the Silkworkers Company.'

Monk strode off, cursing himself for his folly. But worse was to come. Henry Wood, Number Twelve, missed the evening meal in the dining hall because of a doctor's appointment in the village. He took a pie supper in the Rose and Crown and began telling everyone about his conversation, just as Johnny Fitzgerald arrived, full of cash and curiosity. Johnny let the conversation take its course at first.

'You can't be serious, Number Twelve,' said Freddie Butcher, Number Two. 'You're not suggesting that the Warden has been playing tricks with our wills?'

'I'm not suggesting anything,' said Number Twelve, taking a long draught of his beer, 'but if you had a couple of thousand, or even a couple of pounds, would you leave half of it to Monk?'

There was a pause while the old gentlemen thought about this. Most drank deeply to aid the thought processes. So rapid was the decline in the level of the glasses that Johnny felt obliged to order another round. The barmaid, unaware of the passions she roused in the old men, smiled sweetly at him as she pulled the final pint. Christy Butler, Number Thirteen, a printer in his previous existence, could not take his eyes off her, especially when she leant forward over her work.

'It's a mistake, surely,' said Peter Baker, Number Ten, his hand on top of his head, searching for the few remaining hairs. 'Warden Monk must be remembering things wrong.'

Number Ten was widely believed to be the most stupid person in the almshouse. There was no reply. Then Andrew Snow, Number Eighteen, whose sight had nearly gone, tapped the table with his fist.

'My friends,' he said, with the air of one making a great announcement of state like the Speech from the Throne or the Budget, 'I have an important statement to make.' Everybody turned to look at Number Eighteen, the wisps of white hair left on his head, the deep lines like a map

109

around his mouth and his forehead, the white shirt he always wore under the silkmen's coat. Then he looked confused. 'The only thing is,' he looked around suddenly, 'I'm not sure I can tell you.'

'Why not?'

'Of course you can tell us.'

'Don't be so silly.'

'You can't lead us all up the garden path and then not tell; it's not fair.'

Johnny Fitzgerald wondered how it was going to end. He felt he might be on the verge of discovering something at last. Andrew Snow, Number Eighteen, looked more confused than ever. When he turned to Johnny, an answer to his dilemma seemed to come to him.

'Mr Fitzgerald,' he said, 'you're a man of the world, I should say. Could you advise me on what I should do?'

'I can't really, unless I know exactly what it is you might be going to say. Why don't we hop outside for a moment and you can tell me all about it, if the company have no objection?'

Hop would not be the first word to spring to mind about the progress of Number Eighteen from the back bar of the Rose and Crown to the road outside. He walked very slowly, holding on to the backs of the chairs as he went.

'It's like this, Mr Fitzgerald,' he began, after Johnny had steered him a few paces away from the pub. He paused briefly. 'I had a conversation with Abel Meredith, Number Twenty, a couple of months ago. It's not often I remember conversations these days but I can remember this one very clearly. We were talking about our wills and I said my money, not that there's much of it, was going to my nephews and nieces. He said – I'm certain of this

– that all his money was going to his brother who lived in Canada, Saskatchewan or Alberta, one of those places. What do you think of that, Mr Fitzgerald? Should I tell the colleagues about it?'

'Of course you should,' said Johnny cheerfully, sensing that a profitable hornet's nest was about to open up. 'They have a right to know, those men. Who knows how many other wills have been changed, if that is what is going on?'

There was an expectant air as the two of them returned to the Rose and Crown. Number Twelve was trying to start a flirtatious conversation with the barmaid, whose blonde hair and pale brown eyes looked particularly fine this evening. Jack Miller, Number Three, who had spent his life working in a bank, was staring expectantly at his empty glass as if it might be refilled by the workings of divine providence. Number Eight's head was beginning to slip forward as if an evening nap might be about to start only a couple of hours after the afternoon one had ended.

'Well?' said Freddie Butcher, Number Two.

'What's the news?' asked John Watkins, Number Fifteen.

They all stared at Andrew Snow, Number Eighteen, as he repeated his moves on the way out, holding on to the chairs as he made his way back to his seat. He took his place with a great sigh and took a long pull at the remains of his pint. Johnny Fitzgerald, always quick to detect the advent of thirst in himself and his drinking companions, offered to buy another round before the news broke. He was duly despatched to the bar, where the barmaid showed off her wares once more to the great delight of the old gentlemen.

'I was just saying to Mr Fitzgerald here,' said Number Eighteen, 'that I remember a conversation I had with Number Twenty a couple of months ago. I'd be the first to admit that I don't remember all my conversations that well these days' – there was a general nod of agreement at this point from the company – 'but I do remember this one. I remember it very clearly. We were talking about wills. I said that I was going to leave all my money to my nephews and nieces, not that there was very much of it. Abel Meredith told me he was going to leave all his money to a brother in Canada, Saskatchewan I think he said, wherever that is. They always told us at school that Canada was a very big country so this Saskatchewan place could be anywhere. He didn't say anything about leaving money to Monk, not a word.'

The old men stared at him for a moment as if they had been hypnotized. Then, virtually in unison, as if obeying a hidden conductor, they raised their glasses to their lips and drank deeply. Johnny Johnston, Number Nine, beginning a fresh pint from his refill, had a ring of creamy foam round his mouth. Stephen Potter, Number Fourteen, was wiping beer off his moustache with a bright red handkerchief.

'God bless my soul!' said Number Twelve, the man from the fish trade. 'He didn't mention Monk at all? Meredith, I mean?'

'He did not,' said Number Eighteen.

'Man's a bounder,' said Jack Miller, Number Three. 'Always thought so.'

'Do you think he robs us every time somebody dies? This has got to be stopped.' Josiah Collins, Number Seventeen, the man who read his Bible every morning, made his first contribution of the evening.

'What are we going to do?' said Andrew Snow, Number Eighteen. 'We can't let it lie. Mr Fitzgerald, can you give us some advice?'

Johnny had been tying to make a link between forged wills and murder and found the connection difficult. He established, to his great surprise, that some of the old men delivered their wills into Monk's keeping when they arrived at the hospital. The Warden told them, he was assured, that this way was preferable to the quarters of the recently dead being searched in the quest for a last will and testament.

'Well,' Johnny began, 'the first thing to do, I would suggest, is that all those who have entrusted their wills to his care should ask for them back. Then I think you should take them all to a reputable solicitor close by. That way everybody will know at once where to look for anybody else's will. More important, I think, is that you need to ask Monk for his version of events. So far we only have a guess, a very intelligent guess, mind you, from Henry Wood, Number Twelve, about what has been going on. I think it might be premature to condemn the Warden as a blackguard without any hard evidence.'

'How do we do ask him what's been going on?'

'I'm sure he's a blackguard!'

'The devil! I shan't speak to him ever again!'

'What a thing to do!'

The old men were all talking at once. The barmaid popped her head round the corner to see if anything strange was going on. Johnny suddenly felt very sorry for the inhabitants of the Jesus Hospital. Here they were, away from their families, if they had any left, in a strange place, with decay and death waiting for them. That was all that was left. They were like children, he said to himself, too innocent to know what to do in difficult circumstances. But children grow up, they grow wiser, they put away childish things. They grow into maturity, secure in the knowledge that their powers should increase over time and that their future is in front of them. The future had shrunk to a seventeenth-century quadrangle and evenings in the Rose and Crown for the men of the Jesus Hospital. Even the young knew that death would come in the end, but for them death was so far away they never thought of it. Here it could come tomorrow, a stroke in the night, a failing heart, a murderer's knife.

'Did I give my will to the Warden when I arrived?' asked Christy Butler, Number Thirteen, with a spill from his glass spreading slowly down his shirt. 'I can't remember.'

'Neither can I,' added Colin Baker, Number Six, his wooden leg tucked under the table, staring into his beer.

The old men of the Jesus Hospital fell silent. Memory, as so often, was failing them. They were losing touch with their own past. Johnny Fitzgerald thought the evening might degenerate into melancholy and a pitiful series of complaints about time.

'I don't think you should worry about that,' said Johnny cheerfully. 'I forget my own door keys about once a month. And that's when I'm stone cold sober. Don't worry about not being able to remember, don't worry at all. It happens to us all. I don't think it makes any difference if you left your will with the Warden or not. You can still go and ask if you can have it back. If he hasn't got it, he'll tell you. This is what I think you should do.' Johnny, who had followed Powerscourt's instructions not to mention affairs at the hospital to the letter up till now, felt he had to take command of this strange company of veterans. 'Just go in one at a time after breakfast or whenever you know he's going to be in his office, and ask the Warden if you can have your wills back. When you've got them, take the wills round to the nearest solicitor's office, every single one of them. We can meet here again tomorrow evening and decide how to proceed.'

The old men stared at Johnny as if he were some Old Testament prophet leading them out of the wilderness. They nodded and drank deeply of their beer. The barmaid popped her head round the corner.

'Nearly closing time, gentlemen. It'll be last orders in a minute. Is there anything I can get you?'

Johnny raised his hand. Thirteen old men stared greedily at Barbara Wilson as she pulled another round. Johnny reflected sadly that for most of these inhabitants of the Jesus Hospital last orders were not very far away.

7

The staff at the Athenaeum in London's Pall Mall prided
themselves on their knowledge of their members' wishes,
which bedroom a country member preferred if staying
overnight in town, where the members liked sitting for
lunch, which of them took wine by the glass at lunchtime
and which took it by the bottle. By now they had years
of experience of dealing with the Permanent Secretary at
the Home Office. Sir Fitzroy Robinson Buller liked the
corner table in the garden room for luncheon with his
guests, he always ordered lamb, cooked rare, he usually
took a glass or two of Pomerol with his main course and
if he was in a really good mood he would have a glass
of Barsac with his pudding. Now his overcoat had been
safely deposited in the cloakroom and a glass of the club's
driest Amontillado was in front of him as he perused the
menu and waited for his guest. The Commissioner of the
Metropolitan Police was late. His cab was stuck in traffic.
Sir Edward Henry complained to himself that he was
meant to be in control of traffic movements in the capital.
The two men shared a political master, Herbert Gladstone,
son of the famous Prime Minister of the previous century.

Pleasantries were exchanged over the soup. Light skirmishing began with the main course and the Pomerol. When his lamb was nearly over, Sir Fitzroy made his move.

'Let me tell you in confidence,' he began, 'that I am seriously worried about the Home Secretary and his position in the government. Having a Gladstone in the cabinet may have been a gesture towards the glorious Liberal past, but our Herbert is a pale copy of his famous father. Having one leading institution operating on the hereditary principle might be thought strange, but to have two is surely a mistake. By now, after centuries of experience, the vicissitudes of successive monarchs should have warned us off perpetuating that system anywhere else.' Sir Fitzroy paused for a sip of his wine. 'Forgive me,' he said, 'I digress. My real concern is with these recent murders, the ones where the victims have strange markings on their chests. I fear that knowledge may seep out, and the newspapers will know that the three cases are linked. I fear there may be a public outcry. Three police forces trying to catch one murderer. What a waste of public money! Is it for this that we pay our taxes? Why do we not appoint a single man from the ranks of the Metropolitan Police to take charge of the affair? I have made this suggestion in a memorandum to the Home Secretary but I have had no reply. He sits, yet again, on the fence, Herbert The Unready, unable to make his mind up. What do you say, Henry?'

Sir Edward Henry had realized long ago that politics played as large a role in his job as policing. Over the years he had tried to maintain as much freedom of action for his force without alienating his political masters. In theory the Home Secretary could order him to do something. In practice, if he was careful, he could keep his distance. Occasional scraps had to be thrown down, apparent

117

concessions that might keep the authorities quiet while giving little away.

'I fully understand your anxieties, Sir Fitzroy,' Sir Edward began, thinking about his defences. 'I am sure you would agree that a rational man might organize our policing very differently if he were given a clean slate. Other countries have a national body which can investigate cases which cross the boundaries of separate forces. But, as things stand,' he paused to polish off the remains of his roast beef, 'I have no powers which would enable me to take the case over. I have a most efficient and imaginative man on the case of Sir Rufus of the Silkworkers, murdered in his own hall. But I cannot order the Norfolk Constabulary to hand over the case to one of my officers, any more than I could instruct the Buckinghamshire force to hand over the death in the Jesus Hospital. Only the Home Secretary has the power to do that. The ball, I fear, is in your court rather than mine, Sir Fitzroy.'

'Surely you must agree that such a course of action would be the right one in these circumstances?' Sir Fitzroy was beginning to tap the table with the fingers of his left hand, a sure sign, to those that knew him well, that he was growing angry.

'That's as may be, Sir Fitzroy, but we in the Metropolitan Police have long memories. People still remember the case of Inspector Whicher and the Road Hill murders half a century ago. A detective was called in from the Met. He identified the killer. He was not believed. Indeed, he had to abandon the case and his career in the police force. Local rivalries played a part in that. Only later did it transpire that Whicher had indeed identified the murderer correctly, but his theories were ignored by the local authorities. We do not look forward to a repeat of such incidents.'

'I see,' said Sir Fitzroy, his fingers tapping ever harder. 'This is most unsatisfactory.'

Sir Edward Henry knew that to make an enemy of the Permanent Secretary at the Home Office was as dangerous as making an enemy of the Home Secretary himself. All kinds of minor but irritating obstacles could be put in his way, lack of cooperation over police pay, threats of public inquiries into controversial cases.

'There is one thing I can do,' he said finally. 'I am very concerned about the fact that all these murders have links with the Silkworkers Company. They have a number of properties, particularly almshouses, in the London area. I propose to mount a guard over all of them round the clock until further notice. And I will send a message to the other Chief Constables in southern England that we are proposing to do this. I don't think the writ of the Silkworkers Company stretches as far as Aberdeen, probably not even up to York.'

Surely that, he said to himself, should appease Sir Fitzroy. It's not precisely what he wanted but it's something more than a fig leaf.

'Splendid, Henry, simply splendid. I shall take steps to inform the Home Secretary when I return to the office. That should give him a push in the right direction.' Long experience told him that you seldom achieved your objectives in the jungles of Whitehall by proceeding in a direct line. Crab-like progress was the order of the day. He beckoned to the waiter and ordered a second glass of Barsac for them both.

Inspector Miles Devereux was sitting in a borrowed office in Cannon Street police station with a bunch of papers in his hand. These were the reports of the officers sent to interview all those who had attended the fatal dinner in the Silkworkers Hall. Like so much police work, the details were all here. Devereux was bored by details as he was bored by so much of police routine. But he knew that he had to take them seriously. Otherwise he could make a mistake. Scratching the back of his head, he finished the last report. There was nothing here that could possibly help with their inquiries. He picked up a fresh sheet of paper and wrote 'Silkworkers Feast' at the top. Then he began writing an account of what happened hour by hour until the murderer struck. If you were in a job where details mattered, he said to himself as he reached eleven o'clock and the Haut Brion began to flow more freely, the least you can do is to make sure that your facts are right.

Lord Francis Powerscourt was with his brother-in-law William Burke in his vast office in the City of London once more. Burke was seated behind an enormous desk thick with files in neat bundles that made him look like a First Sea Lord or the Viceroy of India.

'For God's sake, William,' said Powerscourt, 'can't you come and sit in one of these chairs by the fire. You're too terrifying behind that thing. You look like some American tycoon about to ruin his enemies.'

Burke laughed. He took up a sheet or two of paper from his desk and joined Powerscourt on the other side of the marble mantelpiece.

'I have some interesting news for you, Francis, about our friends the Silkworkers. Remaining liverymen still alive, no further deaths overnight, I trust?'

'All left alive, present and correct, as far as I know,' said Powerscourt. 'I wouldn't vouch for tomorrow, mind you. Or the day after.'

Burke grunted and fished around in his pockets for a pair of spectacles.

'There are two ways of looking at what's been happening here, Francis. One benign, the other sinister. You can't take a view until I tell you what's been going on. The Silkworkers have been in existence since the early fourteenth century. Nobody is certain about the exact date of their foundation but various records begin to appear after thirteen thirty-eight or thereabouts. To understand the current controversy in the company, you have to go back to a little known codicil to a document believed to have been written in thirteen fifty, just after the Black Death of thirteen forty-eight. This wretched codicil was only discovered in the Silkworkers archives three or four years ago. All kinds of people have been excavated from their lairs to pronounce judgement on it – university professors, cathedral librarians, every archivist who could be found within a twenty-mile radius of Temple Bar. All of them, with one exception, say it is genuine. I'll tell you about the exception in a moment.'

Burke helped himself to a large cigar from a brass and silver humidor on the table in front of him. 'You have to imagine, these wise men say, what it must have been like just after the Black Death. Thousands and thousands of Londoners were dead. Contemporaries said you could catch the stench of rotting bodies far outside the city walls. The dead were piled so high on some streets that the survivors had to tread on the corpses to continue their journeys. Think most of all, the professors and the rest of them say, of the effect it must have had on men's minds. Their God, they felt certain, had deserted them. Perhaps this was the beginning of the end, the Book of Revelation come to Lombard Street and Cornhill, the number of the beast replacing all the numbers they had in their early ledgers. Maybe the plague would return over and over again until there was nobody left alive.'

Burke paused and blew an enormous smoke ring up to his intricately plastered ceiling. 'With me so far, Francis? You are? Not too difficult? Good. Now to this wretched codicil. Nobody knows who drew it up or to what document it was attached. The bearded ones believe it may have been part of a new version of the Silkworkers' constitution. Certainly the memory of the Black Death must have been paramount in the minds of those who wrote it. I asked one of the few experts who seemed to be under seventy years of age to make me a modern translation. I couldn't make much sense of the original.'

Burke picked out one sheet of paper from his pile and began to read.

'"As we have suffered most grievously in person and in property from the recent onslaught of the Great Mortality" – that's the Black Death to you and me – "we, the Wardens of the Company, have introduced this codicil to assist our successors in time of plague, pestilence or peril. At such times, if the Prime Warden and his three colleagues deem that there is a great danger or threat to the persons, property or families of the Silkworkers, they may take such steps as they think fit to safeguard those persons, property or families for posterity. Thus the ancient misteries of the Silkworkers," I know you're going to ask, Francis, misteries comes from the Latin *ministerium* which means occupation, "may be preserved for the future to rank alongside the other misteries in the City of London. May Almighty God bless our deliberations at this time and preserve us in body and mind until the last days."'

Burke laid down his cigar and blew a further smoke ring in the direction of a Lawrence portrait of an earlier City grandee on the wall.

'That's it, Francis. Except there's a final paragraph after "the last days", like a postscript. "Any changes proposed to the government of the Company in times of plague, pestilence or peril must be supported by the approbation of eight out of ten of the membership of the Company, their names or their marks to be recorded in the Company records. Any monies raised may be placed in property or other places. If the danger is great and the Lord of Hosts appears to have abandoned his people for the second time, the Company may be broken up, the monies divided in the following fashion: one half to the Prime Warden, one third to the Council, the remains divided among the membership according to their length of membership in the company."'

'Well,' said Powerscourt, 'that must have set the cat among the pigeons when the Prime Warden realized the implications. Tell me this, William, what do your wise men think that reference to "have suffered most grievously in person and in property" means right at the beginning?'

'If they're honest with themselves, they don't know. A couple of the professors say it refers to the collapse of property prices at the time of the Black Death. If your friends and relations are dying all around, you're not going to put your house up for sale. Prices would have collapsed, they say.'

'They may just be reading the present back into the past,' said Powerscourt. 'You said earlier, William, that there was a great argument going on among the Silkworkers. Where does this codicil come in?'

'Well, the key section is the bit about the authorities being able to take such action as they think fit if there is a great danger from plague, pestilence or peril. The party for change, led by our mutual friend, Sir Peregrine, think that the threat of war with Germany is such a moment of peril. They point out, quite rightly, that were that to happen, the value of the Silkworkers' assets would fall like a stone thrown from a high building. It would be a financial catastrophe. Why not, says Sir Peregrine, sell up now and buy everything back when the war's over and prices are still very low. They'd make a killing, a real killing, I tell you. I've told you before how rich these livery companies are. They've got properties all over the City, some of them maybe dating back to the Black Death itself, who knows. When you join the Silkworkers as a full member, not like the old boys in the almshouses, you have to promise to leave either monies or securities or property to the company in your will. There are millions of pounds on the table here.'

'So Sir Peregrine is proposing that they sell up. Fifty per cent to the Prime Warden sounds a pretty good deal to me, William. And what's to stop any of them taking all their share for themselves and never giving any back to the company when the peril or pestilence has ended?'

'What suspicious minds you people have,' said Burke, shaking his head sadly, 'but as it happens, you're more or less right. Three months ago, I think, Sir Peregrine proposed this vast sell-off of all their assets. He's been canvassing for votes ever since. They've got a rather unusual membership, the Silkworkers. Most of the livery companies don't want to have too many members on board – you don't want to be paying for elaborate feasts for five hundred or more. But the Silkworkers have an

124

ordinance that says only Silkworkers can be admitted to their almshouses. Rather than go to the bother of changing their statutes, they simply enlist everybody who isn't a Silkworker already into the company when they are taken in at places like your Jesus Hospital.'

'Do you mean to say,' Powerscourt was leaning forward, 'that all the old boys in the Jesus Hospital in Marlow are members of the Ancient Mistery of Silkworkers? That they all have a vote, for God's sake?'

'They do.'

'You're not telling me that all the pupils at Allison's up in Norfolk are members with votes, too?'

'They're too young,' said Burke, 'but I bet many of the masters are members. I'm virtually certain that the late bursar must have belonged.'

Powerscourt rose to his feet and began pacing up and down the room, as he did so often in his own drawing room in Markham Square. Walking the quarterdeck was how Lady Lucy referred to it.

'I think you said earlier, William, that one of your experts had doubts about the authenticity of the codicil?'

Burke laughed. 'Yes, and a most entertaining fellow he is, too. Professor of History at Cambridge, Fellow of Trinity, said by his contemporaries to be the brightest interpreter of the past since Thomas Babington Macaulay. Name of Tait, Selwyn Augustus Tait. He's thought to be unable to write a word of his books until he's taken a pint of claret on board. He read the codicil, the original version, in this room, in that very chair, Francis, where you're sitting now.'

Powerscourt stared at his chair as if a scrap of historical wisdom might have been deposited on it by his distinguished predecessor. 'What did he say?'

'In actual fact, he read it twice. Then he said, "Mr Burke, I would not hold you to any figure, but tell me, what are the Silkworkers worth? Approximately. To the nearest million."'

'What answer did you give, William?'

'I said five or six million, maybe more.'

'What did he do then?'

'He laughed. Then he asked if we had any decent claret about the place. "When my wits have been sharpened by a glass or two," he said, "I shall give you my verdict." Then he went out to stare at the view from that window behind you, the one where you can see St Paul's.'

'I presume the claret arrived in due course?'

'It did, an excellent vintage it was, too. When Tait had consumed two glasses, at a pretty rapid pace, it must be said, he laughed again and poured himself a refill. "It's a fake," he said, "that codicil. I'm almost certain it's a fake." And he laughed a third time.'

'Like Saint Peter with the cock crowing perhaps. Did he explain why he thought that?' asked Powerscourt, fascinated by the account of the claret-drinking historian, a cross between Johnny Fitzgerald and Edward Gibbon.

'He did. Of course he did. For a start he said that people like the Silkworkers always looked after their archives very carefully. He had examined a couple of the livery companies' records in the course of his researches and found them extremely well annotated. He doubted if anything could have been found recently which would have been in existence for six hundred years without discovery. By this time, Francis, most of the original bottle had gone and I felt obliged to order another. The professor's main objection was cynical. You always have to ask this question in these circumstances, he claimed. *Cui bono?* Who benefits? Who stands to gain from it? It was a good question for Cassius and Cicero, he said, and an even better one now for the Silkworkers. Sir Peregrine and his colleagues could make fortunes, possibly millions for Sir Peregrine alone. He was sure the thing was a clever forgery, designed to provide an avenue through which the funds of the Silkworkers could be diverted into the pockets of their officers. Then he took another long pull of his claret and said good afternoon and left to catch his train.'

'Was he weaving on his way out? Steering an uncertain course for the door perhaps?'

'He was not, Francis. Selwyn Augustus Tait seemed as sober as you and I. Maybe there's something in the air up there in the Fens with all that mist and those winds from the Urals.'

'Do we know if there is a timetable for this vote? By God, it'll be more exciting than a by-election. The fate of these vast sums of money in the hands of a group of people, many of whom have never seen a bolt of silk in their lives. A date, William, a date?'

'I'm not absolutely sure,' Burke replied. 'Something tells me it is the middle of February, end of February perhaps? I'll check for you.'

Burke fell silent for a moment. The great seventeenth-century French clock that had once graced the hunting lodge of Rambouillet ticked away the seconds of the late afternoon on the Burke mantelpiece. 'I wouldn't say this to anyone but you, Francis, but I blame democracy and the popular papers for so many of our troubles, I really do.'

'Whatever do you mean, William?' Powerscourt had never heard his brother-in-law as political or as philosophical as this before.

'With democracy as we know it now, with all these extra

voters on the rolls, politics is governed by the whims of the uneducated and the ignorant. The popular papers, especially the *Daily Mail* – God, how I hate the *Daily Mail* – have been exaggerating or inventing the threat from the Germans for years now. You can scarcely open a newspaper but there are these ludicrous scare stories in there. If the country were run by intelligent people like men of business, we could sort out the German problem in a weekend. "You would like a bit more of Africa," we could say. "Well, have another bit. Have this bit here and that bit over there, while you're about it; we've got far too much of it already." So the German men of business would say, "That is very kind. Now what would you like in return? Would you like us to stop building our dreadnoughts up there in Kiel and Wilhelmshaven? Would you like us to halt the arms race at a point where you always have four or five big ships more than we do so you and your people don't feel threatened? Very good. We shall do it." I'm sure it wouldn't even take a weekend. But can you imagine what the newspapers would say back here? "Asquith gives Empire to Germans!" "British Empire handed over to the Hun!" The mass of the population who read the *Mail* and not *The Times* or the *Morning Post* would be up in arms. The government would fall within weeks. They would be pariahs, excluded from polite society, maybe even banned from their clubs, who knows.' Burke sighed. 'It's all too late now, Francis, far too late. People talk about currencies being devalued so they lose their purchasing power and their value. Good government has been devalued by extending the franchise in this country but nobody could stop it.'

Powerscourt thought a diversion was needed. 'William,' he began, 'I think it must be sitting in this chair where that other fellow sat. Have you any decent claret in the house?'

Burke laughed. 'I'll order some now, Francis. We could have the same wine as the professor had.'

Burke stopped halfway across the room and stared at his brother-in-law. 'My God, Francis, how stupid of me. I've forgotten to tell you one of the most important facts of all about recent events at the Silkworkers.'

'What was that?'

'How could I be so foolish! There was a lot of opposition to Sir Peregrine and his friends in the Silkworkers. Can you guess who the leader of the opposition was?'

'I have no idea, William.'

'I'll tell you who it was,' said Burke. 'It was the man recently found dead at the top of the steps leading down to the river in Silkworkers Hall with the strange mark on his chest. Sir Rufus Walcott, he was the leader of the opposition.'

One hundred and twenty miles away Detective Inspector Grime of the Norfolk Constabulary was a very angry man. He had been waiting all day for one of the boys of Allison's School to come and speak to him about the visit of the phoney postman on the day of the murder of the school bursar Roderick Gill. That morning a real postman had retraced what they thought must have been the steps of the killer. The headmaster had addressed the pupils at the end of morning assembly before lessons began.

'Good morning, boys,' he had said, sweeping his black gown behind him as he spoke. 'I know that you will all be as anxious as I am to clear up the recent murder in our midst. This morning I appeal for your help. Less than an hour ago the postal authorities and the police repeated the journey through our school of the murderer who came disguised as a postman. If this second visit by a real postman sparked any memories in your minds of that earlier, fatal trip, perhaps you would be so kind as to speak to Inspector Grime on my left here. He will be in the Officers' Training Corps office for the rest of the day. Please see him if there is anything you remember, anything at all.'

The boys filed out and headed for their classrooms. Many of them stared rather insolently at the policeman as they passed him on their way out. Inspector Grime had made few friends among the schoolboy population of Allison's. He had spoken to them all by now. His bored manner did not impress. With one or two of them he had been downright rude. As the pupils settled into their desks to begin their day's work, the word began to be passed round. It was started by a rather intelligent young man in the Fifth Form who proclaimed to all and sundry that he wanted to be an anarchist when he grew up. 'Don't speak to the policeman. Pass it on,' he wrote and tore the page out of his notebook. He handed it to his neighbour. Inside ten minutes every boy in the room had read it. When the pupils changed classes at the end of the first lesson, those in on the secret told the colleagues they passed in the corridor. The would-be anarchist's note was still travelling by the time of morning break at eleven. Within five minutes of that starting, every single boy in the school had received the message. The policy of non-cooperation with the civil authorities had been established in a little over two hours.

Inspector Grime sat in his temporary office surrounded by literature about the Officers' Training Corps and a succession of military photographs on the wall. Boy soldiers from Allison's marching past the front of the building. Boy soldiers at camp in some dreary part of Norfolk near the sea. Boy soldiers standing steady on parade beneath the Union flag. The headmaster had assured him that the witnesses would probably come during morning break. They did not. The headmaster then revised his opinion and informed Inspector Grime that the boys would come to him during the lunch hour. They did not. After lessons closed for the day the headmaster felt sure that this was the time for the boys to come forward. He asked his deputy if he had heard anything on the school grapevine about the boys' attitude to the police Inspector. The deputy had no intelligence to offer. By now the headmaster was seriously worried. Were the boys in his care obstructing the course of justice? He found it impossible to believe that they had not noticed anything that morning. He wondered if there might be another way of getting them to talk.

Detective Inspector Grime was livid. He had read through all his notes on the case so far. He had learnt from one of the OTC handbooks how to dismantle and clean a rifle. He had read about making progress in open country and through difficult terrain, which was certainly where he felt he was now. Worse was to come. His Sergeant arrived shortly before five o'clock to tell him of a message from the Dean of York, who had promised to make further inquiries about the whereabouts of one Jude Mitchell, cuckolded husband of the mistress of the dead man. The dean and his people had toiled all day for many days and caught nothing. Mitchell was nowhere to be found. They had cast their nets as far afield as Beverley to the east and Lichfield to the south and Ripon to the north, all minster or cathedral cities where a mason like Mitchell might have been able to take on temporary work. He was nowhere to be found.

'Damn it, Sergeant,' said Grime to his subordinate, 'where the hell is the wretched man? You can't just disappear like this. Not nowadays.' The Sergeant resisted the temptation to say that Mitchell appeared to have done precisely that. 'Give me a moment, will you?' the Inspector went on. 'You can take this back and send it off. I'd better send a telegram with the latest news, or rather lack of it, to Lord Francis bloody Powerscourt. Damn the man and his fancy theories!'

Had Inspector Grime been a more sympathetic officer, one that boys might be happy to speak to about what they had seen, he would have heard some things that were not all that important to his investigation. But some sensible boys would have told him that the man was of average height. Others would have told him that the man seemed to be in his middle thirties. Others again would have told of a thick black beard. But one boy had information that would have made the Inspector and Powerscourt very interested indeed. This was a boy called Lewis, David Lewis, who was in his first year in the Sixth Form. Lewis was the best mimic in the school. He could impersonate his headmaster, his housemaster and the chaplain perfectly. When his friends persuaded him, he would deliver wickedly accurate sermons from the chaplain late at night, standing at the end of his bed in the dormitory with his dressing gown acting as cassock. On another famous occasion in Allison's legend he had rung the headmaster, purporting to be his housemaster, about some detentions which were subsequently cancelled and caused a rift between the two schoolmasters which had not been healed to this day.

The phoney postman had bumped into Lewis on the morning of his murder run and had apologized. 'I'm so sorry,' he had said and continued on his way. Lewis probably had the most acute ear in the school. The accent, he declared to his friends, was not English; the man was a foreigner. He was not American either, said David Lewis, having spent six months in Washington three years before. Quite where the phoney postman did come from he could not be sure.

That night the overtaxed men of the Metropolitan Police had another burden added to their load. Word, their Sergeants and Inspectors informed them, had come from the very top. They were to be on guard all night at various properties and almshouses belonging to the Silkworkers Company. The danger, they were told, could come from the inside with the inmates trying to kill each other or from the outside with unknown villains come to murder the residents. Two constables stood in the doorways of grand houses in the City owned by the Silkworkers.

PC James Jones, five years off retirement, spent the night inside and outside the Hospice of the Holy Trinity in Blackheath. He told his wife of long standing he thought it had to do with German spy rings operating in the City of London. PC Albert Smith, who had been married for eight days, was on patrol at the Hospice of St Michael in Richmond. He said to his new wife as he left that he might be away all night, but that he would be at home all day the next day and he didn't expect to be that tired. PC John Walsh, on duty at the Jesus Hospital in Haringey, made himself conspicuous by pacing noisily up and down the little quadrangle. He believed that a gang of thieves were intent on stealing the hospice's magnificent collection of silver, which they left carelessly on display in a cabinet with no lock. That at any rate was the view of his Sergeant, who had made representations about the silver in the past but to no avail. And PC Walter Buchan, at six feet five inches the tallest officer among them, kept vigil over the old men in the Almshouse of St John the Divine in Clerkenwell. He had told his wife before he set off that the world had gone stark raving mad.

The following morning Sir Fitzroy Robinson Buller, Permanent Secretary at the Home Office, sent another memorandum to his master. He reminded the minister about his earlier message regarding the three murders and hoped the Home Secretary would soon be in a position to deliver an authoritative judgement. In the meantime he described the measures taken around the various properties belonging to the Silkworkers. If the government were pressed in parliament or in the newspapers about what they were doing in these cases, the Home Secretary could now point out that all necessary steps were being taken to safeguard the public.

8

There were two telegrams for Powerscourt the morning after the police watch began. One was from Johnny Fitzgerald with the latest news from Marlow and the old gentlemen's wills. The other came from Inspector Grime, and Powerscourt could feel the disappointment and the frustration behind the words about the total lack of information from the boys of Allison's.

'Damn it, Lucy,' he said, stretching out on the sofa in front of the fire, 'I feel like some military Commander miles and miles from the front who has to communicate with his Generals by runner or by telegram. Don't think Napoleon had to go in for this sort of thing. By the time I have taken one lot of information on board, another lot comes in from elsewhere which changes the picture altogether. I suppose I'll just have to get used to it.'

'I'm sure you'll get to the bottom of it, my love,' said Lady Lucy, used to these moments of doubt in the course of her husband's investigations. 'I do think the news about Sir Peregrine and the Silkworkers is fascinating, Francis. Do you think he just wants to make off with the money?'

'I know he's been using the argument about the

Germans all over the place. The headmaster man up in Norfolk told me about that one. I've been investigating things for so long now, Lucy, I always think the worst of everybody. So in my opinion the whole case may be about Sir Peregrine getting his hands on the money.'

There was a discreet cough at the door. Rhys, the Powerscourt butler, always coughed to announce his arrival when he had to make an unexpected appearance.

'Telephone, my lord.' Rhys usually sounded as if he had just come from or was just about to go to a funeral. 'From Norfolk, my lord. The headmaster of Allison's, my lord.'

Powerscourt shot down the stairs to the room looking out over the square that he used as a study. It was gloomy outside, the rain rattling against the windows in Markham Square.

'Headmaster,' he said, 'how nice to hear from you. How are things up there in Norfolk?'

'My apologies for ringing you at home, Lord Powerscourt. I need some advice.'

'Fire ahead,' said Powerscourt cheerfully.

'Yesterday morning we had a real postman retrace the steps of the murderer up the long corridor in the school. At the same time as the earlier visit, of course. I appealed to the boys at assembly, very soon after the visit, to report anything they had seen on the day of the death to Inspector Grime. I told them he would be in the OTC room all day.'

'And?' asked Powerscourt.

'That's just it,' replied the headmaster. 'There is no "and". Nobody came forward. The Inspector waited all day and nothing happened. He was very cross by the time he left, I can tell you.'

'Do you think the boys knew something but didn't want to tell? Or that they hadn't seen anything at all?'

'Damn it, Lord Powerscourt, about fifty or sixty boys must have seen the phoney postman that morning. If they were properly awake – and many may not have been – they must have realized that this was not the normal time for the man with the mail to arrive. And I suspect that they may have taken against the policeman. He can be a bit surly at times, Inspector Grime.'

'Could you or your colleagues talk to the boys individually? Would that work?'

'I don't think they would talk to us either. They'll have decided en masse not to talk to the policeman. They're bright enough to see that if they talk to the staff it's virtually the same as talking to Grime. The information will go straight to the police.'

'I see,' said Powerscourt.

'I'm acutely conscious that the boys in my charge appear at the moment to be obstructing the police in their inquiries. That can't be right. What do I do if Grime turns nasty and takes one or two of my pupils down to the police station?'

Powerscourt could see the serried ranks of parents lining up outside the headmaster's study in the headmaster's mind. He could hear the voices in the headmaster's head.

'I'm not going to stand for this, my son hauled off to the local police station!'

'I'm taking my two boys home immediately, and they won't be coming back!'

'I've known our member of parliament for many years now. You'll be hearing from him very soon!'

'My sympathies, Headmaster,' said Powerscourt.

'You're in a very difficult situation, and it's not of your making.'

'I've had three members of staff laid low by the influenza today. We're going to have to rework the entire timetable.'

Something in what the headmaster said set off a train of thought in Powerscourt's brain. It couldn't work, could it? It would be too difficult to arrange, surely. Or would it? To hell with it, why not? There was nothing to lose.

'Headmaster,' he said, 'a thought has just struck me which might, just might, help us out of some of our difficulties. It is rather a long shot and I don't want to tell you about it until I have had time to think it through. Could I call you back inside the hour?'

'Of course,' said the headmaster. 'I will wait by the telephone.'

Powerscourt shot back up the stairs to tell Lady Lucy the news. Then he put a proposition to her.

'You can't be serious, Francis.'

'I am, my love, I am.'

'Well,' said Lady Lucy, 'it's very unusual. I don't think such a thing is happening anywhere else.'

'I'm sure it is. This is nineteen ten after all, not eighteen hundred and forty.'

'In a way,' said Lady Lucy, 'I suppose it might be rather fun. I'm sure I could do it. Yes, Francis, yes, why not? I shall fulfil my duties in my earlier name of Mrs Hamilton.'

Powerscourt ran back down the stairs. 'Headmaster,' he said, 'I have a proposition to put to you.'

The headmaster listened carefully to Powerscourt's proposals. Then he laughed. 'Splendid idea!' he boomed down the phone as if he were addressing the parents on

Speech Day. 'I propose we put it into action on Monday, the day after tomorrow. A week's service for a start, more if required.'

Thomas Monk, Warden of the Jesus Hospital in Marlow, was awake very early the next morning. Monk was a worried man. Eight of the old gentlemen had arrived in his office the day before and demanded their wills back. Monk had watched out of his window, fingering his pale blue cravat, as the octet marched in line out of the hospital and down the road to the solicitor's offices. Monk still had three of their wills in his possession. He suspected that the owners of those wills had forgotten where they had put them. Any one of those old men could arrive at any time and demand their last will and testament. But that was not the full extent of his problems. Only one of the three wills he still had contained any money, and its owner, in Monk's judgement, was not going to be around for very much longer. Experience at the hospital had left Monk a good judge of how long its members had left to go – if he could have taken odds on the life expectancy of the different inhabitants of the Jesus Hospital with the local bookkeeper in Maidenhead, he would certainly have done so.

The Warden's principal concern had to do with the will of Number Twenty, Abel Meredith. This was the one with slightly over two thousand pounds, originally going to Meredith's brother in Canada. His conversation with Henry Wood, Number Twelve, in which he had implied that half the money went to Canada, the rest to him, had led to Andrew Snow, Number Eighteen, remembering an earlier conversation with Meredith, in which he, Number

Eighteen, was told all the money was going to the brother in Canada. And that had led directly to the old men requesting their wills back. All of them had voiced their concerns about Meredith's will and where his legacy was going. He had said nothing, but he knew he had to do something. Otherwise the old men, led by that slippery Number Twelve, might complain to the Silkworkers Company in London.

The inmates of the Jesus Hospital eased the pains of their days at the Rose and Crown, famed for its barmaid and the smoke. Monk had never visited the place, feeling it would be beneath him to be seen drinking in the same place as the residents of the almshouse. Five minutes' walk in the opposite direction was the Duke of Clarence, a place that was pretending not be a pub at all, but some sort of superior watering hole for people coming for boat rides on the Thames or going for lunch or dinner at the expensive hotel on the island up the road. Even the public bar in the Duke of Clarence looked as though it might contain a couple of stockbrokers from the City. It was here, the previous evening, over two pints of mild and bitter, that Monk formulated his plan for the next morning.

Breakfast was nearly over in the Jesus Hospital. The tomato ketchup and the HP sauce had been sprayed over pairs of sausages and a helping of fried bread this morning, accompanied by what the old men thought were two rather mean rashers of bacon. As the meal came to an end and the last cups of tea were passed round, the Warden came in and knocked on the table nearest the door for quiet.

'Gentlemen!' he said. 'Silkmen, forgive me for interrupting your breakfast, but I felt I had to speak to you on a matter of some urgency.' Monk was speaking quite slowly and very loudly for the benefit of his audience. 'Yesterday a number of you came to see and asked, very properly, if you could have your wills back. I agreed, as I should, to these requests. But some of you also voiced concerns about the will of our late colleague Abel Meredith, Number Twenty. Maybe I am wrong here but I felt that there was an implication that I might have tampered with this will in some way. Nothing could be further from the truth.'

Monk paused at this point and gazed round the old men. He put his hand in his pocket and pulled out a couple of pieces of paper. 'This is Abel Meredith's will. I am going to hand it round so you can all read it. Whatever you might have thought, you will see that all the money goes to his brother in Canada.' With that, Monk handed the documents to Jack Miller, Number Three, and sat down. This was indeed the original will. This was part of the plan Monk had concocted in the Duke of Clarence the evening before. Monk thanked God he had kept the earlier version hidden inside his special floorboard.

It took some time for the papers to be passed round the company. Spectacles had to be found. Meredith's writing was not of the clearest and often needed decoding by a neighbour. The strain of reading through such a paper, surrounded by your fellows in the hospital, made some of the silkmen so nervous they had to stop for a rest in the middle of it. Those who had read it fidgeted uneasily in their chairs, keen to escape into the quadrangle outside for a good gossip about its contents. After nearly an hour they were finished. Number Three, Jack Miller, gave the will back to Monk.

'Thank you very much for your time, gentlemen,' he

said and walked out of the dining room. As he strode back to his office he smiled as he thought of the second part of the plan concocted on his mild and bitter in the Duke of Clarence. This was going to be his revenge on the Jesus Hospital. The original would go back into its floorboard. The will he would send to the London solicitors, however, would be the one he had forged some time earlier, the one that left half the money to the brother and the other half to him. Monk knew how long the legal niceties could take. Correspondence to and fro from Saskatchewan might add a couple of months to the timescale, particularly if the Canadian lawyers, like so many in England, were partners in the well-known firm of Slow and Bideawhile. It might be a year or more before the thing was settled. And by then some of the old men would have forgotten. And the others would be dead.

The silkmen of the Jesus Hospital may have drunk in the Rose and Crown, Thomas Monk may have patronized the Duke of Clarence, but Johnny Fitzgerald was staying in the expensive hotel on the island in the river a quarter of a mile from Marlow. The new owners originally wanted to call it the Champs Élysées after the great thoroughfare in Paris. They settled for the Elysian Fields instead, a name they thought brought a touch of glamour, a suggestion of divine food and wine and maybe a faint hint of naughtiness, Turkish belly dancers perhaps, or girls imported from the Moulin Rouge.

Lord Francis Powerscourt left home early to take breakfast with Johnny Fitzgerald. He planned to visit all his key players in one day to tell them about the Silkworkers codicil, for this, he thought, put the whole case in a different light.

'Good God, Francis,' said Johnny, pausing in his progress through a small mountain of kedgeree, 'you're not trying to tell me that the whole case may revolve round a piece of paper over hundreds of years old written by some bloke who had just escaped the Black Death? And that the bloody thing may be a forgery?'

'I am,' said Powerscourt. 'And there's more. You will recall that stuff I just told you about there being a vote and that eight out of ten of the members had to approve any alterations to the rules?'

'I do.'

'Well, all of your old gentlemen have a vote. They have to become members of the Silkworkers Company when they sign up for the Jesus Hospital. Twenty votes is quite a lot. They could be more important than we think.'

'Nineteen, actually,' said Johnny indistinctly through a final mouthful of kedgeree. 'Dead men don't vote.'

'Sorry,' said Powerscourt.

'For God's sake, Francis, won't you eat something? You're making me nervous sitting there like a high court judge at the Old Bailey, not having anything at all apart from a tiny slice of toast. Have a poached egg or two, in heaven's name.'

Powerscourt began to work his way through the eggs dumped on his plate by his friend.

'I suppose you want me to run this lot up the flagpole with the old boys,' said Johnny, glancing at a very pretty young American lady at the next table whose husband was complaining loudly to the waiter about the coffee. 'I wonder why they haven't talked about it before. I

143

don't recall a single mention of it in all the time I've been marooned down here.'

'Valuable work you've been doing, Johnny, valuable work.' Powerscourt grinned at his friend. 'I suspect they have all been sworn to silence, the old men. The one thing Sir Peregrine can't have is publicity. His whole scheme might collapse once it got into the papers.'

Johnny stared silently at a couple of slices of ham. 'I don't think it'll be any good asking them about it in the Rose and Crown,' he said finally. 'I'll have to try them one at a time. The man Wood, Number Twelve, maybe that's who I'll start with. He's got a pretty suspicious mind.'

'One other thing, Johnny,' said Powerscourt.

'Oh yes?' said his friend. 'What is it now?'

'Could you tell Inspector Fletcher about the codicil and all that? I've got to go back to London.'

'Yes, yes, I'll do that,' said Johnny. 'Don't mind about me. Here I am abandoned on the island like that bloody woman from Crete whose name I can never remember. There was her bloody lover on his bloody boat, just visible from the shore, hull down on the horizon.'

'Never mind, Johnny. At least the abandoned Ariadne was in the company of Bacchus, the god of wine. They tell me there's some pretty good stuff in the cellars here. It's said to come from the Elysian Fields themselves.'

Powerscourt found Inspector Miles Devereux in the council chamber of the Silkworkers Hall, a beautiful room where the inner circle of the company held their meetings.

'If you've got to have a bloody office,' Devereux drawled, 'you may as well have it in a place like this.' He waved a hand at the tall windows looking out over the

144

Thames and a number of full-length Silkworker Prime Wardens lining the walls.

'Look at this rogues' gallery,' he said, pointing at the paintings. 'They look as though oysters wouldn't melt in their mouths. I bet you they were as slippery as eels, mind you, lying about where the silk had come from, the precise location on the Silk Road, just like today, probably.' Devereux scrabbled about in the papers in front of him and pulled out a couple of sheets.

'I'm thinking of staying here,' he said, 'making this my permanent office. As long as we haven't solved the case, that'll be fine. Once we have been successful, a grateful company might leave me here as a thank-you for services rendered. If you get bored you can always go downstairs and jump in the Thames or wait for some assassin to come and slit your throat.'

Powerscourt smiled. He thought boredom might be a permanent problem in the life and times of Miles Devereux.

'Sorry for the waffle,' Devereux said, sitting up straight in his chair. 'This is an account of what happened at the grand dinner the other day. I don't think there's anything unusual except for the amount of Haut Brion they seem to have got through. I've checked with the company manciple and he assured me it was nineteen bottles of the stuff, most of them drunk by only five or six people. My papa would have approved of the Haut Brion, though never in those quantities.'

Powerscourt glanced through the paper. There was little of interest there. He told the Inspector about the Silkworkers codicil and its implications.

Devereux whistled and began pacing about the room. 'This is like something out of a penny dreadful,' he said.

'And Sir Rufus Walcott was the leader of the opposition inside the company? Fascinating.'

Eventually Miles Devereux sat down on the edge of his desk and voiced a concern that had been in Powerscourt's mind since the previous evening. 'I say, Lord Powerscourt. This could be the motive for all the murders. Suppose there was opposition to the changes at the Jesus Hospital as well as in the livery company itself. Suppose there was more opposition at Allison's School up there in Norfolk. Three places where the supporters of Sir Peregrine or indeed Sir Peregrine himself might have had a motive for murder. Maybe they said they were going to make it public, or write to *The Times* or their MP or something like that. There is one further possible consequence.' He stopped suddenly and stared at Powerscourt. 'This might mean that the strange marks on the bodies are a diversion, that they were stamped on the victims to draw attention away from the true motive, greed or preservation of your own position, whatever you might want to call it. Sir Peregrine had in his possession whatever strange instrument caused the marks. Either he or his accomplices then stamped it on the victims, hoping we would all be sidetracked away from the real murderer. Which, in a way, we have been.'

'Exactly so,' said Powerscourt, nodding at the young man. He had been surprised that Johnny Fitzgerald hadn't reached the same conclusion an hour so earlier. Maybe the Elysian cellars had befuddled his wits.

'However,' said Miles Devereux, 'this, as my superior officer would say, is speculation, little better than guesswork. Guesswork, he says about three times a week, never won a conviction at the Bailey. Is it time to interview Sir Peregrine yet, do you think?'

'I think it's too soon. I must be off in a moment. I have to tell our friends in Fakenham about the latest developments. Before we talk to Sir Peregrine I think we need to talk to the experts about that codicil. I don't think we should rely on my brother-in-law's view of the thing, even if he has talked to the man who thinks it's a fake. I'm going to ask him to send you the names of the principal experts who thought it was genuine. I'll call on the man from Cambridge on my way back from Norfolk. I'm not sure we'll end up any the wiser, but we've got to do it.'

'I say, what fun,' said Inspector Miles Devereux, rising from his chair and dancing a little jig in front of a sixteenth-century Prime Warden dressed from head to toe in black. 'I wouldn't dare say it to my fellow policemen, Lord Powerscourt, but I can say it you. Black Death! Ancient codicils! Murder most foul! What fun! What tremendous fun!'

Inspector Albert Fletcher, the officer in charge of the investigation into the death in the Jesus Hospital, was a worried man. Even the news of the Silkworkers codicil did little to cheer him up. He could see that there was at last a motive, a clear motive, but the thought of fourteenth-century documents and clever modern forgers filled him with gloom. He had so far failed to solve his first murder case. He was not living up to his promise, the bright future so many had predicted for him. Nothing he had tried so far seemed to have yielded very much. He summoned his Sergeant and gave more instructions.

'I know we've asked house to house for anything strange or any strange persons seen on the morning of the murder,' Inspector Fletcher began. 'I think I got the times wrong. And the ring around the hospital was probably too small. I want you to get all the men you can find and begin house-to-house inquiries in a five-mile radius of the hospital. And ask about the two days before the incident as well as the morning of death, could you? Some visiting murderer could have hidden himself away down there in those boathouses. Look sharp about it now.'

The Sergeant always knew when his master was in a bad mood. It was pointless to raise any objections. He saluted smartly and left the room as fast as he could. Inspectors, he said to himself, bloody Inspectors. Surely they could remember their own trials and tribulations when they were mere Sergeants. Begging for uniformed men from their superiors to take part in what the superiors would regard as ridiculous fancies was one of the most difficult things in a Sergeant's life. And the keeper of these good men and true, one Superintendent Maurice Trotter, had a very pretty daughter who sang in the Sergeant's church choir. He was thinking of striking up a conversation with her the next time they met.

Johnny Fitzgerald was entertaining Number Twelve to lunch in the Elysian Fields. The members of the hospital had been to the funeral of Abel Meredith the day before. The medical men had finally given up hope of finding anybody who could identify the strange marks on the chest and delivered the body up for burial. The old men had enjoyed the service, singing the hymns with gusto, some of them even managing to kneel down for the prayers, the stern words about the body of Abel Meredith being committed to the ground, earth to earth, ashes to ashes, dust to dust, cheering and reassuring to the old men who were still alive.

The dining room in the Elysian Fields was only half full and Johnny had secured a table next to the tall windows looking out over the river. Henry Wood, Number Twelve, wearing his official uniform of blue coat with white buttons and tricorne hat, was pleased to be asked to such a luxurious establishment but slightly suspicious of Johnny's motives. He was the man who had worked in the fish trade before coming to the hospital. He wasn't quite sure what to make of Johnny. Maybe, Number Twelve thought, he was a pike with those teeth. Sometimes he wondered if he mightn't actually be a shark.

His host was charming, urging more hock with the fish course, and ordering an expensive bottle of Beaune with the veal. They chatted amiably enough over the first course with Johnny encouraging Henry Wood, Number Twelve, to tell him more about what went on in the hospital. Over the apple pie, seeing that the subject seemed unlikely to come up of its own accord, Johnny made his move.

'What are you all going to do about the Silkworkers ballot and those plans to sell off the assets?' he inquired.

'How do you know about that?' replied Number Twelve.

'I've a cousin who belongs to the livery,' Johnny lied cheerfully, 'not that he's ever been near a silkworm in his life. He said there was a lot of argument going on.'

'Well, that's certainly true with us.' Number Twelve looked round him as if he thought he might be under surveillance of some kind. He took a large gulp of Beaune and Johnny knew he was hooked. 'Fact is,' Number

Twelve went on, 'we've all been sworn to secrecy. We're not meant to breathe a word about it to anybody.'

In his long experience of human nature working with Powerscourt, Johnny knew that there is nothing some people sworn to secrecy like better than telling somebody else about it at the earliest possible opportunity.

'Were you all united in your opinions then, up there at the hospital?'

Number Twelve laughed a sarcastic laugh. 'We were not. Absolutely not. I've never known the men so divided as they were about this vote. People came to blows once or twice.'

'Really?' said Johnny.

'It was that bad.' Number Twelve, Henry Wood, finished his glass and looked expectantly at the Beaune. Johnny topped him up and ordered another bottle.

'So where does opinion stand now?'

'I'm not quite sure, actually. To begin with, nearly everybody seemed to be in favour of selling up. Warden Monk was particularly keen on the plan. I've often wondered,' Number Twelve leant forward at this point and whispered, 'if he wasn't in the pay of that horrible man Sir Peregrine Fishborne!'

'Seriously?' said Johnny.

'Very seriously. That man is capable of anything. I wouldn't be surprised if he turned out to be the murderer.'

'You said informed opinion was initially for selling up. Did some people change their minds?'

'Well,' said Number Twelve, admiring the colour of the wine in its splendid bottle, 'the opposition were very clever. They said they could see all the attractions, money in our pockets from our share of the sale of the assets, that sort of thing. But, they said, there was no guarantee about what was going to happen to the Jesus Hospital later on. If the Silkworkers effectively ceased to exist, even though some people said it would come back again when the war was over, who was going to look after us in the meantime? Who was going to pay all the bills? They said, the opposition, that our situation would become untenable. The Prime Warden and his cronies could kick us out and sell the hospital off to the highest bidder and turn it into houses or flats. We would become notorious, they said, decrepit old men walking the streets of Marlow and Maidenhead with begging bowls in our hands and nowhere to rest our weary heads at night.'

'That must have put the fear of God into some of the men,' said Johnny. 'But tell me, what of your own position? Which side were you on?'

Johnny thought he knew the answer to that. He did.

'I was with the opposition, myself. Any change in the position of something as marginal as an almshouse must be risky. People probably wouldn't pay for them to be built if they didn't feel they had to. The founder, the original Gresham back in sixteen whatever it was, must have thought it would improve his chances of getting into heaven. Otherwise he wouldn't have bothered. I wouldn't think Sir Peregrine and his friends think they might be going to hell. They wouldn't behave like this if they did.'

'And who was the leader of the opposition, as it were, the main voice against Sir Peregrine?'

'Well, it was Number Twenty, actually. He was very persuasive when he was alive, Abel Meredith.'

And now he's dead, Johnny said to himself. He opposed the changes and now he's dead, just like that other one, up there in the Silkworkers Hall.

9

Powerscourt felt like a naughty schoolboy waiting for an unpleasant interview with the headmaster. He was indeed in the outer office of the headmaster of Allison's School, but the naughty boys, three of them, he was told, were in the inner sanctum, facing the wrath of the authorities for drinking two bottles of prohibited wine behind the cricket pavilion. The headmaster, however, was affable as Powerscourt was ushered in and the miscreants sent back to their classrooms.

'Lord Powerscourt, how good to see you. And Lady Powerscourt is at her station, I trust?'

The Powerscourts had arrived in Fakenham the evening before and were comfortably settled in the Crown Hotel, a few minutes' walk from the school.

'I hope so,' said Powerscourt. 'She was certainly going in the right direction when I last saw her. Do you have any further news, Headmaster? Are the boys still refusing to talk?'

'I'm afraid they are,' replied the headmaster. 'Let's hope they change their minds soon.'

'There is one development on which I'd like to hear

your opinion,' said Powerscourt. 'It concerns the constitution, if that's not too grand a word, of the Silkworkers Company. We did talk about it when I was here before, but without mentioning one key legal fact. As I understand it, Sir Peregrine Fishborne, in his role as Prime Warden of the Company, wants to sell off the assets and distribute the proceeds among the members, with a view to reacquiring the assets at a later, unspecified, stage. He claims, so I'm told, that the justification for this course of action is an ancient codicil, only recently discovered, which gives him the right to do this in times of great peril, like a possible war with Germany. That, I think, is the key legal fact we did not discuss at our earlier meeting, Headmaster. I wonder what you feel about this, as head of a school which has been in the care of the Silkworkers for centuries?'

'I have to tell you, Lord Powerscourt, that we at Allison's were divided about the plan. We still are. Some people thought it most unwise. According to the bursar, who was, if you like, the leader of the opposition, it could endanger the future of the school.'

'So Roderick Gill was the leading man in the hostile party?'

'He certainly was. He thought it most imprudent, an attempt by the authorities in the livery company to enrich themselves at the expense of future generations. Pure greed, he called it.'

'I see,' said Powerscourt. 'Were there a lot of votes here in the school?'

'Twelve. Myself and my deputy, the bursar and the other nine votes were spread out among the senior members of staff. Allison's has always had a dozen votes; it goes back for years and years.'

153

'Did they all oppose the plan?'

'I'm terribly sorry, Powerscourt, I feel my obligations to the Silkworkers don't allow me to answer that. I was in breach of covenant when we had our earlier discussion. I would prefer not to do that again.'

'Do you know if Sir Peregrine and his friends were aware of some opposition here? Was there any attempt to change your minds?'

'It's curious you should ask that,' said the headmaster, gathering his gown behind his back and strolling over to the window. 'We were still waiting for Roderick's final report on the affair. But I know he wrote to Sir Peregrine as a matter of politeness to let him know his views. The school, after all, is an important part of the role and responsibilities of the livery company. Gill told him, as I understand it, that he did not see how the Silkworkers' duties to the school could be fulfilled if its assets were all sold off and distributed among the members. I think he actually asked if Sir Peregrine proposed to sell the school off as if it were a house on Lombard Street. But he was polite. He invited the Prime Warden to come and talk to us whenever he felt able to. He said it might help clear the air.'

'How long ago was this, Headmaster?'

'Five days ago. It was the first day of the snow. I met Gill on his way into town to post the letter in person, slipping and falling over as he went.'

Mrs Hamilton's first class that day was with the Lower Sixth. She told the boys she was a temporary replacement for their normal French oral teacher, who had a bad attack of influenza. She expected to be with them for a week, maybe more. Then she took the register in French and made a note by each name to remind herself who they were. Fettiplace Jones, red hair. Johnston, prominent nose. Jackson, curly brown hair. Kingham, very tall. She announced that she was going to speak French to them all the time. And she proposed that they should read together, each boy taking it in turns to read a page. She had brought the book with her and said they were going to start with 'A Scandal in Bohemia', the opening story in *The Adventures of Sherlock Holmes*, translated into French the year before. Mrs Hamilton had tracked it down to a small bookshop in Bloomsbury specializing in French literature and translations the day before.

Ellis opened the bowling. '*Pour Sherlock Holmes,*' he said examining every word very carefully as if it were a bomb and might go off at any moment, '*elle est toujours La Femme.*' He staggered on to the end of the page and passed the book to his neighbour. As with most Englishmen, Mrs Hamilton reckoned, they probably understood about three quarters of it and could guess the rest, but she doubted if they could book themselves a hotel room in Brittany, let alone order supper.

Jackson was adequate, Smythe quite fluent if rather slow, which he was. David Lewis, the mimic, had a perfect accent and impeccable diction. His passage told how Dr Watson, returning home from a case via Baker Street, sees Holmes at the window of 221b and goes up to speak to him. Lewis told her, in almost perfect French, that he had been twice to France on holidays and had picked up his accent listening to the French middle-class discussing the food in hotel dining rooms.

The story moved on through the lesson with the King of Bohemia revealing his true identity and the mysterious

Irene Adler making her presence felt. But it was not the woman in the story who fascinated the boys; it was the woman teaching them, here in their own classroom. Women at Allison's made the beds, they cleaned the floors, they prepared most of the food and looked after the washing. What they had never done until this moment was teach, and look glamorous at the same time. Mrs Hamilton had wondered beforehand if she would remind most of them of their mothers. They were so starved of female company and so full of teenage energy that they saw her in quite a different light.

For Lady Lucy, of course, masquerading here in her earlier name of Hamilton, the object of the detective story was quite simple. After a couple of days, maybe even before the end of *'Une Scandale en Bohème'*, she could turn the conversation to murders generally. Had any of the boys been unfortunate enough to come across a murder? What, they had only recently had one right here in the school? *Vraiment? Mon Dieu! Quel horreur*! Maybe they would tell her something then, something they had not told the police or their teachers.

'Alors, le papier ici,' West Minor at the end was not one of the fluent ones, *'est fabrique en Bohème! Et le monsieur qui a ecrit le petit mot, il est Allemand . . .'*

Mrs Hamilton was quite pleased by her first lesson. David Lewis, the finest mimic in the school, couldn't take his eyes off her. After school, he decided, his imagination working overtime, he would follow her home and find out where she lived.

Inspector Miles Devereux thought he would have liked to go to university. His two eldest brothers had managed it before the money ran out, one to the sedate quarters of Selwyn College, Cambridge, the other to more romantic pastures, Worcester College, Oxford, with its lake and its fifteenth-century monks' cottages. As he made his way up Gower Street towards University College he wondered what it would be like to be a student right in the heart of London. William Burke had sent him the name of a Professor Wilson Claypole, an expert in the period around the Black Death, who had been one of the academics vouching for the authenticity of the Silkworkers codicil.

The Inspector expected some aged figure, dry as dust and dull as ditchwater, who would soon lose him in the intricacies of fourteenth-century script and idiosyncrasies of expression. Claypole, in fact, turned out to be only a few years older than he was. He wore a very smart suit and a Garrick Club tie. With his polished boots and expensive haircut he looked more like a society solicitor or a successful barrister than an academic.

'Come in, come in,' he said and waved Devereux to a chair. 'Welcome to University College. We don't have the ivy climbing up the walls and the ancient port maturing in the college cellars like they do at Oxford and Cambridge, but we like to think we're more modern here, more in tune with the latest thinking and the latest scholarship. Now then, I haven't got much time. I've got to be at the House of Lords in forty-five minutes. That codicil you've come to talk to me about, I perfectly understand why you've come. You can't take somebody else's word for it being genuine, you've got to come to the horse's mouth. Which in this case, as it happens, is me! I am the horse!' Professor Claypole snorted heartily at his quip.

'I'm not an academic like yourself,' said Devereux.

157

'No indeed,' said Claypole and laughed again.

'But I would like to know how you're sure it's the real thing.'

'Good question, Inspector. Let me try an example from your own field. When you charge a man with murder, are you always one hundred per cent sure he did it? Would you still arrest him if you were eighty-five per cent sure? Seventy-five per cent sure? You don't have to reply to that question, by the way, I'm not sure I'd really like to know the answer. But with the codicil, of course, you can't be absolutely certain either. Not with a thing that old. It's not possible. There's a man called Galt at St Andrews up there by the sea in Scotland who's done a lot of work on fourteenth-century documents and their use of language. He's certain it's real. The thought behind the codicil, that emergency measures may be needed in the aftermath of the Black Death, that's absolutely typical of the time. I've always thought it is impossible to over-estimate the influence of the Black Death, your friends and family decimated, divine punishment arriving for your sins, never sure if you're not going to wake up with nausea, vomiting, lumps all over your body. That, for me, was the most convincing aspect of the thing, the fact that the author, who was probably a lawyer of some sort, was so frightened by what had happened, so unsure of what the future might hold, that he thought his livery company should be prepared, should be ready to take whatever steps might be needed in the face of a second catastrophe, of God abandoning his people to their fate all over again, the last days coming to Threadneedle Street and London Wall. If you believed in God, and as far as we know most of them did, the Black Death must have seemed the Great Betrayal.'

'Am I right in saying that the main opposition to your view comes from our friend in Cambridge?' Devereux had heard about academics being rude about each other. This was the first time he had seen or heard it at close quarters.

'Well, you could say our friend in Cambridge is the only opposition. I suspect he hasn't even read Galt's work, for a start. They're quite restricted in their attitude to scholarship up there in the Fens. If it wasn't invented in Cambridge, it doesn't really exist. Tait's main argument concerns who might benefit from it. That doesn't carry as clear a message for me as the textual analysis of the wording. I think the benefit question is more or less irrelevant. Man's barking up the wrong tree.'

Inspector Devereux had one last card to play. He wasn't hopeful about it. 'Tell me, Professor, and remember you are speaking to an ignorant outsider here, what are the financial arrangements in matters like this? Do you get paid for the consultations and so on?'

Claypole laughed again. 'Of course we do, Inspector, of course we do. I never thought I'd be advising a rising police Inspector about the ways of the world but here we are!'

'How much?' said Devereux, and there was something about his tone that made the professor wonder if he had underestimated the man from Scotland Yard.

'Well, we fixed the fee up beforehand, before I'd done any work.'

'How much?' said Devereux, suspecting suddenly that there might be a gold seam lurking here.

'Five hundred guineas for me, if you must know. I charge rather like a Harley Street doctor. And one thousand guineas for the College Development Fund. That'll be most useful. And I'd be most grateful if you wouldn't bandy those figures about, Inspector. I've got my reputation to think of.'

'Of course,' said Devereux. 'I'm most grateful for your time and I wouldn't want to keep you from your appointment at the House of Lords. I'm afraid we policemen do not have the resources to pay for information. A very good day to you, sir.'

As he made his way back to his office, Inspector Miles Devereux wondered what a good barrister would make of the figures. Who benefits indeed, he said to himself. He resolved to send a telegram as soon as he reached his office. He felt Powerscourt would be very interested in the five hundred guineas.

The sun was shining in Cambridge as Powerscourt made his way to Trinity College and the rooms of Selwyn Augustus Tait. Sunshine in February was not what he remembered from his time here, usually cold, damp, strands of fog swirling round you as you made your way up King's Parade. Tait had rooms next to the chapel in Trinity Great Court, the largest quadrangle in either Oxford or Cambridge.

'Damn it, man, no point being indoors in the sunshine at this time of year. Let's go for a walk. We can talk as we go and have some coffee on the way.'

Tait led the way past the Master's Lodge, which Powerscourt even in his undergraduate days had thought was far too imposing to be called a mere lodge, as if it were a hunting or shooting outpost, past the Hall into New Court and over the Garret Hostel Lane Bridge. He was wearing a three-piece suit with a cream shirt but he was not one of those men who fit comfortably into their clothes. Selwyn Augustus Tait was not a virtual scarecrow like the Allison's teacher Peabody, but he gave the impression that none of his clothes fitted him properly.

'Bloody codicil,' said Tait. 'Sorry you've had to flog all the way out here for me to tell you it's a fake. Well, it is. There are many strange things about academics – odd dress, eccentric mannerisms, terrible shoes. Historians are probably the worst. What you have to remember about medieval historians, Powerscourt, is that there are precious few documents, hardly any original pieces of evidence. It's not as bad as ancient history, mind you. If you set your mind to it, you could probably read all the original sources for most of classical Greek history in less than a fortnight.'

Powerscourt smiled. He had been reading history here all those years ago, enveloped in the embrace of the colleges and the beauty of the river. They were now facing the Back Lawn of King's where the famous chapel was flanked by the classical elegance of the Gibbs Building.

'So what happens to all these medieval historians when a new piece of evidence, or what seems to be a new piece of evidence, turns up?' Tait was rubbing his hands together as he walked. 'They go wild with excitement. Judgement goes out of the window. There are just two questions you have to ask yourself. One, is there anything else like it in the surviving stuff we do have? These livery companies were a form of self-defence in a way, but they will all have known what the others were doing. If one company was incorporating a get-out clause from their constitution, then the likelihood is that some of the others would, too. But nobody did. I'm not saying that's conclusive, mind you, but it's significant.'

Tait stopped to look at the herd of cows who lived in these fields on the far side of the river from the colleges.

'Just like the cows,' he said with a laugh, 'medieval historians, chewing a cud that's six hundred years old all day. The other thing is much more important. Who benefits? The Prime Warden benefits. All his chums in the inner council, or whatever it's called, benefit. The ordinary members are thrown a few scraps. It's a fraud, quite a clever fraud, but a fraud nonetheless.'

'Who do you think did it, the fraud, I mean?'

They had now reached the café in the Silver Street basin, lined with bedraggled punts waiting for the summer, and were taking coffee at a corner table looking out over the water.

'Hard to tell,' Tait replied. 'Not too difficult to find some academic who'd cook the whole thing up for money. Maybe they found somebody in Europe nobody here has ever heard of. I'm sure some of the dons back in Trinity haven't left the college in years. Nobody might have heard of the fellow.'

A totally new thought suddenly struck Powerscourt. 'Can I ask you another question, Professor? I've only just thought of it and it may be complete nonsense.'

'Of course,' said Tait, 'fire ahead.'

'One thing that's always puzzled me is why the bar is set so high, if you like. Why did eighty per cent of the Silkworkers have to approve of the changes before they could be carried out? Why not fifty per cent or even sixty?'

'Good point,' said Tait. 'Those livery companies were always keen to carry the membership along with them, unanimity in face of the foe, that sort of thing.'

'But surely,' said Powerscourt, 'the eighty per cent is still very high. Let's just try standing the whole thing on

162

its head, if I may. Suppose it is genuine. And suppose that the point of the codicil is not to enable the authorities to sell everything off and make loads of money, but the opposite. The bar is set so high to make the thing virtually impossible. Nobody would ever get eighty per cent of the votes. The codicil, on this theory, becomes not the means of enriching the Prime Warden and his friends, but the opposite. It's designed to make it impossible. The assets will remain locked together. Nobody will ever get a large enough majority to steal them.'

Tait paused and inspected the ducks circling round the punts in the Silver Street basin. Powerscourt thought he could almost see Tait's brain working, little grey cells marching at top speed across his cranium, cerebral lights flashing at each other like the dials on the bridge of a ship.

'My God, that's smart, Powerscourt. Very smart. Wish I'd thought of it myself. But your theory, elegant though it is, depends on the codicil being genuine. I still believe it to be fake. I'll think about it, mind you, and let you know if I change my mind.'

'One last thing,' said Powerscourt. 'Can I ask you about money?'

'Do you mean, did the Silkworkers offer me a fee for my opinion? Well, yes, they did. But I didn't take it. It didn't seem right when I was saying the whole thing was rubbish.'

'Might I ask how much they were offering?'

'You may indeed. They were offering twenty guineas, which was quite generous for such a job. Why are you so interested in the money side of things if I may ask?'

'Of course you may. Did you know that a man called Claypole, Wilson Claypole, also gave advice on the codicil?'

'That man from University College? How much was he paid?'

'He was paid,' Powerscourt paused for a moment for effect, 'the princely sum of five hundred guineas with a thousand going to the College Development Fund.'

Selwyn Augustus Tait laughed. 'That's it, Powerscourt. You need look no further. You've found your forger. Why, for five hundred guineas I might have forged the bloody thing myself!'

Inspector Albert Fletcher would have had little time for theorizing academics in London or Cambridge or anywhere else. In his hand he had what he believed was the most important piece of evidence discovered so far in this case. His house-to-house search of the wider environs of Marlow had produced one piece of real value, discovered by Constable Jack Perkins. Initially, an informant who lived close to the Elysian Fields Hotel reported a very large black car going down the road to the hotel late in the evening before the murder. Further investigations with the night porter revealed to Perkins that the car and its occupants were regular visitors. Sir Peregrine Fishbone had been in the hotel that evening. He had a meeting with a person or persons unknown. His chauffeur had been waiting in the car.

'Sergeant!' he yelled. 'Come quickly, man! We've got to go to the Elysian Fields!'

Sergeant Donaldson thought his master had gone mad. Were they going to heaven on a wet afternoon in February?

'It's that big hotel down by the river, the one where the rich people go. Sir Peregrine bloody Fishborne was there the night before the murder!'

Ten minutes later the two policemen had dismounted from their bicycles and were waiting for the hotel manager to join them.

'My name is Sebastian Briggs, gentlemen.' A dapper young man of about thirty years in a very smart suit with an MCC tie escorted them into his office. 'I am the manager here. To what do I owe the pleasure of this unexpected visit?'

Inspector Fletcher explained that they were investigating a murder at the Jesus Hospital.

'I do not see what the Jesus Hospital has to do with us,' said Briggs. 'It is not part of this establishment.'

'The hospital, as you probably know, is run by the Silkworkers, a livery company in the City of London. The Prime Warden, Sir Peregrine Fishborne, is the officer responsible for looking after the almshouse. We have reason to believe that he was in this hotel late in the evening on the day before the unfortunate silkman was killed. And that he had a meeting here that evening with somebody.'

The hotel manager's reply took a lot of the wind out of the Inspector's sails.

'What of it?' he said. 'Sir Peregrine is a director of the company that owns the Elysian Fields. The Silkworkers have invested heavily in this establishment. Sir Peregrine has a permanent set of rooms here, the Baron Haussmann Suite on the first floor, at his disposal. He is a regular visitor.'

Fragments of French history from school floated through Sergeant Donaldson's mind. Was there a Sun

165

King Suite upstairs? A Danton Room where you could get murdered in the bath?

'Nobody saw Sir Peregrine leave,' said Inspector Fletcher, feeling he was being cheated of his prey.

'Come, come.' Briggs sensed that the initiative in this conversation had now passed to him. 'What if nobody saw him leave? This is a free country. We run a hotel here, not a police station. You're not suggesting that Sir Peregrine committed the murder, are you?'

'I'm not suggesting anything,' Fletcher stuck to his guns, 'just trying to establish the facts. Will any of your staff have known he was here that night?'

'The night porter will have known what was going on during his watch. But that particular night porter is not on duty at present. He will be here in a couple of hours' time.'

'When he appears,' said Inspector Fletcher, 'could you ask him to come down to the police station as soon as he arrives? Tell him it's very urgent. Good day to you, Mr Briggs. You haven't heard the end of this, not by a long chalk.'

'Do you think it's a woman, sir?' asked Sergeant Donaldson as the two men made their way back to the police station.

'Woman? What woman?' snapped the Inspector. 'We haven't got a bloody woman in this case. Not yet at any rate.'

'Sorry, sir, I meant the room permanently available to Sir Peregrine back there at the hotel. Do you think he takes a woman there? Maybe women plural?'

'God knows,' said the Inspector. Try as they might, neither of the two policemen could imagine Sir Peregrine engaging in amorous dalliance in hotel rooms by the Thames.

The back bedrooms in the great house by the sea did not have the grand views of those at the front, the waters of the harbour, the sea off to your right, the yacht *Morning Glory* riding peacefully at her moorings. The back bedrooms looked out over what might once have been a rock garden as the ground rose steeply up the cliff. The man with the great black beard took out two pairs of sharp scissors he had purchased some weeks before. He had only reached the house that afternoon after lying low for some days now, out of sight and out of contact with any human beings at all.

Blackbeard stared at his reflection in the mirror. He would have rather liked being a pirate, he thought, all those raunchy wenches and the stolen rum. Very gingerly he began his work with the larger pair of scissors. Snip. A large chunk of beard fell to the floor. Snip. He worked his way down the cheek and up from the neck until he reached his mouth. Snip. He looked at himself again, one side of his face a straggly mass of his remaining hair, the other a rich and curly black. Snip. He disposed of most of the moustache and the hair beneath his mouth. Snip. He worked his way up the remaining cheek and the right-hand side of his neck. Piles of black hair were lying across his lap and down on the floor, as if some latter-day black sheep had come in to be sheared. Snip. The man repeated the process with the smaller, even sharper pair of scissors. Now at last the shaving soap and the razor. When he had finished, the man in the mirror inspected himself closely. He doubted if anybody he had met in the last two months would have recognized him. He smiled at his alter ego in the mirror.

That evening more policemen joined their brothers in London on duty outside the buildings owned or run by the Silkworkers Company. Constable Mick George of the Surrey force stood guard on the Earl of Northampton's almshouses in Camberley. Sergeant Jacob King stood at ease all night long outside the Philip Trevelyan Hospital for the Working Poor in Guildford. Constable John Lawley watched over the old men of the St Peter and Paul Almshouse in Woking. The Chief Constable of Surrey wasn't taking any chances, not with three victims already dead and warnings from the Commissioner of the Metropolitan Police.

10

Lord Francis Powerscourt was entertaining a brace of police Inspectors in his drawing room in Markham Square. Rhys the butler had just finished serving coffee. Neither of his guests asked Powerscourt where his wife was. Draped across a chaise longue by the window, Inspector Miles Devereux of the Metropolitan Police looked as if he might have been born in this house and into this social circle. Inspector Fletcher of the Buckinghamshire Constabulary was less at home, sitting nervously by the edge of the fire, twirling his hat in his hands. Both had reported their latest developments to Powerscourt, Fletcher the astonishing discovery of Sir Peregrine in the vicinity of the hospital late in the evening the day before the first murder, Devereux his equally surprising encounter with the history man from University College London who was paid such a large number of guineas for his advice on the codicil.

'Let's think about Sir Peregrine first, shall we?' said Powerscourt. 'Inspector Fletcher, have you any theories about what was going on?'

The Inspector gave his cap another twirl. He paused for

a moment or two before he spoke. 'I do, my lord, I certainly do. The first theory – we have to consider it, however unlikely it sounds – is that he really was at the hotel on business. He is a director, after all. His normal activities in the City kept him occupied all day so he had to drive over in the evening. My second theory is that he was there on Jesus Hospital business. Maybe he had come to see Warden Monk to discuss the votes in the Silkworkers ballot. Fishborne may have been trying to devise a way to persuade all those who would have voted against his plans while Abel Meredith was still alive to change their minds. Maybe Monk was telling Sir Peregrine how much money he would have to spend to buy the votes.' Inspector Fletcher looked round for approval.

'I like that theory,' said Inspector Devereux, 'but I still find the whole thing pretty incredible. Late in the evening, Sir Peregrine, travelling by night in case anybody recognizes him perhaps, a meeting with person or persons unknown at that time of night, nobody seeing him leave. In my book there's one likely explanation for this behaviour. If it barks, it's a dog. If it mews, it's a cat. If it's an elderly rich man charging round in the middle of the night to a hotel where he has a permanent suite, it's a woman. Suppose the mysterious man was actually female? And suppose the meeting took place not in some private room downstairs but between the sheets in some vast bed in the Baron Haussmann Suite upstairs? What do you say, my lord?'

Powerscourt laughed. 'It's certainly possible. I don't think we could rule it out. But it's a pretty odd coincidence. Inspector Fletcher, you are the only one of us who has actually met this potential Casanova by the Thames. Do you think it likely? Possible?'

'I tell you this, my lord, when my Sergeant and I were talking on our way back from the hotel, neither of us even considered it. Later on we did, and we thought it impossible. He's not a nice man, my lord, that Sir Peregrine. I'm not an expert on what makes women tick, far from it, but it's hard to see any female jumping into bed with Sir Peregrine.'

'Forgive me,' Miles Devereux stretched and moved to a sitting rather than a recumbent position on his chaise longue, 'isn't that the point? The women are dealing in a currency other than love. They're dealing in money, possibly in gold. Maybe Sir Peregrine brought a high-class tart with him in the car, or his secretary perhaps. I'm sure there may be some form of crime involved, procurement, prostitution, God knows what's going on, but this isn't relevant to the murder. Or is it?'

Powerscourt took another sip of his coffee. 'It's very unlikely that it is relevant, but it might be. I don't think we should dismiss it altogether. If nothing else it might be a useful lever against Sir Peregrine. Now then, somebody has to talk to the wretched man, ask him what he was doing down there in Marlow late at night. Maybe we should talk to the chauffeur, too. What do you say, Inspector Fletcher?'

Inspector Fletcher turned a bright shade of pink. 'I'm happy to do that, my lord. The thing is' – he paused and gathered his courage – 'I don't think he thought very highly of me when we met before. In fact he complained about me to my Chief Constable. I know he did.'

'I think that's commendable, your telling us that,' said Powerscourt, 'I really do. But don't you see, we can turn that to our advantage. If I go and see him, it'll put him on his guard. Same with Devereux here. But if it's you, he won't bother to put up his defences at all if he has a low opinion of you already. Much better from our point of view.'

Inspector Fletcher managed a small smile. 'Right, my lord, I shall go and call on him tomorrow and see what he has to say for himself. I'll take my Sergeant for protection and moral support.'

'Good man,' said Powerscourt. 'Now then, what do you think of this codicil business, gentlemen?'

'Before we do that, my lord, I've just thought of something.' Inspector Devereux looked excited all of a sudden. 'Why don't we just arrest Sir Peregrine now? He was on site at the Silkworkers Hall the night of the murder there. We only have his word for it that he left when he did. He was in the vicinity hours before the first murder. In both cases he had a very powerful motive for killing his victims; they stood between him and a fortune. I'm sure any jury would look kindly on such a prosecution, my lord.'

'Maybe they would,' said Powerscourt. 'I have wondered myself if we shouldn't arrest him. But I don't think our case is strong enough. We have a possible motive, we have proximity to the deed itself, but we don't have any hard evidence. Not yet at any rate. And if we picked him up now, London's finest solicitors would be on our backs straight away. London's finest barristers would be on parade at the Old Bailey. For the time being, I think we should consider the codicil. Inspector Fletcher, you have not been exposed in person to the academics who are arguing about the thing. What is your view of the matter?'

'We don't have much to do with codicils and livery companies down in Marlow, my lord,' Fletcher began, and inspected his boots for a moment. 'What strikes me as curious is the discrepancy in the payments. Twenty guineas for the man in Cambridge, five hundred for the man in London. That sounds pretty damned fishy, even in Buckinghamshire.'

'Your man in Cambridge, Lord Powerscourt,' said Devereux, 'he said that the London fellow must be the forger with that sort of payment. Why on earth did Claypole tell me that in the first place? He didn't have to, he didn't have to say a word about it. "My financial affairs are private," that sort of thing.'

'Vanity?' said Powerscourt. 'He seems to have been pretty keen to tell you he had to be in the House of Lords very soon. Very clever people can get superiority complexes; they think they're above everybody else. I'm very certain of one thing though. It makes a great hole in any possible defence for Sir Peregrine in court.'

'How?' said the two Inspectors, more or less in unison.

'Suppose you are the counsel for the prosecution, gentlemen. You line up a little collection of these academics who gave their views on the codicil. Up comes Professor Number One, he does his stuff. "How much were you paid?" "Twenty guineas." Professor Number Two. "How much were you paid?" "Twenty guineas." Up comes Professor Number Three. "How much were you paid?" "Twenty guineas." Now it's Professor Wilson Claypole's turn in the witness box. "How much were you paid?" "Five hundred guineas" "Five hundred guineas? Would you just like to repeat that figure, Professor Claypole, so the gentlemen of the jury can be in no doubt of it?" "Five hundred guineas." With a skilful barrister the jury would be left in little doubt that Claypole was the forger.'

'And once we know that Claypole was the forger,' Miles

Devereux was now walking up and down the room, 'the whole codicil sideshow disappears. Sir Peregrine's plans collapse like a pack of cards. The man's a crook.'

'He may be a crook,' said Powerscourt, 'but that doesn't necessarily make him a murderer.'

The headmaster of Allison's School was a worried man. Even now, many days after the murder, no boy had come forward with any details of the fake postman who had arrived in the school to strangle its bursar. The boys had been invited to speak to Inspector Grime after the second visit. None had done so. The headmaster had tried speaking, in confidence, to the boys he considered most influential with their schoolfellows. Nothing had happened. He had enlisted the help of the local bishop, the Bishop of Norwich. That mighty churchman had preached an eloquent sermon on the theme of render unto Cesar the things that are Caesar's and render unto God the things that are God's from St Matthew's Gospel. He spoke of the obligations on Christians to pay their taxes, to support the civil authorities, to be law-abiding citizens. The headmaster thought at the time that short of telling the boys to tell what they had seen on either of those days, the bishop had done all he could to persuade some boys, impressed by the weighty presence of a prince of the Church among them, to tell what they knew. The bishop's message fell on stony ground. Now the headmaster's last hope lay in the slender figure of Lady Lucy Powerscourt, pretending to be Mrs Hamilton, the French language teacher. The headmaster had little hope in that direction.

That evening Inspector Grime, at Powerscourt's suggestion, was taking dinner with Lady Lucy at the Crown

Hotel in Fakenham. The Inspector was wearing his best suit for the occasion. But he, like the headmaster, was in despair. He was not making any progress, he told her sadly. His principal suspect, Jude the stonemason, seemed to have vanished off the face of the earth. The boys of Allison's School would tell him nothing. His Chief Constable was making ominous noises, threatening, so Grime had heard on the grapevine, to take him off the case altogether. When Lady Lucy moved the conversation on to Inspector Grime himself, a sad picture emerged. His wife had died some years before. There had been no children. He had his aged mother living with him and her memory had gone; she was liable to wander off into the fields or on to the main road if she was not watched twenty-four hours a day. The Inspector paid a woman to look after the old lady when he was at work. At weekends he did it himself. It was, he said, running his fingers through the remains of his dark hair, getting him down. Lady Lucy listened with a sympathetic ear and congratulated the Inspector on caring for his mother. Apart from expressions of sympathy, she felt there was little she could do. To tell Inspector Grime about her one tiny glimmer of good news would, she thought, give him false hope and, perhaps, false optimism. The boy who had followed her to the hotel might be sufficiently besotted to tell her something important. But she would certainly tell Francis when he came the following day. The tiny glimmer would come, if it was going to come, the following afternoon shortly after four o'clock.

Inspector Fletcher checked once more the polish on his boots. He fiddled yet again with his tie. He and Sergeant

Donaldson were in the reception of Sir Peregrine's vast headquarters in the City of London. Teams of secretaries and stenographers and dark-coated financiers hurried in and out of the building with an air of great purpose. Sergeant Donaldson thought to himself that he much preferred the quiet backwater of Maidenhead where the police knew most of the people and life passed by at a much slower pace. Here everything moved so quickly.

Earlier that day the policemen had received a valuable piece of ammunition for their interview with Sir Peregrine. Warden Monk had replied to their messages and presented himself at the police station. Yes, he admitted readily enough, he had been seeing Sir Peregrine at the hotel, late the other evening. He had met him there before at that time. It was, he said belligerently, a free country, wasn't it? A man could go where he wanted and talk with whomever he wanted, couldn't he? As far as he, Thomas Monk, was aware, there weren't any laws against any of that, were there? Not yet at any rate. He and Sir Peregrine had been discussing Jesus Hospital business. No, he did not want to tell the officers exactly what had been discussed. That was private. Both Inspector Fletcher and his Sergeant were sure that Monk was hiding something, but they could not tell what it was. Inspector Fletcher felt sure that news of the interview would reach Sir Peregrine long before he and Sergeant Donaldson crossed the portals of his domain. Not for the first time he cursed the invention of the telegraph.

A tall slim young lady in a fashionable trailing skirt brought them up to Sir Peregrine's office on the top floor. The room was huge, with spectacular views over the City of London. Many of these captains of industry filled their walls with hunting prints or views of English cathedrals.

Sir Peregrine's walls were hung with battles. Before he sat down, Inspector Fletcher caught a glimpse of a sweaty Leonidas holding the pass at Thermopylae.

'Thank you, Miss Davis,' boomed Sir Peregrine, as the young lady ushered the policemen on to a couple of chairs. 'Tea, Miss Davis.' She had almost reached the door when the qualification came, 'For one.'

Bloody rude, thought Inspector Fletcher. Bloody rude.

'Well, gentlemen, what can I do for you?' Sir Peregrine addressed his visitors as if they were the lowest variety of office boy in his employ.

Inspector Fletcher had agreed with Inspector Devereux that the Marlow police would confine themselves to the murder at the Jesus Hospital. The complicated questions of the authenticity of the codicil could be left to Devereux and Powerscourt. Now Inspector Fletcher could feel his nerves rising. No pauses between sentences, he said to himself. No hesitations. He thought he might start to shake quite soon if he didn't get a grip on himself. He began taking a series of deep breaths as his wife advised.

'We would like to know,' he began hesitantly, 'what you were doing in the Elysian Fields Hotel outside Marlow the other evening.'

The Inspector had gained in strength as his question progressed. He felt slightly better. Maybe it was going to be all right.

'Who says I was there?' Sir Peregrine remembered Inspector Fletcher from the day of the murder at the Jesus Hospital. He had thought little of him then. He saw nothing to make him change his mind.

'Your car was seen on the road leading to the hotel, Sir Peregrine. And the hotel manager confirmed your presence.'

'What if I was? I'm a director of the damned hotel. Man can visit any damned hotel he likes, especially if he's on the board.'

'Could we ask who you saw when you were there, Sir Peregrine. At the hotel, I mean.'

'That's none of your damned business either.' Sir Peregrine paused while Miss Davis placed an ornate tea tray in front of her master. As a further insult to the visitors, it was laden with scones and sandwiches and three alluring slices of cake. 'Man can see who he likes, damn your eyes.'

'I put it to you, Sir Peregrine,' Inspector Fletcher was feeling almost confident now, 'that the man you went to see was Thomas Monk, Warden of the Jesus Hospital which, as you know as well as I do, is run by your own livery company the Silkworkers.'

'I do wish you would mind your damned business. Monk or no Monk, it's got nothing to do with you.' Sir Peregrine paused to eat an enormous mouthful of chocolate cake. For some reason, Fletcher was to tell his Sergeant later, the sight of the chocolate cake made him very angry indeed.

'I do not feel, Sir Peregrine,' he said firmly, happy in the knowledge that he had not paused for the last five minutes or so, 'that you are taking our questions as seriously as you should. There was a murder at the Jesus Hospital a matter of hours after your car was seen at the nearby hotel. We have no reports of anybody seeing the car leave. For all we know, it, and you, could still have been there at the time of the killing. There was a second murder at the Silkworkers Hall in the City of London. You were the last person to see the victim alive. Your position is more serious than you seem to think, Sir Peregrine.'

'Are you saying that I am a murderer? Am I a suspect?'

'I am not saying that you are the murderer. As to whether you are a suspect or not I leave that up to you to decide for the moment. Now, if we could return to the business in hand, perhaps you could tell us, Sir Peregrine, when you left the Elysian Fields the night before the murder?'

'Are you deaf as well as stupid? It's none of your damned business!'

'Then we can assume, can we, Sir Peregrine, that you were still there on the morning of the murder?'

Sir Peregrine made a mighty noise that sounded like a cross between a howl of pain and a yell of triumph. He rose to his feet. His face had turned purple. He was pounding his enormous fist on the table. 'Get out! Get out now! You insult me in my own office! How dare you? A couple of failed police officers from the back of beyond! Ignorant clodhoppers! Get out! Go on! Clear off!'

Oddly enough it was Sergeant Donaldson who had the last word in the interview. 'Good day to you, Sir Peregrine,' he said, opening the door. 'So glad you enjoyed your tea.'

Sir Peregrine sat down and took a quick swig straight from the half bottle of whisky concealed in his bottom drawer. He pressed a button underneath his desk. Miss Davis appeared as if by magic.

'Get me the bloody solicitors,' he snarled. 'And get them now!'

Mrs Hamilton's spoken French classes were going well. The Lower Sixth were well advanced into 'A Scandal in Bohemia'. They had passed the point where the King of Bohemia reveals himself to Holmes and Watson and they have made the acquaintance of Irene Adler, the well-known adventuress. Mrs Hamilton wondered if she had picked too exotic a story, if she wouldn't have done better with some more domestic problem set in Surrey with governesses and gamekeepers. She hadn't yet tried to change the subject to murder at Allison's – she rather feared there was no actual murder in 'Scandal in Bohemia' – as she hadn't deemed it appropriate.

The boys read their section of the story or gazed long-ingly at Mrs Hamilton when they were not on duty. She had become the focus, the depository of the teenage longings and the teenage fantasies of an entire class. As she made her way back to the hotel that afternoon she checked behind herself a couple of times. It was as she thought. She was being followed. Francis had told her years before of a tingling sensation when somebody is coming after you. For Mrs Hamilton this was the second day of the pursuit. It was as she had predicted. She smiled slightly as she went into the hotel. Then she ran up the stairs and turned all the lights on in her suite of sitting room, bedroom and bathroom. After that she went out of the side door of the Crown, round the back of the green and tapped David Lewis lightly on the shoulder. 'Come and have some tea,' she said sweetly. 'You'll catch your death of cold out here.'

David Lewis followed his new teacher into the hotel. He thought he had turned red permanently. He suspected his face might never return to its normal condition. His eyes still had the look of puppy-like devotion they had shown in class.

Lady Lucy ordered tea and scones. The room was large with Georgian windows looking out over the green.

'You'll never make a detective like Sherlock Holmes if you follow people like that, David,' she said with a smile. 'I think you need to be more subtle, not so much sudden jumping behind trees.'

'I just wanted to be close to you, Mrs Hamilton. I don't quite know how to say this. I've never felt like this in my whole life, not ever . . .'

Lady Lucy was saved by the arrival of the tea. The maid poured two cups and handed them round before she left. Lady Lucy had been wondering how to extricate herself from this situation which could prove so embarrassing.

'My husband should be here in a minute,' she said brightly, buttering a scone. 'He's on his way up from London.' She thought that might buy some time. She watched as David's face fell. Maybe he hadn't thought of her with a husband at all. Lady Lucy decided to take a gamble, a huge gamble.

'He's a detective, my husband, like Sherlock Holmes, only he's real, my husband I mean.'

'Really?' said David Lewis. 'And is he working on a case at present?' There had been mention in the school of a detective who had talked to the headmaster and to Inspector Grime. What was his name? David Lewis didn't think it was Hamilton.

Lady Lucy got there before him. 'My married name is Powerscourt, Lady Lucy Powerscourt,' she said. 'Before that I was called Hamilton. And my husband's called Francis.'

'And are you detecting something up here?' David Lewis had temporarily forgotten about love in favour of crime and investigation. This was like one of those shockers that passed round the school.

181

'Of course we are, silly. And we'd like you to join us, to become part of our team. It depends, of course, on your being able to keep a secret.'

'Of course I can keep a secret, Lady Powerscourt, Mrs Hamilton – dear me, what should I call you?'

'You'd better go on calling me Mrs Hamilton, I think, David. In case the other name slips out in class.'

David Lewis stared at Lady Lucy for a moment. 'You're here because of the death of the bursar, aren't you? Mr Gill. Is that the secret?'

'Part of it, David, just part of it. There are other matters I can't tell you about just yet. Very deep, very dark matters.'

'What can I do to help? I'll do anything, Mrs Hamilton, I'm so happy to be a part of the team.'

Lady Lucy cut him off. She thought he might be about to go back on to dangerous ground.

'There is one thing,' she said, 'that would really help the investigation.'

'What's that?'

'You remember there was a lot of talk about the false postman who came to the school, and who was almost certainly the murderer? And how the police repeated the exercise a couple of days later, exactly like the first visit?'

'I do.'

'The strange thing is that nobody has come forward with a description of the fake postman. Somebody must have seen him. If you're looking for somebody, it helps if you know something of what he looked like. Was he short, was he tall, was he clean shaven, was he bald, did he have a crutch and a parrot on his shoulder, that sort of thing.'

David Lewis gazed helplessly into Lady Lucy's eyes. 'Some of us have felt badly about this for some time,

182

Mrs Hamilton. It's just that Inspector Grime rubbed so many of the boys up the wrong way. They decided not to cooperate.'

'Of course,' said Lady Lucy, unwilling to be drawn on the matter of the Inspector, 'but what a way to begin your work with us, David. The information would be so very valuable. And inside our little band of investigators you would get the credit.'

This was it, David Lewis thought to himself, he was becoming part of a secret society like the Red-Headed League in the Sherlock Holmes stories. 'Well, I was one of three or four people who got a good look at the man on the day of the murder,' he began. 'He looked about thirty to thirty-five, just under six feet tall, I would say, with an enormous black beard.'

'Anything else?'

'Just one tiny thing. He bumped into me quite heavily and said, "I'm so sorry." The thing is, Mrs Hamilton, I have a bit of a reputation for being a mimic which means I always listen very carefully to how people sound when they talk. This chap didn't come from round Norfolk way. I don't think he was English at all. And he wasn't American either. I lived in Washington for a while when my papa was at the embassy there and I can tell a Southern drawl from the sound of New York.'

'Fascinating,' said Lady Lucy. 'That's really useful, David. What a way to join the team! Francis will be so pleased when I tell him.'

'Would it have been easier if he had been English, Mrs Hamilton? Easier for the detecting team, I mean?'

'I'm not quite sure I follow you.'

'Well, if he had been English, he would be here in England, wouldn't he? But think of all the other places he could have come from. Australia? New Zealand? South Africa? What happens if he's going home? Or if he's already gone home? That would make our lives very difficult.'

Lady Lucy thought that young David Lewis might have a promising career in the detection business.

'Just think of them as fresh fields to conquer, David. Fresh fields to conquer. Now then,' she said, smiling at the boy, 'we need to make a plan. We need to secure our communications. I think it would be best if we kept our meetings absolutely secret. You mustn't tell anybody, not even your best friend in school.'

'Of course, Mrs Hamilton. If I told anybody it wouldn't be a secret.'

'Quite right. I think we should meet here every other day. If we made it every day then somebody might notice. And there is one thing I would like you to do before our next meeting.'

'What's that, Mrs Hamilton?'

'I want you to find out everything you can about the man who was killed, Roderick Gill the bursar. I know he didn't teach you or anything like that, but there's usually some gossip or scrap of information that might be useful.'

As the lovestruck David Lewis returned to school, Lady Lucy wondered if she could be prosecuted for corrupting the young.

Inspector Miles Devereux was back in the Silkworkers Hall. This time there were no bodies by the water, only a hard-working cleaning lady and a pervasive smell of floor polish. He had come to meet the Silkworkers Secretary. He would be the man, in Devereux's judgement, most likely to know about the voting patterns and the voting timetable of the Silkworkers Company. Fletcher had informed him of his sulphurous interview with Sir Peregrine and the solitary teacup. Devereux wondered if it would be morning coffee for one on this occasion.

The Secretary, Colonel James Horrocks, a retired military man with an enormous moustache and a faint hint of the parade ground still lingering about his person, was not alone. 'Buckeridge, Inspector, Antony Buckeridge of Buckeridge Johnston and Forsyte, Lincoln's Inn Fields, solicitors.' He pronounced the word solicitors very solemnly indeed. 'Here to keep an eye on things, don't you know!'

Miles Devereux shook hands with his opponent pleasantly enough, like a man before a duel. He didn't think there was much the solicitor could do to prevent him finding out what he wanted to know. Buckeridge was in his forties, tall and slim, and he interrupted the proceedings from time to time by sneezing loudly after a pinch of snuff.

'Colonel Horrocks,' Devereux began, 'we would like to know more details of the forthcoming ballot among the members of the Silkworkers Company.'

Horrocks began tapping on the table with his pen. He looked over at his solicitor.

'I see,' said Buckeridge. 'I fail to understand how the internal procedures of my client's company can be of interest to the police.'

Miles Devereux had seen this tactic before. You could use an interview like this one to discover how much the police knew and where they had obtained the information.

'It is,' he said with a wintry smile, 'for us to decide what is and what is not relevant to our inquiry. I repeat, Colonel Horrocks, we would like to know more details about the forthcoming ballot of members of the Silkworkers Company.'

'And it is for his legal advisers, Sergeant, to advise on when it is or is not necessary to answer questions. And I am advising him that he need not reply to your request.'

The one thing you must never do in these situations, Miles Devereux said to himself, is to lose your temper. Much better to make the other man lose his. 'Colonel Horrocks, could I remind you of two things? The first is that we are dealing with a murder inquiry here. And the second is that there is an offence known as obstructing the course of justice. Police officers like myself are perfectly entitled to arrest people who are actively hindering the police in the course of their inquiries. Magistrates do not look kindly on those who hinder the work of officers of the law, particularly in murder cases. I say again, we would like to know more details of the forthcoming ballot among members of the Silkworkers Company.'

There was a pause. Buckeridge shrugged his shoulders and helped himself to some more snuff. Devereux wondered if they had a fallback plan if the initial objections failed to work.

'There is to be such a ballot,' Horrocks said finally.

'Thank you, sir,' said Inspector Devereux. 'Thank you for cooperating. Now perhaps you could tell us when the ballot is to take place or the date when the relevant papers have to be lodged with the company.' Devereux didn't know if the election was going to take place on a single day, or whether the papers were sent out beforehand to

186

all potential electors with a date by which they must be returned.

'The closing date has not yet been finalized,' Horrocks said after another long pause.

'But the voting papers have been sent out?'

'They have.'

'But with no fixed date for the return?'

'Not exactly.'

'What does not exactly mean?'

Horrocks looked at Buckeridge once more. The solicitor shrugged. Devereux doubted if he had decided to keep quiet for long.

'The papers had to be returned by the end of February or possibly a little later. That is the date not yet fixed in stone.'

'Does that mean that the vote could be closed if the organizers decided it had gone the way they wanted? Even if all the votes weren't in?'

'Come, come, Sergeant,' Buckeridge was back, snorting and sneezing, 'that's a question of motive or intention, not a matter of fact. I advise you not to answer it, Colonel, there is no need.'

'And where are the votes kept? The ones that have been sent in?'

'They're kept here in this office,' said Horrocks.

'And who has access to the papers, the votes?'

'Well, the senior members of the company, naturally. They all have keys to the safe over there by the window.'

'Really, Colonel, really? So Sir Peregrine or anybody else with a key could come in and check on the votes? It's like the cabinet checking on the ballot boxes on election day before the polls have closed.'

'I object, Sergeant!' Anthony Buckeridge was getting cross now. Inspector Devereux thought he might be on the verge of losing his temper. 'The procedures here are all governed by ancient statute. Your assumptions are totally unwarranted and potentially slanderous.'

Ancient statute, Devereux said to himself, that's good. That wretched codicil. About as ancient as nineteen hundred and eight, if the man from Cambridge was to be believed.

'Another question for you, Colonel, if I may.' Horrocks was looking like a boxer who has had quite enough for one day. 'Did the voting slips mention the place they were going to, if you follow me. Would they have said, Thomas Dixon, Jesus Hospital, Marlow, that sort of thing? Or would the location be omitted?'

'I object, Sergeant.'

'It's Inspector, actually.' Devereux smiled beatifically at the solicitor. 'Let's get our facts right, shall we? I was promoted two years ago.'

'You are imputing motive to my clients.'

'What motive am I meant to be implying?'

'You are implying that my clients might be forging votes if there was no specified location on the ballot paper.'

'What a suspicious mind you have, Mr Buckeridge! I hadn't thought of that before. Thank you for drawing it to my attention. I've nearly finished, Colonel, just a couple of small points to clear up. What was the total number of those entitled to vote, the size of your electorate, if you like?'

'Just over seven hundred and fifty,' he said, 'seven hundred and sixty-three, including the outstations like the almshouses and the school and so on. The location is specified at the top right-hand corner of the ballot paper.'

'And do you know how many have voted up until today? There must be some sort of a tally, I presume.'

'I object.' Buckeridge had returned to the ring. 'The voting figures are a private matter for the Silkworkers Company. You do not have to answer that, Colonel.'

'I'm afraid he does, Mr Buckeridge. Let me repeat the question with another one. Do you know how many have voted up until today? And have the votes come in from the Jesus Hospital in Marlow and Allison's School in Norfolk?'

'You do not need to answer that, Colonel. That is private information for the company,' Buckeridge was looking pleased with himself now.

'You could probably argue that it should be classified information in normal times, gentlemen.' Inspector Devereux wasn't about to lose his temper but he was angry. 'But these are not normal times. One murder would be bad enough. We are dealing not with one or even two but with three murders, one in this very building, one at the Jesus Hospital and one at Allison's School in Norfolk. For the last time. How many votes have been cast up till today? And have the votes come in from the Jesus Hospital in Marlow and Allison's School in Norfolk?'

'I object.' Buckeridge was off again. Devereux cut him off.

'I wouldn't pursue your objection any further if I were you, Mr Buckeridge. Any further refusal to answer questions, or advice to the same effect, and I shall arrest you both right now for obstructing the police in the course of their duty. It's your choice. You can spend the rest of the day at liberty. Or you can spend it in a police cell.

Our formalities can sometimes take a very long time to complete. In cases like this I have known them spread out into the following day or even the day after that. It's entirely up to you.'

There was a pause. Eventually the Colonel cracked. 'Six hundred and eighty votes have been received so far. No votes have been received from Marlow or Fakenham.'

'Thank you, Colonel, thank you very much indeed.'

PART THREE

THE FARMER'S ARMS

11

Inspector Grime pounded the table with his fist when Lady Lucy and Powerscourt told him the news. 'By God!' he said. 'You've managed to find out what a police Inspector, a headmaster and a bloody Bishop couldn't manage; you've got us a description. Now we can get going!'

He shouted for his Sergeant and strode over to a map of Norfolk on his wall. 'Now then, Sergeant Morris,' he began. 'First of all I want a house-to-house search of Fakenham and the surrounding villages. Does anybody remember seeing a man, middle thirties, average height with a great black beard on the days before the murder or on the day itself? Suspect may have had foreign accent but we can't be sure. Blighter must have got here the day before. Blighter must have stayed somewhere. All hotels, boarding houses, you know the drill. Blighter must have got here somehow. God knows where he came from; we'll just have to try all stations. Cromer, Holt, Swaffham, King's Lynn, Norwich, I want signs put up in all those places asking anybody who remembers seeing our bearded friend on the day of the murder or, more likely, the day before to report to their local police station. I'll send a wire to all those stations directly after this meeting.' Inspector Grime stopped. 'Is that clear? Any questions?'

'Only this,' said his Sergeant. 'We know he came here to kill the bursar. But he must have gone away, too. Should we ask people who were on the trains if they saw him leaving too? Same journey, only both ways? Travelling on a return ticket, if you like?'

'You'd better include that,' said the Inspector grumpily, reluctant to admit he might have forgotten something important. 'Please amend the instructions accordingly.'

The Sergeant departed to organize the manhunt. Only the police had the manpower to undertake such a search, Powerscourt said to himself. But he did wonder if they hadn't missed the obvious point. The murderer might have been sporting a large black beard on the fatal day. How long had it taken him to grow it? In other words, how long before the event had he known that he was going to come to the school and kill the bursar? And, more important still, did the murderer still have the beard? Or had he shaved it off? He mentioned his reservations to Lady Lucy as they walked back to the hotel. He didn't say anything to Inspector Grime. He didn't want to spoil his enthusiasm. As he took a cup of tea, another thought struck him. If you were the murderer, maybe you would suppose the police's first assumption would be that the killer would shave the beard off. But suppose the murderer was playing double bluff? Suppose he was still wandering around with a great black beard, reckoning that the police were now looking for a clean-shaven man. Maybe the beard would be his best form of disguise after all.

Johnny Fitzgerald had been approaching the old men of the Jesus Hospital one at a time. He had become a familiar figure in the almshouse, popping his head round a door one moment, inviting an elderly resident for coffee or lunch at his hotel the next. He had realized by now that you could discount the first ten, maybe the first fifteen minutes of any conversation with a silkman resident at the Jesus Hospital. Once he had uttered the familiar words *how are you*, the man would be off. It reminded Johnny of cavalry officers he had known in his army days who always spent the first part of any conversation talking about their horses. So he knew by now that Nathaniel Jones, Number Five, known as Jones the Steam from his days as an engine driver, was troubled with the gout, not that he drank a lot, only four or five pints a night and a couple of whisky chasers, and that he had trouble sleeping. There followed a list of all possible remedies from counting sheep to listing the names of all your classmates in your last year at school. Christy Butler, Number Thirteen, had trouble with his back. Sitting down for meals, he told Johnny, had become very difficult. Maybe he would have to eat standing up. But he couldn't go to sleep standing up, could he? That Dr Ragg, he was no more use than a teetotaller in a saloon bar; he never gave you proper medicine. William Taylor, Number Sixteen, usually referred to as Pretty Billy, a nickname that had followed him throughout his life, true in his youth, ironic in old age, said he just felt ill most of the time. He ached. He sweated. He limped. He had headaches. He was, he told Johnny, like some old engine that has been run for too long and is just about to collapse. Looking at him, Johnny thought Number Sixteen was probably right.

There was one topic Johnny always came round to in these conversations. He never approached it head on. He came in from the side or from the back; he never knocked on the front door. On the question of the Silkworkers' vote – Devereux had passed on the news about the dates – Johnny found opinion undecided. He noticed a reserve in the old men, as if some further injunction had been added to the earlier demands for silence.

That evening Johnny was at his usual position at the table in the Rose and Crown nearest the bar. This was where the old men liked to sit, closest to where the pretty barmaid would be as she pulled pints for the silkmen. The talk was of minor ailments at first. When he judged that all were present who were going to come, Johnny took the initiative.

'Gentlemen,' he said, 'I would like to ask you about something that has been troubling me. You see, I have a relative in the Silkworkers Company up in London and he has been telling me about the vote that's coming up. Now, it's for you to decide how to cast your vote, obviously, but I think there is a risk that you could make a terrible mistake. But I can only say that when I know how you are going to vote. I think most of you were against it when Number Twenty was with us. Is that still how it is today?'

Silence fell over the saloon bar. The old men looked at each other but did not speak. The barmaid even looked in from the public to see if one of the old gentlemen had actually died halfway down a pint of Wethered's Best Bitter. Eventually Jack Miller, Number Three, the former bank clerk, broke with the discretion of a lifetime and spoke up.

'We're not meant to speak to anybody about this,' he began.

'Who says so?' said Johnny, draining his glass.

196

'Well, it's Warden Monk, Mr Fitzgerald, sir, but seeing as it's you, I think we can make an exception.'

'Has he been saying this all along, or only recently, the Warden?'

'Well, he did say it at the start, but he repeated it very definitely only the other day.'

Curiouser and curiouser, Johnny said to himself. Sir Peregrine comes to the hotel at night. Monk puts the frighteners on about speaking to anybody the next morning. What else had Monk and Sir Peregrine been cooking up in the ornate splendour of the Elysian Fields?

'That's very interesting,' he said, 'but tell me, are you still of the same mind? To oppose the changes, I mean?'

One or two of the old men glowered at each other. Johnny wondered if they might come to blows. Even the barmaid pulling another round failed to distract them in the usual way.

'It's like this, see.' John Watkins, Number Fifteen, who had lost two fingers of his left hand in some battle long ago, rarely spoke and was therefore regarded as a fount of very deep wisdom by his fellow silkmen. 'Some people have changed their minds, and that's a fact. I shall mention no names and no numbers. I leave that to others. But I do believe that there are special circumstances regarding those who have changed their minds and betrayed all our futures for thirty pieces of silver. I shall say no more.' Number Fifteen returned to his tankard.

Johnny waited for somebody else to speak.

'We don't know what to do for the best, Mr Fitzgerald,' said Edward Cooper, Number Seven, 'and that's a fact. We don't understand about codicils and things from hundreds of years ago. We're simple folk here, so we are. What would you advise us to do?'

Not for the first time, Johnny felt a great wave of sympathy for the silkmen. Here they were, abandoned by their families, if they had any family left, thrown together with a group of people they had never known before, complicated arguments about money and codicils they did not properly understand swirling around over their heads, still frightened there might be a murderer in their midst, poised to strike again. They're parked, he said to himself, in death's waiting room, hanging on for the last train.

'Gentlemen, gentlemen, I am perfectly happy to give you advice though I would warn you that I have no more experience in financial matters than most of you. But first I would like to know what's going on. What did John Watkins, Number Fifteen, mean when he talked about thirty pieces of silver? You can tell me, gentlemen. I'm not going to let you down.'

There was a pause. Considerable amounts of beer were poured down the silkmen's throats as they wondered what they should do. Sometimes one draught was not enough. A second was needed, and in two cases a third was required to set the thought processes into full working order.

'Very well,' said Peter Baker, Number Ten, 'I'll tell you, if nobody else will. Just the other day it was, Monk calls a meeting straight after breakfast. Funny how they all make their announcements first thing in the morning. Maybe they think our wits leave us during the course of the day. I suppose they might be right. Anyway, Monk says he has a special statement to make. It concerns the ballot, he says. He has been given to understand – pompous fellow, that man Monk, always was – that all those who vote in favour of the changes will receive what he called

198

a discretionary emolument. He had to explain that, of course. Basically, if you vote yes, in Monk's presence and he sees you do it, then you get ten pounds. That's a lot of money, Mr Fitzgerald. It's more than I have to live on for a year and I'm sure that holds true for many of my colleagues here.'

'Discretionary? Emolument?' James Osborne, the locksmith, Number Nineteen, had risen, rather unsteadily, to his feet. 'It's just another word for bribe. That's all. They're trying to buy us off!'

'I don't suppose anybody asked Mr Monk how much he would be getting if he delivered the votes?' Johnny was ordering another round with a wave of his hand as he spoke.

'Nobody did, sir, though I think we should have done.' This was Henry Wood, Number Twelve, the man Johnny had lunched with at the hotel, lubricated by a couple of bottles of Beaune. 'I'm going to say what I think. This is all very difficult for the people in the Jesus Hospital, Mr Fitzgerald. Time has a lot to do with it. None of us are going to last very long. If the livery company is broken up, we all receive a payment for that, because we're all members of the Silkworkers Company. We're like shareholders, getting our cut when the company is sold on. Mr Monk says nobody can be precise as it depends on the state of the stock market and the property market when the assets are sold. He claimed it could be between thirty and fifty pounds. Now there's this extra money on top of that. Some of the men here would have more money in their hands than they have ever had in their lives. And if things start to go wrong in the hospital after a couple of years – even though they have always said it will be protected, whatever that means – it won't matter very much. Half of us will be dead. It's all very well to talk of doing the right thing for posterity and voting no, but I don't think you feel virtuous when you're in your coffin, six feet underground, with the lid screwed down.'

'It's all a question of timescales,' said Christy Butler, Number Thirteen, staring hard at the low level of his beer in the glass. 'If you think you're going soon, within a year or a year and a half, say, vote yes and enjoy the money while you can. If you think you might still be drinking this excellent bitter in ten years' time, you'd better vote no or you might not be able to afford it. Short time left means yes; long time left means no.'

'That's all very well,' said Johnny Johnston, Number Nine, the former postman, whose glass was completely empty, 'but how on earth are we meant to know how long we're going to last? Even the bloody doctors aren't going to tell us that.'

There was another silence. Johnny Fitzgerald remembered being told that Number Nine had been conducting a vendetta against Dr Ragg for years over the treatment, or, as Number Nine maintained, the lack of treatment for his gout. He called for refills. He wondered what the assets of the Silkworkers were worth on the open market. He wondered if Inspector Devereux had found out. Johnny rather liked Miles Devereux. He decided that the best thing to do would be to keep this particular ball in play. Maybe Sir Peregrine Fishborne would have to make another trip to the Elysian Fields late at night.

'Gentlemen,' he said, 'you were kind enough to ask me for my advice. I do not think we have sufficient information to form a balanced judgement. I think you need clarification on one particular point. While I agree with my friend Number Twelve that it must be difficult to feel virtuous in the grave, I do feel that we owe certain obligations to our successors. You are all good men and true.' Are you sure? he said to himself. One of them might be a murderer. Better press on. 'I do not think that you would want the Jesus Hospital to close its doors for ever just so that you could receive what one of your colleagues referred to as thirty pieces of silver. When I say clarification, I mean this. You should ask to see the full accounts of the hospital for the last five years. Then you take an average of the figures. Then you ask for a legally binding document, signed in the presence of solicitors, which guarantees that an amount of capital capable of producing that amount of annual income with a fifteen per cent safety margin will be placed in a reputable bank and is only to be used for the maintenance of the Jesus Hospital.'

Johnny took a monster pull on his beer. He realized he might have made it too complicated. He heard various mutterings among the old men. What did he mean by average? Surely capital referred to places like London or Paris. What was it doing here? What was a fifteen per cent safety margin?

'Basically,' said Johnny, 'it means that you ask them to guarantee that there will be enough money to keep the hospital going in the future.'

Old heads began to nod in agreement at this moment. The barmaid announced in her sweetest voice that the Rose and Crown was closing for the night. The old men shuffled slowly back to the hospital. Johnny made his way back to the Elysian Fields. A taxi passed him as he neared the front door. Johnny had a brief glimpse of an enormous black car discreetly parked under the trees. A very pretty young woman got out of the cab and fiddled with her gloves. As she entered the reception area, Johnny caught a hint of very expensive perfume. 'The usual keys, madam?' the night porter behind the desk said. 'The Baron Haussmann Suite?'

Johnny was astonished. Sir Peregrine had indeed come once more to the Elysian Fields but not to plan more bribes for the old men of the Jesus Hospital. Johnny looked at the girl's back as she disappeared up the stairs. She seemed to be very pretty indeed. Johnny didn't think she had come all this way at this time to discuss share options or exchange rates. I'll be damned, Johnny said to himself. The old devil. Lucky bugger.

Inspector Grime's Sergeant, a young man called Peter Morris, had nurtured hopes of becoming a draughtsman or an artist before being claimed by the more mundane appeal of the police force. This was his first murder inquiry. But he liked to keep his hand in when he could. He had constructed for his Inspector a great chart which stood proudly on one wall of Grime's office. It was a time-line, with the days before and after the murder marked in different colours. Black, in harmony with his beard, marked the suspect's movements. Blackbeard, as all the policemen referred to him now, first appeared in the chart on the day before the murder. He had arrived in the town at seven o'clock in the evening on a train from King's Lynn. The policemen noted glumly that he had arrived in the dark. Then he seemed to disappear. No bar or hotel or bed and breakfast establishment remembered such a man. The black entry appeared again the following morning, entering the school and killing its bursar early in the morning. Then he vanished once more.

The Inspector and his Sergeant were having a conference by the chart the morning after Sir Peregrine's night visitor arrived at the Elysian Fields. 'Right,' said Inspector Grime, 'we've had seventy replies so far and this is all that stands up. Is that right, Sergeant?'

'I'm afraid it is, sir. I think some members of the public are too ready to offer help. We've had reports of all sorts of men with black beards but most of them were the wrong age or the wrong height. Some more reports should come in today, sir.'

Inspector Grime snorted. He had had such high hopes when the original description was provided by the sixth-former David Lewis. Now it seemed to be turning to dust in his hands. 'Where did the bugger sleep, for God's sake? Are there any empty houses or cottages he could have used? He can't have disappeared between seven in the evening one day and eight o'clock in the morning the day after, can he?'

'I've got people checking on all the empty dwellings, sir, to see if any of them might have been occupied. I don't have the answers yet. Could I make a suggestion, sir?'

'If you must,' said Grime whose reluctance to listen to subordinates made him unpopular with his men.

'I tried this the other day, sir, on my way home. If you skip over the fence at the side of the school football fields you could be in Allison's School grounds without anybody knowing you were there. There are all kinds of outbuildings there, cricket pavilions, football changing rooms, a couple of barns, a great shed full of mowing machines and things. I checked with the school, sir, and they say they don't bother to lock them at night. Blackbeard could have spent the night in there. There's running water in some of them so he could have washed and things like that. It's possible, sir.'

Inspector Grime snorted once again. 'That's as maybe. But how did the bugger get away? Nobody saw him getting on to a train out of Fakenham the next morning. I doubt very much if he would have wanted to hang around just after he'd killed the bursar. And he must have dumped the postman's uniform somewhere along the way.'

'He could have dumped the uniform anywhere as he was getting away,' said the Sergeant.

'So how do you suggest he got away then?' The Inspector repeated his question. 'Did he have supernatural powers, do you suppose?'

Inspector Grime's sarcasm was as unpopular as his dislike of suggestions. Sergeant Morris just carried on.

'He could have walked, sir.'

'Walked? Where could the man have walked to, for God's sake?'

'Norwich, sir, perhaps.' The Sergeant noticed that his Inspector was turning red and reaching in his pockets for his pipe, usually a bad sign. 'I know it's a long way but you'd be much less visible there with all those people in the railway station. He could have gone anywhere from Norwich, sir, as you well know.'

'Would you like to take over the entire investigation, Sergeant? Use your vast experience in murder cases to solve the mystery of the vanishing Blackbeard?'

'Certainly not, sir, but could I just make one last suggestion and then I'll keep quiet. I've got the highest respect for your position and your experience, sir, as you know.' Sergeant Morris was well aware that the Inspector had to write a report on his conduct in the next ten days. More or less continuous helpings of humble pie were usually required at this point. Sergeant Morris thought yet again about requesting a transfer to a different part of the county.

'Let's hear it, if I must.'

'Well, sir, I'm sure you must have thought of this already. You've got so much more experience than me. But suppose this Blackbeard is our man. He travels up here from we know not where, could be anywhere in the country. That suggests to me that the motive, the reasons behind Gill's death, may have nothing to do with the school, or the Silkworkers or his affair with the married woman and the disappearing stonemason husband. The motive might lie elsewhere.'

Inspector Grime blew out an enormous mouthful of smoke. The tobacco was relaxing him.

'That's perfectly possible,' he said. 'It's equally possible that Blackbeard was a hired killer. You can pick up people like that in London very cheaply these days, a hitman who'll kill somebody for a couple of hundred pounds. The real murderer could still be local, but he could be a man who has decided to hire Blackbeard to hide his own identity.'

'Do you believe that, sir?'

'Do you know, Sergeant, I'm not sure what I believe any more.'

Inspector Miles Devereux had removed his feet from the desk and hooted with laughter when Johnny Fitzgerald telephoned with the news about overnight visitors at the Elysian Fields. He asked Johnny to see if the visitor was coming back to London by train. If so, once Johnny told Devereux the time of the train, she could be intercepted at the London end. Inspector Devereux looked forward to questioning her.

But his main concern that morning was with the two principal characters in his section of the investigation, Sir Peregrine Fishborne who was very much alive and Sir Rufus Walcott who was very much dead. He had decided two days before that he needed more information about them, about their past, about anything that happened some time before that might give rise to sudden death years later. Two of his brightest men had been given the task of finding as much as they could about the life stories of the dead man and the one who had succeeded him as Prime Warden of the Silkworkers Company.

'It's all very conventional,' said David Lawrence, the constable assigned to Sir Peregrine. 'I started in *Who's Who*. That's not much use really – a whole lot stuff about his progress through the livery company. I talked to a couple of reporters who write about the City, sir, and they said his life only got interesting with this row about the Silkworkers and the codicil. He's well connected, Sir Peregrine, one cousin on the board of one of the big banks, another runs a shipping company, a third is a big noise in Lloyd's the insurers. You could, one of these reporters said, coast along quite happily in the slipstream of those relations if you kept your nose clean and played your cards right. Sir Peregrine's chairman of a middling sized insurance company, plenty of money, but not as much as the other members of the family. The other reporter thought this was what started him off on the codicil and the selling off of the assets.

He has to keep up with Cousin Rupert at the bank and Cousin Jeremy at the shipping and Cousin Nigel in Lloyd's.'

'Would Sir Peregrine become richer than the others if he sold off the assets?' asked Devereux, thinking perhaps of his own family, where the brothers proliferated but the assets had long since disappeared.

'Richer, probably,' said Constable Lawrence, 'but I didn't ask that question, so that's a guess.'

'And what of Sir Rufus?' Inspector Devereux was hoping for better things from his second sleuth, Constable Conrad.

'He's pretty conventional, too,' said Conrad who was, at twenty-two years of age, the youngest member of Devereux's team. 'There is one curious thing about him, sir, and that's his entry in *Who's Who*.'

'What on earth has happened to his entry in *Who's Who?*'

'There's this gap, sir. St Paul's School, Christ Church, Oxford, then a gap until he's thirty-five years old. At that point he turns up on the board of the Town and Capital Insurance Company and never looks back. My informants said he was a whizz with figures, sir. Calculate the likely profit on any takeover in a second or two once he knew the share price and the sales figures and the state of the balance sheet.'

'Have you been able to trace anything at all in the missing years?'

'Not a thing, sir.'

'God bless my soul,' said Devereux, 'I never heard the like.'

'As I said, sir,' Constable Conrad pressed on, 'once word got out about his ability with figures, he was on boards all over the place. And, to be fair to him, most of his companies prospered.'

'Are there any links between the two of them? Apart from service with the Silkworkers?'

'There's a Norfolk connection, sir.' Constable Lawrence had returned to the fray. 'We only realized it when we were comparing notes just before we came to see you. Sir Peregrine has a house in Norfolk, near Melton Constable. Big place, peacocks on the lawn, lots of gardeners.'

'And my man, Sir Rufus, he's got a great pile just outside Aylsham. I don't know about peacocks but they say the garden is by Capability Brown. The places can't be more than ten to fifteen miles apart.'

The telephone rang. Inspector Devereux's face broke into a wicked grin. 'No sign of her at all, you say? Disappeared? Not gone off in the boot of the big car? Never mind. Keep me posted, Johnny. Happy watching.'

Inspector Devereux told his men about the late-night visitor to Sir Peregrine's suite at the Elysian Fields, and that she seemed to have disappeared. Johnny Fitzgerald could find no trace of her this morning.

'Only one thing for it, sir,' said Constable Lawrence cheerfully. 'You need a permanent vigil at that hotel. Apprehend the young lady once she appears. Have a serious talk with her, then bring her in for questioning.'

'Quite right, sir.' Constable Conrad was keen to join the hunt. 'With that kind of watching operation, you need twenty-four-hour cover, sir. A man on watch every hour of the day, sir. I'm sure the two of us could handle it.'

The Inspector laughed. 'Get away, the pair of you. If there's any handling of this young lady to be done, then it must be carried out by the senior officer on the

208

case. That's me. I shall, of course, let you know how I get on.'

Lord Francis Powerscourt was walking from the railway station to the Jesus Hospital in Marlow. A light rain was falling. He suspected that two if not three of his Inspectors felt sure that Sir Peregrine was the murderer, and were close to arresting him. Earlier that day he had sent a wire to Inspector Grime, asking him if there were any reports that Sir Peregrine had been at his house in Norfolk at the time of the bursar's murder, or if the huge black car had been seen near the school at that time. Powerscourt was not convinced that Sir Peregrine was the killer. In his mind he always came back to the strange marks on the dead men's chests, surely not only a link between the murders but a shout of defiance, a taunt to anybody investigating them.

As he approached the building, he stopped suddenly and drew back to the side of the road. Fifty yards from the front door Warden Monk was having a conversation with a man Powerscourt had not seen in this case before. Indeed it was a couple of years since they had last met. Monk seemed to be nervous, rubbing his hands together over and over again. The man had been Powerscourt's contact point when he had worked for the government a few years before. His name was Colonel James Arbuthnot and he was a senior officer in the British Secret Service.

12

Powerscourt saw Monk turn on his heel and head back towards the front gate of the hospital. Colonel Arbuthnot was coming his way. He was small, about five feet eight inches tall, with a handlebar moustache and a Roman nose. He fiddled constantly with a white rose in his buttonhole, as if he was on his way to a wedding. Powerscourt stepped out of the shadows into the middle of the road.

'Good morning, Colonel,' he said cheerfully, 'and what brings you to Marlow today?'

Arbuthnot looked at him carefully. 'Ah, Powerscourt,' he replied. 'I'd heard you were involved in this matter.'

What on earth, Powerscourt said to himself, was a senior British intelligence officer doing at the Jesus Hospital? It didn't make sense.

'I am indeed,' he replied, 'and what, pray, has the death in the almshouse got to do with you or with your department?'

'I don't feel obliged to answer any of your questions, Powerscourt. This is a matter of state security. You, of all people, know the rules.'

Powerscourt remembered that these people made Trappist monks seem talkative.

'For God's sake,' he went on, 'was Abel Meredith one of yours? I find that scarcely possible.'

'In the world of intelligence, Powerscourt, there are more things in heaven and earth than are dreamt of in your philosophy. Now, if you'll excuse me, I must get back to London.'

'I will not excuse you, Colonel, until you have told me something of your business here.'

Arbuthnot gazed up and down the little road as if he suspected German agents might be lurking behind the trees. He twisted the rose in his buttonhole once more. 'This is all very difficult,' he said finally. 'Under the terms of the paper you signed those years ago you are still committed to serving the interests of the department whenever you are called to do so. It will be much more convenient for me if I can learn whatever you have discovered from your lips rather than having to make repeated trips to this bloody backwater. Are you happy to do that for your country?'

'I am, but only on condition that you tell me what the department's interests are with the late Meredith.'

Arbuthnot paused again. A lone horseman galloped slowly down the road. When he had passed out of sight, the Colonel spoke again. 'We do not like having to conclude bargains with people who are, in effect, our own agents. But I will make you an exception in this case. If you tell me what you know about the death of this wretched man, I will tell you something of our interest in him.'

Was this a genuine offer? Would Arbuthnot take on board all he knew and give him nothing in return? How much did he know already? For all Powerscourt knew, he could have been in touch with one or more of the Inspectors on the case already.

'Well,' he said finally, 'the first thing to say is that I have, for the present, no idea at all who killed him. There is one thing you should know. Meredith's body had a strange series of marks on his chest. The same marks were found on the bodies of two other men, murdered in the days after the death in Marlow, both connected with the Silkworkers Company. One was a former Prime Warden of the Silkworkers, whose body was found by the water at the Silkworkers Hall near Tower Bridge. The other was the bursar of Allison's School at Fakenham in Norfolk which has always had very close links with the Silkworkers. The existence of the strange marks is known only to those at the very heart of the inquiry. It has not been made public.'

'Do you believe that the marks hold the key to the mystery, or mysteries?'

'I do not know, Colonel. There is a plan, organized by the current Prime Warden of the Silkworkers, to sell off the company's assets and distribute them among the members. This plan has proved contentious. There are disagreements about the provenance of some ancient documents which would seem to give sanction to the sale of the assets. The members here, like the members at the school, were mainly opposed to the sell-off. The chief opponent, the figurehead of the opposition, was the body found by the Tower, Sir Rufus Walcott. Apart from that, we have little to go on. So far we know very little about the past lives of the men in the Jesus Hospital. Maybe you could enlighten me on that.'

'You have been very frank, Powerscourt. Thank you for that.' The Colonel took another furtive look up and down

212

the road. Secrecy, Powerscourt thought, their own secrecy will be their undoing. 'Let me try to give you such information as may be useful to you. The department, shall I say, has always had an interest in the Silkworkers. They are able to travel to and from Europe freely, ostensibly to meet with other guilds and similar ludicrous organizations. It's bizarre, the extent to which the middle classes of Europe like dressing up in uniforms and livery from the distant past.'

'You mean they are messengers? Picking up reports from agents? Dropping off requests for more information?'

'You may think what you will,' Arbuthnot smiled a glacial smile. 'It is not for me to comment.'

'Was Meredith a messenger for you? How long had be been working for you then?'

'That is a difficult question to answer. I am now going to tell you the most sensitive part of our position, in return for your earlier and future help. If you agree to the future, that is?'

Powerscourt felt he had little choice. 'I do,' he said. Visions of endless future meetings, held like this one, on the nation's side roads or in derelict buildings in the capital flashed across his mind.

'Meredith was originally employed by us as a courier. We now suspect the Germans may have turned him, through bribery or brute force, to work for them. But we are not sure.'

'Heavens above, man, are you saying he turned into a double agent? Do you think the Germans might have killed him? God in heaven.'

'You may think what you will. I have told you the relevant points. It is not for me to comment any further. We shall meet again.'

Colonel Arbuthnot adjusted the rose in his button-hole once again and set off towards the railway station. Powerscourt watched him go.

Lady Lucy was taking tea once again with David Lewis, her agent inside the schoolboy population of Allison's. She was now in her second week as French conversation mistress, the permanent holder of the position ostensibly still down with flu. The boy was nervous, rocking slowly to and fro in his chair.

'Look here, Mrs Hamilton, I've been thinking about things and there's something I've just got to say . . .'

His words tailed off. Lady Lucy didn't like the sound of this one little bit.

'More tea, David? What do you think of this chocolate cake? The staff here recommend it highly.'

Reluctantly the boy tried out a large piece of cake.

'Now then,' Lady Lucy went on brightly, 'have you anything further to report from the classrooms and the corridors of Allison's? Your last piece of information was most useful. I was asking then if you could find out anything about the late bursar, Roderick Gill.'

David Lewis spoke indistinctly through a mouthful of cake. 'Yes, I have, but you have to understand the rules about the Sixth Form.'

'I see,' said Lady Lucy.

'Once you are over eighteen you are allowed to go and have a pint of beer in the evenings on Fridays and Saturdays, not on the other days. If you come back drunk or anything like that, the privilege is withdrawn from everybody in the school. It works pretty well on the whole.'

'But you're not eighteen yet, David, are you?'

'No, I'm not. I'm seventeen and a half, actually. But the older chaps bring back some gossip about what they've seen in the town, if any of the masters are getting drunk, any new motor cars to be seen.'

The boy paused to brush some chocolate crumbs off his trousers.

'There are three pubs in Fakenham itself, and one, the Farmer's Arms, a little way out on the Cromer Road. It used to be a pub; now it's been turned into a smart hotel but they still have a bar where people who wouldn't be seen dead in an ordinary pub can go and have a drink. Here in the town, there's the Crown where we are now. Some of the masters use it, so the boys don't come here very much. It might be a touch embarrassing all round. There's the Green Man, which is a dump, and the Royal Oak, which is said to be haunted but has the cheapest beer. That's the school favourite.'

'More tea?' said Lady Lucy.

'Thank you,' said David Lewis, and continued his story. 'For some reason, two of the chaps got fed up with the Royal Oak and went to the Farmer's Arms instead. Every time they went there the bursar was in the place with a woman.'

'What sort of woman?' asked Lady Lucy, trying to remember the details of the stonemason's wife. 'Was she young? Pretty?'

'Well, Longford and Fairfax said she must have been very good looking when she was young.'

Male cruelty begins very young, thought Lady Lucy. 'Age?'

'Well, they thought she must have been fairly old, well over forty. The thing is they were behaving as if they were twenty-one, all over each other. Longford said it was rather vulgar, not the way proper people that age ought to behave. And she looked like she had plenty of money. They used to leave together and she had a car waiting outside with a chauffeur.'

Whatever else she might have had, Lady Lucy said to herself, the stonemason's wife did not have a car and a driver.

'I don't suppose your friends managed to catch a name for the lady?'

'Only a Christian name, I'm afraid. Maud, that's what the bursar called her, Maud.'

Lady Lucy thought that with the name of the pub and the man and the Christian name of the woman, it should not be too difficult to find a name and an address. 'Well done, David, that's very useful. I'm so proud of you!'

'Do you think she might have killed him?' David Lewis was beginning to enjoy the many possibilities of detective work. 'Now I think about it, mind you, she's not likely to have dressed up as a man with a great black beard and walked up the school corridor first thing in the morning. Did she go to London to hire a killer to do it for her?'

'I don't think we should assume that just because she was seen having a drink with Mr Gill that she had anything to do with his death. It sounds from what your people said that they were friends, not enemies.'

'Hmm,' said the boy, in that tone of voice people adopt when they don't believe a word of what they've just been told. 'I must go to my piano lesson in a minute, Mrs Hamilton. Is there anything you'd like me to make inquiries about?'

Lady Lucy poured herself a final cup of tea. 'Well, there is, but I don't know how you'd set about finding the answer. We'd like to know what Mr Gill was doing before he came to the school. Maybe somebody at Allison's who was already in post when he arrived would know.'

'I'll see what I can do,' said David and rose to leave.

'Do you like playing the piano? Are you good at it? Any favourite composers?'

The boy stopped by the door. 'The piano? It's the best thing for me at the school next to cricket. I just love Mozart, Mrs Hamilton. It makes me think I'm in some elegant building where all the rooms and everything are perfectly proportioned. The windows are open and there's a garden outside, drenched in sunshine. Mind you, I like Tchaikovsky too.'

'I shouldn't think you're in a Georgian jewel of a house then, David.'

The boy laughed. 'No, it's dark and there's a storm outside. I'm striding out over the moors with that chap Heathcliff, tortured by unspeakable thoughts.'

Powerscourt and Johnny Fitzgerald were taking coffee with Inspector Fletcher and his Sergeant in the garden room of the Elysian Fields Hotel. They were the only people in the room. A constable had been placed on watch near the front door to check the entrances and the exits. Powerscourt told his colleagues about his encounter with the secret service man earlier that day.

Inspector Fletcher was astonished. 'I find it impossible to believe that intelligence work has been going on at the Jesus Hospital. It's such an unlikely place for it.'

'Maybe that's the point,' said Johnny Fitzgerald. 'It works because it's so improbable. What do you think we should do, Francis?'

'My man,' Powerscourt had been careful not to mention Arbuthnot's name, 'didn't say if there is any connection with the other two murders. Maybe the intelligence people used the Silkworkers indiscriminately, wherever they were to be found. I just don't know. Did Meredith join the hospital of his own free will? Or did the secret service place him there for reasons of their own? It would be a good place to hide people, if you think about it. Known largely by your number not your name, hardly ever out of the building apart from expeditions to the Rose and Crown. All strangers immediately visible and probably suspect. If you were looking for somebody, you wouldn't necessarily think of an almshouse, or, put it the other way round, if you didn't want to be found, what better place to hide than an almshouse? Damn it,' he looked round at his companions, 'there are too many questions and not enough answers. The first thing we need to do, and this, I feel, is going to fall on your shoulders, Inspector, is to find out as much as we can about Abel Meredith's past life. Where he was born, how he earned his daily bread, wives, children, criminal convictions, spells in prison, you know, the works.'

'Fine,' said the Inspector. 'We've done this before.'

'Not like this, I think you'll find. I don't think my friend has stopped yet. There's more to come.'

'How did you know, Johnny?' said Powerscourt.

'I'm like our friend the Inspector; I've been here before too.'

'I don't understand, my lord.' Inspector Fletcher was looking confused. 'What else do you want me to do?'

'I'm afraid I think we need the past lives of more than Abel Meredith, Inspector.'

'Which ones?'
'All of them in the hospital.'
'Great God!'

The man they called Eye Patch was looking out to sea in the daytime just as he did in the night. As then, he kept well back from the windows. The sun was shining this morning, dancing over the water, lighting up the pretty buildings on the seafront. Eye Patch was pleased. Most of his mission had been successfully accomplished. There was only one task left for him to perform, and he could do that once they had a really dark night. He found he was no in hurry now. At the start, with nothing accomplished, he had been unusually nervous. Now he was so near the end he felt calm. He had grown very attached to the little town, not that he had met any of the inhabitants – the closest he came to contact with them was when the locals came to the door to deliver supplies of food and drink. Very soon, maybe in a couple of days, he could close his operation down and go home. He thought he would go through a city where you could buy women by the hour or the after-noon, so much quicker than the boring rituals of flirtation and conquest. Eye Patch smiled and stared out at the water.

'Which of these two knights of the realm would you like to start with?'
'Let's start with Sir Peregrine. At least he's still alive.'
Inspector Miles Devereux had gone to the home of a

retired newspaperman. Sammy Wilson had covered the City of London for a variety of newspapers for over forty years. Even in retirement he kept his hand in, composing short biographies of financial grandees for small but welcome sums. He was a small man, who looked, even his friends admitted, remarkably like a gnome, a benevolent one, but nonetheless a gnome. Devereux had known him for years. He was always a useful source of information, much of which had never made its way into the public prints. Now they were drinking Mrs Wilson's finest tea, and consuming her lemon cakes in front of the fire, the walls lined with prints of famous cricketers and famous matches from long ago.

'Well,' Sammy Wilson began, 'I'm not surprised you're asking questions about Sir Peregrine. I've thought for years that he might get into trouble for some of his activities.'

'What do you mean?'

'I mean, my young friend, that Sir Peregrine has often sailed pretty close to the wind. I don't think he's gone in for massive fraud against the public, against the people who've invested in his companies. Rather, it's the way that he gets to the top of them that's always interested me. It's happened twice, as far as I know. There may well be more examples that I don't know of. And these are only rumours, you understand, just rumours, nothing you could issue an arrest warrant for, if you follow me.'

'You're talking in riddles, Sammy, and you know it,' said Inspector Devereux, popping his second lemon cake into his mouth. 'Can you be more specific? We're talking off the record here, for heaven's sake.'

'I'm glad to hear it,' said Sammy Wilson. 'The pattern is the same in both cases. Sir Peregrine gets himself appointed to the board of some medium-sized outfit; London Wall Insurance was the first one. He sits there for a while, good as gold. Doesn't query the accounts or anything troublesome like that. Eighteen months in, there's an emergency meeting of the board, called by our friend. A vote of no confidence in the managing director is passed by a small majority. Sir P, surprise, surprise, becomes the new managing director. The word on the street is that his supporters were either bribed or blackmailed into following him. His supporters' club, surprise, surprise again, are given large increases in salary under the new regime. The cynics said that a promise of future cash would not have been enough to persuade his colleagues to vote the previous man out. Money must have changed hands beforehand. Or they were blackmailed. Or both.'

'What happened to the previous managing director? Did he make a fuss?'

'I can see the way your devious mind is working, young Devereux. Previous man loses job, loses income, bears a grudge against Sir P for years, bumps him off in the basement of the Silkworkers Hall. Well, Sir Peregrine was too clever for that. Not long after his expulsion from London Wall Insurance, the previous managing director, Young was his name, Randolph Young, gets another job in a different company specializing in shipping. Guess who was on the board there? Finding it difficult, are you? Too tricky a problem perhaps? Let me enlighten you. Sir Peregrine was on the board there, too. Seemed to have no problem working with the man whose job he'd stolen, as you might put it. Rum, that, I thought, rum.'

'Nothing ever came out about what had been going on? Not a word?'

'Well, as you might imagine, there was a lot of whispering and muttering around the City. Terrible place for the speed of rumour, as you know. But no, nothing firm ever emerged; just one more strange happening in an environment where strange things happen all the time.'

'And the second time, Sammy? I think you said there were two examples.'

'You're quite right, I did. The second was slightly different. But once again it happened at a company where Sir Peregrine was on the board. Lombard Electricity, they were called, installing and researching electric supply, that sort of thing. Doing very well, it was, too. Still is, I think. Anyway, Sir Peregrine is on the board again, as before. Very well behaved again to start with. Then there's another extraordinary board meeting. The charge is that the managing director has been fiddling the books. Hand in the till, that sort of thing. Poor man says all the documents are forgeries but the monies do seem to have been extracted from the company's bankers and transferred over. The board, led, with great reluctance, more in sorrow than in anger, by Sir Peregrine, how unfortunate that one of our best and brightest should have had a temporary fall from grace and what probity he has always displayed in the past, the board don't believe this unfortunate managing director. Out he goes. In comes our friend, Sir P, top dog once again, the man who overcame his friendship with the previous incumbent to restore that honest dealing for which the City is famed. Hypocrisy was being handed out in ladlefuls and Sir Peregrine was the chief beadle.'

'Were the documents forged?' The Inspector was on his fourth lemon cake.

'I was told,' Sammy Wilson was talking very quietly at this point as if even his own wife should not be privy to such sensitive material, 'told by a source very close to the action, that they were forgeries. Clever forgeries, but forgeries none the less. Certainly that managing director, man by the name of Ibbotson, never admitted anything.'

'Where is he now?'

'Ibbotson? I knew you were going to ask me that. I don't know, to be honest with you. I think he just dropped right out of the Square Mile altogether. Would you like me to find out where he is?'

'I would. Very much so.'

'My God, Inspector, you've got a very suspicious mind. Are you fitting him up already for the handcuffs and the rope?'

'Certainly not. Far too soon. Inquiries, as my colleagues are fond of saying, will have to take their course. What of the other man, Sir Rufus Walcott? Let me tell you for a start that there are fifteen years or so missing from his life in *Who's Who*. Any idea what that's all about?'

'You don't want to pay too much attention to what's in there, young man. They only print what their subjects tell them, those *Who's Who* people; they don't check anything out or do any research of their own. If I were compiling some of those entries they'd be a lot juicier than the ones that appear, I can tell you.'

'But why do you think Sir Rufus left this great blank in his life?'

'Could be any one of a number of things. Failed business ventures? Founder and managing director of Croesus Holdings, went bankrupt towards the end of the last century? I don't think you'd want people knowing about that. He could have gone to the colonies or to America and gone bad rather than good, if you see what I mean. Failed gold prospector somewhere or other? I don't

223

think you should bother too much about those missing years. The thing about Sir Rufus is that in so many ways he was the exact opposite to Sir Peregrine. Sir Peregrine, you might say, is a rather slippery character, one or two doubtful episodes in his past. Sir Rufus was completely different. I doubt if there was even a small bone let alone a skeleton in his closet. He was a man of honour. He was known for his integrity. That's why he ended up on so many boards and being appointed Lord Lieutenant of Norfolk. You've got to be clean as the driven snow to hold a position like that with its links to the monarchy. I doubt if anyone would appoint Sir Peregrine Lord Lieutenant of Wandsworth Prison even if there was such a post.'

'How odd that two such different characters succeeded each other as Prime Warden of the Silkworkers.'

'I spent a lot of time years ago on a story about the City of London School, Inspector. Fellow there told me that it is almost a tradition at the public schools that the man taking over is as unlike his predecessor as possible. Maybe that applied to the Silkworkers too.'

Inspector Devereux rose to go. 'I am most grateful for your help, Sammy. If you could find out the name of the managing director supposed to have cooked the books, I'd be grateful.'

'Would you like me to arrange a meeting with you if I find him?'

'Yes please. And could you pass on my thanks to your wife for these lovely lemon cakes? I look forward to more of them when I return.'

'They're infuriating, Lucy, just infuriating.'

'Who is infuriating you now, Francis? I haven't seen

you this furiated for a while.' Lady Lucy smiled at her husband, pacing up and down the imaginary quarterdeck that masqueraded as a drawing room in their hotel in Fakenham.

'Sorry, Lucy, it's those secret service people. I told you I met one of them, a man called Arbuthnot, outside the Jesus Hospital. They don't tell you anything. The late Meredith may have been a courier for them. Or he may not. Other silkmen in the hospital or elsewhere may also have been couriers. Or again, maybe not. They never give you anything concrete to work with. It's the same as the time I worked for them before. They nearly drove me mad then. I suspect they're going to do it again.'

'Can't you just ask the old men if they have worked for the government in the past, Francis? They can't have been major spies, surely, just messengers or couriers.'

'I don't know, Lucy. Arbuthnot implied the dead man might have been turned round from being a British agent into a German one. If you wanted to hide the ace of spies away somewhere, you could do a lot worse than the Jesus Hospital.'

'Is there nobody you can talk to, Francis? Are there any retired spies? People who have left the service and might be more able to talk?'

'I don't think there are any of those. The service has only just been founded. Hold on a minute, though.' Powerscourt stopped by the fireplace and stared at Lady Lucy for a moment. Then he smiled. 'I've just thought of something, Lucy. It's a long shot, but it might just work. I'm going to go to Paris to see a man in the Place des Vosges.'

'Who is this French gentleman, Francis?'

'I met him when I was working on the death on the Nevskii Prospekt, my love. His name is Olivier Brouzet and he is the head of the French secret intelligence service.'

Inspector Grime swore violently when he heard the news of Roderick Gill's meetings in the Farmer's Arms. He despatched a young constable who lived round the corner from the pub and knew the landlord well for more information.

'Bloody man Gill,' he raged at his Sergeant. 'Why isn't one woman enough for him? Why does he need to have two on the go?'

'Don't know, sir.' His Sergeant had long ago decided that the minimum number of words were the safest course of action on these occasions.

'Do you suppose we would find yet more women if we went on a trawl round the pubs of Holt and Swaffham? Is the bloody man never satisfied? I'm beginning to suspect this womanizing may have been the death of him.'

Constable Parrish, all of twenty-four years old, returned from his trip to the Farmer's Arms.

'Well, Constable, what's the news?'

'The woman's name is Lewis, sir, Mrs Maud Lewis. Widow, thought by the publican to be in her late forties.'

'You don't often hear them say they're in their late fifties, do you?' The Inspector was scowling at a picture of Queen Alexandra on his wall. 'Some of these women have been in their late forties for years.'

'Yes, sir.' Constable Parrish carried on, 'She lives in a huge house a couple of hundred yards from the pub. She only moved there about six months ago, sir. The publican thinks she lived in Birmingham before that. Plenty of money, sir. Kind to the servants apparently.'

'Never mind whether she was kind to the bloody servants or not for now – did she have any family?'

'She does, sir, sorry, sir. She has two sons in their early twenties. The publican believes they live in London now.'

'Do they come to visit their mother? Devoted sons perhaps?'

'Well, sir, this was one of the most interesting things. I should have mentioned it earlier. Two or three weeks ago the two boys were having a drink with their mother. There was a row. The publican wasn't in the room himself at the time but one of the bar staff told him about it when they'd gone. They were arguing about the money in her will. The boys kept saying they couldn't see why they should lose out in favour of somebody she hardly knew.'

'My God,' said Inspector Grime, 'if that's not a motive for murder I don't know what is. Sergeant, take yourself off to interview the merry widow this minute. Don't leave without an address for her sons.'

13

The old men of the Jesus Hospital had been summoned
to a special meeting in the Maidenhead police station.
Black police vans brought those thought unfit to walk
the seven hundred yards from the almshouse. The silkmen were kept in the police canteen until it was time
for their interview. Afterwards they were free to leave
or to wait for the police to take them back home. Under
no circumstances were the men who had been through
the interview allowed to speak to those who had not.
Inspector Fletcher had decided that the easiest way to
obtain the information needed about their past lives and
their past connections was to ask them. He dreaded to
think what might happen if he asked them to write anything down. He had looked at the records of the old men
held by Monk in his little office and decided to start again.
The Inspector and Sergeant Donaldson were seated side
by side at the table in the interview room.

'Thank you very much for coming,' Inspector Fletcher
began, 'and thank you for agreeing to answer our questions about your lives before you came here. This will be
useful in our investigation.'

There was usually a murmur of dissent from the silk-men at this point. The old gentlemen didn't like being called out to the police station at ten o'clock in the morning. They didn't like change to their routines in any shape or form. They didn't like having to give details of their earlier lives. The Sergeant had given it as his opinion that any of them with criminal records or other misdemeanours in their past were hardly likely to tell a police Inspector and a Sergeant just yards away from the cells.

'I am going to ask you a series of questions,' Fletcher went on. 'All you have to do is to tell me the answers.' For once the Inspector's pauses and hesitations worked to his advantage. The old boys had more time to take in what he was asking. 'First, this is just for the record, could you give us your full name – that means all your Christian names if you have more than one – and your date of birth.'

Sergeant Donaldson was scribbling furiously in his notebook. He was to remark later that all of them could manage their names but about three of the silkmen were having trouble remembering their birthdays. They would stare blankly at the wall and scratch their heads. The Inspector waited.

'If you can't remember your precise date of birth, the year will do,' he said, wondering if the whole exercise was going to come to nothing, defeated by the ravages of time and old age's ability to wipe out people's memories. Two out of the three who had forgotten the exact date managed to tell him the year. The third, Number Four, Bill Smith, known as Smithy, with his shock of white hair, gave up.

Inspector Fletcher took them through the names of their parents, the names of their wife or wives, if such were still alive, which he doubted, and the names of any children and where they were now. He asked for details of the jobs they had held and the places where they had lived. Had any of them, he asked, ever been employed by the government in any way? The post office perhaps? Most important, he said, what was the name and nature of their last job before they came to the Jesus Hospital.

Most of the old men were slow and suspicious, trying to remember some post they might have held thirty or forty years before. The Sergeant took pity on them. He had a father the same age as these men, after all. This, he felt, was asking too much of the old boys, reminding each and every one of them how mentally frail they had become and the things they could no longer remember. When they had finished, they sat patiently in their places waiting for the Inspector to dismiss them. He had one last request for them all. 'Thank you very much,' he said. 'My final inquiry does not relate to any of you, but I would like you to tell us anything that Abel Meredith may have said to you about his year of birth or his parents or his own family, if he had one, and any jobs or positions he might have mentioned to you. And one other question' – this, in fact was the point of the entire exercise, heavily disguised under a cover of personal information – 'did Abel Meredith, Number Twenty, ever ask you to go with him on a journey, to London perhaps, or maybe even abroad?' Most of the old men looked blank at this point. Most of the information they gave was of little value, but in two cases the answers to this final question were pure gold.

Number Six, Colin Baker, said he had gone with the late Abel Meredith, Number Twenty, to Hamburg for a few days three months before. They had stayed at a modest hotel and seen the sights of the city and its many drinking establishments. Number Twenty had paid all the bills.

230

'Were you with him all the time?' asked Inspector Fletcher.

'I don't understand,' said Number Six.

'Was there ever a time when you were left on your own? When Abel Meredith, Number Twenty, could have gone to a meeting or something like that?'

There was a long pause while Number Six marshalled his thoughts. Sergeant Donaldson thought he might be about to fall asleep.

'There was something strange, I suppose, now I come to think about it. It was on our first morning there, just before nine o'clock. I remember that because they had an enormous clock in the dining room where we were having breakfast. Not that you can get a decent breakfast in Hamburg; even the Jesus Hospital can do better than them. Anyway, Number Twenty, says he is just going to look for an English paper. I sat there trying to eat some disgusting cheese and a smelly sausage or two. Number Twenty came back after twenty minutes or so and said there were no English papers to be had. I suppose he could have met somebody in that time. I never thought about it.'

The Inspector and the Sergeant exchanged meaningful glances but made no comment. 'Did you get the impression that he had been there before? Was he able to speak to the natives in German?'

'Well,' said Number Six, 'they certainly knew him at the hotel. I'm sure he'd been there before. And he could certainly jabber on to the locals in their ridiculous language, though I'm not qualified to say how good he was.'

That was all. Colin Baker, Number Six, the man with the wooden leg, could remember no more. Any attempts to obtain more details of this strange holiday were met by a shake of the head and a plea to be allowed to go home.

The other nugget came from Pretty Billy, Number Sixteen, who told of going to London for a day with Abel Meredith the month before he was killed. They had gone to an address in central London where Meredith said he had to see a man about some business to do with his investments. He, Number Sixteen, had been parked in the saloon bar of the Three Horseshoes, virtually next door.

'Number Twenty left me with two large glasses of port – I remember that now,' said Pretty Billy. 'I don't normally like port but I just fancied it that day. Isn't it strange how these whims come over you!' Number Sixteen sank back into a reverie of past port.

'How long before he came back?' asked Sergeant Donaldson gently.

'What was that? Where was I? I see, how long before he came back. Half an hour? Both my glasses were empty by then and I was looking forward to another. But that was not to be. Not that day, anyway. Number Twenty was in a furious temper. "Bastards, bastards," he kept saying to himself over and over again. He didn't speak a word to me all the way back to Marlow. Then he went straight to the Rose and Crown and didn't come out till closing time. I don't think I can remember any more, Inspector.'

Number Sixteen was the last man to be interviewed. Inspector Fletcher scribbled a rapid telegram to Powerscourt with the news of Hamburg and the meeting in London and sent Sergeant Donaldson off to dispatch it. He leant back in his chair, considering the relevance of the German mission, when a stout constable knocked on the door and headed straight for him.

'Sorry, sir,' he began, 'it's that woman, sir, the one at the Elysian Fields, sir.'

'What woman? What are you talking about, for God's sake?'

'Sorry, sir, it's the lady who goes up to Sir Peregrine's quarters, sir, the suite on the first floor. Constable Jones has apprehended her, sir, on her way out. She's waiting to talk to you now, sir.'

Inspector Miles Devereux was waiting to meet James Ibbotson in a private room at the Midland Grand Hotel at St Pancras Station. Ibbotson was the managing director ousted by Sir Peregrine from his post at a leading insurance company some years before. The Inspector's reporter friend Sammy Wilson had not only located the man, but also set up the meeting here today. Ibbotson was a short, nervous fellow, with a fancy waistcoat and very small eyes.

'Good day to you, Mr Ibbotson, how kind of you to come.'

Devereux told him about the murder of Sir Rufus Walcott at the Silkworkers dinner hosted by Sir Peregrine as Prime Warden of the Company.

'Got the wrong man, didn't he, our friend the murderer,' said Ibbotson.

'What do you mean?'

'Should have bumped off bloody Sir Peregrine rather than the other fellow, if you ask me. Would have been a public service, don't you know.'

Inspector Devereux had wondered before now if the intended victim might not have been Sir Peregrine, the death of Sir Rufus a mistake.

'We believe this murder may be linked to one or two others, one in Buckinghamshire where Sir Peregrine was spotted some time before the killing took place, and the other in Norfolk, near to where Sir Peregrine has a house.'

'Arrest him then,' said Ibbotson, with rather a vicious smile. 'It's about time the man was put behind bars. One thing's rather a pity, mind you. If he killed all of them he can still only be hanged once. Three times would have been more satisfactory. No chance of bringing back disembowelling, I suppose?'

'I take it, Mr Ibbotson, that you are still protesting your innocence about the so-called forgeries at your previous place of employment?'

'I am indeed, sir. I am as innocent as the newborn babe. I was cheated out of my position, sir, cheated. It's a scandal.'

'Forgive me for asking, but what is your occupation now?'

'You may ask,' said Ibbotson. 'Indeed in your position you must ask. It took me eighteen months, sir, to obtain a new post. My name had been blackened right across the City of London. I now have connections with the National Trust through my wife's family. I am employed by them as senior accountant.'

'I have to ask this question, too, Mr Ibbotson. Where were you between ten o'clock at night on the twenty-first of January and nine o'clock the following morning?'

'I was at home,' said Ibbotson. 'We had two friends from the Trust to supper. I suppose they went home about half past ten. My wife and I turned in shortly after that. The following morning I went to work in the usual way. I reached my office about half past eight and was there, or in meetings, all morning.'

'And your friends and colleagues would support your account?'

'They would. I shall give you their names.' The former

managing director entered three names into Devereux's notebook. He turned back at the door. 'Please let me know when you arrest Sir Peregrine, Inspector. I would be most interested.'

'What would you do?' asked Inspector Devereux.

'Revenge,' the little man said, 'is a dish best eaten cold, according to the Spanish. I have spent years with the prospect of revenge getting colder every year. It's so well refrigerated by now, my lust for revenge, it's practically turned to ice. I would, of course, visit Sir Peregrine in prison. I don't think I'd bother saying anything. Just looking at him behind bars in prison clothes would be enough, I think. I'm sure I could look at him all day.'

Sergeant Morris wasn't looking forward to his interview with Mrs Maud Lewis, christened the merry widow by his Inspector. The Sergeant wasn't as hopeless with women as the Inspector, but he thought he might have to ask her a number of very personal questions. As he passed the Farmer's Arms and set off up the road, he consoled himself with the thought that she might be one of those talkative women only too happy to tell her entire life history once they have a captive listener. The Sergeant had met a number of those in his time.

She was all charm as he arrived, showing him into an enormous drawing room lined with paintings and photographs of dogs. Mrs Lewis was about fifty years old and dressed from head to toe in black. She was a nervous woman, forever fidgeting in her chair or clasping and unclasping her hands. The Sergeant had an aunt with exactly the same mannerisms. A servant was ordered to bring them tea at once.

'Sergeant Morris, did you say? You must be all worked off your feet just now with this terrible murder. What a business! And to think that I knew the deceased! I've never known a deceased before! My own dear Roderick, cut off in his prime in that dreadful way!'

The Sergeant saw that he might have trouble steering the conversation in the direction he wanted it to go.

'Perhaps you could tell me how you came to be living here in Fakenham, Mrs Lewis? Of course there's no reason why you shouldn't be living here, but I don't think you've been with us very long.'

'You're quite right, Sergeant, I haven't been here very long, but I do like to think that Fakenham has taken me to its bosom! Such kind people! We lived in the Midlands before where Horace had his business. He was my late husband, Sergeant, bless him. Horace had a chain of stores, you know, clothing shops, shirts, blouses, undergarments. Horace always said that ladies' undergarments were his top sellers. Give them the right stuff and the customers will always come back, that was his motto. The shops were in and around Birmingham but we lived in a better sort of neighbourhood, Edgbaston Park. We had a very tasteful residence there. Do you know Edgbaston Park at all, Sergeant?'

The policeman shook his head.

'It's rather like one of these Norfolk towns, Edgbaston Park, quite superior people living there. We were so happy in the place, Horace with the shops, the boys off our hands, all our friends.' Mrs Lewis paused briefly to pour some tea. 'But then, two years ago to the day next Wednesday, we were struck by tragedy. Well, Horace was, really. He was up a ladder in the back storeroom of the main shop, checking on the supplies of some items of hosiery when he was struck down! Quite what Horace was doing up this ladder when he had all those people on his staff I don't know. Anyway the young lady with him tried to bring him round on the floor where he'd fallen. No use, no use at all. Horace had had a heart attack up the ladder and that was the end of him. He'd often talked of heaven being like an enormous shop where you could buy everything without paying. Well, now he'd gone there. By express. He'd always been fond of expresses, Horace.'

She took another mouthful of tea. The Sergeant wondered how the unfortunate Horace had coped with this very talkative wife. Had she gone on like this all evening in the tasteful residence at Edgbaston Park?

'It took such a long time to get things straight, Sergeant. The staff in Horace's shops did ask me on a number of occasions if I would take over the management of the business but I said I would find the memories of Horace too painful. They understood that, bless them. I still own some shares, mind you, so Horace keeps me supplied with dividends from beyond the grave! I'm sure he would be pleased about that. And then I came here. And then I met Roderick. My fiancée, you know. We hadn't told anybody about it, well, hardly anybody, but you are the law, aren't you, Sergeant, so it's only proper I should tell you. Render unto Caesar, Roderick used to say. Do you know, Sergeant, I've never known what that meant, and I've never liked to ask in case people thought I was stupid. Do you know what it means, Sergeant?'

'I think, Mrs Lewis, that it's a quotation from the New Testament. Render unto Caesar the things that are Caesar's, render unto God the things that are God's. It means you should pay your taxes to the state like a good citizen, and you should go to church and worship God as well.'

'I think that's very fair, Sergeant. I expect you have to know things like that in the police force. Come to think of it, you are like Caesar, the law of the land, and the dear vicar is like God.'

'Could I ask, Mrs Lewis, forgive me if this seems a personal question, how you came to know Mr Gill?'

'I met him through the church, of course – appropriate now we are talking of rendering unto God. He was often in the church, looking after the accounts, counting the collection money. The Reverend Williamson is a very conscientious man, but I don't think he knew anything about money. He used to say that Roderick was his right-hand man. Horace had a chap in the shops who did the figures, not a nice man like my Roderick, but he knew all about the taxes and how, sometimes, you could avoid paying them. Dear me, I shouldn't have told you that, should I! Horace would be so cross with me. If you've got one sin, Maud, he used to say, it's that you open your big mouth without thinking about it!'

'Don't worry about that, Mrs Lewis,' said the Sergeant. 'We're engaged on a murder investigation here, nothing to do with taxes.'

'Thank goodness for that,' said Mrs Lewis. 'Now where was I?'

'You were talking about your meeting with Mr Gill.'

'Ah, yes. I think we grew close when we were working on the arrangements for the Harvest Festival. It was as if love was blossoming among the fruit and vegetables dotted around the church. After that Roderick used to come to my house after we had a few drinks in the Farmer's Arms together. Roderick would drink Guinness and I would have a glass of port – Horace introduced me to port years ago – and things progressed from there.'

'When did you become engaged, Mrs Lewis?'

'I'll always remember that, Sergeant. It was after the midnight carol service on Christmas Eve. We were sitting together near the front. I remember thinking that Roderick was coming close to me during "Oh Come all ye Faithful". Then he came even closer when we were singing "Hark the Herald Angels Sing". And then, would you believe this, Sergeant, he actually held my hand while we were singing "Silent Night"! Discreetly, of course, not so people could see. I wondered if he was going to propose while we were in church, in "It Came Upon the Midnight Clear" perhaps, but he waited till we were home again.'

The Sergeant wanted to ask if the school bursar stayed the night on these romantic evenings, but he thought it better not.

'Have you told your children about this?'

A small cloud seemed to pass across Mrs Lewis's features. 'Well, I did, actually. I think it's fair to say that neither William nor Montague ever understood Roderick. They never liked him. It was so unfair. Roderick tried so hard.'

'Did you have rows about it, Mrs Lewis? Sorry, but we have to ask questions like these.'

'I expect somebody has been telling stories out of school at the Farmer's Arms. Quite why these snooping people have to listen in to private conversations I'll never know. Yes, there was a row.' For the first time in the conversation Mrs Lewis seemed to have lost the power of speech.

'Was the row about money? About who you were going to leave the shares to?'

'My goodness, they were listening carefully, weren't they! Yes, it was. What you must understand is that Horace left the two boys very well off. Each of them has as many shares in the business as I have, if not more.

239

Neither of them has to work at all. So I can't see why they were so cross when I said I was going to leave my shares to Roderick after we were married and I made a new will.'

'But you didn't. Get married, I mean, did you, Mrs Lewis? You didn't have much time between the engagement and the murder.'

'No,' said Mrs Lewis sadly, 'we didn't. Such a pity as I'd seen a very beautiful hat over in Norwich. I was so looking forward to getting married in that hat.'

'And tell me, pray, the will you already had in place, the one that was valid when Mr Gill was killed, where did that leave the money?'

'That went to the two boys, all of it. I hadn't even met Roderick when I made that will.'

'I've nearly finished, Mrs Lewis. Just one last thing, if I may. Could you just give me the address or addresses for the boys? I don't think they live locally, do they?'

'Montague lives at fourteen North Road in Highgate near the school, and William lives at thirty-four Noel Road in Islington. Such pretty houses they have. Now then, will you take a glass of Madeira before you go, Sergeant? A small sherry? I usually have a little tipple about this time!'

The Sergeant declined. As he made his way back to the station he wondered if Mrs Lewis realized the import of what she had told him. She had just pointed out that her two sons, singly or together, had very powerful motives for murder.

Powerscourt discovered to his great delight that M. Olivier Brouzet, Director General of the French secret service, was not at his elegant headquarters in the Place des Vosges in Paris. He was in London, conferring with his English counterparts. He met Powerscourt in a charming room, hung with Gobelin tapestries, in the French Embassy.

'Thank you for your note. How pleasant to meet you again, Lord Powerscourt.' Olivier Brouzet was still slim and dapper with a charming smile. 'You mention you have been having trouble with secrecy in your secret service? Is that so, Lord Powerscourt?'

Powerscourt explained about the murder at the Jesus Hospital and the two further murders at places connected with the Silkworkers Company. He mentioned the strange marks on the dead men's chests. He told Brouzet about meeting Colonel Arbuthnot outside the almshouse and his great reluctance to give any details of his interest in the victim and the manner of his death. And he passed on his latest intelligence about the highly suspicious trip to Hamburg and the meeting in London that infuriated Abel Meredith. He complained about the secrecy in the organization he had served.

'Maybe you should make allowances, my friend. This secret organization of yours is very young. Perhaps they do not yet know how to behave.'

'Colonel Arbuthnot hinted that Meredith might have been turned into a double agent by the Germans. Do you think that is possible?'

'Anything is possible in this secret world, my friend. This Meredith would seem to have been used as a courier, but then the Colonel more or less admitted that, did he not, when he said his service sometimes used the Silkworkers as messengers. It's quite smart, I think. Maybe we should infiltrate our winegrowers' fraternities

241

and use them to take messages to and from Germany under cover of friendly visits to the vineyards of Hock and Moselle. In the world of espionage, Lord Powerscourt, if you look at things very closely for a long time you may end up entertaining the most fantastical notions. You can think you are going mad, and some of us do. It becomes like a repeating image in a hall of mirrors. The man is a double agent; no, he is a triple agent. You can go on for ever. Certainly the British have turned quite a lot of people in recent times. Betraying your country is often preferable to four years in some ghastly English prison where the inmates will beat you up all the time for being a German spy. Patriotism flourishes in the most unlikely places.'

'What would you advise, Monsieur Brouzet? Should I take this spying business seriously or not?'

'That is a difficult question, my friend. Part of the difference between our two countries on espionage-related matters is that of geography. You have the waters of the North Sea between you and the Kaiser. For us, he is, literally, next door. That is why I think these matters are taken more seriously in France than in Britain. Let me ask you a question. From what you have told me, you think these mysterious marks hold the key to the crimes, the fact that all three corpses have been defaced in the same way. Is that right?'

'It is,' said Powerscourt, wondering where this French logic might be taking him.

'Well, my friend, it seems unlikely to me that all three dead men were involved with the secret service and acting as couriers to Germany and back. I do not believe the Germans would come all this way to kill all three of them. I think that's very unlikely. So I think you should not close your mind to the possibilities of espionage in

242

this case, but I do not think it should be at the forefront of your mind either. I tell you what I will do. Quite soon I have a meeting with the superior officer of this Colonel Arbuthnot. I shall ask him about events at the almshouse. I shall tell him that we had an agent holidaying at your Elysian Fields Hotel who heard about the murder inquiry and reported back to us. I shall, of course, let you know what he says.'

Inspector Fletcher had never interviewed a professional mistress before, if that was what she was. He wasn't quite sure if she had committed any crimes. The young lady had blonde hair and bright blue eyes and went straight on to the attack as if she were a professional boxer.

'Hey,' she said, 'are you in charge round here? That man of yours, Constable whatever his name is, he seems to have lost the power of speech.'

'I am the senior investigating officer, looking into a case of murder. Fletcher is my name. I'm an Inspector.'

'Good for you. Well done. Nobody's mentioned murder round here to me. Everybody's still alive in this hotel as far as I know. Some of them may be bloody old but they're not dead yet. Not quite. My name's Francesca, by the way; my friends call me Frankie. I don't know nothing about this murder, wherever it was. Why can't I go home? You've got no cause to hold on to me. I've got work to do.'

'I'm sure you do. What kind of work do you do, Miss Francesca?'

'I'm a masseuse. And I do occasional escort work sometimes. If the money's right. Do you need a massage, Inspector? You look pretty tense to me.'

'I'm fine, thank you,' said the Inspector. 'I wonder if

you could tell me about your relationship with one of the directors here, Sir Peregrine Fishborne.'

'What's it got to do with you, my relationship as you call it, with old Fishcake? None of your bloody business.'

'There you're wrong. The murder we are investigating took place at an almshouse not far from here. Sir Peregrine was here at the hotel the night of the murder. We think you may have been with him. The date of which we speak is January twenty-second.'

'I may have been with him that night,' Francesca said, 'and I may not. I can't be expected to remember exactly where I was all the time. I still don't think it's any of your business.'

'Did you come down with Sir Peregrine in his car? Or did you make your own way here? It was a Saturday. The hotel people remember you being here. In the Baron Haussmann Suite.'

'What if I was?'

'Could I ask you what you were doing with Sir Peregrine so late at night?'

'You may. He needed a massage. He often sends for me here when he needs a massage. He's got a terrible back, old Fishcake, just terrible.'

'I see,' said the Inspector. 'And does the treatment involve you staying the night?'

'You're the nosey one, aren't you? Course it does. Sometimes the treatment doesn't work first time round. You have to do it again. "Frankie," old man Fishcake would say to me, "despite your best efforts, I'm afraid it hasn't taken. One more time if you please." And usually he needs it again in the morning. Help him through the day, that sort of thing. What's he done anyway, my client? You're not suspecting him of the murder, are you?' With that Francesca began to laugh. 'All the time he's lying there, scarcely able to move, you think he's off up at the almshouse killing somebody? Don't be ridiculous!'

'Can you remember, Miss Francesca, if Sir Peregrine required further treatment in the morning? Can you remember what time he left the hotel?'

'There is one thing you can say about old Fishcake; he's very regular in his habits. He always wants it in the morning, the treatment, I mean. Never known him not to. He usually left very early in the morning after I'd seen to him. Seven o'clock? Eight o'clock? Sometimes earlier, sometimes later. His back was so bad one day recently I had to stay till ten o'clock.'

'Has this masseuse duty been going on for long, Miss Francesca?'

'Long enough, Inspector. There are times when a girl might like to be pummelling something younger, if you follow me, but I can't complain. I've been seeing to him for about six months, I should say.'

'How does he get in touch with you, Miss Francesca?'

'You're getting very cheeky, young man. I shall answer this question and then no more. He's lent me a flat so I can treat him there when he needs me to. Just off the Strand. And he's installed one of those telephone things so he can call when he needs me. That's your lot, sunny Jim. I'm off.'

The constable and the Inspector made their way back to the station.

'Do you know, sir, I'm not feeling too good,' said the constable.

'I'm sorry to hear that,' said Inspector Fletcher. 'What seems to be the trouble?'

'It's my back, sir. I seem to have twisted something. I think I need a massage.'

14

Inspector Grime of the Norfolk Constabulary hated London. He had hated it ever since his father took him there as a treat when he was seven years old. Master Grime had been accidentally separated from his father in a huge shop in Oxford Street and it had taken four very frightening hours before they were reunited. He disliked the noise, the clamour of streets too full of cars and carriages and carts and humans. He disliked the crowds rushing around on missions he did not understand. He disliked Londoners. He thought they were slick, superficial, devious and would rob you of your last farthing if they had a chance.

Now, stuck in a cab at eleven o'clock in the morning between Liverpool Street Station and Noel Road in Islington, home of William Lewis, son of the merry widow in Fakenham, he cursed the traffic that was making him late for his interview, arranged by telephone the afternoon before. Damn London, said the Inspector. At least I'll be out of here this evening after I've seen the other Lewis up in Highgate.

William Lewis ushered him into an upstairs drawing room that looked out on to a garden and the Regent's

Park Canal. 'You've come a long way to see me, Inspector, it must be important. Would you like some coffee?'

'Thank you, but no,' said the Inspector. 'I'm sorry to have to ask you personal questions, but this is a murder inquiry. I wonder if you could tell me about how your mother coped after your father died. In a general way, if you see what I mean.'

'Have you met my mother, Inspector?'

'I'm afraid I haven't had that pleasure yet, Mr Lewis. My Sergeant went to talk to her and reported back.'

'Pity, that,' said William Lewis. 'Things might have been easier if you had. Let me try to answer your question, Inspector. My mother is a creature of fancy. My father once referred to her as being blessed with an iron whim. She gets ideas into her head. And unlike a lot of women who are content to leave the idea where it is, she acts on them. Not all the time, just most of the time. My brother and I – he's the elder, by the way – tried to persuade her to stay where she was after our father passed away. The house was more than adequate for her needs. I'm not saying she had a lot of friends, but she knew a lot of people round there. But no, that wouldn't do. Sell the house, move to Fakenham – why Fakenham, for God's sake? She was going slightly mad.'

'When you refer to her going slightly mad, sir, what do you mean? Was she behaving out of character?'

'I think you could say she was behaving entirely in character; that was the trouble. Who in their right mind would want to get involved with an ageing bounty hunter who stalked his victims over the flower rotas and the Harvest Festival at the local church?'

'I hope you won't mind my asking, sir, but did you meet Mr Gill the bursar? What did you think of him?'

William Lewis snorted. 'He was awful. Creepy, sucking up to my mother all the time, calling her darling and my love and all that sort of stuff. You could tell a mile off that he was only interested in the money.'

'So what did you and your brother do about it?'

'We tried, Inspector, we tried. God knows we tried to talk some sense into her. What did she think she was doing, marrying this useless specimen of humanity? And if she did have to marry him, why did she have to leave him all her money? What would Father have thought of it?'

Inspector Grime had a sudden vision of Horace Lewis, obsessed with the sale of his undergarments, supposedly up a ladder in the stockroom with a very pretty girl beside him.

'We can get the exact figures from the solicitors, Mr Lewis, but I wonder if you could tell us exactly how much money we're talking about here. In the shares and the property?'

William Lewis looked out of the window. A barge was making slow passage towards the long tunnel at the top end of Noel Road. 'You may find this hard to believe, Inspector, but I don't know. Truly I don't. I could never keep up with the numbers at school. My brother Montague looks after all that. I know I have enough to live comfortably off the shares.'

'Could I ask you to tell me how you felt about Mr Gill, sir? Did you dislike him? Did you hate him?'

William Lewis wasn't going to own up to hatred. 'Dislike would do it, Inspector,' he said. 'Extreme dislike, maybe.'

'Did you kill Roderick Gill, Mr Lewis?'

'I did not.'

'Could you tell me where you were on the afternoon and evening of January twenty-second?'

'Of course. In the afternoon I went for a walk, as I usually do, Inspector. I spent the evening with my brother. We played chess.'

'Who won?'

'I did, Inspector. It was quite a long game. In the end I captured his queen with a fork and that was the end of my brother. On the chessboard, I mean.'

Forty minutes later Inspector Grime was in the small library at 14 North Road, Highgate, home of the mathematically minded Montague Lewis, elder son of Mrs Maud Lewis of Fakenham. The conversation followed remarkably similar lines to the earlier interview in Noel Road. Montague Lewis, like his brother, thought his mother had gone slightly mad. He could see no reason why she wanted to marry this wretched bounty hunter. The Inspector noted that they used exactly the same word to describe Roderick Gill. It could have been collusion before he arrived, or it could have been the way they had talked about him for months.

'How would you describe your feelings towards Roderick Gill, sir? Dislike? Loathing? Hatred?'

'I don't think I'd go as far as that, Inspector,' said Montague Lewis. 'I despised him, that's the best way to put it, I think. I despised him for creeping round my mother the way he did; I despised him for insisting they get married as soon as possible.'

'Did you kill him?'

'I did not.'

'Could you tell me your whereabouts on the afternoon and evening of January the twenty-second?'

'Of course, Inspector. I spent the afternoon at the

London Library. The staff there will confirm that. I spent the evening at my brother's house.'

'And what were you doing at your brother's house, sir?'

'Sorry, we were playing chess, Inspector.'

'Who won?'

Montague Lewis looked cross all of a sudden.

'I did,' he said. 'I usually beat William at chess.'

Inspector Grime didn't know what to make of it. For now he said his farewells. He wondered how much collusion there had been between the brothers, all wasted by a silly mistake, not agreeing a common line on the chess match. Both of them must have been lying, he thought. Heaven knew what they had been doing that evening but one lie was not enough to convict anybody of murder.

As he made his way towards his train, Inspector Grime cursed London with greater fury than ever. Somewhere on his travels around the capital, probably in this very station where he now stood, swearing loudly, his pocket had been picked. The Artful Dodger had his wallet and the train ticket to take him home to Fakenham.

The old men of the Jesus Hospital were in rebellious mood in the days after they talked about their lives and their jobs to Inspector Fletcher and his Sergeant. Even a new dress for the barmaid in the Rose and Crown had been unable to staunch their anger. The fit among them agreed to hold a meeting in the pub at seven o'clock in the evening. Three of their number were confined to bed on doctor's orders. Two could see little point in wasting their money in the pub. Another two were teetotal and had never tasted a drop of alcohol in their lives. Their companions never tired of pointing out that this appeared to have done little to improve their health. On the contrary, these two were considered by the experts as the most likely to join the late Abel Meredith in the Jesus Hospital section of the graveyard. The rest made their way at varying speeds to the Rose and Crown where they were welcomed by the barmaid, pulling pints as fast as she could go.

They discussed various means of registering their protest. Hunger strikes were considered until those still in possession of normal appetites realized they might be having pap forced down their throats for days, if not weeks. Eventually they decided on a march, in their best coats and hats, to the Maidenhead police station to hand in a letter of protest about their treatment. Even then, taking note of the frail condition of many of the silkmen, they resolved to travel most of the way by bus.

Lord Francis Powerscourt was staring moodily at the fire in his drawing room on a Sunday afternoon in Markham Square.

'I wish I'd never taken on this case, Lucy. I've never had one that spanned three different locations before. I can't seem to get a grip on it.'

'Do you still think they're all the work of one man? And that the mysterious mark on the dead men's chests is the key to the whole thing?'

'Yo ho ho and a bottle of rum, fifteen men on a dead man's chest,' said Powerscourt with a smile. 'I do think that, Lucy, yes I do. I doubt if any of the three Inspectors believe me any more on that point, mind you. Inspector Grime is very excited about the sons of that Mrs Lewis who Roderick Gill was going to marry. It seems they both lied to him about where they were on the evening before the murder. He's writing to all the theatrical costumiers he can find to see if any of them hired a big black beard at that time.'

'Are you going to come to Fakenham with me tonight? I've got to be teaching again in the morning. This is my last week.'

'I shall come up with you this evening, Lucy, and return the next day or so. Your work up there in the school has been invaluable, my love. Who knows, maybe you'll turn up even more information. I'm going to have a meeting with all three of those policemen here early next week. The Three Inspectors, it could be a pub, Lucy; coppers lurking everywhere to make sure there's no drunk and disorderly behaviour.'

'You're not going to forget next weekend, are you, Francis?'

'What's happening next weekend?'

Lady Lucy pointed at an embossed card on the mantel-piece above the fire. 'Why, it's Queen Charlotte's Ball, Francis. I'm so looking forward to it.'

Powerscourt made a face.

'Now, now, Francis, you always complain about these things but you enjoy them once you're actually there. I remember distinctly you saying in the taxi home the last time we went to a ball, years ago now it must have been, how much you enjoyed the dancing.'

Inspector Miles Devereux thought there was only about a week to go before the results of the Silkworkers' vote were declared. The only thread he could see between all three murders was this strange election in the Silkworkers Company. As he made his way towards the Secretary's quarters on the first floor, he wondered if he would find a lawyer there, as he had on his previous visit.

Anthony Buckeridge of Buckeridge, Johnston and Forsyte was indeed in attendance. He managed what might have been a smile at the policeman as he walked in.

'Good morning, Colonel, Mr Buckeridge,' said Devereux. 'I was wondering if the votes were all in, if the result is known now, that sort of thing.'

'Things are proceeding according to plan,' said Colonel Horrocks, the Secretary to the Silkworkers. 'There are still six working days to go before the ballot is closed.'

'But do you know how many votes have been cast and in which direction?' Devereux persisted.

'We do,' the Colonel replied. Devereux thought the men were much more relaxed than they had been on the previous occasion.

'I think you'll find that your interest in this matter will close very soon,' said Buckeridge.

'I don't follow you,' said the Inspector. 'You sound to me as if you know who has won already.'

The two men looked at each other. 'It would be premature to declare that we already know the result,' said Horrocks. 'However, we would be failing in our duty to act as responsible citizens and give all the assistance we ought to the officers of the law if we did not say that it is virtually certain that Sir Peregrine's proposals, for which he has campaigned so hard and so long, are likely to prevail.'

Damn it, Devereux said to himself, the old bastard has won. The only question is, did he commit murder to get his way? 'You're sure of that, Colonel? Sir Peregrine is going to get the eighty per cent he needs?'

Horrocks placed a set of papers in front of him. 'There is still a possibility that the no campaigners could triumph.

But the voting patterns that we have seen from everywhere else would have to go into reverse on the final votes. It looks most improbable.'

Inspector Devereux was thinking of the bribes offered to the old men of the Jesus Hospital. 'Have the old men of Marlow voted yet? Have their papers come in?'

'I'm afraid that the details of individual votes are not available to the public, even to the police,' said Buckeridge, reverting to pompous mode. 'Nobody asks you, Inspector, how you voted in the last general election and I hope that in this country they never will.'

'I see,' said Devereux. 'It's just that it would save a certain amount of police work and public expense if we knew if the almshouse had voted or not. You would be doing us a favour.'

Once more the two men exchanged glances. 'Oh, very well, I don't think it can do any harm. The silkmen of the Jesus Hospital have cast their votes. It may interest you to know that they voted in favour of Sir Peregrine's proposals. Every single one of them. As yet we have no figures from Allison's School.'

Bribery, Inspector Devereux said to himself, bribery could get you everywhere. He realized suddenly that it was too soon to ask the other important question. If the votes of Allison's School were also in favour, had those two institutions pushed Sir Peregrine's proposals over the eighty per cent threshold? In other words, if they had voted the other way, would the plans have been defeated?

Powerscourt found Inspector Grime active on many fronts. He was still pursuing Blackbeard round the railway stations of northern Norfolk. He had launched additional inquiries, asking if either of the two Lewis brothers, age, height, general characteristics, had been seen in the Fakenham area at the time of the murder. He was awaiting replies from theatrical costumiers in Norwich, Cambridge and London as to whether they, or anybody else they knew, had hired out a black beard at any time in the last six weeks, and if they had a name and address for the customer. He had been in touch with the high commissioners and senior representatives of Australia, Canada, New Zealand and South Africa, asking them to send him a man of their country who could speak with a pronounced accent. The man would need to be in his thirties. Inspector Grime explained that they would be assisting in a murder inquiry at a leading public school in Norfolk. Two of their number, the New Zealander and the Canadian, had already reported for duty. Grime arranged for them to be wearing postal uniform and to walk up the same corridor as the murderer on the day of Roderick Gill's death. They were to bump into David Lewis and apologize as their predecessor had done before, using exactly the same words. After that they were to bump into other boys and apologize in case that brought forgotten memories to the surface. Neither of the two colonials on duty so far had brought any response from the pupils. The Inspector had taken the New Zealander and the Canadian into his OTC office afterwards to talk to David Lewis but the boy had been definite that theirs was not the accent he had heard on the fateful day.

An elderly Sergeant came into the Inspector's office. 'Forgive the interruption, Lord Powerscourt, Inspector, this has just come back from Melton Constable. A local man who has been away for a fortnight visiting his sick mother says he saw Sir Peregrine's car, or one very like it, in Melton Constable outside Sir Peregrine's house on

255

the day of the murder, sir. He says he's seen the car before with Sir Peregrine in it, so he's fairly sure he's right.'

'God in heaven, Sergeant, this is dramatic news.' Inspector Grime was pounding his fist into his other hand as he strode up and down his office. 'This could change everything. Tell them over in Melton Constable to bring the man in and hold him till I get over there. Do you want to come with me, Powerscourt?'

'Thank you for the invitation, Inspector. I think I am going to call on somebody else. If you think about Sir Peregrine's activities, a lot of them have been concerned with the votes in this affair of the Silkworkers. I wonder if he popped up here to have a word with the bursar. And I doubt very much if he would have seen the bursar on his own. I'm going to call on the headmaster, Inspector, if that's all right with you.'

'That's fine by me,' Inspector Grime replied. 'I say, Powerscourt, do you think Sir Peregrine brought that girl with him, Francesca, wasn't that her name? I've never met a masseuse before.'

The headmaster was in a meeting about the cost of repairing the cricket pavilion when Powerscourt arrived.

'My dear Lord Powerscourt,' he said, ushering him to a chair, 'how good to see you again. And let me say how valuable the work your wife is doing for us is. The boys are progressing in leaps and bounds. We shall be devastated when she has to leave on Friday. Now then, does your presence among us signal that the crime has been solved, that we can offer our congratulations?'

'Would that it did,' said Powerscourt ruefully. 'Believe me, Headmaster, I wish we could have found the answer by now. Life must have been very difficult for you all up here with this hanging over the school.'

'I rather think we have got used to it, though getting used to murder can't be good for any of us. Is there anything particular you wish to speak to me about today?'

'There is, Headmaster. It is rather a delicate matter, I fear. One of the important players throughout this inquiry, in all three locations, is Sir Peregrine Fishborne, Prime Warden of the Silkworkers Company.'

'We know Sir Peregrine here. He is on the board of governors. I think we could say we know him quite well.'

'Indeed so,' said Powerscourt. 'It has just been reported that Sir Peregrine's car, with, presumably, Sir Peregrine himself inside it, was seen at Melton Constable on the day of the murder.'

'What of it? The man has a house there, for God's sake.'

Powerscourt thought that the headmaster's usual urbanity might be giving way to tetchiness.

'A great deal of Sir Peregrine's time in those days was spent in canvassing for votes for his reorganization of the Silkworkers.'

'So?' said the headmaster.

'I just wondered if he came here to talk to you and your bursar about how you were going to cast your votes, that's all.'

There was a pause. The headmaster fiddled with his gold pen. Powerscourt looked out of the window, the playing fields stretching far into the distance, a phalanx of tennis courts closer to home. A buzzard was hovering over the playing fields, searching for prey.

'I can't lie to you, Lord Powerscourt. Yes, he did come here. Yes, we met with the bursar. I would have told you before but he asked us to keep it a secret, Sir Peregrine, I mean. I don't think it has anything to do with the murder, I'm absolutely sure of it. Let me tell you what the meeting was about.' The headmaster put down his pen. He brushed his hair back over his forehead.

'What you have to understand, Lord Powerscourt, is how much these schools cost to run. There are the staff to pay. The fabric of the buildings is in almost permanent need of repair. The grounds are another drain on resources. Just before you came in I was given an estimate for repairing the cricket pavilion that, at present, we cannot afford. There was a suggestion that the Silkworkers Company might like to re-endow the school to enable us to carry out repairs and to embark on a new building programme which would open a new chapter in the long history of Allison's.'

'Might I ask who made this suggestion, Headmaster?'

'You may. It was my suggestion.'

'And was the quid pro quo that the votes of the school would go Sir Peregrine's way?' Don't mention blackmail, Powerscourt said to himself, don't even think about it.

'It was,' said the headmaster.

'Sir Peregrine must have been pretty desperate for votes if he was prepared to spend all that money on rebuilding and so on. I suppose it wasn't his money, mind you, not his personal fortune. And what did your bursar think of all this?'

'That was part of the problem, Lord Powerscourt. That was why Sir Peregrine came all this way to see us. Roderick was opposed to the scheme, to all of it. He said that if the Silkworkers Company effectively dissolved itself, there would be no guarantees of any Silkworker money coming to the school ever again. He was unmoved by all the talk of new buildings. He used to describe them as being promises made with fool's gold. We should stay the way we are, he would say. It's much safer. Sir Peregrine tried his hardest but Roderick wouldn't budge. Sir Peregrine got rather cross, actually.'

'I'm afraid I have to ask you this, Headmaster. Which way did you and your colleagues vote in the end?'

'We voted for Sir Peregrine, all of us, all of our votes. I sent the paperwork off this morning. We voted for change, a change that will do much to restore the fortunes of the school.'

'So you voted against the advice of your bursar, Headmaster?'

'It was the first time I had ever disagreed with Roderick on a question of finance, Lord Powerscourt.'

'But Mr Gill, the bursar, was actually dead by the time the rest of you cast your votes, was he not? He couldn't have a vote where he'd gone, could he?'

'That is correct.'

'Thank you for telling me all of this,' said Powerscourt. 'Is there anything you would wish to add?'

'I don't think so. I will give the matter some thought. I wouldn't like to feel you had not been kept in the picture a second time. I can find you at the Crown, I presume?'

As Powerscourt strolled back towards the police station he felt that another name had been added to the list of suspects. There were the two sons of Mrs Maud Lewis, lying about their chess game. There was Sir Peregrine Fishborne and his chauffeur who drove him everywhere, there might be shadowy members of the British or German secret service, there might be unknown opponents of Sir Peregrine's schemes, and now another late entrant in the Fakenham stakes, the headmaster himself, keen to remove the last opposition to his grand schemes of expansion and glory.

15

Inspector Grime was astonished when Powerscourt told him the details of his conversation with the headmaster of Allison's School.

'I thought I was doing well, my lord, with this new witness confirming that Sir Peregrine's great black car has been seen in Melton Constable. But the headmaster, that's virtually blackmail. You build me a new school, I'll give you my votes. Pity the bursar didn't stay around to hold his ground.'

'I think we have to include him on the list of suspects, the headmaster I mean, but I don't think he'd have carried out the murder. He had far too much to lose. Did you say you were coming to London tomorrow, Inspector, for further conversations with the Lewis sons? I could give you a lift, if you like. I hope to have a summit meeting with all three of you Inspectors at my house late tomorrow afternoon if that sounds convenient for you?'

'Thank you, my lord. That would be most helpful. I have been wondering about whether to interview the Lewis boys in a police station or in their homes. Would you have any advice?'

'Talk to them in their homes, that would be my suggestion. That way, they won't suspect anything. Call them into the police station and they'll think they're on their way to the Old Bailey.'

'I'll give that further thought, if I may, my lord. Tomorrow morning we have the last of the colonial gentlemen coming in to the school to see if anybody remembers their accents.'

The amount of noise generated by some hundred and fifty boys trying to make their way up or down the principal corridor of Allison's School was deafening. Inspector Grime, sheltering in a side corridor, thought a hundred and fifty policemen, even wearing their best boots, would not be able to equal it. Odd snatches of homework questions floated past him on the morning rush.

'Who was Prime Minister after Peel, for heaven's sake?'

'*Alea jacta est*. What's the *alea*? Do you know?'

'Who was Elizabeth the First's spymaster?'

Then he saw him. Today's colonial was a burly man with black curly hair who looked as though he might be a prop forward in rugby. He elbowed his way past a number of boys, including David Lewis, saying sorry as he went. For the boys, bumps and collisions en route to the first lessons of the day were nothing new. It was just part of the daily routine. They had been warned beforehand that another stranger would be in their midst this morning. One or two of the naughtier ones made it their business to crash into their visitor, but his bulk ensured that they came off worst.

'Well,' said Inspector Grime to David Lewis when the visitor had passed through the corridor into the

Inspector's temporary quarters in the Officers' Training Corps room, 'what did you think?'

'I'll tell you that in a moment, sir. Could the gentleman read something for me so I could be sure?'

'Of course,' said Inspector Grime. The visitor began to read in a clear voice from the current school prospectus. When he reached the section about the high quality of the meals provided, David Lewis held up his hand.

'That's enough, sir,' he said. 'What a pack of lies about the school food, mind you.'

'Do you recognize the accent, David?'

'I do, sir. That is the accent of the man who bumped into me as I was walking along the corridor on the day of the murder, sir.'

'Do you know where the accent comes from, David?' asked Inspector Grime.

'Well, sir, we know from the previous riders and runners that he wasn't Canadian or Australian or New Zealander. So he must have been South African. Is that right?' He addressed his question to the visitor.

'Yes, I am South African,' said the prop forward.

'God help us all,' said Inspector Grime, and he wished for a moment that he had paid more attention to the maps on the walls of the geography classroom where he had interviewed the boys. Even those bloody globes would have helped, he said to himself, if I'd taken any notice of them. Where exactly was South Africa? And how far away was it?

Lady Lucy thought you would not have known that the three men all belonged to the same profession. A two-day exercise for the OTC involving all the boys in Allison's meant there was a break from Sherlock Holmes in French in Fakenham. She had wondered in her time up there if Holmes would have liked Fakenham. On the whole, she thought, probably not. Irregular supplies of cocaine would not be acceptable. She welcomed the Inspectors to the Powerscourt family home in Markham Square. The twins, Christopher and Juliet, peeped down at the visitors from the landing on the top floor. They had been mightily impressed to learn that there would be no fewer than three police Inspectors in their house. Their behaviour had taken a brief turn for the better but, as Powerscourt remarked to Lady Lucy, he did not expect it to last.

Inspector Fletcher looked out of place. He was wearing his best uniform, buttons polished, boots gleaming, but he still hopped uncertainly from place to place until Powerscourt suggested he sit down on the sofa next to the fire. Inspector Miles Devereux looked relaxed in an old tweed suit and had parked himself in an armchair by the bookcase. Inspector Grime was wearing an old and rather shiny suit but he looked at home in the first-floor drawing room with the paintings of Lady Lucy's ancestors on the walls. Powerscourt himself was leaning on the mantelpiece, with a drawing of the strange mark on the dead men's chests in his hand.

'Thank you all so much for coming,' he began. 'I thought it would be helpful if we all heard how everybody else is coming along. Perhaps you'd like to start, Inspector Fletcher?'

Fletcher had made notes in the train on what he was going to say. 'I think it fair to say, my lord, that the picture at the Jesus Hospital is far from clear. We know that somebody broke in during the night, or hid himself away the evening before, and murdered Abel Meredith. Or he was killed by one of the other inmates. One of the old men heard noises but did not see anything. So far we have not received any reports of strangers being seen in the immediate vicinity of the hospital. We know that Warden Monk was operating a racket of some sort with the old people's wills, but that does not seem to be an adequate motive for murder.' Inspector Fletcher paused and looked round at his little audience. Lady Lucy gave him a smile of encouragement.

'We know from you, my lord, that the dead man, Abel Meredith, may have been used as a courier by the secret service to travel to Germany to bring back information, and our own inquiries in Marlow tell of at least one trip to Hamburg which may have involved him acting as a messenger. I have to say that we have no idea if he was taking messages or instructions from England to Germany or vice versa or both. It is possible that his intelligence activities led to his death, though I cannot see how at the moment. We know, largely thanks to the activities of Johnny Fitzgerald, that there has been a lot of anxiety about the changes proposed to the constitution of the Silkworkers by Sir Peregrine Fishborne. We know that Sir Peregrine was staying at the hotel on the island in the Thames, the Elysian Fields, on the night before the murder. We know that he was accompanied by a masseuse called Frankie who was a regular visitor to his suite at the hotel.'

There was a snort or two from the other Inspectors at this moment. Lady Lucy looked demurely ahead.

'We do not know much for certain about what time he left in the morning, though the girl says he was usually away by seven o'clock. There is always the possibility that some internal feud between Meredith and another resident of the hospital led to his death, though I have to tell you that there are doubts about whether any of the old boys would have the strength to work the knife with sufficient force to cause death in the manner inflicted. And I would remind you that the knife used in the Jesus Hospital may also have foreign connections. One of the doctors thought the wound was caused by a weapon called a kris, commonly found in places like Ceylon and Thailand. Inquiries continue into the past life of Abel Meredith and the other residents. My colleague and I have had one interview with Sir Peregrine in his office. It was the only time in my professional career, my lord, where the suspect has ordered tea for himself but not for his visitors.'

Inspector Miles Devereux was next into the lists. He spoke as if he were describing an afternoon in the hunting field.

'I would have to agree with my colleague that the picture concerning the murder in the Silkworkers Hall is not clear either. One of the interesting things about the victim is that there is a long spell missing from his career as described in *Who's Who*. The subjects, you will recall, make out their own entries. Fifteen years of his early adult life are simply not accounted for, and so far all attempts to fill in the blanks have failed. I, too, have had dealings with Sir Peregrine's people. Twice now I have been to interview the Silkworkers Secretary about the ballot in the livery company. On both occasions the Secretary was accompanied by a rather disagreeable lawyer who tried to make my life as difficult as possible. They have told me one important fact. Sir Peregrine is going to win the ballot. Not all the votes have arrived yet, but most of them have and they believe that he already has enough support to carry the day by the required majority. His principal opponent in the company was, of course, the dead man. Sir Rufus was bitterly opposed to the plans. So, in two of the locations we have opposition to Sir Peregrine which might have been enough to derail his scheme. I expect we will hear the same story from Norfolk.'

Inspector Grime had been making notes as his colleagues spoke. Now he shut his notebook and put it in his breast pocket. 'Well, gentlemen,' he began, 'in some ways we have more information about the killer in Allison's School than we do for the other places. But I should tell you first of all that Allison's School, with its twelve votes, also voted in favour of Sir Peregrine's plan. We know that the murderer came to Fakenham the evening before on the train. He could have come from more or less anywhere. We do not know where he spent the night. One suggestion is that he passed it in one of the outbuildings of the school, such as the cricket pavilion, which were not usually locked. We know that he entered the school disguised as a postman early the following morning. I think he must have brought the postman's uniform with him. The murderer entered the main school corridor at a time when it was full of boys and bumped into some of them. One of those boys claims he spoke with a South African accent. After the murder, our suspect disappears. And there may have been a personal link with our friend Sir Peregrine as well. His car was seen at his house at Melton Constable on the day before the murder. He attended a meeting with the headmaster and the bursar at the school the evening before the killing. Once again, the subject was the Silkworkers' vote. The bursar was opposed to any changes to the statutes. Once he was out of the way, the headmaster voted for the changes in exchange for some new buildings. I am grateful to you, Lord Powerscourt, for that last piece of information.' Inspector Grime paused for a moment and wiped his glasses. His Sergeant always maintained that the more suspects he had in his sights, the more cheerful he became.

'Up in Norfolk, my lord, we have not one suspect, Sir Peregrine, but two, or possibly three. Let me explain. We have heard of the masseuse called Frankie plying her trade at the Elysian Fields. We have no masseuses but we have a victim with two mistresses. One, Mrs Hilda Mitchell, is married to a stonemason who went away before the murder and has not been seen since. He is definitely a suspect. His wife, like the other lady, was collected up by the deceased, Roderick Gill, at church functions. He was known in cynical circles as the Groper in the Vestry. It seems you weren't safe at innocuous events like the Harvest Festival and the Christmas carol service. Mistress number two, Maud Lewis, is a widow with considerable property left by her late husband. She was going to marry Gill and leave her money to him. She has two sons, both in their twenties, both of whom regard Gill as a bounty hunter of the worst sort. When I interviewed the two of them separately at their homes recently their alibis stood up well until it came to a chess game they had supposedly played the evening before the murder. Both of them have different accounts of who won. To sum up, you could say we have a surfeit of suspects, the cuckolded stonemason, Sir Peregrine, one of the two sons of Mrs Lewis. I don't know which one I'd back in the Fakenham murder stakes myself.'

'Well done, Inspector, well done everyone,' said Powerscourt with a smile. 'Can I ask you all the same question? Do you think Sir Peregrine is the murderer? Inspector Fletcher?'

'My answer has to be that I just don't know, my lord. There are perfectly innocent explanations for his appearances at the various murder sites. Well, not entirely innocent if you include Frankie the masseuse at the hotel. He had to be at the Silkworkers Hall for the dinner – he is Prime Warden of the Company, after all. And it sounds as though he had to go to Norfolk to try to persuade the bursar of Allison's School to change his mind. He can't have been sure about the votes, Sir Peregrine. It sounds as if his proposal could have gone either way. But there's nothing to link him directly with the actual murders.'

'Everything you say is true,' said Miles Devereux, still with his languid air, 'except there is one fact we should never forget about Sir Peregrine Fishborne. He stands to make an enormous amount of money if his scheme is approved. He will become one of the richest men in England. People say he has been stacking the livery company with his supporters for years. He may have spent a decade dreaming up this plan. If it succeeds, he need never work again. He could employ a whole netball team of masseuses if he wanted.

'Sir Peregrine was certainly in the vicinity of the places where all three murders were committed,' Inspector Devereux went on, 'and I think we should remember one crucial piece of information about him. The old men at the Jesus Hospital were going to vote against the scheme. Now, with Meredith out of the way and the bribes in place, they voted in favour. Sir Rufus Walcott at the Silkworkers Hall was the leader of the opposition to his plans. Heaven knows how many of Sir Rufus's supporters have been bribed or changed their minds; we simply don't know, but he was not around to vote against. And at the school, more bribery. I suggest that without the murders Sir Peregrine might well have lost the vote. With the murders, he has won the day.'

'Well put, Inspector,' said Powerscourt. 'That is a compelling argument. Well done indeed.'

'I know there has been one unfortunate encounter,' Miles Devereux went on, 'the meeting with tea for one, but I think we should pick him up again, Sir Peregrine, I mean. Leave him to rot in the cells for a couple of hours this time. Hold up his solicitor when he arrives. I don't think he'd ever confess, Sir Peregrine, but he might incriminate himself.'

'I think we should investigate that chauffeur of his,' said Inspector Fletcher. 'The man goes everywhere with him. What happens if he has a dual role for Sir Peregrine? Driver by day, murderer by night? I'll put one of my men on it when I get back to the station.'

'Good idea,' said Powerscourt. 'There are a number of lines of inquiry still proceeding in all three cases. I do think the most important thing we have to decide this afternoon is what to do with Sir Peregrine. What about you, Inspector Grime? What are your views on the Prime Warden of the Silkworkers? Do you think we should bring him into the police station for questioning?'

'I'm honestly not sure,' said Inspector Grime. 'There is a great deal of circumstantial evidence against him – as my colleague said, the bloody man was on the scene of all three murders. But he had a reason for being there on all three occasions. We don't have anything that links him specifically to the dead. The motive, of course, is very strong, but I wonder if we shouldn't wait for something more concrete. As things stand we might just have a fruitless conversation with the lawyers, causing confusion all round.'

It was Inspector Devereux who brought up the most

difficult point. 'I recall, my lord, that you used to believe that the strange marks on the bodies were the key to the whole affair. Could I ask if you still believe that?'

'Well,' said Powerscourt, 'I realize I may be in a minority of one here, but yes, I still do believe that, however unpopular that makes me in present company. I have always thought that the murderer, undoubtedly an arrogant murderer, was sending some kind of message with those marks that only the recipients would understand. So far, of course, nobody has been able to identify the stigmata at all. But I haven't given up hope.'

'I believe I have mentioned it to you before, my lord,' Miles Devereux had raised himself from a recumbent to a sitting position, 'but do you not think it possible that Sir Peregrine, or some other possible murderer, has merely used this device to throw us off the scent?'

'I think it's possible, but not likely.'

'I think we should let Sir Peregrine stew in his own juice for a few days longer,' said Inspector Fletcher. 'Our investigations into the chauffeur may come up with something. I might speak to that masseuse Frankie again and see if she has anything more to tell us.'

'Very well,' said Powerscourt. 'I think we agree that we should leave Sir Peregrine a little longer.'

'I'm with you there. Now, if you'll excuse me, my lord,' Inspector Grime was checking the ornate clock on the mantelpiece, 'I have to go and interview one of the Lewis sons. I'm going to call unannounced at six o'clock. My Sergeant will be knocking on the door of his brother at exactly the same time so they can't concoct some more lies about chess matches.'

The meeting broke up with Inspector Devereux offering the use of a couple of cells to Inspector Grime for the incarceration of his suspects. 'We've got one cell in particular where you can listen in to what they're saying to each other from next door. The carpenters have made the wall in between completely hollow to let the sound pass through without the suspects knowing. It's a low trick but we are dealing with murder here.'

The Rolls-Royce Silver Ghost swept silently across the streets of Mayfair. Rhys, the Powerscourt chauffeur, was wearing his best blue uniform with his cap sitting plumb centre in the middle of his head. Lady Lucy was sitting in the back seat in a new dress from Worth that swept down to the floor in a single graceful line. Powerscourt was in full evening dress, even down to his medals.

'Do I have to?' he had asked, as they were preparing for the ball.

'I think you do, Francis. You always look so handsome in evening dress and you'll look even better with your medals. Besides, lots of men will be wearing their decorations on a night like this. It's what people do.'

Reluctantly Powerscourt had complied.

'I don't think we've been to the Queen Charlotte's Ball for years, Francis. I'm really looking forward to it.'

Powerscourt grunted and fiddled with his tie. He had to go through with it. He knew how much Lady Lucy loved dancing.

There was a great throng waiting outside the main entrance of Grosvenor House. Rhys had to wait five minutes before he was able to draw up at the right spot. Powerscourt and Lady Lucy stepped over the threshold into the vast reception hall which was festooned with flowers. Lady Lucy was to learn later that a special train had brought them over from Paris, roses and lilies and tulips and every sort of ornamental flower that money could buy. There was a reception line snaking out across the hall and into the drawing room on the left. One room beyond that on the left-hand side of the house was the ballroom. Strains of a polka drifted out into the great hall. Supper was laid out in the salon to their right. The room was awash with colour, the blues and reds and the white sashes of the military, the dashing colours of the ladies' dresses, the tiaras and necklaces that sparkled with diamonds and rubies. Powerscourt was surprised to see so many military men there. He wondered fancifully if they had returned to the Duchess of Richmond's ball on the eve of Waterloo.

> There was a sound of revelry by night,
> And Belgium's capital had gathered then
> Her beauty and her chivalry, and bright
> The lamps shone o'er fair women and brave men.
> A thousand hearts beat happily; and when
> Music arose with its voluptuous swell,
> Soft eyes looked love to eyes which spake again,
> And all went merry as a marriage bell;
> But hush! hark! a deep sound strikes like a rising knell!

They made their way slowly up the reception line. There was a sprinkling of Knights of the Bath and one or two Victoria Crosses on display. The man immediately in front of them said that the King and Queen had been expected to attend. The King always liked going to balls where he could wear his field marshal's uniform and his vast collection of decorations from all over Europe, but his doctors had recommended he go to Biarritz for his health.

'Not much chance of the Prince of Wales showing up,' the man said gloomily. 'Probably spending a happy evening at home sticking more stamps into his albums.'

The Duke of Westminster told Lady Lucy that he had first met her at a dance in Scotland some years ago when she had been accompanied by her grandfather. The Duchess told Powerscourt that she had followed one of his recent cases, the death of a wine merchant, with great interest. Then they were through. Powerscourt thought that it had been rather like going through some obscure border crossing in a distant part of Empire where you were never safely on the far side until the leading official had given his blessing.

Lord Rosebery, one of Powerscourt's oldest friends, former Foreign Secretary, former Prime Minister, was leaning against a pillar, glass of champagne in hand.

'Francis, Lady Lucy, how good to see you. I wondered if you would be here. May I introduce Sir Charles Holroyd, Director of the National Gallery, and Lady Holroyd?'

Polite bows were exchanged. Sir Charles was a tall, slim gentleman of about fifty years with piercing blue eyes. 'I believe you're an investigator, Lord Powerscourt. May I ask if you are investigating anything at present?'

'By all means,' said Rosebery, 'you may listen to my friend's account of his latest case, but think how dull that would be for Lady Lucy here, who has heard all about it many times by now. Will you do me the honour of this dance, Lady Lucy?'

'Of course,' said Lady Lucy and was led away to the mazurka. Great swathes of coloured sashes were passing Powerscourt and the Holroyds. It was as if an entire regiment was on the march towards the dance floor. Powerscourt explained the nature of his latest case. The

Holroyds had heard of Sir Peregrine Fishborne and obviously thought little of him. But it was on the mention of the strange marks on the bodies that the National Gallery director grew really interested.

'Nobody can tell you what they are?' he said. 'Who have you been trying?'

'Medical men, policemen; all kinds of inquiries have been made but nobody has got a clue.'

'How very odd,' said Sir Charles.

'You don't suppose it's the emblem of some secret society?' said his wife, who was known to be a tireless worker in the cause of improving native conditions in India.

'Like the Freemason's handshake, you mean?' said Powerscourt doubtfully. 'But even if it is secret, somebody must know about it. Somebody must have inside knowledge of the thing, almost certainly including the victims. Except nobody does.'

'I tell you what, Powerscourt. I'll place a bet with you. You say you have some drawings showing what these marks look like. You let me have them on Monday morning. When my experts have finished with them, if we don't have any answer, I'll drop them round to my friend and colleague Sir Frederic Kenyon at the British Museum. Between us we've got a lot of expertise at our disposal. If we can't solve the mystery, we buy you and your wife lunch at the Savoy Grill. If we can, you pay for the lunch. What do you say?'

Powerscourt laughed. 'I say thank you very much, Sir Charles. I'm delighted to accept your offer. I only wish I'd thought of it sooner. I'm obliged to you, sir, and I shall see you on Monday.'

Powerscourt escorted Lady Holroyd to the dance floor. It was filling up well now, with a beautiful couple

274

the centre of attention, dancing as if they had danced this dance for the last fifteen years, eyes only for each other, the girl sinking into her partner's arms in a sort of swoon from time to time. Against the walls the old ladies watched from their chairs and smiled and remembered being swept off their feet by some dashing young man when they were eighteen years of age. For one or two of them the memories were so vivid it might have been yesterday. Lord Rosebery was guiding Lady Lucy with great elegance combined with a sort of weary resignation, as if dancing, like so many other things in his life, had lost its appeal. Lady Lucy always said Rosebery had never been the same since his wife Hannah Rothschild died and left him so much money and so many houses.

Shortly after eleven o'clock Powerscourt was tapped lightly on the shoulder. Inspector Miles Devereux had come to the ball in fashionable clothes and with a very beautiful young woman on his arm.

'May I introduce Hermione Granville, Lord Powerscourt.' After a moment or two of pleasantries, they glided off. Powerscourt remembered that the young Inspector might not have any family money but he had family connections that branched out all the way down Park Lane. He looked as much at home here as any of the dowagers chatting merrily in the drawing room. And the girl on his arm was one of the prettiest at the ball. Powerscourt wondered how she felt about being escorted round London society by a man who spent his days in pursuit of criminals and murderers. Perhaps she rather liked it. She was chatting with one of the dowagers now. Her consort was sweeping Lady Lucy round the floor.

The supper room was packed with hungry dancers. It was, Powerscourt remarked to Lady Lucy, a tribute to the world's growing ability to overcome the limits of time and space. Two vast tureens exuded a delicate perfume from the soup they held. There was caviar from the Black Sea, piled up carelessly in great bowls as if it were rice or mashed potato. There was a flotilla of lobsters boiled alive, pink and red under the great chandeliers, delicate Dover sole lined up round the edges of a giant serving dish, great sides of beef, dripping with blood and marbled fat, each with its attendant server, knife and carving fork at the ready. There were hams from Italy and Spain, waxy dishes of veal, plump chickens from Bresse in France, ducks from Aylesbury, woodcock that might have come from the Grosvenor estates, felled by Grosvenor staff with Grosvenor guns.

M. Escoffier's assistant had excelled himself with the puddings, cakes sprinkled with almonds or chocolate or ground coffee, ice creams and sorbets of every flavour known to man, and one or two new ones, invented for the occasion, zabagliones invented in Sicily, rum babas and Mont Blancs dripping with whipped cream, delicate pastries with a hidden promise of cream or sorbet inside, a pair of trifles half the length of a cricket pitch, small delicate cakes with pineapple and pistachio and pine nuts. The room was full of people praising the food or returning for seconds or even thirds. Dancing made people hungry. The champagne still circulated round the diners, accompanied now by the offer of iced homemade lemonade fresh from the kitchens which, it was thought, might deal better with the thirst than champagne.

'Do you think the guests will eat all this lot, Lucy?' asked Powerscourt, staring at the mountains of food.

'I should think they'll have a good try,' said Lady Lucy.

'The supper room's going to be open for hours yet. Come too late and the lobsters will have all gone.'

'But what will they do with the remains?'

'I heard Sybil Grosvenor say they're going to give them to the local hospital.'

'God help them, Lucy, the patients I mean. There you are, lying on your hospital bed, wondering if your end is nigh, feeling like death warmed up, and a nice nurse comes along waving a great lobster claw at you. I think they'd probably throw up, or die on the spot.'

'Never mind,' said Lady Lucy. 'Come along now, Francis, you've only danced with me once all evening. And you look so handsome, too.'

The orchestra was playing the 'Kaiser' waltz, yet another composition from Johann Strauss, the man they called the King of the Waltz. Powerscourt was dazzled by the light pouring from the candles in the chandeliers and from the batteries of electric lights hanging on the walls. Shadows, like the people, seemed to float over the boards. He glided happily, Lucy in his arms, across the sprung floor. The musicians were growing tired, wiping the sweat from their brows on the sleeves of their evening jackets. They danced on. Powerscourt suddenly remembered the first time he had danced with his Lucy, on their honeymoon at a great ball at one of the most beautiful old houses in Savannah. He remembered thinking they were trying to put the clock back, the good ladies and gentlemen of Savannah, to the golden years before the Civil War changed America for ever. Mint juleps flowed like water, he recalled, and the steaks were the size of tennis rackets. Even then, long after it ended, the horrors of war were still present, large numbers of men still on crutches from the great battles like Gettysburg and Antietam.

They had danced at a coronation ball given for Edward VII when he announced to the world that the days of mourning that marked Victoria's last years were over, to be replaced with a reign of gaiety and, some said, dissipation. But the musicians on that occasion were not as deft with their waltzes as the Grosvenor ones, now embarking on the 'Emperor' waltz. Lady Lucy's eyes were half closed. 'I wish I could dance until the morning, Francis,' she whispered. 'Do we have to go home at all?'

'This waltz goes on for ever, my love,' said Powerscourt, whirling her round into the very centre of the dance floor. For Lady Lucy, the music, the brilliant lights, the flowers on the walls, the beautiful people streaming round her had thrown her into a sort of trance. The faint perfume from the banks of roses seemed to her to come from the gods themselves. In front and beside her, the sashes of the men looked like pennants being carried into battle, and the sparkles from the diamonds and the rubies made the ballroom look like a treasure trove waiting to be discovered. The sprung floor made her think of standing on a perfect English lawn in the spring before it was hardened by the sun. Some rough fellow had backed into one of the baskets of roses against the wall. Petals of white and pink lay abandoned on the floor like confetti after a wedding. As she looked at the other couples, Lady Lucy thought that love was everywhere. It was all around her, in the smiles of the young women clinging tightly to their partner's hand, in the arms of the young men pulling their girls ever closer, in the stolen embraces that took place from time to time at the edges of the ballroom. Lady Lucy looked across at the beautiful ladies from the Grosvenor past on the walls, who seemed to her to have left their places in their picture frames and joined the crowd on the dance floor, a countess painted underneath one of Gainsborough's trees with the leaves shimmering in some invisible breeze, a duchess in pale green with feathers in her hat and long white gloves fastened at the wrist with glittering diamonds, the current Duchess painted by Whistler years before, a glittering pageant of blues and greens by the edge of a lake. Lady Lucy had risen above the ballroom glories of Grosvenor House and was floating over Mayfair, greeting three or four other Peter Pans as they drifted across the night skies of London. She never wanted to go home. She wanted this dance, this 'Emperor' waltz, to last for ever. Her very own one, Emperor Francis, bent down every now and to give her a gentle kiss on her neck. She wanted to stay in Francis's arms until time itself ended, being whirled across the dance floor to the music of Johann Strauss.

The first hints of dawn were appearing across the gardens when the music finally stopped.

'Francis,' said Lady Lucy, coming back to earth with a smile and squeezing her husband's hand, 'that was a wonderful evening. Just wonderful. I think we'd better go home now.'

16

Powerscourt dropped his drawings in to the National Gallery at nine-thirty on the Monday morning. The director's office suggested he return at midday by which time, they told him, they would have had a preliminary search through whatever materials they thought relevant. On his return he was shown up to the director's office where a very slim young man was sitting beside the director.

'Good morning, Powerscourt,' said Sir Charles Holroyd. 'May I introduce one of my assistants, Orlando Thomas?'

As Powerscourt shook the young man's hand, Sir Charles added, 'Orlando is one of our foremost experts on paintings of battles, principally since eighteen hundred. You'd be surprised how many of those we have here. Military men often leave us their paintings in their wills. Young Orlando has been down in the basement where most of our holdings are stored.'

'When I looked at those markings, Lord Powerscourt,' Orlando Thomas began, 'I wondered if they might have come from a weapon used in some forgotten war.

I thought I'd seen something very like it before. I've brought you up a present.'

He rose from his chair and placed a small rectangular painting, about four feet by two, on an easel behind him. Powerscourt saw what looked like a mountain in the background, the upper sections rising up to a grey cliff on the right. All the action was taking place on the ground in front of it. British redcoats seemed to be conducting a desperate defence. On the attack were large numbers of black warriors who seemed to have the British surrounded. A number of redcoats were lying on the ground, the warriors stabbing them furiously. A lone British colour was still aloft inside a circle of defenders.

'Do you know the painting, Lord Powerscourt? Do you know what's going on?'

'I don't know the painting at all. I don't think I'd like to have been there. It looks as if our men are going to be wiped out.'

'I'm afraid they were,' said Orlando Thomas. 'It's one of the worst defeats suffered by the British in the whole of the nineteenth century. Painting's the work of a man called Fripp, C. E. Fripp. The battle and the picture took their name from the hill in the background, called Isandlwana, in Zululand in South Africa. The black warriors are Zulus who outnumbered our men by about ten to one.'

'If you look closely, my friend,' Sir Charles wasn't going to let all the glory accrue to his colleague, 'you will see that most of the Zulus have short stabbing spears called assegais. Their idea of battle was to close with their enemies and rip their guts out with these spears. But some of the others have a short stick with a kind of pimpled knot at the end. They are striking faster than their colleagues with the assegais because it is so much shorter. You can't see any of the marks they leave in the painting but if you look at the end of the weapon through a glass you can see all the bits sticking out rather like a thistle.'

Powerscourt took the glass and peered at the weapon. Was this the answer to the riddle of the strange marks on the victims' bodies? Did it end here? In this painting of a dreadful massacre?

'It's called a knobkerrie, Lord Powerscourt.' Orlando Thomas seemed to have picked up a lot of military information on his travels round the gallery basement. 'It was one of the Zulus' favourite weapons.'

'Why haven't we heard more about this battle? How many men were killed, do we know?'

'Over a thousand lost their lives.' Orlando was now checking his facts in a little notebook. Very few got away.

'There are a number of theories as to why we know so little about it, Lord Powerscourt,' Orlando carried on. 'The first is that it happened on the same day as Rorke's Drift where a small band of British soldiers held off repeated attacks from an enormous band of Zulus many times their number. We must have ten or twelve large paintings of Rorke's Drift compared with this one little chap of Isandlwana.'

'Didn't the General commanding the whole British force secure lots of Victoria Crosses for the Rorke's Drift people? I seem to remember being told by some veteran that they were flying around like chocolate bars at a children's party.'

'If you were of a cynical disposition, Lord Powerscourt,' Orlando Thomas was looking as innocent as the day is long at this point, 'you could say that Lord Chelmsford, officer commanding, used the success at Rorke's Drift to conceal the earlier catastrophe. And you'd have to admit that he has been more or less successful.'

'How long have you had the painting, Sir Charles?'

The director of the National Gallery smiled. 'That's a curious tale, Lord Powerscourt. It used to belong to a man called Smith Dorrien, Horace Smith Dorrien. He was actually present at the battle of Isandlwana and one of the very few to get away. The painting used to hang on the wall of his drawing room. But he found people looked at him very strangely when they asked about the battle and were told he'd survived. They all thought he must have run away, which he didn't do at all. He was only obeying orders when he left. The last straw, he told us, was when he was entertaining some French military man as part of the Entente Cordiale, and the Frenchman actually said to him, "Run away then, did you? Probably best thing you ever did. Means you're still here. Discretion better part of valour, *c'est vrai, n'est ce pas?*" So he packed the thing up and sent it off to us. He said he hoped we'd look after it. Which we have.'

'And where is this Smith Dorrien person to be found now?' asked Powerscourt. 'Is he still alive?'

'Very much so,' said Sir Charles, 'He's still with the army but he's now General Officer Commanding, Aldershot. I took the liberty of telephoning him before you came. He'll be more than happy to see you this afternoon or tomorrow morning. Then he has to go to Sandhurst for a few days.'

'Did you tell him about the marks?' Powerscourt asked.

'I just told the General there was something of a mystery involved and that he should be able to help.'

Powerscourt rose to take his leave. 'Thank you very much indeed, Sir Charles. I cannot say how grateful I am for this news. I feel a whole new shaft of light is opening up in my investigation. Quite where it's going to take me I have no idea, but without your help I couldn't even start. Thank you again.'

'I think you may have forgotten something, Powerscourt. Lunch at the Savoy when your investigations are complete? I think we should add young Orlando to our party as he's done this excellent research, don't you? They tell me the chef at the Savoy Grill has found a miraculous new source for oysters.'

Inspector Grime had brought the Lewis brothers to Inspector Devereux's police station. When questioned again about their whereabouts on the day and night of the murder in Fakenham they had stuck to their story about the chess, even though their accounts of the result were incompatible. They had tried to laugh off their inconsistencies by saying it was easy to forget such a thing. Could Inspector Grime, Montague Lewis asked, remember what he had to drink the last time he was in a pub? Well, the results of chess matches were like that for him and his brother. Inspector Grime was not impressed. The two men were now locked up in the cell where a person next door could hear every word that was said.

'This is a right pickle and no mistake,' said William, staring unhappily at the bars on the cell window.

'Do you think we should ask for a lawyer?' said Montague. 'Aren't they bound to let us have one?'

'As far as I understand it, they are and they aren't. I mean they will say yes, of course, but then the man will be sent to the wrong police station, or they won't pass the message on immediately. He'll get held up.'

'Did that horrid policeman tell you how long we're going to be kept here?'

Inspector Grime, on the other side of the wall, grimaced.

'No, he didn't,' William replied. 'He just said we could be locked up for a long time.'

'Do you think they have food in a place like this? Or do we just starve?'

'God knows. I've not been in a police cell like this before.'

'Do you think we should tell them the truth?' said Montague.

Inspector Grime turned his ear ever closer to the wall.

'Certainly not,' said William. 'Very bad idea. Think of what might happen then.'

'I think we should try the lawyer,' said Montague. 'At least we'd be doing something useful rather than fretting ourselves to death in this bloody cell. Damn the policeman! Damn his Sergeant, too!'

'Damn the whole bloody lot of them,' agreed William.

Inspector Grime decided to leave the Lewis brothers where they were for the time being. The only thing he had gleaned from his sojourn up against the wall was that both of them were lying about their activities on the night before Roderick Gill was murdered. But then, he reflected, he'd known that already.

Aldershot, Powerscourt thought, had that air of impermanence that hangs over garrison towns all over the world. Headquarters of the British Army, it could send thousands of the soldiers based there off to distant wars across the globe. Dick Turpin and Springheeled Jack may have graced the place with their exploits in the past, the

Duke of Wellington on his enormous horse and enormous statue might dominate the streets today, but a quarter of the population could disappear in a week or less.

The General Officer Commanding's office was in an imposing building facing the parade ground. Powerscourt was escorted to the office of General Horace Smith Dorrien by a handsome young Lieutenant who looked rather embarrassed as he asked him to wait. They could hear a fist banging on the table next door and a mighty roar of disapproval.

'What do you mean you missed parade because you didn't wake up in time?' Crash! Bang! 'What does the army give you a bloody servant for if not to make sure you can get out of your bloody bed when the time has come? What do you have to say for yourself, man?' Crash! Bang! 'Speak, dammit! Or have you lost your voice as well as your wits?' Crash!

'I'm afraid the General does have something of a temper on him,' whispered the young Lieutenant.

'How long do these turns go on for?' Powerscourt whispered back, remembering some veteran shouters in his time in the military, who seemed able to go on for an hour or more in a single rant.

'Hard to say, sir,' the Lieutenant murmured. 'Form book's not much use on these occasions.'

'Have you lost the power of speech? Have you? Well, you'd bloody well better find it! Fast!'

'Yes, sir. Sorry, sir.'

'Is that the best you can do, for God's sake? Look here, Captain Morris, not that you're likely to be Captain much longer if I've got anything to do with it, what do people join the army for? What do they want from the army, the King and the Prime Minister and all those damned politicians up at Westminster? I'll tell you what they want. They want us to protect the country from attack and defeat the King's enemies. Defeat means fighting, you bloody fool. Fighting, for God's sake. Why do you think the army has people doing drill until their arms nearly fall off and their feet swell up in their boots? Discipline, that's what it means. Discipline!' Crash! Bang! Crash! 'And why do we need discipline? I'll tell you why we need discipline, you pathetic wreck of a human being. With discipline, soldiers will do what they're told however dangerous it may seem. They'll die where they're sent if they have to. Those poor unfortunate soldiers under your command know that. Discipline also includes getting out of bed in the morning on the day when your men are on parade.'

Powerscourt and the Lieutenant heard a low muffled sound that might have been a man crying. Then there was an almighty crash accompanied by a tinkling sound that lasted a few seconds and then died away.

'Great God,' the Lieutenant whispered, 'there goes the telephone. That's the fourth one this year. Heaven knows how I'll get another one out of the engineers.'

Even the General seemed taken aback by his assassination of the telephone. There was a brief silence.

'For God's sake, stop blubbing, you fool! Nothing gets my goat more than people supposed to be officers of His Majesty blubbing. More lack of discipline. You're pathetic. Just get out of here, before I throw something at you. Go on, clear out.'

A red-faced Captain fled the field of battle. Powerscourt was to learn later that he had resigned his commission that very afternoon and complained to his MP about Smith Dorrien's behaviour. Nothing was heard of Morris again in the town of Aldershot.

Inside the office, the volcano seemed to have been turned off. The fires of fury had abated. The Lieutenant introduced Powerscourt and left the room. General Horace Smith Dorrien was well over six feet tall. He had a long thin face with a small well-trimmed moustache, a prominent nose and pale blue eyes. He wore his uniform with the air of a man who never takes it off.

'Powerscourt,' said General Smith Dorrien, 'Powerscourt. Boer War. Military Intelligence. You did very well, as I recall.'

'I did have that honour.'

'Now then, that man at the National Gallery, Holroyd I think he's called, tells me you're investigating a series of murders where the victims have mysterious marks left on their chests. He thinks I may be able to help. Is that right?'

Powerscourt told him the story of the three deaths in chronological order, leaving nothing out. He included all the details of Sir Peregrine Fishborne and his plans for the funds of the Silkworkers Company.

'Fishborne, did you say, Powerscourt? Man who drives around in an enormous motor car as if he's an American tycoon cruising down Wall Street?'

'That's the man.'

'Good God, we had a son of his through our hands here a couple of years back. Slippery fellow. Never paid for his round in the mess, slightly suspect when dealing at cards, if I remember correctly.'

'What became of him?' asked Powerscourt.

'We managed to pack him off to Ireland, actually. Never a popular posting, Ireland. Natives not friendly, always liable to take a pot shot at you when you're not looking. Come, we digress.'

Powerscourt recalled the ability of the best trained

military minds to concentrate totally on the matter in hand and not be diverted into other channels. He produced his drawings of the marks left on the victims' chests. Smith Dorrien stared at them carefully. Then he produced an eyeglass from the drawer in his desk and gave them some more detailed attention.

'Good God, Powerscourt, now I see why you were in the National Gallery in the first place. You'd gone to look at that painting I gave them some years back. Isandlwana. What a terrible place. What a terrible battle. It was the first one I ever saw, you know. I presume the people at the National Gallery have been suggesting that those short weapons you can see in my picture, the knobkerries, could have been the cause of these marks. Am I right?'

'Absolutely, General. I have been thinking on my way here about the various explanations a man might come up with for the presence of such marks.'

'Such as?'

'Well, the most obvious, I suppose, is that the murderer had one of these knobkerries lying about in his house or in his attic, left him by a parent or an uncle perhaps, picked up maybe at some country house auction, and he put the marks on to throw mud in our eyes, to make us wonder about the marks rather than other aspects of the killing.'

'I don't think you really believe that, Powerscourt, do you?'

'I'm not sure that I do, actually. The thing is that the doctors say the blows with the knobkerrie probably occurred before death, but they can't be sure. Doctors can be as difficult to pin down as lawyers sometimes. That says to me that the marks are central to the stories of all three killings, that there is a link binding them together.'

'We are not meant to speculate too much in the military, as you know, Powerscourt, apart from thinking about what your opponent is going to do next. But it sounds from what you say that all three victims were roughly the same age, fifties in the case of the Jesus Hospital man and the bursar, rather more in the case of Sir Rufus.'

'That is correct. I should have told you that there is a blank space of fifteen years in the early life of Sir Rufus, according to his entry in Who's Who.'

'Never trusted Who's Who myself. They never check anything, those people, just take a man's version of himself at face value. Odd. Pretty damned odd, if you ask me.'

Powerscourt was looking at an enormous calendar on the wall behind Smith Dorrien's desk. There were rings round various days in different colours, red and black and green, each one presumably denoting some military activity of fixed date. He told Lady Lucy later that day that the idea came to him as he wondered if any of the circled dates might denote a family birthday in the general's household.

'Do you know the date of the battle of Isandlwana, General?'

'I do, or rather I think I do. I'll just check it so we can be sure.' He delved into some grey military almanac on the side of his desk. 'Thought so, memory not going quite yet, thank God. The battle was fought on the twenty-second of January, eighteen seventy-nine.'

Powerscourt stared at him for a moment. His mind shot back to the painting he had seen that morning, brave redcoats hemmed in against a grey mountain, being slaughtered by the bloodthirsty Zulu warriors.

'Out with it, Powerscourt, what's so upsetting about the date, for heaven's sake?'

Powerscourt wondered if the General might be about to start shouting at him. 'It's just this, General. The first murder, the one at the Jesus Hospital, took place on the twenty-second of January this year. The chances of that being a coincidence must be about three hundred and sixty-five to one.'

'Good God, how very strange. Speculation must come more readily to a man in your profession than it does to me, Powerscourt. How do you think these events could be related?'

Powerscourt was looking at the calendar again. 'God knows,' he said. 'Maybe the murders have something to do with the battle, though it's hard to think what after thirty-one years. Tell me, General, can you remember how many are said to have died at Isandlwana?'

'That's a tricky question,' said General Horace Smith Dorrien. 'You must remember that I was ordered from the field to take a message to the rear. I wasn't there at the end. I didn't see most of the carnage. Certainly over a thousand of our men were slain by the Zulus. They didn't take any prisoners. They hardly left any wounded; they finished them off as they lay on the ground. And after that the dead were disembowelled to a man. Their clothes were stripped from their bodies. Any number between five and fifty were said to have survived but those figures are very unreliable.'

'Why is that?'

'Well, it wasn't going to be good for your career if you were a member of one of the regiments there to have survived. You could only have done that by running away earlier and faster than everybody else. Some men made a stand where they stood. They were all slaughtered. But another body of men tried to save themselves. Many were cut down by the Zulus who ran faster. But if you did escape – and I heard stories of a number of people in this position – you wouldn't be in any hurry to return to the military. You might be court-martialled and shot if you did. So a lot of people could have drifted off and never rejoined the army at all.'

'And if you did that, would you be registered as a deserter?'

'Well, you might have been, if anybody had been keen to establish a true record of what happened. I don't think anybody ever conducted a proper review of the battle-field to establish the identities of the dead. They just lifted the names out of the regimental rolls and assumed they had all been killed. Commanding Officer Chelmsford was off looking for a different bunch of Zulus when the battle happened. So he wasn't keen to establish the facts as they didn't reflect too well on him. Most of the other officers were dead and the living in other regiments who hadn't been at the battle were happy to record all those whose whereabouts they didn't know as killed in action. Much neater that way. Close the account down, that sort of thing.'

'Am I right in thinking, General, that you could have survived Isandlwana but that everybody would think you were dead?'

'You are. There is a further complication about those regimental rolls, mind you. They were completely up to date at the time they were taken, but that could have been months before the battle. In the interim people went home sick or were discharged and new recruits whose names were not on the rolls joined up in their place. There were a number of cracks where people could fall through the system.'

'And where would I find those regimental rolls now, General?'

'Hold on a moment, Powerscourt.' The General returned to his almanac which he seemed to regard as the fount of all knowledge for things military. 'Bloody politicians,' he said with feeling. Powerscourt suspected that bloody politicians could be worth a whole afternoon of ranting invective. Two telephones might end up in pieces on the floor. 'They will keep changing things for no apparent reason. Many of the men at the battle came from the Twenty-fourth Regiment of Foot, known as the Warwickshires. They're now known as the South Wales Borderers, God knows why, headquarters at Brecon, God help you. Unless you can find a copy in the War Office, though I rather doubt that. Are you going to see if any of your victims are on the last regimental rolls before the battle? Bloody thankless task, if you ask me.'

'If I think it necessary, General, then I will head off to Brecon. Do you think it possible that one or all of the victims could have been present at the battle?'

Smith Dorrien paused and stared out at his parade ground, his mind back on the battlefield in South Africa. 'Judging from what you told me about their ages, yes, it is possible.'

'I want to ask your advice on another related matter, General. Where could I lay my hands on a knobkerrie? I need to show it to one of the medical men to see if it caused the marks. That is the most important thing for me now.'

'Well, I don't have one myself,' said the General, 'but I know a man who does, or who almost certainly does. Fellow by the name of White, Colonel Somerset White. He's retired now, lives in a big house near Marlow. I'll let him know you're coming. He's got an enormous barn full of weapons he's picked up in his career, much of it in Africa. I know he's got Zulu spears and assegais so he'll almost certainly have a knobkerrie. The Colonel's been saying for years that the government should have an army museum where the public could come and see all his stuff but nothing ever happens. Bloody politicians.' The General looked up an address in a small black book on his desk.

'Here we are. The Oaks, Marlow, Buckinghamshire. I'm sure he will be able to help. Now then, I've got another useless officer coming to see me on a charge. I would ask one thing of you, Powerscourt.'

'Of course.'

'If you need further advice or assistance, then you must come back to me. I'd be delighted to help in any way I can.'

'Thank you so much, General. And thank you for all your help today.'

As Powerscourt gathered up his drawings, he felt the fires of wrath were being stoked again. Smith Dorrien was reading some report in front of him and making furious marks with a black pen. The General was turning red in the face. He began squeezing a different pen in his left hand very hard. His left foot was tapping angrily at the leg of his desk. Powerscourt managed to escape to the comparative sanctuary of the outer office.

'For what we are about to receive,' a tubby Captain was saying to the Lieutenant, 'may the Lord make us truly thankful.'

There was a bellow from the far side of the door. 'Murphy! Murphy, you bloody fool, come in here at once!'

'I think,' said the young Lieutenant, 'that what the gladiators are supposed to have said on their way into the Coliseum is more appropriate, actually: "*Ave Imperator, morituri te salutamus*. Hail, Caesar, we who are about to die salute you."'

Inspector Grime and Inspector Devereux made their way back from the listening cell to Devereux's office.

'It nearly worked, dammit,' said Inspector Grime. 'I wonder if they suspected we were listening in.'

'What do you think they were up to?' asked Inspector Devereux. 'Do you think they popped up to Fakenham and slew the bursar?'

'I don't think they went to Fakenham, but I could be wrong. It would have been incredibly risky to walk up that corridor first thing in the morning, even if you were disguised as a postman. They must have been known by sight to some of the pupils from the time they spent around the town with their mother. But I'm not ruling anything out just yet. I just need to find out what they were up to that evening.'

'Something to do with women, perhaps,' said Inspector Devereux darkly. 'Maybe they were having a joint massage with the fair Frankie. I can't see her being too particular about the clientele if the money was right.'

Inspector Grime bent down to tie up a shoelace. 'I know what I'll do,' he said. 'I'm going back to that cell right now. I've tried this before and it usually works. I should have thought of it before.'

'What are you going to tell them? That you suspect them of consorting with prostitutes? Seducing young women beneath the age of consent?'

'Worse than that, Devereux, much worse. I'll give them an hour to make up their minds. If they don't tell, their mother will be notified that they've been arrested.'

'On what grounds?'

'I shall tell them that as they are so reluctant to admit what they were doing, I shall inform their mother that they are being held under suspicion after being arrested in a brothel. A homosexual brothel. That might do the trick.'

A letter from Paris had arrived for Powerscourt. Lady Lucy watched him open it at the breakfast table.

'It's from my friend, Monsieur Olivier Brouzet,' he told her, munching absent-mindedly on a piece of toast.

> My dear Powerscourt,
>
> Please forgive me for not replying sooner to your inquiries about the unfortunate man at the Jesus Hospital. Urgent business brought me back to Paris in rather a hurry. I have spoken to the superior officer of the man you mentioned, Colonel Arbuthnot. I have also involved one of our agents in Berlin. The dead man, Meredith, made four trips to Hamburg in the last few years, always staying in the same hotel. He was a courier, taking messages from his masters in London to their people in the field. He was not a spy. The idea that the Germans might have turned him into a double agent is nonsense. The Colonel was trying to lead you up the garden path there.

In short, I doubt very much if his activities in the murky waters of intelligence had anything to do with his death.

With best wishes,

Yours sincerely,

Olivier Brouzet

Powerscourt handed the letter over. 'Another door closes, my love.'

'What do you think this bit means, Francis?' said Lady Lucy after she finished reading the letter. '"I have also involved one of our agents in Berlin." What sort of agent would know in this level of detail about somebody else's secret service?'

'There's only one thing it can mean, Lucy. The French must have an agent inside the German intelligence outfit. That's the only place they could have confirmed their information.'

'Great God,' said Lady Lucy. 'Do you think we have an agent in there in Berlin, too? Do the Germans have a spy inside our outfit?'

Powerscourt smiled. 'I wouldn't be at all surprised.'

PART FOUR

THE BAR AT SALCOMBE

17

'Lord Powerscourt, delighted to meet you.' Colonel Somerset White had a head shaped like an egg with a few wisps of hair above the ears. He had a solid moustache and a red complexion as if he spent a lot of time out of doors. The Oaks was a modern house, looking, Powerscourt thought, as if its owner might have designed it himself after a long spell in the Deep South of the United States. A great veranda ran round the building, as if the inhabitants of Buckinghamshire needed deep shade for half the year.

'How is my friend Smith Dorrien?' he inquired. 'Temper under control, eh?'

'I'm not sure I'd go that far,' said Powerscourt. 'One fellow seemed to be getting well roasted before I went in and there was another man being trussed for the oven as I left.'

'Dear me,' said Somerset White. 'He should be more careful, he really should. The pity of it is that he's done more than anybody to improve the lot of the ordinary soldier. It's the officers he has the rows with.'

'He was very helpful to me,' said Powerscourt. 'Now then, let me tell you what my business is about.' For the second time that day Powerscourt went through the catalogue of murders, the list of suspects, the marks on the bodies that he was now beginning to suspect might have been inflicted by knobkerries from the Zulu wars.

'We'd better go over to the barn, Lord Powerscourt. I think I've got a couple of them over there. I just hope we'll be able to find them.'

Powerscourt wondered what conditions in the barn-cum-museum would be like if their owner was unsure about finding his exhibits.

The first section of Somerset White's building was all order and neatness, row upon row of ancient swords and shields and lances and daggers, all neatly lined up on trestle tables down one side of the barn. Each item had a label in Somerset White's spidery hand beside it. Along the other side were pistols, guns, flintlocks, blunderbusses, Baker rifles from Wellington's time, even, to Powerscourt's great delight, an early version of Congreve's rockets from the Peninsular Wars which usually caused more panic in the companies of their owners with their boomerang flight path than they did in the ranks of their enemies. Once more the labels bore witness to hours and hours of research, with a description of the firepower of each weapon, its probable date of construction and a list of the battles where it would have been used.

In the middle of the barn there was a rough partition with a door in the centre. On the far side it was chaos. There was a great pile of stuff in the centre of the floor, weapons of every shape and size, bits of uniforms, regimental colours, small pieces of artillery, curved swords, straight swords, krises and tulwars from Ceylon and India. And that was just the surface. God only knew, Powerscourt thought, what was underneath.

'Sorry about this,' said Somerset White. 'You need to understand how I collect all this stuff. Auctions maybe in provincial towns, never in London, house sales where the owners sell everything in the place after a death, a few advertisements in the local newspapers in places near Aldershot and Camberley. Our ancestors were a pretty rapacious lot. I don't know if you were aware of that, Lord Powerscourt. Sometimes I have thought that there must have been some enormous emporium by the quayside, Harrods International perhaps, or Harrods India, where the victorious officers and men could buy up booty to take home with them. The raw material, if you like, for a triumph, not through the streets and temples of Rome, but at the Limes or the Old Rectory in Bracknell or Pangbourne. Anyway, if you keep records of annual deaths in *The Times*, you can work out that more people die in the time between October and April than they do in the rest of the year. Pretty obvious, I should say. So that's when I do my collecting, attending the auctions and so on. In the summer I sort it all out so I can display the stuff on the shelves. I've got a sword and gun man from the Wallace Collection up in London who comes down to give me a hand with the dates.' Somerset White paused and wiped his hand on the side of his trousers. Powerscourt wondered what was going to happen next.

Somerset White grabbed a couple of aprons from a hook on the back of the door. 'You'd better put this on,' he said. 'It's amazing how much dirt and dust these old weapons collect on their journeys here. Now then, this what I always say to myself on these occasions; rummage, rummage!'

With that Somerset White got down on his hands and knees and began riffling through the heap of assorted weaponry in front of him. A collection of tunics, sashes, spears and cutlasses began forming another pile to his left. Powerscourt, on the opposite side of the mound of weapons, began to do the same.

'It's amazing the stuff people hang on to,' said Somerset White, pausing briefly to examine a long straight spear with a lethal blade. 'Do you know, I've got three white shirts worn by Charles the First on the morning of his execution at the Banqueting House. I've got four pairs of boots as worn by Lord Cardigan at the charge of the Light Brigade. And I've got five nightshirts as worn by Admiral Nelson during his time with Lady Hamilton. Not exactly sure he'd have bothered with nightshirts myself.'

'Colonel,' said Powerscourt, his right arm deep into his vast heap of stuff, 'you don't, I suppose, have any idea where your knobkerries might be? I mean, can you remember when you bought them and where they might be in our treasure trove?'

'I haven't a clue,' said Somerset White cheerfully. 'If I'd known where the bloody things were, we wouldn't have had to embark on this fishing expedition, would we?'

Powerscourt reflected bitterly that it was like fishing without bait. He felt his hand touching the hilt of a sword. Pulling firmly, he drew the weapon out of the pile. It was like no sword he had ever seen. It had a short blade. One side had been cut away in sections so that a row of serrated indentations like irregular teeth ran down the blade to the tip.

'What in God's name is this contraption, Colonel?' said Powerscourt, waving the object above his head like some demented warrior from long ago.

'Do you know,' said the Colonel, sitting on the floor rather than rising to his feet, 'that's only the second one of those things I have ever seen. It's Italian, I think, and it's called a sword breaker. Your enemy's sword would be destroyed in the teeth. All you'd have to do would be to finish him off. It's as if you've disarmed your opponent, effectively.'

Powerscourt put it to one side and plunged back into the pile. He had decided to try a new policy now. Rather than going straight into the section in front of him, he decided that a better approach might be to open everything up, to scoop out great swathes of weaponry until the top resembled the surface of a volcano, a shallow shape like a dish, that enabled you to see much more of the assorted memorabilia. He was just sitting back to enjoy his new creation when there was a shout of triumph to his left.

'I told you there were a couple of the bloody things here!' said Colonel Somerset White, pulling out a pair of sticks with thistle-shaped markings on the circular ball at the top. 'This one has twice as many spikes or studs as the other one; not sure what that means for your corpses. But you'd better have these, Powerscourt; as you said, you'll need them for the medical men to pronounce one way or another.'

'Can you remember where you got them, Colonel? Something might come back to you if they're a fairly recent purchase.'

Somerset White got slowly to his feet. He looked as though he might have trouble with his back. He took off his apron very slowly.

'I think I've got it. They were at an auction in Basingstoke, property of a Major Digby Holmes, who had recently passed away. The auctioneer, I remember now, said the knobkerries had come back with the Major from the Zulu wars. Mind you, bloody auctioneers would say anything to sell you things. I've had one or two real disasters from dodgy auctioneers. Maybe Major Holmes fought in that battle with the unpronounceable name you were telling me about. Never fought in Africa myself, even managed to avoid the Boer War. Served in India all my time. Enough of this. I expect you want to be on your way with our little friends here, Lord Powerscourt. If I can help in any other way, please let me know.'

'Thank you so much, Colonel. There is one thing. Does the major leave a widow behind him, or was he single at the end?'

'There is a widow, a Mrs Laetitia Holmes, I believe. They said at the auctioneers that she'd been wanting to throw out all her husband's military stuff for years. His end was an opportunity not to be missed.'

Johnny Fitzgerald was beginning to think he had been abandoned, rather in the fashion of Robinson Crusoe. True, the rather louche purlieus of the Elysian Fields, illuminated from time to time by the visitations of Frankie the masseuse on missions of mercy to Sir Peregrine, were more than comfortable, certainly better than Crusoe's island. Johnny had noticed that Frankie carried a large handbag on occasions, filled, he presumed, with the instruments of torture of the masseuse's trade. He still spent a number of evenings in the Rose and Crown entertaining the old men of the Jesus Hospital. He had continued his policy of lunching the silkmen one at a time and it was on one of those occasions, on a bleak day in Buckinghamshire with the rain lashing against the windows of the hotel, that he hit the jackpot.

He was entertaining Freddy Butcher, Number Two, a cheerful little man who had once been a bus driver by trade and had family connections with the Silkworkers.

Number Two was clean-shaven with a great red mark down the right-hand side of his face. One section of informed opinion in the almshouse said that he had crashed his bus on the Clerkenwell Road, killing a couple of elderly passengers. The other view was that he had been caught misbehaving with the wife of a well-known criminal who had set about his face with a knuckleduster.

By this stage the first bottle of Pomerol had come to an end, and Johnny, who had only had a couple of glasses, ordered a refill. Something told Johnny that Number Two wasn't used to this amount of alcohol at lunchtime. Maybe he would let slip something important. Johnny poured him another glass. Two plates of roast duck arrived, groaning with apple sauce and roast potatoes and parsnips.

'I've felt for some time,' said Johnny, 'for all the convivial evenings in the pub, that people are holding back on me. There's something they're not telling me. If somebody would tell me, maybe the mystery would clear up and you could all be left in peace.' Johnny had been a foot soldier in the great demonstration to the Maidenhead police station, reasoning that there needed to be somebody able-bodied present in case one the old boys had a heart attack or keeled over from some other ailment. In the event the old boys had cut quite a dash, marching the last hundred yards in their best uniforms, attracting a good deal of public sympathy for their efforts and an article in the local newspaper.

It was the red wine that did for Freddy Butcher, Number Two, and possibly for Number Four, Bill Smith, known as Smithy, as well.

'You're quite right, of course,' said Number Two, holding up his glass for a refill. 'We have been holding something back.'

Johnny waited for a forkful of duck and parsnip to go down.

'There was a feud, you see. It had been going on for months.'

Johnny remained silent, hoping for more intelligence.

'Number Four and Number Twenty, the man who was killed, they had been at each other's throats, you see.'

'What was it about?'

'Well, nobody knew for certain, I think it had to do with something in Number Twenty's past. I think he may have told Smithy about whatever it was and Number Four took against Number Twenty from then on. Number Four was forever telling anybody who would listen that Number Twenty was a bloody coward.'

'When was the last time they fell out?' asked Johnny.

'The day before Number Twenty was killed actually. This time they had the row in the middle of the quadrangle, nearly coming to blows.'

'Did anybody hear what they were saying?'

'Oh yes. It seems odd now, but that Abel Meredith, Number Twenty, was shouting at Number Four, "*if* you call me a coward once more, I'm bloody well going to kill you, so I am."'

'Wrong way round,' said Johnny

'I beg your pardon?'

'Well, it wasn't Number Twenty who did the killing. He was the victim, wasn't he? What happened then?'

'What happened then?' Number Two, Freddy Butcher, who had been making his way pretty steadily down the second bottle, sounded suddenly as though the drink might have got the better of him. Then he seemed to get a second wind, cheered on by another large draught of the Pomerol. 'Well, Warden Monk came out of his office wearing his best blue cravat and told them to shut up. He said that if there were any more rows like that, he would have them thrown out of the hospital, dumped outside the front door with their belongings in a paper bag. He sounded as though he meant it, too.'

'How very interesting,' said Johnny. 'Did Warden Monk also tell you all not to mention the row to the police or anybody else?'

'How did you know that? He did, as a matter of fact. He said that anybody who told the police would also be thrown out, dumped by the front gate and the rest of it, complete with possessions in a paper bag. It's a pretty powerful threat, Johnny. Most of us don't have anywhere else to go. That's why we ended up in the Jesus Hospital in the first place.'

'And nobody knows any more about what they were arguing about?'

'No. You know what it's like in these places, Johnny. If anybody heard any more detail, every single person in the hospital would have known all about it before you could brew a cup of tea.'

When Johnny had seen his guest off the premises after a large helping of apple pie and a glass of calvados, he took a taxi to Maidenhead police station. He thought Inspector Fletcher would be keen to hear his news.

Powerscourt left the knobkerries with the doctor at the Maidenhead Hospital who had examined Abel Meredith, with a request that he telephone Powerscourt as soon as he had reached a decision. There was something at the back of his mind that he couldn't quite retrieve, something he thought was important. He tried to remember which of the three murders it concerned. Not the Jesus Hospital, he felt sure. Not the murder in the Silkworkers Hall. It had to be something to do with Roderick Gill up at Fakenham. But what? With the boys running up and down the corridor? With Blackbeard himself, sidling into Gill's office and killing him? With Gill's papers in their box files lined up by the wall? Hold on a minute. It certainly had to do with Gill and with Gill's maths teacher friend whose name he could not for the moment remember, but who had told him as they patrolled the school grounds that Gill had been frightened of something in the days before he died. The teacher had never discovered what had frightened him, but the merry widow, who regularly entertained her friend from the church, might know. Powerscourt grabbed his coat and fled into Markham Square, looking for a taxi to take him to Liverpool Street Station and north to Fakenham.

'Did you say your name was Lord Francis Powerscourt? And that you are an investigator with our policemen?' Mrs Maud Lewis was inspecting her visitor from London as if he might just have landed in an extraterrestrial vehicle on the edge of her garden.

'I did, Mrs Lewis.'

'And are you really a lord? I mean Lord isn't just some unusual Christian name your parents gave you when you were born?'

'I'm a real lord, I'm afraid, Mrs Lewis. But I'm what's called an Irish peer because the family estates were there. I don't have the right to sit in the House of Lords. Just as well probably, with all the trouble up there at the moment.'

'Goodness me, how very exciting. I don't think I've ever had a lord, even one who couldn't sit in the House of Lords, in my humble abode before! And we never had anybody like that in the house when we lived near Birmingham. I don't think they do lords in Birmingham. Lord Powerscourt, should I call you Lord Powerscourt or Powerscourt or just Lord?'

'Lord Powerscourt would be fine, Mrs Lewis. Don't worry about it.' By this stage they had reached the drawing room, with a fire and a couple of dogs asleep on the hearth. Mrs Lewis showed Powerscourt into a chair on the left of the fire.

'That's where dear Roderick used to sit, in that very chair. He never sat anywhere else. Such a lot of trouble everybody seems to be having trying to find the murderer.' Mrs Lewis produced a deep-blue handkerchief and began to dab at her eyes. Powerscourt began to fear for the worst.

'That's what I wanted to talk to you about, Mrs Lewis.'

'About the chair where dear Roderick used to sit?'

'Not exactly,' said Powerscourt. 'More about his state of mind in the weeks leading up to his death.'

'Forgive me for interrupting, Lord Powerscourt, but I normally partake of a little refreshment at this time of day. Sherry, sweet sherry, naturally. Could I interest you in a glass?'

Powerscourt wondered suddenly if she and the late Roderick Gill spent their evenings taking refreshment of one sort or another.

'That's very kind, but no thanks.'

Mrs Lewis made her way to a drinks cabinet by the window and came back clutching what looked to Powerscourt to be one of the largest sherry glasses he had ever seen. She settled back into her chair and beamed at her visitor.

'Sorry, Lord Powerscourt, for the interruption. Horace – he was my first – used to say I was incapable of sitting still for any length of time. Forgive me. You were saying about Roderick?'

'I was wondering about his state of mind in the weeks before his death, actually, Mrs Lewis. Whether he was upset or depressed, that sort of thing.'

'That's a very good question, Lord Powerscourt. He was, I'm not sure if I would call it depressed, he was certainly upset. A woman can usually tell these things, particularly with their loved ones. I thought it had some-thing to do with the church accounts actually; he'd been worried about those in the past. But it wasn't; it was something even more serious.'

'What was it, Mrs Lewis? Did he tell you?'

'Well, at first I thought it had to do with that other woman he used to consort with, the one married to the stonemason who's disappeared. I saw her looking at my Roderick in church one Sunday and it was so brazen you couldn't believe it. You could not believe it. She was practically lying down on the ground in front of him. But it wasn't that, or I don't think it was that.'

Powerscourt thought Mrs Lewis must have some pretty good intelligence sources if she knew all about the other woman. He was beginning to see what Horace, her first, meant when he said that she was incapable of sitting still. It wasn't so much a physical sitting still, but a mental one.

'So what was it, Mrs Lewis?'

There was an uncharacteristic pause. For a second Powerscourt wondered if the woman might be ill.

'I'm trying to remember exactly what Roderick said,

Lord Powerscourt. I think there was a letter that caused the problem. It came from so long ago, he told me, that he had virtually forgotten about it. And that was all he said. He tried to keep up his spirits. He talked of going away for a while but he wasn't definite. I could never work out if I was included in his plans for going away and so on and I never got an answer, not a satisfactory one anyway. It was all very strange.'

'Did he show you the letter? Were you able to read it?'

Mrs Lewis shook her head sadly. 'I never saw it.' Powerscourt wondered about the collection of files and written material all over Roderick Gill's office at the school. He hoped they had not been disturbed. He wondered about the papers that had been burnt.

'Do you keep a diary at all, Mrs Lewis? I wonder if that might jog your memory.'

'How very clever of you, Lord Powerscourt. I do have a diary. I'll just go and fetch it from the morning room.'

Powerscourt wondered how to proceed in the affair of the diary. Should he ask if he could take it away, as an important piece of evidence to be returned later? Or should he ask her to read the relevant excerpts?

They were pink, the diaries, two of them, each with a great bow on the front. 'Here we are, Lord Powerscourt. I thought you should have last year's as well. How nice to think that one's diaries are an important piece of evidence in a murder trial! You will let me have them back, won't you? Will you change your mind about that glass of sweet sherry now?'

Powerscourt arranged with the headmaster's office that he could come to inspect Gill's papers first thing the following morning. He arranged to see Inspector Grime in an hour. He proposed to fill in the time with an inspection of the pink diaries and their contents in his hotel room. He decided his life would not be the poorer if he omitted all the entries before the entry of Roderick Gill.

Sunday, 19th September. Went to church this morning. First visit to morning service in Fakenham! Was welcomed afterwards by a most charming man called Roderick Gill, bursar at the school. He was most attentive! Also met vicar, nondescript little man who preached a dreary sermon, and his mouse of a wife.

Sunday, 3rd October, church, matins. Talked again to Mr Gill, who is taking a most Christian interest in my settling down in Fakenham. Has asked me to meet him in the church for another chat on Wednesday afternoon. He has to do things with the money for the vicar. How kind, seeing he does all that already for the school!

Powerscourt wondered what the secret of Roderick Gill's success with women might be. He suspected he flattered them; he made them feel better about themselves so they thought better of him.

Wednesday, 6th October, called on Mr Gill at the church. He bought me tea and a slice of cake at that café by the square! My new neighbours invited me to tea. Quite pleasant, except we finished at six-thirty and not a drop of drink was offered! Maybe they're too poor. House poky, so-called dining room so small you couldn't swing a cat. I should be ashamed to be offering hospitality in such a place. Maybe they're too poor for that, too! Oh dear, hope I'm not being uncharitable to my new neighbours!

Sunday, 24th October, met that nice Mr Gill at church again. Vicar's wife has excelled herself this morning, wearing a pink creation with frills that was most unsuitable. Have asked Mr Gill to dinner a week on Thursday! He says he'll come!

He's off the mark now, Powerscourt said to himself. I wonder if she knows what she's getting herself into. He skimmed some more dates and found an interesting entry.

Thursday, 4th November, Roderick came to supper! He brought me a bottle of wine and some perfume from Norwich! I hope he thinks I made it worth his while!!!

There were a number of further entries about his visits with triple exclamation marks. And in one case, four.

Saturday, 25th December, 1909, what joy! What happiness! That this should happen to me! Dear Roderick has asked me to be his wife! After the midnight carol service yesterday! And I have said Yes!!!!

Powerscourt flicked on to the days before Gill's death in the diary.

Friday, 14th Jan. Dear Roderick has not been himself today. He has been withdrawn and rather uncommunicative. Naturally I tried my best to fill in the gaps in the conversation. He will not say what the trouble is. I hope he is not sickening for something.

Sunday, 16th Jan. For the third day running, dear Roderick has not been himself. He tried to laugh everything off but I can tell he is not himself. The boys came and were most unpleasant about Roderick, saying he was just a bounty hunter and other horrid things. I shall leave my money where I want to. They've got plenty of it anyway.

Monday, 17th Jan. Boys gone back to London. Dear Roderick still not well. Jumpy, staring out into the garden as if he thinks there's somebody hiding there. He's talking of going away for a while and it's not clear whether I am to be a member of the party or not. Don't suppose he's been canoodling with that stonemason woman again. Or has he? Said hello to the vicar in the town this morning. He's got a hole in his trousers, right where his knees are meant to be.

Friday, 21st January. At last managed to get sense out of Roderick. It's something from his past, he says, something so long ago that he can hardly remember it. He won't tell me what it is. But he says there might be some unpleasantness, that's why he might go away on his own. He doesn't want me to be upset, he says. I think that's very gallant of him, to save me from unpleasantness. Had another cup of tea with the neighbours this afternoon. They can't even serve proper tea over there, their stuff tasted like warmed-up soap.

Some unpleasantness, Powerscourt thought, I'll say there was some unpleasantness, enough unpleasantness to kill him. Not long to go now.

Sunday, 23rd January. To church for matins. Roderick very jumpy on the way, peering round corners as if he were some sort of hunting dog. Vicar preached a sermon on the text of it being easier for a camel to pass through the eye of a needle than for a rich man to enter the king-dom of God. And he said the definition of rich was any person who had so much money they didn't have to work! Idlers and wastrels, he called them, the wretched vicar. That means me! Denounced from the pulpit of my own church to which I give generously out of the kindness of my heart! I shall write a stiff letter to the vicar when I have calmed down.

Monday, 24th January. Poor Roderick still very worried. The headmaster's wife, he says, has called him in to see if she can offer any help. That means the headmaster must be worried about him too. He says the wife is a very supe-rior sort of person. Well, she may seem like that to him, Vera Staunton. The vicar's wife told me of the times when her family hadn't two pennies to rub together and lived in a one-bedroom railwayman's cottage by the side of the train tracks.

Roderick has to go to a late meeting at the school. He is very worried when he comes back, not so much about himself now but about the future of the school. He says there is a plot by some wicked man from London to take away all the money that comes from the Silkworkers. Roderick is in despair.

25th Jan. Some wicked person has killed Roderick at the school this morning. I cannot write any more.

Powerscourt put down the second volume of diaries, most of whose pages were still awaiting further entries. He felt he would be intruding on private grief if he read any more. Just before he went to meet Inspector Grime he asked the hotel reception if they could put him through to his home telephone number. Rhys, the Powerscourt butler-cum-chauffeur, greeted him in his normal telephone manner, that of one welcoming a colleague back from the dead, and put Lady Lucy on the line.

'Francis,' she said, 'how good to talk to you. Listen, there's been a development. The doctor in Maidenhead called about half an hour ago. He's going to get a second opinion tomorrow, but he's virtually certain that a knob-kerrie, similar to the ones you sent him, was the weapon used to make those marks on the dead men's chests.'

'Did he really, Lucy? Yo ho ho and a bottle of rum. That's very interesting, very interesting indeed.'

18

Powerscourt felt cheerful as he sat down for an early evening drink with Inspector Grime. He hadn't found the actual murder weapon but he knew now what had caused the marks on the dead men's chests. He could suggest that there might be some sort of a link between a battle in Africa thirty-one years previously and the deaths of three people in southern England, all members of the Silkworkers Company. He would have been the first to admit that he had, at present, no clue at all about the possible links between the battle, the knobkerrie and the livery company but there were many avenues left to explore.

Inspector Grime listened to Powerscourt's ideas with little enthusiasm. He had never put much faith in the theory that the marks were the key to the investigation. Now he felt they were all going to be dragged down an alleyway with little hope of success. He didn't mention any of his misgivings but Powerscourt felt them emerging from Grime's body language and general suspicions like a hand signal.

'I suppose we'll have to go through all those papers again, the ones in his room and his office.' Grime sounded even more melancholy than usual this evening.

'I'm afraid so,' said Powerscourt. 'I could do it on my own, you know, if you've got better things to do.'

'That's kind of you, my lord, but the fact is that the investigation up here is stalled. We still haven't found the stonemason, but he's due to report back to York Minster any day now.'

'What happened about the two Lewis boys and their lies about the chess match?'

This time, Powerscourt thought, Inspector Grime definitely cheered up. 'It was only when I threatened to tell their mother what was going on that I got the truth out of them. I said I was going to inform Mrs Lewis that her sons had been arrested in a homosexual brothel. You remember Sir Peregrine and his masseuse in that hotel on the Thames? Well, it seems that something similar was going on in Montague Lewis's house. They were entertaining a former servant girl of theirs called Nellie and her friend Matilda.They eventually admitted that the discussions were horizontal rather than vertical, if you follow me. The girls confirmed it, though they refused to say if they had been paid, which makes me suspect that they probably were. But we couldn't hold on to them for that. The stonemason is hot favourite now, unless, of course, we find out more about this letter that frightened the bursar.'

That night Powerscourt had a strange dream. He was alone, in military uniform, in some vast open country he did not recognize. From his time with Military Intelligence he thought it might be South Africa. About a hundred yards behind him were a group of about fifty native warriors. They were dressed for combat wearing only their loincloths. Their bodies glistened in the sunlight. In one hand, he saw, they were carrying assegais, the deadly spears they used to stab their opponents to death at close quarters. They were singing some terrible battle cry which throbbed and throbbed until you felt it might be about to enter your bloodstream. Every now and then one of the warriors would raise his spear and utter some blood-curdling war cry. Powerscourt's companions seemed to have melted away. Perhaps they had already been picked off and were lying on the harsh ground waiting for the vultures. He had two loaded pistols in his jacket, each with six rounds. He doubted if he would be able to find the time to reload once they were upon him. He would be surrounded, stabbed to death in a country a long way from home. When the war cries sounded again, closer this time, much closer, he woke up.

'Why don't I take his sitting room, if you take the office?' Inspector Grime seemed to be in a better frame of mind the next morning, as they walked up the drive to the school.

'Thank you,' said Powerscourt. 'I looked at those files in his rooms before, but I might have missed something.' They were entering the long corridor where the fake postman had made his way to Roderick Gill's small office. Powerscourt was struck again by the noise. Lady Lucy had mentioned it, too – at its worst, she said, when all the pupils were moving about at the same time. Twenty or thirty, she said, would be bearable but once it gets over a hundred it's impossible.

The headmaster strode into view and the boys parted in front of him like the waters of the Red Sea. 'Morning, gentlemen. I wish you luck in your quest today.' Quest, thought Powerscourt. Bloody man must think we're looking for the Holy Grail.

Powerscourt thought that he might have got the better of the deal. He remembered Gill's room as being packed with papers, including that strange gap where a couple of decades seemed to have disappeared. But when he applied himself to Gill's office after the head porter opened it up for him, he realized that things were no better here. You can't jump about on these sorts of paper chases, he told himself. Even if some stupendous attack of boredom threatens to overwhelm you, you cannot abandon your post and jump ahead to another file further down the line. One step at a time. The files here were in the bottom two shelves of Gill's desk, and lined up on a long shelf behind it. He began with the bottom drawer. It was concerned entirely with catering. Powerscourt remembered that one of the junior boys had complained about the bursar because he had sacked the previous head cook who at least provided edible food, unlike his successor who was, the boy claimed, trying to poison them all.

When he got the hang of Gill's filing system, Powerscourt could see why the man before had been fired. Considerable sums of money had been abstracted from the funds provided for the catering and had simply disappeared. It was impossible to prove theft from the figures, but the assumption was unavoidable. The next drawer dealt with the ancillary staff: the porters, the cleaners, the ladies who made the beds, the gardeners. Powerscourt thought these people were all paid less than they would be in London. The first four files on the wall all dealt with the teaching staff: recruitment, contracts and pensions, records of their annual meetings with the headmaster. One whole file dealt with the recruitment of the present head. Reading through the way the process was handled, Powerscourt thought that the Silkworkers held the key to the appointment. Then there were six files dealing with the pupils, going back for a period of some ten years. Powerscourt read them all in case there was some earlier pupil who had left with a grudge against Roderick Gill, but he found nothing. After a break outside the main entrance, he returned to the remaining paperwork, all of which had to do with the Silkworkers. Gill had done a great deal of research, with accounts of the foundation and constitution of the livery company. He remembered that Gill was working on a report about the proposed changes to the constitution of the Silkworkers Company but he did not find it here. The last contained detailed accounts of the working of the sick bay and the appointment of matrons. He realized that he had thought he would find a letter somewhere in here. Grime, virtually certain they were on a wild goose chase, had probably found nothing in Gill's room either or he would have come to tell him. Damn, damn, damn, Powerscourt thought to himself, where is the bloody letter? Where has it gone? Was there a letter at all? There had to be a letter, he told himself, or else a visit to make Gill so jumpy. And of those two, a letter was much more likely. He made his way round to the headmaster's office to see if there was a copy of Gill's report on the possible changes to the constitution of the Silkworkers Company. There was not.

Inspector Grime, he discovered, had also found

nothing. The investigation appeared to be stuck. Just before eleven o'clock, he made his way round to Mrs Lewis's house to return the diaries. He had already copied the relevant passages into his notebook. He found her dressed from head to toe in black.

'Good day to you, Lord Powerscourt,' she trilled. 'How can I be of assistance to you this morning?'

'I've brought your diaries back,' said Powerscourt. As a final throw of the dice he asked one last question, with little hope of success. 'Did Mr Gill leave any papers here, a file or anything like that?'

She looked at him slowly. Then she turned pale. 'My goodness, my mind must be going. I've completely forgotten about it. Yes, he did. Roderick said that if anything happened to him I was to give it to the headmaster. Aren't I hopeless, forgetting all about it!'

'Could I have a look? I could drop it down to the head's office when I've seen what it says.'

Powerscourt was ushered into the chair by the fire once more. Mrs Lewis returned with a slim grey folder. Powerscourt looked through the pages. This was the long-awaited report on the Silkworkers, eight pages of closely reasoned argument, all of it hostile to the proposed changes. Hiding behind the last page was a letter, two pages long. There was no address and no date at the top.

Dear Gill,

I expect you and your colleagues have forgotten all about me. It is now thirty-one years since your treachery, since you left me at the mercy of those black bastards underneath that mountain nobody could pronounce and still fewer people could spell. Do you remember? Before the battle we swore that, whatever happened, we would look after each other, that we would be all for one and one for all. Some bloody chance. You left me to die and ran away to save your own skins. It would have been perfectly possible to have carried me from the field or put me on the back of a horse. But no. You hadn't time for that. I was stabbed twice more after you ran away, once right next to the eye. Only three other dead men falling on top of me saved me from the disembowelling and the vultures. The Zulus couldn't have believed anybody was left alive at the bottom of the heap.

Damn you to hell for what you did. I have thought of those events every day for the last thirty-one years. You may see me again or you may not. But you can be sure of one thing. Vengeance is mine, saith the Lord. I will repay.

There was no name and no signature at the bottom. A letter possibly sent by a madman who didn't say where he was or who he was, but who promised revenge. Powerscourt was inclined to believe every word of it. He took his leave of Mrs Lewis. The file containing the report he delivered to the headmaster's office. The letter he put in his pocket.

'You'll find the Records Office in that big building on the right, looking rather like a barn, sir.' Johnny Fitzgerald had been dispatched to Brecon to inspect the records of the 1st and 24th Regiments of Foot, part of which had been involved in the disaster at Isandlwana. Here, Powerscourt had assured him, he should find records of those who lived and those who perished in the battle. He wasn't surprised to see the building, set apart from the main block, like an isolation ward in a fever hospital. Real military men, and Johnny knew all about them from his years in the Intelligence Corps with Powerscourt in India and South Africa, didn't think records had anything to do with soldiering, not real soldiering. It was women's work, but if you had to find men to do it, then you could be sure, Johnny reminded himself, that the unfit, the undesirable and the useless would be despatched to serve there, sad Captains who couldn't control their men, Privates who couldn't shoot straight or couldn't shoot at all, Corporals with drink problems.

Johnny saw a long series of shelves laden with files. He mentioned the request he had telephoned about yesterday, that he wished to inspect the records of the men who had fought at Isandlwana from the 1st and 24th Regiment of Foot.

'Never heard of the First or the Twenty-fourth Regiment of Foot,' said the surly-looking Corporal who seemed to be the keeper of the records. 'This is the South Wales Borderers here. You've come to the wrong place.'

'No, I haven't,' said Johnny, smiling at the repulsive little man. 'It is you who are mistaken. The First and the Twenty-fourth, previously known as the Warwickshires, were amalgamated into the South Wales Borderers by some fool in the War Office about thirty years ago. Now, I rang up yesterday to ask somebody to look out those files for me. Has that been done?'

'How many times do I have to tell you? We have no feet here, with or without numbers. Just Borderers.'

'God in heaven, man,' Johnny's voice had turned very cold, 'how many times do I have to tell you that they're the same thing?'

'What's going on here?' A fat old Captain was advancing slowly towards them, clutching a glass of what Johnny thought looked like malt whisky. 'Who's shouting at my men? Who the devil are you?'

'Fitzgerald, Captain, formerly Major Fitzgerald, over ten years in the Intelligence Corps with Lord Francis Powerscourt, India and South Africa.'

'I see.' The little man sounded slightly more amenable now. 'And what is your business here, may I ask?'

'You may indeed, Captain,' Johnny had decided to call the man Captain as often as he could. 'I am here on the suggestion of General Smith Dorrien, GOC Aldershot, to look at the records showing who died and who survived at the battle of Isandlwana. The General, as you know, was one of the few who lived to tell the tale. I telephoned yesterday, asking for the relevant papers to be prepared. Your colleague the Corporal seems not to have understood that, Captain.'

'Wait here, please.' The Captain drained his glass and took the Corporal off into the interior of the building. Johnny thought you could go mad in one of these places, surrounded by the records of the fallen like some Egyptian priest with the Book of the Dead. He wondered how different the atmosphere would be in the Officers' Mess. He checked that he had his pocket book with him containing all the names Powerscourt thought he might find in one list or the other. After fifteen minutes the fat Captain reappeared.

'My apologies, Mr Fitzgerald, there has been a misunderstanding here. We have the documents for you in the study area. Please come this way.'

The Corporal resumed his position at the entrance. Johnny and the Captain made their way down passages lined with innumerable files to a small area with a couple of tables and a fire. Johnny wondered if this was where the Captain came to enjoy his solitary whiskies. He sat down.

'This thicker folder obviously lists those who perished at the battle,' the Captain said. 'The smaller one lists the names of the survivors. I should tell you that the lists were compiled based on the last rolls taken before the battle. The authorities knew who had survived. They could only assume that all the rest were dead.'

'And how long before the battle were the last rolls compiled?'

The Captain looked down at a black notebook. 'The rolls were taken in October, four months before Isandlwana.'

'Thank you very much,' said Johnny. 'So the records might not have been totally accurate about the people who died. In the gap between the rolls in October and the battle in January, some men may have left; others, not recorded here, may have arrived. Is that right?'

The Captain smiled. 'You are absolutely correct. That is the position.'

The names had been handwritten. They were in alphabetical order. As he worked his way down the pages – Abbot, Acland, Addison F., Addison W. – Johnny thought that most of these men would still be alive if they hadn't signed up for the colours. He wondered about their parents and how they would have been told the news. He expected these sad battle rolls would have been published in the relevant local newspapers, worthy of notice today, forgotten tomorrow. He knew there was an impressive memorial to the men who had fought in the Zulu wars in Brecon Cathedral, close to the barracks. Davis, Davidson, Davies, Denby, the names rolled on. When he reached the halfway point at the letter L, he paused and took a stroll up the corridor. Outside he could hear the regimental band playing 'Men of Harlech' rather badly. The Captain waved at him, glass in hand, from a distant piece of shelving. When he reached the end, he checked through the names he had brought with him and the notes he had made to make sure he had not missed anything or made a mistake. He flipped through the list of survivors, and wrote them all down on Powerscourt's instructions. The Captain reappeared.

'Tell me, Captain, if you can, allowing for the time difference between October and January, how accurate do you think these records are?'

The Captain stared at Johnny as if nobody had ever asked him such a question before. 'I don't think anybody knows the answer to that. Nobody ever went round the battlefield writing down the names of the dead. Basically, as I understand it, though the military historians would never admit it, if you didn't show up at the regimental HQ after the battle, they would list you as dead.'

'And which do you think is more likely, Captain? That you could have been listed as dead when you were alive or listed as alive when you were dead?'

The Captain took a large draught from his glass. 'I could be wrong, but I think it is more likely that you could be listed as dead when you were actually live.'

'Thank you,' said Johnny, grateful that the man had in the end proved a helpful guide. 'Let me buy you a drink,

Captain. But could you lend me a phone first of all? I have to relay an urgent message to London.'

The three police Inspectors gathered in Powerscourt's house in Markham Square at half six in the evening. Inspector Grime had read the letter on the way down to London and returned it to Powerscourt without saying a word. The other two Inspectors went through it as soon as they sat down.

'Well, gentlemen, you could say that this letter, taken with what we now know of the knobkerries from the medical men, shows a possibility at least that this battle long ago may hold the key to the murders. What do you think, gentlemen?'

'I have never held out much hope for the marks on the victims' chests being a significant clue, I'm afraid,' said Inspector Grime, confirming himself in the role Powerscourt thought he would play at this and any other significant meetings, that of Doubting Thomas.

'I'm not sure at all,' said Inspector Fletcher after a long pause. 'There could be a connection with this battle but it's all so long ago and so far away. It's very distant, if you know what I mean, while the murders are right in front of us.'

Two against so far, Powerscourt said to himself.

'I'm not sure I agree with my two colleagues on this one.' Inspector Devereux was stretched out on a sofa, smoking a small cigar. 'I think this new information about the weapons and the letter is very promising. I could well feel like murdering some people who abandoned me to the mercy of the Zulus on the battlefield, if that's what happened. But the letter does make a chap rather cross. There's no date on it. There's no address. There's no signature. I presume there's no sign of the envelope. Did the author send it from England or from somewhere else? And if it is somewhere, where? And going back to the knobkerries and the battle, why should somebody wait all those years to take revenge? Surely if you thought about the betrayal every day, as he said he did, you wouldn't wait this long, would you?'

'I think,' said Powerscourt, 'that there are a number of things we could do. We should return to the people who knew the victims, even Mrs Lewis, I'm afraid, and ask if they ever mentioned the battle and what happened there. And there's one other thing we should do. Let us suppose that the man who wrote the letter lives somewhere else, say in South Africa. How does he know how to find the addresses of his victims? In fact all he would need to do would be to ask the Silkworkers if they knew the addresses for Meredith, Walcott and Gill, but how would he know about the Silkworkers?'

'I can look after that, my lord,' said Miles Devereux. 'I was involved in a case last year that involved a number of private detective agencies. They owe me a favour. I'm sure I'll be able to find out if anybody has been inquiring about our three friends.'

There was an apologetic cough and Rhys the butler sidled into the room. 'I'm terribly sorry to interrupt, my lord, but Johnny Fitzgerald is on the telephone for you, my lord. He says it's very urgent.'

Powerscourt made his apologies to the Inspectors and hurried down a flight of stairs to the room he called his study.

'Johnny?' he said. 'How is Wales?'

'Wales is wet, Francis, and the beer is very poor. I've

had better in the Hindu Kush. Do you have a piece of paper handy? You may want to write this bit down. It's quite surprising, really.'

'I'm ready, Johnny.'

'Fine. Here goes. Two of the names you gave me, two of the victims in fact, are mentioned in the records – Private Abel Meredith and Corporal Roderick Gill, both of the Twenty-fourth Foot.'

'I presume they're in the survivors' column, Johnny?'

'There you'd be wrong, Francis. According to the records of the South Wales Borderers into whom the Twenty-fourth Foot were drafted some years ago, Private Meredith and Corporal Gill were indeed at the happy event. But they're not listed in the survivors' column, Francis. They may have been murdered earlier this year, but according to the army rolls they've both been dead for thirty-one years.'

19

There was general astonishment when Powerscourt brought the news back to his drawing room. Even Inspector Grime, for so long the Doubting Thomas of the party, seemed interested.

'How very strange,' he said

'It can't be true, surely,' was the verdict of Inspector Fletcher.

'How very odd,' said Inspector Devereux. 'Do you think it's true, my lord, or do you think there has been some mistake?'

'If by do I think it's true you mean do I think their names are recorded in the death column over there in Brecon, then, yes, I do believe that it is true. Johnny Fitzgerald wouldn't have got that wrong. But do I think those two, Meredith and Gill, were killed in the battle, then no, I don't. I think there has been some mix-up. I shall have to go to Aldershot tomorrow to speak to General Smith Dorrien again. From what he's told me already I think Meredith and Gill may have run away, possibly with Sir Rufus, and did not want to rejoin what was left, if anything, of their units in case they were tried for cowardice. Johnny has a list of the survivors. Not very many of those, I'm afraid.' Powerscourt paused and looked round at his three policemen. He had always suspected that there could be problems with such a number. He had always operated with one single senior police officer in the past.

'Look here, gentlemen,' he began, 'I think we should be honest with each other. I hold no official position with any of your forces. I was asked to look into the murders by Sir Peregrine Fishborne in his role as Prime Warden of the Silkworkers. I do not know how many of you would wish to concentrate on these recent leads about the knobkerries and the battle long ago. I suspect that most of you don't. That is a matter for you to decide. You are, after all, responsible to your own superior officers and your own Chief Constables. You are not responsible to me in any way at all. So, I put it to you, if you wish to ignore these latest developments and concentrate on your own inquiries, then feel free to do so. I could not stand in your way. I shall always be grateful for the help you have given me so far.'

There was a pause in the drawing room in Markham Square. Inspector Grime was the first to speak.

'That's very generous of you, Lord Powerscourt, very generous indeed. I shall certainly ask the relevant people in Fakenham, the headmaster, Mrs Lewis and the teacher Peabody if they remembered the late bursar mentioning the battle of which you speak. And I shall let you know the results of those conversations as soon as possible. But on the question of the Zulu weapons and the battle I can't pronounce or spell, I'm afraid I don't agree with you at all. I still think those marks were a red herring, designed to confuse us. I suspect the killer picked the thing up at an auction or in a junk shop and thought the marks would put us off the scent, which, to a certain extent, they have. My main suspect remains the vanishing stonemason whose wife had an affair with Roderick Gill in the past. I'm sure he's our man. And now, if you'll forgive me, I should like to return to Fakenham before I miss the last train. I've got work to do.'

Rhys the butler appeared as if by magic to escort the policeman from Norfolk out of the house. Powerscourt wondered if he had been listening by the door.

Inspector Fletcher was next to speak.

'I'm afraid I have to tell you, Lord Powerscourt, that I agree with my colleague from Norfolk. And now that we have the news about one of the men in the almshouse having a feud with the late Abel Meredith, I am confident that we will be able to clear up the murder in the Jesus Hospital very soon. I shall, of course, like my colleague, ask around for you about whether Meredith ever mentioned the battle to which you seem to attach so much importance to any of his fellow silkmen. I have to say I think it is highly unlikely, but we will do it nonetheless. I should tell you that Sir Peregrine's chauffeur has a satisfactory alibi for the night of the murder at the Jesus Hospital. He is now in the clear. It has been a pleasure working with you, Lord Powerscourt. I am sure we shall keep in touch about these murders. For the moment, I too feel that I should return to my duties from which perhaps I have been detained too long.'

Rhys materialized once again to show Inspector Fletcher to the door.

'Mysterious chap, that butler of yours,' said Inspector Devereux. 'How does he know when to come into the room like that? Do you think he listens at the door?'

'I've never asked him,' said Powerscourt. 'Let me just say that Rhys, like God, moves in mysterious ways.'

'Lord Powerscourt, it seems to be my turn now. I think our two colleagues were premature in their early departures like players sent off at a football match. But let me put two questions to you, if I may. The first is this, and relates to why I think the others were wrong to reject the South African link altogether. There has to be a common link between the three murders, the marks on the dead men's chests. It is surely impossible for three different killers to be carrying around with them one of these knobkerries and use them on their victims. It can't be possible, surely. Do you agree?'

'I do, of course I do. In some way I've always felt that the most significant thing about the murders was these strange marks. They're the killer's calling card, left on the body as you might leave your card in somebody's house. It's the murderer's signature tune, if I may mix my metaphors. And your second question, Inspector?'

'My second question,' the Inspector had risen from his chair and was leaning on the mantelpiece, 'has to do with the time gap. Our friend, if it is the murderer, says in his letter to Gill that he has thought about revenge every day, every day for the last thirty-one years. Why has he left it so long?'

'I've thought a lot about that,' said Powerscourt, 'and I can only give you some guesses. I intend to raise it with Sir Horace in the morning. Maybe the boy at Allison's School in Fakenham was right and he comes from South Africa – let us leave to one side for the moment the age difference between a fake postman in his thirties I think it was, and the man who wrote the letter. For whatever reason, our mystery man seems to have stayed in South

Africa after the battle; he didn't return to Britain. Now why the gap? I can only speculate. Perhaps he thought he would never find any of them again. Then, maybe, he heard quite by chance of one of these men, probably Sir Rufus. Maybe he was married with a family and didn't want to put his life in danger with a mission of multiple murder. All kinds of things, personal as well as professional, might have held him up before he could embark on his long-delayed mission of revenge and retribution.' Powerscourt paused and stared into the fire. 'It's all so flimsy you could blow it away.'

'Maybe we'll never know,' said Miles Devereux. 'First thing in the morning, my lord, I'm going to talk to these private detectives. I'm with you on this case until the end.'

The only sound to be heard in the outer office of Sir Horace Smith Dorrien, General Officer Commanding at Aldershot, was a fly failing to escape through a closed window. Powerscourt raised an eyebrow at the young Lieutenant who acted as the guardian of the office.

'Very quiet today,' the young man said with a smile. 'Much better than yesterday, thank God.'

'Was yesterday bad? Very bad?'

'Well, not to put too fine a point on it, we had a Krakatoa of a dressing-down yesterday afternoon. Did you know, Lord Powerscourt, people claimed to have heard the real Krakatoa erupting three thousand miles away, the sound travelling almost to Western Australia? It's a bit like that here. The General got so worked up that the doctor man had to come round and speak to him. As far as I know the doctor told the General that if he went in for many more of these shouting matches he'd drop down dead in the middle of one of them.'

'How come the doctor came round? You didn't by any chance call him in, did you?'

'I didn't hear that question, Lord Powerscourt. I've gone deaf all of a sudden.'

The General was writing busily at his desk when Powerscourt was ushered in. 'Paperwork, my friend, always paperwork. Not surprising Napoleon had a mobile desk he carried round with him in his coach. Paperwork will be the death of us all. What news from the Zulu wars?'

Powerscourt told him about the records of two of the murder victims registered among the dead at Isandlwana, Meredith and Gill. The General laughed. 'I'm not surprised at that. Those records aren't like the ones you'd find in hospitals or places like that. I shouldn't pay any attention, if I were you. Just ignore it.'

'But how do you think they ended up in the records as dead?'

'Some army clerk may have made a mistake, that's the most likely explanation. Have you met many army clerks in your time? You have? Then you'll know as well as I do that they're not likely to end up as scholars or exhibitioners at Balliol.'

'Is there any other explanation, General?'

'Well, there is the one I think I mentioned the other day, that they ran away and then deserted. They could have thought that if they went back to their units they would be accused of cowardice. So they never presented themselves. Mind you, the units they might have presented themselves to had all disappeared anyway, slain by the Zulus in the battle. At that point the army would have assumed that they were among the dead. Some of them, I gather, were unrecognizable.'

'Good God,' said Powerscourt. 'Could I ask you about one other matter, which I don't think has to do with the military, but where I'd welcome your thoughts as a man of wide experience. I'd like you to read this letter, which was sent to one of the victims shortly before his death.'

Powerscourt handed over the letter found in Roderick Gill's memorandum to the headmaster of Allison's School. General Smith Dorrien put on a pair of tortoise-shell spectacles and read it quickly. 'Not sure I'd like to get one of these myself. So what's your question?'

'It's this, General. If you've thought of revenge every day of your life for thirty-one years, why wait this long? Why not try to take your vengeance earlier?'

The General looked out at his parade ground for a moment. A small detachment of horse in bright red jackets was cantering across the square. 'I don't think that's very difficult, actually. We don't know where the chap who wrote the letter is, do we? I mean, he could have stayed in South Africa or he could have gone to Australia or Canada, virtually anywhere. Expensive business travelling back from there to here and maybe he had to support a family before he could go away on revenge business. And then there's the question of priorities, Powerscourt. Your man may have had his work cut out earning a living, supporting a wife and children perhaps. People are always saying that one day they'll climb Mont Blanc or write a novel or see the pyramids, that sort of thing. I've talked for years about going to Rome. I don't know if I'll ever get round to it now.'

Powerscourt had a sudden vision of the General ranting at Michelangelo's paintings on the roof of the Sistine Chapel.

'Maybe the man's circumstances changed so he could fulfil his dream,' the General went on. 'Whatever prevented him taking his revenge before has suddenly gone away. It could have been like that, don't you think?

'I think that's very possible, General. I'm grateful to you.'

'There's just one other thing, Powerscourt. Didn't you say there is a livery company mixed up in all this? Mercers? Grocers? Some outfit like that?'

'There certainly is, General,' said Powerscourt. 'It is the Silkworkers actually. Victim number one was resident in one of their almshouses. Victim number two was the bursar in a school run by the Silkworkers. Victim number three was killed after a very grand dinner in the Silkworkers Hall. Why do you ask?'

'Do you suppose the Silkworkers might be another clue in some way? Some of those livery companies do have links with the military, with particular regiments, you know. I'm not quite sure what they do, but it wouldn't be difficult to ask them. They might even have some records. And I suspect they're more accurate than the ones you found at Brecon.'

'I didn't know that, about their links with the army, General. I'm much obliged to you.'

'Much more interesting detecting things,' said the General cheerfully, 'than ploughing through the army's paperwork. The bureaucrats seem to think they can win battles on a sheet of paper, or rather sheets of paper. You must come and see me again with your latest news, Powerscourt. It cheers me up.'

Powerscourt thanked him and moved off. As he left

the room he could see a very nervous young Captain being ushered in. It looked as though he was expecting a telling-off. A couple of minutes later Powerscourt realized that the medical man had given his advice in vain. The rant had reached the far edge of the parade ground. You could probably hear it, he said to himself sadly, on the far side of the town, but he doubted it would reach Krakatoa.

Number Four, Smithy, the man who had a row with Number Twenty the day before he was murdered, was sitting on a hard chair in a room inside the Maidenhead police station. It was now three o'clock in the afternoon. The police came for him just after breakfast. He had now been under questioning for five hours. He had managed to bring with him, as friend and representative on earth, Edward Cooper, Number Seven. Number Seven, a small wiry man with a crafty look about him, had spent eighteen months some years before as a guest of Her Majesty in Wormwood Scrubs, and was widely believed in the hospital to be an expert in the workings of the law. It wasn't his fault, Cooper said, if some fool of a footman had left the door of the big house open. Nor, he would continue, was it his fault that the valuable silver was on display in the first room he had come to. He was, his apologia went on, just picking up some of the pieces and admiring them when the butler reappeared with two sturdy footmen. The fact that two of the pieces had found their way into his pockets was pure coincidence. His friend Smithy, Number Four, acting on Number Seven's counsel, had proved totally and absolutely obdurate in his dealings with Inspector Fletcher and Sergeant Donaldson, saying nothing at all wherever possible. 'You've got a right to silence, my friend. Once you tell the police anything at all you'll find they twist it round to what they want you to say. That's why it's good to have me here as another witness.'

'I repeat my question, gentlemen,' said Inspector Fletcher. 'Will you please tell us about the row you had with Abel Meredith, commonly known as Number Twenty, the day before he died.'

'Like I said, mate,' said Number Seven, 'you don't have to say nothing.'

The Inspector was furious. His Sergeant had asked all the old men if any of them had heard the row between Number Four and Number Twenty. It had happened, after all, right in the middle of the quad. Anybody who opened a window would have heard every word. But nobody had heard a thing. Even Freddy Butcher, Number Two, who had told Johnny about the feud over lunch at the Elysian Fields, had now recanted and claimed he had so much drink poured down him that he could not remember anything. The Jesus Hospital had closed ranks on one of its own.

The Inspector and the Sergeant were taking a break, leaving the silkmen under the watchful eye of a young constable.

'What are we going to do, Inspector?' asked the Sergeant. 'We can't go on like this.'

'We can't charge Number Four with anything,' said Inspector Fletcher after a long pause. 'He hasn't said anything at all, apart from his bloody name and number.'

'What about locking them up indefinitely? Refusing to assist the police with their inquiries. A couple of days in the cells might make them more amenable.'

'Maidenhead Inspector locks up old men from alms- house?' said Fletcher. 'Days in solitary for not talking to the police? You know how angry the Chief Constable gets if there's bad publicity in the newspapers. Bad for his chances of a knighthood probably.'

'Well,' said the Sergeant, 'maybe we can't lock them up overnight. But we could give them three or four hours in solitary. Each man to his own cell. Then we could question them again about seven. They might be more prepared to talk then. Particularly if we don't tell them we're going to let them go later on.'

'Do it,' said Inspector Fletcher. 'I don't like it, mind you. I wonder what Powerscourt would recommend in these situations, if he wasn't preoccupied with his ludicrous theories.'

Powerscourt had written to the Secretary of the Silkworkers and had received a speedy and courteous reply indicating that if he cared to call the following morning at eleven o'clock they would hope to have the relevant information for him. So, as Inspector Devereux was talking to the superior private detectives on the fringes of the West End, Powerscourt was in the Court Room of the Silkworkers, drinking coffee with the Secretary under the watchful eye of a couple of Lawrences and a Zoffany.

'You are, I think, temporarily one of us,' said the Secretary, 'by which I mean that we employed you to look into these distasteful murders and your task is not yet accomplished.'

Powerscourt was sure the Secretary, Colonel Horrocks, with his enormous moustache and efficient manner, was an effective administrator. Maybe he had been an adjutant in the army. So many former officers found employment in gentlemen's clubs or livery companies or major charities. A former colleague of his, once the fiercest and most bloodthirsty man he had ever seen on a battlefield, was now in quieter quarters working in a charity for orphans. The Secretary had clear brown eyes and wore his regulation City suit as if he was still in uniform.

'How right you are,' said Powerscourt with a smile. 'I'm sorry it has taken so long. I have a new ally in my military researches, at least, General Smith Dorrien, General Officer Commanding at Aldershot.'

'Horace. How is dear Horace? I served under him for three years some time ago.'

Powerscourt wasn't sure 'dear' was the first word he would have chosen to describe the irascible officer in Aldershot.

'He is well, or he was well yesterday when I saw him. Little trouble with his temper, I'm afraid.'

'It was ever thus,' said the Secretary. 'He was always very calm in battle, oddly enough, no yelling there.'

'What news do you have from your records, Colonel? I have to confess that until the General told me, I had no idea livery companies were involved with the military.'

'Well,' said the Secretary, 'if you look at their long history, it's a fairly recent development, by which I mean the second half of the last century. With us, it started with the wounded returning from the Crimea and it continued from there. Most of our work was with help for the injured or with the widows whose husbands had been killed on active service for Queen and country. I've checked all those names you sent me and couldn't find anything at all that goes back to eighteen seventy-nine. We have records for all three of the deceased but their involvement seems to have begun at a much later date.'

'I see,' said Powerscourt, feeling as if a fish had just escaped from his clutches and was swimming happily away from his line.

'There is one thing that might interest you, my lord. I don't know if it's any use; it probably isn't. Sir Rufus was a regular visitor to South Africa in his later years. He was involved with a big investment trust that did a lot of business over there. He used to go once every couple of years. I think he went to Australia and Canada too, if that helps.'

Powerscourt wondered if the arrival of Sir Rufus and a couple of articles in the local newspaper might have reawakened a thirst for revenge.

'That is most useful, Secretary. Thank you very much. If anything else occurs to you, please get in touch.'

Lady Lucy was drinking tea when Powerscourt returned to Markham Square. She had been feeling rather left out of things since her spell as temporary French teacher at Allison's School. Her husband dropped into his chair by the fire.

'Any luck with the Silkworkers, Francis?'

'Well, yes and no,' said Powerscourt, running a hand through his hair, as he told her what the Secretary had discovered.

'I've been thinking about this case, Francis, and I've got a theory; well, theory might be too grand – a guess, a piece of speculation.'

'Fire ahead, Lucy, fire ahead. Your guesses are usually more useful than other people's theories.'

'Have you read a novel called *The Four Feathers* by a man called Mason, Francis? It came out seven or eight years ago, I think.'

Powerscourt confessed that as yet he had not read the book.

'It's about four British officers about to go off to an African war. One of them, Harry Feversham, changes his mind at the last minute and decides not to go. He's got a perfectly valid reason; he just doesn't tell anybody what it is. The other three think he's a coward and each one sends Harry a white feather as a symbol of Harry's lack of courage. His fiancée also sends him a white feather so he's now up to four. Eventually he decides he has to redeem himself, so he goes off to Africa where he performs various heroic deeds and gradually has the feathers cancelled. And in the final scene he gets the girl back, too.' Lady Lucy sat back and looked expectantly at her husband. 'Don't you see, Francis, this could be like the Four Feathers in reverse?'

Powerscourt still looked confused.

'Let's look at it this way, Francis. These four young men, well, they were young then, the three dead ones and the murderer, are all part of the same unit in South Africa. You can tell from the letter that they've had some motto going between them – the letter talked about one for all and all for one, like those dreary musketeers. But when the battle starts, everything falls apart. Three of the men don't send the fourth a white feather; they leave him for dead on the battlefield. It took Harry Feversham a long time, not thirty-one years admittedly, to work his way back. Our mystery man takes rather longer to have his revenge. Maybe he falls in love. That would stop you thinking of revenge for a while, even for a man, I would have thought. Then, years later, something, maybe one of those visits from Sir Rufus, brings him back to thoughts of revenge.'

'I say, Lucy,' said Powerscourt, 'do you suppose Sir Rufus mentioned that he belonged to the Silkworkers Company when he was in South Africa? If he did, our man from the the Revenger's Tragedy might have thought that all three men, very close at the time of the battle, belonged to it, too. His principal problem, how to find his victims, would have been solved.'

'Well, you know what you have to do, Francis.'

'Sorry, Lucy, I don't understand.'

'It's simple, surely. All you have to do is to ring the Silkworkers Secretary again and ask him to check back over the last six months to see whether anybody has been making inquiries about Sir Rufus or Abel Meredith or the dead bursar Gill. If you are really lucky, we might get a name and an address.'

'Great God, Lucy! Well done, well done indeed. I'll go and call him now. I think I'll say that the approach may have been oblique, somebody searching for a long lost friend, that sort of thing. I don't think an intelligent murderer is going to leave his real personal details behind at this stage.'

Powerscourt shot down the stairs to the little study with the telephone. 'We'll have to wait a while,' he said on his return. 'The Secretary's assistant looks after the correspondence and it may take an hour or so. The Secretary is going to check every letter to see if it mentions one or more of the three men. He's quite excited about the whole thing, Lucy, he says it's better than writing out the monthly newsletter to all Silkworkers, which was his task for the day.'

Inspector Grime was, for once, a happy man. He had sent to York to have the errant stonemason, Jude Mitchell, brought back to face justice in Fakenham. Mitchell's wife was believed to have had or be having an affair with the murdered bursar Roderick Gill. Mitchell himself had disappeared for well over a week between two different assignments working at York Minster. Now he was waiting for the Inspector in the most unpleasant cell in the building. No police cells are ever going to win prizes for design and beauty, but the one holding Jude Mitchell had only a slit for a window and a smell nobody had ever been able to identify or remove. The police officers tended to conduct their interviews in short spells before escaping for a reviving burst of fresh air.

'Now then, Mitchell, you could start by telling us where you've been all this time. Your wife has been worried sick.'

'Is that what she told you? Lying bitch! She wouldn't have minded if I'd dropped down dead or fallen off a big ladder at the minster. More time for her to misbehave herself all over the town.'

'You haven't answered my question, Mitchell. Where have you been all this time?'

'I told that rude colleague of yours up in York where I've been. He's had plenty of time now to check out what I told him. I was with my sister. She lives a mile or so to the north of York. I was with her all the time.'

'So why did your wife not tell us about your sister?'

'There's nothing that woman would like more than to have me locked up and hanged for a murder I didn't commit. Surely even you can see that, Inspector.'

'I don't want any lip from you or you'll never get out of here at all. Even if you were up there near York you could still have given yourself a little holiday and come back down here to murder Roderick Gill.'

'How many times do I have to tell you, I didn't do it.'

'You can stay here as long as you like. I just hope you'll see sense and tell us how you did it next time I come back for a little friendly conversation.' Inspector Grime stormed out of the cell.

Rhys the butler picked up the phone before Powerscourt could reach it. Powerscourt thought Rhys liked saying, 'The Powerscourt Residence,' into the machine.

'Powerscourt?' said the Secretary to the Silkworkers Company. 'I have some interesting news for you. I think you're going to like it.'

20

'Please put me out of my misery,' said Powerscourt.

'Very well. What we have is a letter, dated about three months ago from a firm of solicitors in South Africa called Rutherford, Rutherford and Botha. It's quite short. This is what it says. "Dear Sir, we are acting for the estate of a recently deceased businessman. In his will the gentleman left considerable sums of money to two colleagues who had served with him in the British Army some years ago. We are anxious to trace these two people, an Abel Meredith and a Roderick Gill. Both should be over fifty years old. We have reason to believe that the men may be members of, or have links with, the Honourable Company of Silkworkers. Thanking you in advance for your cooperation, Yours sincerely, Thomas Rutherford."'

'Great God, Secretary, that's astonishing news. Do you have a copy of your reply?'

'I have it in front of me, my lord. It acknowledges receipt of the letter and gives the addresses as the Jesus Hospital in Marlow and Allison's School in Norfolk. There was no further correspondence.'

'And I presume that there is no indication as to the name of the businessman, if he ever existed?'

'None at all. You could try the firm on the telegraph and see if they are willing to say anything.'

'Is there,' said Powerscourt, 'any indication of where they were based, this firm of solicitors?'

'Sorry, I should have mentioned that, my lord. There is an address in Johannesburg on the notepaper, though that may not exist any more than the dead businessman.'

'I'll see what we can do,' Powerscourt replied, 'though I don't hold out much hope. Thank you so much, Mr Secretary.'

He bumped into Inspector Devereux on his way back upstairs, being escorted to the drawing room by Rhys. There was general excitement when Powerscourt told him and Lady Lucy the good tidings from the Silkworkers Hall. And that was not all. 'I too have news,' said the Inspector. 'I have been on a sort of Cook's Tour of London's private investigators. Few, I regret to have to tell you, inhabit districts as superior as Markham Square in Chelsea. They all have one well-appointed room, fire in the grate, hunting prints on the walls, that sort of thing, to talk to their clients. The rooms behind, where they do most of their work, are much more squalid. I'd been to about to six or seven, many of them grouped around Lincoln's Inn Fields for some reason I cannot fathom, and had no success at all. But as I moved east I struck a small piece of gold. In one of those little alleys off Fleet Street there is a one-man outfit – most of the others have half a dozen staff or more – called Joshua Wingfield Wallace and he had a tale to tell. Four or five weeks ago Wallace received a letter with no address and no signature but containing a ten-pound note and asking for maps and directions and general information about two particular places. Our Joshua was a bit suspicious about the lack of name and address, but ten pounds is ten pounds so he did what he was asked. You'll never guess where the two places were.'

'Jesus Hospital,' said Lady Lucy.

'Allison's School,' said Powerscourt.

'Top of the class, both of you,' said the Inspector.

'Where did he send the information?' Powerscourt was walking up and down the room now. 'Did somebody come and collect it?'

'Our friend was far too canny for that, my lord. The reply was to be sent to await the arrival of a Mr Smith at the Paddington Hotel round the corner from Paddington Station. The man who was on duty at the hotel reception that day is not due to clock in again until five o'clock this evening, when I have arranged to go and talk to him.'

'Excellent,' said Powerscourt, 'excellent.' He was now walking up and down the room so fast that Lady Lucy worried he might be about to crash into a wall.

'Passenger lists,' he said suddenly.

'Passenger lists?' said Inspector Devereux, looking at Powerscourt in that concerned way people have when their friends or relations are falling ill or going mad.

'Passenger lists? Are you feeling unwell, Francis?'

'Passenger lists,' said Powerscourt. 'I repeat, passenger lists.'

He strode down the drawing room and settled on the edge of the sofa by the fire. 'Consider what we have just learnt, Lucy, Inspector. I don't mean our friend the one-man band near Fleet Street; I mean the letter found by the Silkworkers. We have one faint indication from the school that points to South Africa. Now we have this letter, real or not, from a firm of solicitors, real or not, supposed to come from Johannesburg. It seems to me quite likely that even if all the other information is false, the point of origin may be the real one. So Mystery Man sends out his initial inquiries from his home town. But he has to get here. And the only way to get here, unless you can find yourself a spaceship, is by boat. Mystery Man must have boarded a liner in Durban to come here. I think Durban is the nearest big port to Johannesburg but I could be wrong. But his name will be on the passenger list of the liner that brought him here.'

'You are quite right, my lord,' said the Inspector, 'or he could have boarded the ship in Cape Town. I became rather an expert in these sailing lines when I was a boy, I'm afraid. I had about eight toy ships I used to play with in the bath. Union Castle Line, my lord, formed by a merger of two companies in nineteen hundred.' The Inspector closed his eyes for a moment as if some great feat of memory was upon him.

'She probably sailed on this route,' he said, frowning in concentration. 'Southampton, Madeira, Cape Town, Port Elizabeth, Durban, Port Elizabeth, Cape Town, St Helena, occasional, Ascension occasional, Las Palmas, occasional, Southampton. There was a round-Africa service you could take if the other ships were full, but it took longer. The route I've just mentioned took over a fortnight from Cape Town to Southampton, longer from Durban.'

Powerscourt was reminded of Leith, Lord Rosebery's train-obsessed butler, who was a walking timetable for the great railway routes of Europe. It looked as though the Inspector was his maritime equivalent.

'Whatever the route,' Devereux said, looking slightly embarrassed, as if he'd shown too much of himself, 'they will have passenger lists, as you said, my lord. Whether they're kept in Southampton or in London I'm not sure.'

'Do you know, Inspector,' said Lady Lucy, 'exactly what information these lists contain?'

'I'm afraid I do,' Devereux replied. 'The lists contain the passenger's name, the port where he or she boarded the ship, the class they are travelling in, and the amount they paid for the ticket.'

'Do they, by any chance,' said Powerscourt, 'contain the address in England the passengers are going to?'

'They do not, my lord. But I suspect we might not necessarily believe any information Mystery Man entered on that score.'

'I think,' said Lady Lucy, smiling at Inspector Devereux, 'that you are going to be able to answer every single question we can think of about passenger lists. Do you know how often the great liners travel from South Africa to London and how many people they have on board?'

Inspector Devereux groaned. 'I should have spent my time more usefully when I was a boy, Lady Lucy. Think of all the things I could have memorized – kings of France, presidents of the United States, all the known elements in the periodic table. I think I said before that the journey takes a little over a fortnight, so there will be two passenger lists every month. On average' – Devereux was adding up the passenger numbers of the different ships but he wasn't going to tell his audience that – 'I should say that there are about two hundred in first class, another two hundred in second, and about a hundred in third.'

'So,' said Powerscourt, 'given that the first murder took place on January the twenty-second, the anniversary of Isandlwana, we should go back to the beginning of December. I doubt if our Mystery Man would have arrived a day or two before his first killing. I think he would have given himself time to settle down. So there could be three sailings on which he could have travelled from South Africa, giving us about six hundred first-class passengers and another six hundred in second class. I think we can omit third class for now.'

'But there won't be six hundred names for us to wonder about, surely,' said Lady Lucy. 'Some of the passengers will have boarded the ship at places other than Cape Town or Durban, some may have got off at Madeira if the ship stops there and not all the ships will be full at this time of year. Then there's the fact that the Mystery Man or MM will be over forty-five if not over fifty. We can rule out anybody younger than that because they couldn't have been at the battle.'

'There might be another avenue we could explore,' said Powerscourt. 'Suppose we end up with eight or nine possible murderers from Durban – my knowledge of these liners is non-existent but I can remember a little of the geography from my time there in South Africa. It's a long journey from Johannesburg to Durban but it's about twice as long to Cape Town. I think you'd be on the train for two or three days. But our Mystery Man must have bought his ticket somewhere. Maybe the Union Castle have an office or an agent in place in Johannesburg or maybe he will have got it from a big travel agent. Could we hire somebody to look into that for us, Inspector?'

'I don't think we'd have to hire anybody, my lord. I'll set the wheels in motion when I get back to the station. South Africa is only one hour ahead in the winter. We have reciprocal arrangements with their police on major investigations. They will go and make the inquiries for us – they will, in any case, be better acquainted with the means of buying tickets on their home turf and so forth.'

'Just think, Lucy, think, Inspector,' said Powerscourt,

rubbing his hands together, 'we might actually get a name at the end of this process. For so long I have wanted a name. Now at last we might be able to get one.'

Inspector Devereux left for Paddington Station and an evening of preliminary telegraph traffic with Johannesburg and Durban. At the Paddington Hotel he discovered that the answer from Joshua Wingfield Wallace, the private detective, had been picked up shortly before seven o'clock the day after it was posted. The man on reception was new and eager to impress his customers and his bosses. He had, he said, tried to engage the Mr Smith in conversation, but with little success. The only information he got out of Smith, after handing over the letter, was that he, Smith, had to go back to the west of England on business the following day. He had gone to his room and not been seen until his departure the following morning. Smith had taken no meals or drinks of any kind in the Paddington. God knows, the man on reception at the time said, what he had done for food. He must have gone elsewhere by the back entrance. There was just one other thing, the young man on reception told Inspector Devereux. It would be easy to remember this Mr Smith, if that was his real name, which the young man doubted. The accent, the young man thought, was foreign though he couldn't place it. He was of normal height, in his middle thirties, but he had a great black beard that reached down almost to his chest.

The passenger lists from Durban to London came early the following morning. Inspector Devereux came with them, three lots of passenger lists with two copies of each one, produced at remarkable speed by the Union Castle line's staff in Southampton. The Powerscourt drawing room had been turned into a battle headquarters with two desks facing each other, one for the Inspector, one for the Powerscourts. Devereux's Sergeant, he told them, was still engaged in telegraphic conversations with the Johannesburg and Durban police.

'None of the ships were full,' Devereux said. 'The *Alnwick Castle*, the *Dover Castle*, *Walmer Castle* all had plenty of space left. They told me, the Southampton people, that there was an average of about one hundred and twenty passengers in first class and about a hundred in second class. That means we've got six hundred and sixty names here. I suggest we begin with the *Alnwick Castle*.' He handed a sheaf of papers to Powerscourt.

Lady Lucy had always been a believer in lists and notebooks and careful records. She had produced from her stores three brand-new dark blue notebooks, one for each of the participants. After a while, Powerscourt thought, the names and the numbers became hypnotic.

Of the first ten passengers only one deserved to have his name entered in the notebooks as a possible – Mr Raymond Armstrong. All the rest were the wrong age or the wrong sex and even Mr Ramon might have been too old at seventy-one.

'Inspector Devereux,' said Lady Lucy, 'why is this Harry Jones person paying twenty-six pounds eleven shillings for first class when some of the others are paying one hundred and fifty-one pounds each?'

'Size of cabin, sea views, state room or not, those are what usually sends up the price. Shouldn't think this Jones has got a sea view at all.'

'What do you say to the seventy-four-year-old Captain Cooper, Inspector?' Powerscourt asked.

'I think not. He's too old. There's only Mr Davies, the businessman, and Dr Hodge, the politician, left in the running for us here and I think we can ignore the doctor. No politician, wherever they come from, is going to risk killing three innocent people, however great their grudge. It would finish their career. So I think we can strike him out, just leaving us with Mr Davies.'

After an hour and a half they were nearing the end of the list of second-class passengers in the final liner, the *Walmer Castle*.

'I say, Francis, Inspector,' Lady Lucy was drawing doodles of glasses, wine glasses, champagne flutes, port glasses, brandy glasses on the left-hand page of her handbook. 'I wonder if there mightn't be another way of reducing the number of names we end up with. Do you think, Inspector, that we will be able to discover where most of the tickets were bought?'

'I hope so,' said the Inspector.

'And am I right in saying that even though the ship goes round in a circle in a way, always returning to where it started, the tickets from here will be marked as going from London to Cape Town or London to Durban?'

'That is correct.'

'But some of the tickets will be for a return journey. You would pay for such a ticket all together, maybe with a slight reduction, even if you got two separate pieces of paper as you do with a train ticket. But even though it might say that you boarded the ship in Durban, you could be going home. You could have started out in London. And if a lot of the tickets were returns, bought in London, and even though some of the passengers would be marked as having boarded in Durban, and though they would obviously be travelling from South

Africa to London, they'd be coming home again. They'd have bought their tickets in London. Mystery Man, on the other hand, would be coming on a ticket almost certainly bought in South Africa, maybe Durban Southampton Durban, but his journey would be the first leg, not the second of the trip. All of which, I think, means that if we can find out where the passengers bought their tickets, we can discount all those return tickets bought at the London end. That should eliminate quite a lot of people.'

'Well done, Lucy,' said Powerscourt. 'That should save us a heap of trouble.'

Ten minutes later Lady Lucy drew a stream of bubbles coming out of an enormous champagne bottle on her pad. 'We're through, Inspector. We've got thirty-one names of the right age and sex in the first- and second-class accommodation on the three ships.'

'Excellent,' said Devereux. 'I've got thirty-two but one of mine is a minister so I think I'll get rid of the holy man. Some pretty strange occupations on board these vessels. Did you get the chap who was a musical instrument vendor, for heaven's sake?'

'We did,' said Powerscourt, 'and a quarryman and a fishmonger and a house painter.'

'Well, if you'll excuse me, I'll take these names to our telegraph office and set to work. I'll wire over to Thomas Cook to see if any of their branches sold the things. Once we've eliminated the people who bought their tickets here I'll launch the South Africans. The Inspector looking after us in Durban is a famous rugby player – he was on their inaugural tour here four or five years ago. He says he has very fond memories of playing in England.'

'Dammit, Lucy,' said Powerscourt after the Inspector left, 'there's something niggling at the back of my mind and I can't get my hands on it. It's slipped away. I think it might be important.'

'Well, Francis, you know my views. If you worry away at it, whatever it is, it won't come to you. If you think of something else altogether, it'll make its own way to the front of your brain. Think of the latest sins and wickednesses of our precious twins. That should do the trick.'

Powerscourt never heard the end of the sentence. He had shot out of the room and returned almost at once with an enormous atlas under his arm. He took a notebook from his jacket pocket and riffled through the pages. Then he opened the atlas at a page showing the west of England. 'Contrary to popular opinion after my announcement about passenger lists, Lucy, I have to repeat that I am not going out of my mind. You will recall that the Mr Smith, correctly named or not, said he had to get back to the West Country. And I have just remembered what I was searching for in my mind. When I first met Inspector Devereux in the Silkworkers Hall he was looking at a collection of rubbish that had been collected after the dinner. Among the objects was a part of a ticket, whether bus ticket or train ticket I know not, from a place ending in "be". Now that is pretty useless in itself, there are a great many place names ending in "be". And I remember thinking at the time that it could have been the murderer himself who dropped the ticket stub – all the Silkworkers who were there that night came from central London. Now let's have a hunt for places ending in "be". I think it means valley in Celtic. Let's look at Dorset. Here we are. Kingcombe, Barcombe, Loscombe, Melcombe Horsey, riding centre presumably.'

'Combe Fishacre,' Lady Lucy took up the chase,

'Thorncombe, Combe Almer, Motcombe, what a lot of Combes.'

'Let's try Devon,' said her husband. 'Ellacombe, Maidencombe, Overcombe, Widecombe, Babbacombe Bay.'

'Holcombe, Harcombe,' said Lady Lucy, 'Boscombe, Salcombe, Combe Buckfastleigh, Branscombe.'

'I'm sure there's a whole lot more. I'm going to contact the London Library in a minute. The librarian there is an expert on British place names. I think he even wrote a book on them a couple of years back.'

'Forgive me, Francis, I'm being dense. What can we do with this list of place names?'

'We can't really do anything with them until we have narrowed down the list of names. Now I think about it, mind you, they might help produce the names. This is one of the great beauties of having an Inspector on board, my love. He brings entire police forces with him. We suggest to the good Inspector Devereux that he contacts his brothers in Christ in the counties of Devon and Dorset and Cornwall and ask them which, if any, of the places might be large enough to be issuing tickets, and in which place a man intent on murder might want to hide himself. If the murderers, and I now think there were probably at least two of them, have arrived in one of these places recently, the police should either know about it or know who will tell them, estate agents or hoteliers, those kind of people.'

March 5th 1910. 10.35 From: Inspector Devereux Metropolitan Police.

To: Ticket Offices, Union Castle HQ Southampton.

Re: Triple Murder Inquiry.

We are anxious to discover where the following passengers bought tickets for voyage from Southampton to Durban, single or return, in December last year or on the first voyage in January. Allen, Briggs, Bell, Cameron, De Villiers, Dixon, Dalrymple, Fish, Gibbons, Grant, Hughes, Jackson, Jones-Parry, King, Kruger, Lowther, Macaulay, Matfield, Middleton, Newton, Peters, Poundfoot, Randall, Smit, Steyn, Strauss, Trumper, Turnbull, Vincent, Williams, Winder.

March 5th 1910. 10.45 From: Inspector Devereux, Metropolitan Police. Same inquiry to Messrs Thomas Cook.

March 5th 1910. 11.25

Lord Powerscourt to Charles Hagberg Wright, Librarian, London Library.

Re: Place Names ending in be.

Currently engaged on triple murder inquiry. Suspect villains may have been based in West Country in a place ending in be. Have suspicious bus or train ticket found at one murder site ending in be. Villains may not wish to advertise their presence. Which villages or towns would you recommend we contact. Regards Powerscourt.

March 5th 1910. 12.45

From: Thomas Cook.

To: Inspector Devereux, Metropolitan Police.

Of 31 names sent, two bought their tickets through our West End branch. Dalrymple, Jones-Parry. Returns Southampton Durban Southampton. First Class. Regards.

March 5th 1910. 13.50.

From: Union Castle Ticket Office, Southampton.

To: Inspector Devereux, Metropolitan Police.

Of 31 names mentioned in your wire, seventeen purchased their tickets in England through our offices or by post: Briggs, Cameron, de Villiers, Dixon, Gibbons, Grant, Jackson, Lowther, Macaulay, Middleton, Newton, Peters, Poundfoot, Randall, Trumper, Turnbull, Williams. All return, Southampton Durban Southampton, except de Villiers and Trumper who were single, second class. All except Cameron, Gibbons, Grant, Newton first class, those four second class. Good luck. Union Castle Line.

March 5th 1910. 14.25.

From: Inspector Devereux, Metropolitan Police.

To: Inspector Paul Roos, Durban Borough Police, South Africa.

Request info on type of ticket, first or second class, and route, single or return, held by the following passengers Union Castle Cape Town or Durban – Southampton – Durban or Cape Town in the two sailings last December 1909, and first sailing Jan 1910: Allen, Bell, Fish, Hughes, King, Kruger, Matfield. Smit, Steyn, Strauss, Vincent, Winder.

March 5th 1910 15.10.

From: Charles Hagberg Wright, Librarian, London Library.

To: Lord Francis Powerscourt.

Re: Place Names ending in be.

Many place names ending in 'be' across West Country, mainly Devon and Dorset, virtually none in Cornwall. Many too small to be good hiding places. Have four for preliminary consideration. Boscombe, next to Bournemouth. Railway station, mineral water, pier, hotels. Ilfracombe, North Devon coast. Tourist town fed by ferries along Bristol Channel. Many hotels, houses owned by naval personnel. Railway station. Babbacombe Bay, smaller than others. Tourist area with many hotels. On coast near Torquay. Served by buses not by trains. Salcombe on its own estuary leading to Kingsbridge. Growing in importance as holiday centre with hotels, large villas for rent, etc. Sailing town, GWR bus serving Kingsbridge railway station. If these don't work, come back for more. Regards. Good Luck, Hagberg Wright.

March 5th 1910. 15.50.

From: Inspector Devereux. Metropolitan Police.

To: HQ Devon Constabulary, HQ Dorset Constabulary.

Re: Triple Murder Inquiry.

Am looking for party of two or three foreigners, probably South African, who may be staying in one of the following resorts in your jurisdiction, Boscombe, Babbacombe Bay, Ilfracombe, Salcombe. Principal suspect over fifty years old, others probably younger. They could be staying in hotel or rented house. Probably arrived mid to late December. All extremely dangerous. Do not approach unless it can't be avoided. Regards.

March 5th 1910. 18.15.

From Inspector Paul Roos, Durban Borough Police.

To: Inspector Devereux, Metropolitan Police.

Re: Triple Murder.

Results so far. All tickets except Bell and Fish, purchased Durban. Bell, Fish singles ex Cape Town. Families related, believed to be going to family function in Oxfordshire and tour of England. Durban passengers Hughes, King, return tickets originating London. All businessmen, known to South African authorities. Smit, Steyn, travelling return Durban Southampton Durban. Pastors with Dutch Reformed Church going to conference in Holland. Information on rest later. Regards.

March 5th 1910. 19.05.

From Inspector Galway, Torquay Police Station.

To: Inspector Devereux, Metropolitan Police.

Re: Triple Murder:

Babbacombe Bay part of our beat. No trace in hotels or guest houses there of your suspects. Regards, Galway.

March 5th 1910. 19.40.

From: Inspector Harkness, Boscombe Police Station.

To: Inspector Devereux, Metropolitan Police.

Re: Triple Murder.

All Boscombe hotels and guest houses checked. No trace of your suspects here. Sorry. Good luck.

'I don't think we're going to get any more cables today,' said Inspector Devereux, fresh from the Metropolitan Police telegraph room. 'You should have had copies of all them,' he went on, stretching his legs out in front of the fire in Markham Square. 'What do you think of the news so far?'

'Normally,' said Lady Lucy, 'I'm a hopeful sort of person. But here we are. We've eliminated most of the people travelling Durban or Cape Town to Southampton. There's absolutely no sign of the people we're interested in, or might be interested in if we knew who they are. Half of the place names in Devon and Dorset have reported back and there's no sign of the suspects there either. The field is contracting all the time. What happens if we've got it all wrong? What happens if they're not South African at all, if they didn't need to come here on a great liner because they lived here already? What happens if the strange mark on the dead bodies is just a decoy, a red herring designed to throw us off the scent? What happens if we've got everything wrong?'

'You're very pessimistic this evening, Lucy,' said Powerscourt. 'I think it's too soon to give up the ghost. We're not out of the hunt yet. Let's wait and see what news tomorrow brings.'

'But what happens if I'm right and we've got everything wrong?'

'I don't believe we have got everything wrong, Lucy, my love. But I tell you what I would do if we were wrong.'

'What's that, Francis?'

'I should present my compliments to the Honourable Company of Silkworkers and resign from this case with apologies for failure. And then I should retire completely from all investigations of every sort. Like the man in *Candide*, I should cultivate my garden.'

21

'How many more of these calls do we have to make, Sarge? We did about fifty yesterday.' James Robertson was the newest recruit to the Devon Constabulary, currently being inducted into the skills required in the force by an experienced Sergeant, John Pickles, based at Ilfracombe police station in the county of Devon.

'Calm down, young man. You'll never get on if you're too excitable; that's what I was always told at your age.' Pickles glanced round the little harbour where many of the hotels and guest houses were located. 'We did most of the work yesterday evening. Not long to go now.'

'We had to work until after eight o'clock last night as you well remember,' said the young man. 'My tea was cold and my mother was just about to go down the police station and ask what had happened to me. What are these people supposed to have done, anyway? Lifted the Crown jewels? Tried to assassinate Mr Lloyd George?'

'Never you mind what they're supposed to have done. They're dangerous criminals. That's all we need to know. Now then, why don't you stop complaining and go and make inquiries in the Hotel Bristol across the road. I'll take the Wellington just here. Off you go now.'

Just over a hundred miles to the south another Sergeant was making his way into the heart of Salcombe. He had lived here all his life, Sergeant Mark Vaughan, apart from an unhappy year on loan as a junior constable in the Met. The local Inspector, based in the mother ship at Kingsbridge, knew at once he was the man for the job. 'Pop into Salcombe in the morning, Sergeant Vaughan, and see if there's anything in this,' he'd said the previous afternoon, handing over the wire from London. 'I can't imagine a more unlikely place than Salcombe for a party of villains to hide, but we'd better check.'

Inspector Devereux was back at his command post with the telegraph machines. The first message came from Ilfracombe and it reported that there was nobody of the descriptions given to be found in the town. A thorough search had been carried out and no strange persons discovered apart from a couple of Greek sailors who appeared to have jumped ship. Even the Inspector was growing worried now. There were only a couple messages more to come. Had they made an enormous mistake? He resolved not to tell Powerscourt yet about the news from Ilfracombe. He took comfort, very small comfort, from the fact that a reference book in the police library said that both Boscombe and Ilfracombe had much greater populations than Salcombe, which had yet to report. Maybe they had found something down there among the shrimp nets and the fishing boats.

Salcombe, close to Plymouth on the Devon side, is surrounded by the sea. Through the centre of the little town runs the harbour, part of the estuary which ebbs and flows each day as the tide travels the six miles back and forth from the larger town of Kingsbridge and then out into the English Channel. Tiny, perfect beaches line the sides. A ferry runs every day in summer, taking passengers up and down from Kingsbridge. As it reaches the open sea, the waters are guarded by Bolt Head on the Plymouth side and by Prawle Point on the Dartmouth side. The sea is in Salcombe's blood. Over the years the men of Salcombe have sailed against Philip of Spain's Armada, smuggled brandy and tobacco to be hidden in secret caves in the cliffs, and sent fast sailing ships, fruit schooners, to bring in fresh oranges and other exotic fruit from Spain and the Azores. In recent years its beauty and the mild climate had been bringing in more and more visitors.

The estate agent's office, open only in the mornings two days a week in the winter and spring, was manned this morning by Jimmy Johnston, another young man whose job took him regularly between offices in Kingsbridge and Salcombe. Mark Vaughan and Jimmy Johnston had been at school together and were still friends in their late twenties. Sergeant Vaughan was tall and slim with piercing blue eyes. He was a feared centre three-quarter in the county rugby team, famous for gliding through the opposition lines like a man who seems to have left the room without actually opening the door, as the rugby correspondent of the *Western Morning News* put it.

'Good to see you, Marky boy,' said Jimmy, six inches shorter than his friend with a shock of red hair. 'Are you here on business or dropping in for a chat?'

'Business, I'm afraid,' said Sergeant Vaughan, lowering himself into an ancient armchair, 'and it might be serious.'

'I see,' said Jimmy, going to the door and closing it with a sign saying back in half an hour on the side facing the street. 'Fire ahead, my friend.'

'The inquiry comes from an Inspector in the Met. He's investigating a triple murder, I don't know where. He is interested in a party of two or three people, who might or might not be South Africans, who might or might not be staying in a place in the West Country like Salcombe. They would be in a hotel or a rented house. If troubled, they could be extremely dangerous. Does that ring any bells, Jimmy?'

'Holy Christ,' said Jimmy Johnson, 'I think it does. Just give me a minute to think about it.' He began pulling papers out of a drawer in his desk and placing them on the table. 'I've been wondering if I should let you know about these people for some time,' he said. 'You could say I've been expecting you. We have a party of three foreigners, staying in Estuary House just up the road from here, between the Marine Hotel and the Yacht Club. Bloody enormous place, Estuary House, owned by some rich industrialist in Birmingham who asks us to let it for him when he's not here. They came,' he consulted his paperwork, 'at the beginning of January. They took the house for three months. Strange thing was, we never saw any of them at all. The deal was organized through a man from Chesterton's in London who came down to sort everything out for them. It was if they didn't want to be seen.'

'Have you had any dealings with them since? Do they wander about the town and so on?'

'Not exactly, no. I mean there have been sightings, but only of them inside the house. Every inhabitant of Salcombe now peers up at the windows when he or she goes past. I have no idea if this is correct or not, but the gossip goes that there are three of them, one in his fifties or a bit older, one in his thirties, the last one a bit younger.' Jimmy paused for a moment and looked at his door as if one of the visitors might be about to walk in. 'They say,' he went on, 'that one of the younger ones has a great black beard, but he hasn't been seen for a while. The other younger one is clean-shaven. But the really strange thing, and I don't see how anybody could have invented it, is that the older man has only got one eye. He wears an eye patch on the other, as if he's some pirate on the Spanish Main.'

'Can we just go back a moment, Jimmy? The lease on Estuary House, whose name is that in?'

'It's in the name of the man from Chesterton's.'

'Are you telling me that nobody's got an idea what these people are called? For all we know it could be Shadrach, Meshach and Abednego looking out at the harbour from that great house up there?' Sergeant Vaughan's granny used to read to him from the Scriptures last thing at night.

'It could, though there are no rumours of our three having been sent into the burning fiery furnace.'

Sergeant Mark Vaughan looked around the office 'You don't have a telegraph here, I suppose?'

'Place is too small,' said Jimmy. 'They've got one up at the Marine Hotel.'

'Look, Jimmy,' said Mark, 'this could be very serious. I need to tell my bosses here and the police in London need to know all about it. Could you look up what paperwork you have about these people? The man from Chesterton's, for instance, he must have had a bloody name even if his clients didn't. And he must have an address. I'm going up to the hotel now. I may have to take a peek at Estuary House on the way.'

Sergeant Mark Vaughan stopped in the middle of the road and stared up at Estuary House. It was on three storeys with great tall windows on the first floor looking out over the harbour. A balcony ran most of the width of the house. On the top floor there were a couple of rooms with smaller balconies and elaborate railings. The curtains were still drawn on the first floor. On top there was a tiny gap, as if somebody needed room to stare out at the harbour and the little town.

Horace Ross, general manager of the Marine Hotel on the other side of the road, lived next door to Mark Vaughan's aunt in a house near the waterfront.

'Horace, you old rogue,' said the Sergeant cheerfully. 'Why didn't you report that you had some very strange people staying across the way? People have gone to jail for less, you know.'

Horace Ross laughed. 'I'll say they're strange, young man. Do you know, to this day I've only set eyes on the youngest one.'

'Let's get down to basics then. How many of them are there and what sort of ages?'

'There are three of them. I'm sure of that because one of the waiters here saw them all sitting down together once. For the last couple of weeks there seem to have been only two of them. The third one has disappeared, or he's not been seen.'

'What on earth was your waiter doing over there?'

'Sorry, Mark, I should have said. They have a lot of their meals delivered to them from the hotel here. Normally one of our waiters takes the food over on a big tray, two if there are a lot of courses, leaves it by the front door and rings the bell. The time they were all seen together the door was left open and our chap assumed he was meant to bring the supper inside.'

'Age? Appearance?' Sergeant Vaughan was writing very quickly in his notebook. Outside the windows in

Ross's office the seagulls were performing their dance to welcome the spring, swooping and soaring and shrieking above the water.

'Oldest one, mid-fifties perhaps? Middle one with the great black beard, thirty-five or thereabouts, I should think. Youngest one mid-twenties. Oh, and I nearly forgot. The oldest one has lost an eye somewhere along the line. He was wearing a crimson eye patch the day our waiter spotted them all.'

'See here, Horace, I need to ask you some more questions in a minute. But for now I need your telegraph machine. Right now, if you please. I think we're going to make a Detective Inspector in the Met very happy indeed.'

Mark Vaughan sent his preliminary report to his Inspector in Kingsbridge. He suggested, and was later instructed, to stay in Salcombe for the rest of the day and gather as much information as he could about the mysterious guests in Estuary House.

This time Inspector Devereux did ring Markham Square with the latest news. 'Lord Powerscourt?' He was almost shouting with delight. 'I think we're in business. Let me read you this wire from Inspector Timpson in Kingsbridge near Salcombe in Devon.

'"From Inspector Timpson, Devon County Constabulary. To Inspector Devereux, Metropolitan Police. Re: Triple Murder. Sergeant reports from Salcombe three males staying in Estuary House, large villa by the sea. House lease arranged by London estate agent, address to follow. Eldest, mid-fifties, has lost eye, wears eye patch. Middle one, middle thirties, has long black beard, not seen for some time. Youngest twenty-five to thirty. No contact with the town. Stay in villa. Meals delivered from local hotel. No names known at all. Locals believe they are plotting a major crime somewhere, man with eye patch the mastermind." What do you think, my lord?'

'Excellent news, excellent, Inspector. I think we should pack our buckets and spades and prepare for a holiday by the seaside. Devon is usually bracing at this time of year.'

'I think we should wait for the news from South Africa, my lord. Then we might have some names. I've asked the Kingsbridge police to seal Salcombe off, discreetly, of course, so nobody can get in our out without our knowledge. Their Sergeant is making further inquiries in the town. Is there anything you would like to suggest for them?'

'Laundry?' said Powerscourt. 'Is there a laundry facility in Salcombe? Or do they send it over to the hotel? And do they have access to a boat? There must be a reason for going to a place right on the water.'

'I'll pass that on, my lord. Hold on, there's another message coming in. Looks like it might be from South Africa. I'll call you back.'

Powerscourt stared out into Markham Square. Green was returning to the trees and there was a blaze of daffodils at the King's Road end. The traffic was stuck again, a line of four red buses seemingly impaled in the middle of the street. He looked again at his atlas, establishing in his mind the precise whereabouts of Salcombe in relation to places like Torquay, Exeter, Brixham and Plymouth. He went to his telephone and placed a call to one Fruity Worthington, a close relation of Lady Lucy's. By night Fruity was one of the leading lights of the West Country social scene, a tireless frequenter of hunt balls and dinner parties, and, a great boon to hostesses with a surplus of ladies, he was still single. By day Fruity was a naval Captain, based in His Majesty's Western Fleet Headquarters in the City of Plymouth.

March 6th 1910. 14.10.

From: Inspector Paul Roos, Durban Borough Police, South Africa.

To: Inspector Devereux, Metropolitan Police.

Re: Triple Murder.

Think we have man you want, Wilfrid Allen, 57, rich businessman ex Johannesburg. Widower. Only one eye, circumstances of loss as yet unknown. Also paid for ticket first class of William James Strauss, same address as Allen in Johannesburg, twenty-four years old, and one Elias Harper, labourer, second class. All singles Durban Southampton. Inquiries will continue about the others, and in Johannesburg where my colleagues are collecting information about Allen. Regards.

Regards? Regards? I'll say regards fifty times over, Inspector Miles Devereux said to himself, as he telephoned the news from South Africa to the Powerscourts in Markham Square. The reaction was swift.

'I've been checking the trains,' said Powerscourt. 'There's a fast service that leaves Paddington in an hour or so. Could you catch that? And I'm sure you'll leave a competent man on duty with those machines in case some more news comes through.'

'Don't worry, my lord, I shall join you on the train. I'm going to book us all in at the Marine Hotel. I'll tell them that you're a private investigator, in case they're not sure what you're doing in our team, and I'm going to take over the telegraph there for the duration of our stay.'

Once Powerscourt had finished speaking, Johnny Fitzgerald commandeered the telephone. He had to wait a long time for the recipient of his call to find what he wanted but he joined Powerscourt and Lady Lucy in the drawing room with a huge grin on his face.

'Thought I'd just make a little inquiry of my own about this fellow Allen,' he began. 'It's not conclusive as there are plenty of Allens about. I've just been talking to the army records people in Brecon. I bought a lot of malt whisky for a Captain there who seemed to have a couple of brains to rub together, saying as I left that I might call back later or want more information. The last records of the First and Twenty-fourth Regiment of Foot, the Warwickshires, taken three or four months before the battle of Isandlwana, unfortunately, do show an Allen in the ranks.'

'Did he have an initial, Johnny?' asked Powerscourt.

'He did.'

'And what was it?'

'It was W. He could have been a William or a Walter or a Waldo or a Willoughby. And he could, of course, have been Wilfrid.'

There was one further message from Devon before Inspector Devereux set off for Paddington Station and the West Country.

March 6th 1910. 14.30.

From: Inspector Timpson, Devon Police.

To: Inspector Devereux, Metropolitan Police.

Re: Triple Murder.

Reluctant to bring another corpse to your attention, but two weeks ago body of a male in his mid-thirties was found at sea. Death by drowning. Despite appeals throughout this and neighbouring counties, nobody has been reported missing.

The man with one eye had made his fortune by taking great care over his business deals, never leaving any stone unturned and never taking any unnecessary risks. Now in his splendid house overlooking Salcombe harbour he stood by a minute gap in the curtains on the great first-floor windows and thanked God he had taken precautions. Early on during his stay he had secured the services of the head porter at the Marine Hotel. In return for large sums in cash that official had promised to keep him informed of any developments that might not be welcome. So he knew now that the police were making detailed inquiries about him. He knew there were plans to close off the town with officers posted across all the roads leading in and out of Salcombe. He knew, too, that more police and an investigator called Powerscourt were on their way from London. He looked again at the two notes he had received from the hotel that morning and finished one of his own, to be taken to the Marine by the waiter who came to collect the remains of the lunch. He had consulted his train timetables and discovered that the train he thought the London people would arrive on should reach the town shortly before seven. Ever since he arrived in Salcombe he had a plan of escape if the need arose. He looked up at the sky. Dusk, that would be the time. As the light began to fade over the town and the harbour, he would make his move.

Sergeant Mark Vaughan had been very busy. He had taken over the two rooms on the Cliff Road side of the Marine Hotel with the best view of Estuary House. When his forces grew more numerous, a constable would be on watch there twenty-four hours a day. He discovered the answer to the laundry question, that the clothes were washed in the hotel and transported to and fro in an enormous wicker basket. He had secured from his friend in the estate agents the name, Giles Coleridge, and the address on the King's Road, Chelsea, for Chesterton's Estate Agents who had arranged the lease on Estuary House and sent them to London. About four o'clock he began wondering why a man with murderous intent would come to Great Britain and choose to stay in a place like Salcombe. Surely London or Bristol or even Southampton where the liner came in would provide better places to hide. The answer might be linked to London's questions about a boat. Why had these people come to Salcombe?

Perhaps, Sergeant Vaughan said to himself, they are thinking of escaping by sea. You could sail out into the English Channel and reach Plymouth in a couple of hours. If the boat was a good one with an experienced crew you could sail more or less anywhere. He suspected a mere Sergeant would not be very welcome at the Salcombe Yacht Club, where they had a reputation for looking down their noses at most of the population. He was right. A superior sort of flunkey told him that they had no idea of any visitors with boats or yachts. It was all they could do to keep tabs on their own vessels. When the Sergeant pointed out a large and handsome yacht on the East Portlemouth side of the harbour, clearly visible from the club's windows, the man from the Yacht Club said it had nothing to do with them, and did the Sergeant mind, there was rather a lot on today with a dinner for eighty people in the evening.

Praying quietly that some god of the sea, possibly Poseidon himself in a bad mood, would wreak a terrible vengeance on the Salcombe Yacht Club, Sergeant Vaughan made his way to the solicitor's where a friend of his worked who was a member of the local Lifeboat. Freddie, for that was the name of the lifeboat man, told him that they had only discovered the details of the boat the previous week.

'She's called *Morning Glory*,' Freddie told him. 'And here's the strange thing. Nobody knows the name of the owner. Well, he's not properly the owner; she's rented from some man in Southampton for three months. Even then, whoever the man is, he got a firm of ship's agents and chandlers in Southampton to do the deal.'

Just like the estate agents from London and the house, the Sergeant said to himself.

'Tell me this, Freddie, has she been out for a sail since she's been here?'

'Well, yes, she has, a couple of times. You know Nat Gibson, that chap who's almost a professional ship's Captain? Lives in Island Street round the corner from here? The chandlers in Southampton commissioned Nat to go there and sail the boat back here. He's paid to be ready to go at a moment's notice.'

'Have you seen Nat around recently?'

'I have, as a matter of fact. But he won't say a word to you or anybody else. It's written into his contract that he's not to speak to a single human soul about his work on the *Morning Glory*.'

'Not even a policeman?'

'Especially not a policeman. Look here, Marky, what's going on? Is there some wicked gang hiding out in the York Hotel? Up at the Marine with the quality perhaps? Planning to steal all the fish?'

'I can't tell you, Freddie, I really can't. But can I ask you a favour? Whatever is going on may involve the *Morning Glory* later on. And we, the police, may have need of a vessel of our own at very short notice. Could you put the word out among the lifeboat crew to be ready to go this evening?'

There was an air of scarcely concealed excitement in one of the first-class carriages on the afternoon train from Paddington to Penzance with connections, among others, to Kingsbridge, where the railway company provided their own bus, decked out in the company livery just as if it were a train compartment, to convey passengers the few miles to Salcombe. Inspector Devereux informed the party that they could have gone by boat but the bus was believed to be quicker as long as there weren't too many farm animals on the roads.

Johnny Fitzgerald went to sleep as soon as the train left London. Lady Lucy was busy with a recent E. M. Forster, *A Room with a View*. Powerscourt and the Inspector were deep in conversation, the Inspector trying to construct a timetable for Allen's activities since he left South Africa.

'God knows what's going to happen this evening,' the Inspector told everybody, 'but I think I can promise you one thing with absolute certainty.'

'What's that, Miles?' said Lady Lucy, who had been calling the Inspector by his Christian name ever since she had danced with him at the ball.

'By ten o'clock this evening,' the Inspector said, 'we shall have a visit from a Chief Constable, come to wash his hands in the blood or the glory.'

A tall police Sergeant stopped the bus on its way into the town shortly after half past six. At the sight of Devereux's uniform, they were waved on. Horace Ross had decided to show off his very best rooms in the Marine Hotel to the visitors from London. Who knew how many friends they could tell when they returned to the capital? Powerscourt and Lady Lucy were in the Imperial Suite with a vast sitting room complete with balcony looking out over the harbour. On either side of them, like sentries on parade, were equally luxurious rooms for the Inspector and Johnny Fitzgerald. The telegraph quarters were one floor above. Ross had already provided an office in the shape of the spare dining room, with great glass windows looking out over the waters. A wind was getting up, causing ripples on the surface. Inspector Timpson and a couple of constables were waiting for the visitors.

Inspector Devereux cleared his throat. 'Gentlemen, Lady Powerscourt,' he began, 'this is what I propose should happen immediately.' There were, as he was well aware, regional proprieties and regional sensitivities to be addressed here. 'With your permission, Inspector Timpson, I think one of your constables should keep watch in that room on the top floor overlooking Estuary House. You and I should go with the other constable and speak to this man Allen, if that is his name.'

Powerscourt raised a hand and was about to speak.

'With respect, Lord Powerscourt, I think this initial meeting should be handled by the police. You will be more than welcome to join us when an arrest has been secured. But these people are killers. Three people have lost their lives. We are paid to stop bullets, my lord. You are not. And there is one final argument in favour of your staying here for the moment.'

'Which is?' said Powerscourt.

'I could never forgive myself if I made Lady Lucy a widow.'

With that the two Inspectors marched out of the room. Everybody else rushed to the top floor on the landward side. They watched as the two Inspectors ran up the slope towards the front door. They watched as they rang the bell several times. They saw them disappear round the back where a loud crash a few minutes later spoke of some back door being kicked in. They watched as lights went on all the way through the house, from the basement to the huge living room with the harbour view to the top rooms with their own little balconies. Lady Lucy swore afterwards that she heard a mighty volley of oaths shouted into the evening air shortly after the top floor was illuminated. Then they saw nothing until two dejected figure could be seen making their way back to the Marine Hotel.

'There's nobody there,' Inspector Devereux told the company in the Marine Hotel office. 'The birds, as the man memorably said, have flown. We haven't lost yet, but we're bloody close to it. Where have they gone? When did they go? How in God's name did they get out?'

22

Inspector Devereux was looking at his notes. Inspector Timpson was looking at his boots. Powerscourt was walking up and down. He hated failure. Johnny Fitzgerald had purloined the hotel wine list and was inspecting it with some interest. The constable was standing to attention in a corner. They could hear Sergeant Mark Vaughan before they could see him, his boots rattling across the Marine Hotel's well-polished boards. Inspector Timpson was the first face he recognized.

'Inspector Timpson, other Inspector, sirs, madam,' he began, telling himself to present his news in an orderly fashion. The events might be dramatic, but there was no place for drama in the telling of them. 'I believe the people in Estuary House have gone, Inspector Timpson, sir. There is a path from the side of the house leading down to the water that is so overgrown it is almost secret. At dusk or in the dark a man would be virtually invisible. The party from Estuary House have a yacht, sir. It is called *Morning Glory* and is normally moored in the harbour here on the East Portlemouth side across the water. It's not there now. They have also contracted an experienced sailor called Nat Gibson, who's almost a professional boat Captain. He left his house in Island Street about forty minutes ago. It is my belief, sir, that he will have picked up the Estuary House people at the Yacht Club landing stage just round the corner from this hotel.'

'Does anybody know where they might have gone?' Inspector Devereux felt they were back in the hunt now, some way behind the fox admittedly, but not out of contact altogether.

'I haven't told you the most important bit, sir.' Sergeant Vaughan felt he had never had a more interested and interesting collection of listeners. 'The Salcombe lifeboat, fully crewed, is at your service for this evening and however long it may take. They should be by the landing stage in five minutes' time. They can take two people on board.'

'Well done, young man, well done indeed.' Powerscourt was now staring out of the window, up the harbour towards the open sea which lay a couple of miles away.

'Sergeant Vaughan here is a local man, Inspector, Lord Powerscourt.' Inspector Timpson had never known a case like it. It had started the afternoon before with an inquiry from the Met. Twenty-four hours later you were preparing to embark in a lifeboat in pursuit of some murdering villains who have hidden themselves away on your patch for months.

'I'm sure the lifeboat coxswain will have an idea where they might go to, sir.' Sergeant Vaughan was wondering if he might be one of the two people on the lifeboat. It was, in a manner of speaking, he thought, his lifeboat, as he had ordered it into action, but he suspected he might be too junior. 'From here they could go down the estuary towards Kingsbridge if they wanted, but I don't think they will. They'd be sailing into a channel they couldn't get out of. They'd be trapped. I think they'll head for the open sea. If they turn left at Prawle Point they could sail round the coast towards Dartmouth, or Torquay, or Exeter even. Go the other way and they could reach Plymouth fairly quickly. Dock the yacht, or leave Skipper Gibson to sail it home, and they could be on a train in a couple of hours.'

'Could I suggest,' Powerscourt was not going to be left out of the action this time if he could help it, 'that Inspector Timpson, as the local man, and myself go on the lifeboat? Inspector Devereux, your expertise on the telegraph will be sorely needed here. We need to contact various other forces about possible railway escapes. Important information may also come in from South Africa. And in any case, apprehending the villains, if we do apprehend them, is only the beginning. The real interviews start when the suspects are back on dry land, not rolling up and down in the swell out on the open sea.'

Inspector Devereux laughed. 'Very good, my lord. I would just like to ask Inspector Timpson if I could borrow Sergeant Vaughan while he is away. We need to contact the nearby lighthouses and suchlike places to keep watch. His local knowledge will be invaluable.'

'Of course,' said Inspector Timpson.

Powerscourt gave a name and a phone number to Inspector Devereux before he left. 'Tell him it's tonight. Suggest he leaves as soon as he can. God speed.'

Devereux whistled to himself when he read the name of the recipient. 'Come on, Sergeant,' he said to Mark

Vaughan as he led the way upstairs to the telegraph room, 'we've got work to do.'

Powerscourt and Inspector Timpson were ushered to their seats at the rear of the lifeboat with that careful air seamen have with landlubbers they suspect may be about to fall in. The *William and Emma* had a crew of twelve this evening, wearing their uniforms of dark grey trousers and jackets, their oars raised to the vertical position as they sidled up to the landing stage, now back in the water as they headed for the sea.

'We're after that big yacht, young Mark told me, sir,' the coxswain, whose name was Robbie Barton, said to Powerscourt and the Inspector. Barton was a cheerful little man in his early thirties who worked as a fisherman by day. 'You mightn't think so, looking at this boat, that it could move quickly but it can. I'm sure we can make up some ground before we reach the English Channel.'

'If you were a villain, trying to escape from justice,' said the Inspector, 'which way would you go once we reached the sea?'

'I don't rightly know. We don't have to decide which way to turn yet.'

They were past East Portlemouth now, little more than a collection of cottages, and were heading towards Mill Bay, a small beach, on their left. The wind was growing stronger. There was a full moon, only visible occasionally through the cloud cover. Powerscourt was shivering with cold. The lifeboatmen were unaffected, pulling vigorously at their oars. As they passed the remains of Fort Charles and Salcombe Castle on the right-hand side of the harbour, the moon cleared for a couple of minutes.

'There she is!' a young lifeboat man at the prow shouted. 'She's just up there by South Sands. By God, she's lovely to look at, that yacht.'

Johnny Fitzgerald had persuaded one of the waiters that it was vital for the success of the operation that he, the waiter, should open one of the hotel's bottles of Chateau Lafite immediately. Johnny felt the Lafite would be wasted on the run-of-the-mill hotel guests with no knowledge of the great wines of Bordeaux. Refreshed by his first glass, he persuaded Lady Lucy to join him on a mission to Estuary House. They might find something useful, he said.

The lights were still blazing on all floors as they made their way round the back and in through the broken door. They started at the top and worked down. It seemed that the three men had separate rooms on the top floor. One was incredibly tidy, so tidy, Lady Lucy discovered, because all the clothes and other possessions had been removed. It looked, she said to Johnny, as if there were only two of them now. The other bedrooms showed signs of hasty departure, the odd sock or jumper left lying on the floor. The biggest room, they decided, must have belonged to Wilfred Allen, if that was his name. There was a powerful telescope by the window, pointing out to sea. Johnny Fitzgerald showed Lady Lucy how the top half of the window had been altered so you could point the device upwards to stare at the stars as easily as you could stare at the sea. Lady Lucy felt a sudden moment of pity for the man who had looked through this lens, hiding in the dark in a tiny English town, thousands of miles from home and consoling himself with visions of the stars turning in their courses across the night sky.

'Look, Lady Lucy, look here!' Johnny Fitzgerald was pointing to a strange wooden implement sitting on a bookshelf next to *The Adventures of Sherlock Holmes*. It was about two and a half feet long, with a circular knob rather like a thistle at the end. 'This must be one of those knobkerrie things that Francis was so excited about. And it's here. This is probably the one used on the victims.'

'How horrible,' said Lady Lucy, staring at the thing as if was a malignant snake. 'Let's have a look at the floor below. That thing makes me feel quite sick.' Johnny put it in his pocket.

On the lower level there was further evidence of a speedy departure. Even in a couple of months, it seemed, people could accumulate an enormous amount of rubbish. Johnny was on his knees, examining a fragment of a letter or a note that had missed the waste-paper basket. 'More police and a private investigator called Lord Powerscourt coming from London early this evening,' he read, 'to be here about seven o'clock.' Johnny read it twice and handed it to Lady Lucy.

'What do you think of this?' he said.

'My goodness! It looks like a note sent to the people here.' Lady Lucy paused for a moment and looked carefully at Johnny. 'Surely it can only have come from across the road? Wilfred Allen must have had an informant inside the Marine Hotel. That's why they left before we got here.'

'Come on, Lady Lucy,' Johnny was running towards the stairs that led to the back door, 'it's time to find out.'

The men in the lifeboat had fallen into a deep rhythm now. They looked as if they could row for ever. The moon cleared once more as the *William and Emma* passed the Pound Stone. Powerscourt suddenly realized that a noise had stopped. Since they left the harbour the principal sound had been the oars dipping in and out of the water and the occasional command of the coxswain. But there had been another sound, coming from further up the channel which he now realized must have been the engine of the *Morning Glory*. They could see the yacht just ahead, not moving now with the engine turned off, nestling in the tiny bay beside South Sands a few hundred yards away. The yacht's sails were being hoisted, Nat Gibson scurrying around the little ship.

'We have to be careful in these waters,' Robbie Barton the lifeboat coxswain said to Powerscourt and the Inspector. 'Over there, a mile or so away on the other side of the channel, is the Bar, a spit of sand that can be treacherous in the wrong conditions. Many a vessel has come to grief there. They say, Inspector, Lord Powerscourt, that this is the bar Tennyson was thinking of when he wrote his famous poem. He's said to have spent time in Salcombe. "Sunset and evening star, / And one clear call for me! / And may there be no moaning of the bar, / When I put out to sea."'

Johnny Fitzgerald and Lady Lucy found Horace Ross, manager of the Marine Hotel, in the dining room, keeping a close eye on his waiters. Johnny beckoned him aside into the room reserved for the police.

'Whose handwriting is this, pray?' he asked, waving the scrap of paper at Ross's face. The manager of the Marine looked at it closely.

'Why, it's my head porter's writing, man by the name of Mills, Timothy Mills. What of it?'

'Simply this, Mr Ross. We found this piece of paper on the floor in Estuary House. It looks as if the recipient was

390

trying to tear the message into pieces and drop them into the waste-paper basket, but he ran out of time. If you read it carefully you will see that it looks as if your Timothy Mills has been sending messages to the enemy, as it were. Could you summon him here for a little conversation, do you think? Now? This minute?'

At Powerscourt's suggestion the lifeboat coxswain had brought the *William and Emma* to within fifty yards of the *Morning Glory*. The men stopped rowing as Powerscourt rose to his feet. The beach seemed to be glistening in the moonlight.

'Mr Allen, I should like to speak to you! My name is Powerscourt,' he shouted across the water between the two vessels. Powerscourt had suggested that they should not get too close in case of gunfire.

There was no reply. Nat Gibson seemed to have completed his work with the sails and was returning to the tiller.

'Mr Allen!' Powerscourt tried again. The lifeboat crew stared as if spellbound by the sirens as a head, then a trunk, then finally a whole person emerged very slowly from the inner cabin of the yacht. The one eye and the red eye patch seemed to Powerscourt to shriek defiance to the world.

'I am Allen,' the man said, glaring at the *William and Emma* with his one eye. 'I know about your activities, Powerscourt. What do you want of me?'

'You must know perfectly well what we want of you, Mr Allen. The police and myself would like to question you about three recent murders carried out on your instructions.'

Allen laughed. 'Are you asking me to give myself up, you fool? I have been in Salcombe all the time for the last three months and I can prove it. You are very stupid indeed if you think I am going to be convicted of anything at all.'

'But what of your associates? Your bearded colleague who travelled here second class to murder your enemies?'

'I have to tell you, Powerscourt, your attentions are becoming very unwelcome. You traced me to this little town. Now you are following me around in that ridiculous wooden boat. You are annoying me, I tell you. I came here to carry out a mission. That mission is now complete. I advise you now to drop the matter, to abandon your inquiries. You may hope to place me in the dock. I tell you that I will never stand in the dock. You hope to beat me. I tell you that you will never beat me. I am going below now. You will never see me again. Gibson, let's move out of here as fast as we can. Goodbye, Powerscourt. It may interest you to know that while you may have troubled me, your activities in my case were like a fly trying to wound an elephant.'

Ten minutes later, with the wind rising and the shelter of the estuary losing its power, the *Morning Glory* had pulled well away from the lifeboat. Neither Powerscourt nor the Inspector could see any trace of the Bar. But Robbie assured them that they were past it now. Dimly ahead, he could see the bulk of Bolt Head which marked one side of the end of the long estuary and the beginning of the English Channel. Now then, he said to himself, which way is the *Morning Glory* going to turn? As the cloud lifted again they could see her, two sails aloft, heading straight ahead.

'She ain't out of the estuary yet, not proper,' said Robbie Barton. 'She's got to pass Prawle Point on the other side before she's really out in the open sea.'

The stereotype for a head porter would be a tall figure, well over six feet in height, solidly built, possibly wearing a top hat, dispensing taxis and greetings by the front door of one of London's great hotels like the recently opened Ritz halfway along Piccadilly. Timothy Mills, head porter of the Marine Hotel, Salcombe, was just over five feet six inches tall and as thin as a whippet. He looked defiant when Johnny Fitzgerald showed him the slip of paper from Estuary House.

'This is your handwriting, I believe,' said Johnny.

'It is. I'm sorry if I've done the wrong thing. My wife's been ill, so very ill, you see, and I needed the money for the doctor's bills. You're not going to arrest me, are you? I couldn't bear to leave Bertha on her own.'

'I'm not going to arrest you, Mr Mills. I'm sorry to hear about your wife. The best thing would be if you could tell us everything you did for the Estuary House people and everything you know about where they've gone.'

'Well now, my main job,' said Mills, 'was to tell them when anybody was making inquiries about them, and sending notes to Nat Gibson about that boat over the way. Oh, I nearly forgot.' Mills, having cheered up a little on hearing he was not to be arrested, looked really anxious all of a sudden. 'I had to go into Plymouth for them shortly after they arrived.'

'And what did you have to do in Plymouth, Mr Mills?'

'I didn't quite know what to make of it, actually. I had to buy a uniform for the young man.'

'What sort of uniform?'

There was a pause and then the words were pulled out like a bad tooth. 'A policeman's uniform.'

'God in heaven,' said Johnny Fitzgerald. 'What on earth did they want with a policeman's uniform?'

'Well, sir,' said Mills, 'there's only the old one gone

off on the boat. The young one's still here, or if he's not, maybe he's going round pretending to be a police officer.'

'Thank you very much,' said Johnny and shot off to the telegraph room to consult with Sergeant Vaughan.

Sharp Tor, Starehole Bay, Shag Rock, Pig's Nose, Ham Stone, Gammon Head, Mew Stone, Robbie Barton called out the names of the landmarks along the coast as they passed. There was no sign of the *William and Emma* changing over to sail yet. The coxswain told his passengers that they probably made better speed with the oars. The wind was rising now, changing direction, blowing hard towards the shore. The moon came out and stayed out for a couple of minutes. Powerscourt saw that the contest was deeply unfair. The odds were stacked in favour of *Morning Glory*, even with the wind against her. She was built for speed and for grace. The *William and Emma* was built to be solid, to keep afloat however bad the storms, to reach the wrecks off the Devon shore and bring the passengers and the seamen home to safety. It was a dray horse against an Olympic sprinter.

'She's not turning to the left or the right, Inspector, my lord. No late supper in Plymouth or Dartmouth by the look of it.'

'My God,' said Powerscourt, 'I've been a fool! Why didn't I think of it earlier. Of course she's going straight out to sea. Once she's three miles from the coast she's outside British territorial waters altogether, and outside British jurisdiction. Inspector Timpson here couldn't arrest them even if we could catch them.'

'Well,' said Robbie, 'she's not three miles out yet. She's

got some way to go. But we'd better start praying for a miracle if we're ever to catch up with her.'

It took Sergeant Vaughan less than half an hour to find William James Strauss, disguised as a police constable, making his way very slowly along the road from Salcombe to Kingsbridge where the railway connected you to a wider world. Lady Lucy took the young man into the Imperial Suite away from the police uniforms. Johnny Fitzgerald had been reunited with his bottle of Chateau Lafite.

'You must be William James Strauss,' said Lady Lucy. 'And the older gentleman is a Mr Allen, a Wilfred Allen, is that right?'

'People call me Jimmy,' said the young man, speaking with a strong South African accent, 'and the older man, as you put it, is Wilfred Allen.'

'And there was a third person, I think, was there not? Elias Harper, if my memory serves me. What became of him?'

The young man turned pale. 'Do I have to answer that?'

'You don't have to answer anything you don't want to,' Lady Lucy replied. 'I'm not a policeman, as you can see. Not tall enough for a start.'

Jimmy Strauss managed a ghost of a smile. 'Can I tell you what happened? What's been going on, I mean. I feel it's all bottled up inside me.'

'Of course,' said Lady Lucy.

The flares lit up the night sky as if some celestial switch had been turned on. Half a mile away from the lifeboat, directly across the path of the *Morning Glory*, lay the nine thousand tons of HMS *Sprightly*, one of His Majesty's destroyers based in Plymouth. There was a roar of gunfire and Powerscourt could see the splashes a couple of hundred yards to the left of the yacht.

'*Morning Glory*!' said a voice trained to rule the waves. 'His Majesty's Ship *Sprightly*, at your service. You are to turn round and return to Salcombe at once.'

The voice from the yacht did not have the same carrying power but the crew of the *William and Emma* heard the words territorial waters and three miles out mentioned at least once.

'Did you bring a measuring tape with you, *Morning Glory*? Don't talk to us about territorial waters,' the voice replied. 'Round here territorial waters are what the Royal Navy says they are. I repeat, turn around and return to Salcombe.'

This time the key word in the reply seemed to be international law.

'Round here, I repeat, international laws are the same as territorial waters, *Morning Glory*. They are what the Royal Navy says they are. Turn around, I say.'

There was another complaint from the *Morning Glory*. There was a brief silence from HMS *Sprightly*. Then there was another roar of gunfire, the shells dropping this time fifty yards on either side of the yacht. Powerscourt thought the spray must have reached the boat.

'Turn around, *Morning Glory*. If you want to see another morning, start turning about right now. Next time I'll sink you. My boys need some shooting practice.'

Another burst of flares lit up the scene. There was another bellow from HMS *Sprightly*.

'Salcombe Lifeboat *William and Emma*! Stay where you are! Our coxswain wants a word!'

The *Morning Glory* was turning round. And at the stern a man was climbing down the steps into the little rowing boat being towed behind her. Nat Gibson, it seemed, had had enough. The little boat set off towards the *William and Emma*. Wilfred Allen, the man come from Johannesburg to Devon, was on his own now.

'It all started with that battle long ago,' said Jimmy Strauss, 'when the three of them left him for dead. A local woman found Mr Allen several days after and nursed him back to health. It took a long time. She thought her gods must have saved him from death. By the time he was well, and his eye had healed out, the other three had all gone back to England.'

'Why did he stay in South Africa? Why didn't he come back?'

'His parents were dead. He told me he wanted a new start. And of course he became very rich through the gold and diamonds. He became one of the biggest traders in the world.'

'Did he indeed. But why did he wait thirty years before taking his revenge?' asked Lady Lucy.

'I think it had to do with his wife. She was ill for years and years with one of those wasting diseases that doesn't actually kill you, but just leaves you weaker and weaker all the time. He would never have left her, Mr Allen. She only died last year. Three days after the funeral he saw Sir Rufus walking down the street in Johannesburg. He told me, Mr Allen, that he didn't know he had that much rage in him. Everything about the battle, the promises beforehand that they would all look after each other, it all came back and flooded him like a tidal wave. That's when he decided to come back and give the three of them their just deserts.'

Lady Lucy thought she would take a chance. She had no evidence at all for what she was about to say but she thought it might be the truth, or close to the truth.

'But he didn't actually kill any of them himself, Mr Allen, I mean. The other man did that, didn't he? Mr Elias Harper, the man who travelled here in second class.'

'How did you know that? Harper did the dirty work all right. Mr Allen was tucked up in Estuary House all the time.'

'And where is Mr Harper now?' Lady Lucy suddenly remembered the drowned man, the corpse that nobody claimed, the body never reported missing. 'He went for a sail, didn't he, Jimmy?'

Jimmy nodded.

'And he didn't come back?'

Jimmy shook his head.

Another voice boomed out across the English Channel from HMS *Sprightly*, that of Captain Fruity Worthington himself this time.

'Francis?'

'Fruity?'

'How are you, my friend. Lady Lucy well I trust?'

'Very well indeed, thank you, Fruity. Thank you so much for coming along. You've saved our bacon.'

'Don't mention it. Pity we couldn't sink her, mind you. We're going to hang around until *Morning Glory*'s tucked up inside that harbour. No point in taking any chances, what?'

'Thank you again, Fruity. We must return to the harbour to talk to the fellow when he's back in Salcombe.'

Morning Glory was just about to go past the *William and Emma*. The vessels were less than thirty yards apart. Allen was holding some long thin object in his left hand. Nat Gibson, the hired skipper, had come aboard the lifeboat, saying he didn't mind sailing yachts for people who might not be one hundred per cent reliable, but he was damned if he was going to be shot at by his own side.

'*Morning Glory*!' shouted Powerscourt as the yacht slipped past. There was a volley of oaths in reply.

'Damn you, Powerscourt! Damn you to hell!' Allen yelled with hatred in his voice. 'If you're trying to ruin me, two can play at that game!'

Powerscourt could just see Allen raise the long thin object to his shoulder and start firing a heavy rifle. It was difficult shooting in the swell but Allen was lucky. One shot hit the man sitting next to Powerscourt in the shoulder and the blood spurted out on to Powerscourt's jacket. Another one seemed to have hit the lifeboat below the waterline as seawater was now pouring into the bottom of the boat. Soon it was over their boots and rising fast. Powerscourt left the sailors to deal with the leak. A very tall man appeared and rigged up a temporary bandage on the wounded shoulder. Powerscourt and Inspector Timpson dragged their pistols out of their pockets and began raking the *Morning Glory* with gunfire. There was a scream to tell them that one of their bullets must have struck home. But the yacht was still under control, turning away from the *William and Emma* and heading for the Prawle Point side of the estuary. When the *Morning Glory* was out of range, Powerscourt realized that the damage to the lifeboat was far greater than he had thought.

The boat was sluggish. His knees were nearly submerged. Only four men were left at the oars. Two others were trying out various different shapes of cork plug to fill the hole where the bullet must have passed through. The rest of them were bailing desperately as fast as their arms would go. Powerscourt was told by the man next to him that the bullet had landed on the overlap between two planks and thus forced a larger hole than it would have done if it had struck in the middle of the board. Powerscourt and the Inspector pulled their shoes off and began to bail. The level still seemed to be rising.

'Should we row, or bail, Coxswain?' Powerscourt shouted.

'Row!' came the reply, as Barton manoeuvred another piece of wood, fished out of a vast locker at the stern, bent into a slight curve to fit over the plug where the bullet had passed through, on to the damaged section of the boat. Nat Gibson had taken the tiller as Powerscourt and the Inspector took their places side by side on the oars. Gibson seemed to be steering, not towards Salcombe, but towards the nearest point of land.

The *William and Emma* was making virtually no headway. Only the wind, strengthening again and blowing towards the shore, moved them along very slowly. Powerscourt wondered if for him, too, this was going to be his last case. He would die, not at the Reichenbach Falls, but here, drowned in the English Channel a couple of miles from the shore. He tried to calculate the distance to dry land and thought it might just as well be the Atlantic Ocean; he could never swim that far. He pulled at his oar, trying to capture the rhythm of the other oarsmen. He wondered about Lucy, in a strange hotel on the coast of Devon, hearing of her husband's death, her children far away.

Inspector Miles Devereux leant back in his chair in the telegraph room at the Marine Hotel. 'Some people in South Africa are working late on our behalf.' He showed Sergeant Vaughan the cables piling up in front of him. 'Johannesburg reports that he was one of the richest men in South Africa. They know from the tickets that he left the country in the middle of December, bound for Southampton. They've even got on to his yacht club in Durban, for heaven's sake. He was a keen yachtsman, our friend Allen. He moored a whole series of boats there, all with the same name: *Cyclops*, after the blinded giant in the *Odyssey*. The latest was *Cyclops Four*.'

'Have they said anything about how he lost his eye at all, sir?' Sergeant Vaughan asked.

'They haven't said a word about that, Sergeant. Maybe they don't know.'

'I was wondering, sir, about the men on duty at the entrances to the town. Should we stand them down?'

Inspector Devereux paused for a moment. 'I think not,' he said finally. 'Think about it. We're engaged on a triple murder inquiry here. We've got an awful lot of guesses but very few facts so far. Keep them there for the time being.'

Sergeant Vaughan cycled off into the night to tell his men to remain at their posts until further notice.

After ten minutes' rowing, Powerscourt felt his palms and his shoulders beginning to ache.

'How much further to go?' he asked the back in front of him.

'It's not the distance that's the problem, my lord. It's this bloody leak. It's getting worse, not better. It must be about two miles or so from here to the coast.'

'That's about half the length of the Oxford and Cambridge Boat Race,' his neighbour on the oars chimed in. 'They do that in about twenty or twenty-five minutes.'

'But their boats aren't full of bloody water, are they? They're not actually sinking, like we are.'

'One of them did sink,' chipped in Nat Gibson from the tiller. 'Cambridge sank in eighteen fifty-nine, I think it was. Bloody boat was too light. She shipped water from the start; went down just after Barnes Bridge.'

The water inside the *William and Emma* was a third of the way up the sides now. Inspector Timpson, a God-fearing member of Trinity Church in Kingsbridge, was saying his prayers very softly. He'd done the Lord's Prayer twice and was halfway through the Creed. Powerscourt thought he would be eligible with these memories for a place at the Jesus Hospital where the ability to recite those prayers was one of the few requirements needed for entry. A short man with a slight limp came to take Nat Gibson's place at the tiller. Gibson went for a conference with the men inspecting the pieces of wood by the leak.

'We can't risk it,' said Coxswain Barton at last. 'I would like to nail one of these pieces of wood into the area around the leak. But putting in the nails might split the side right open. We'd be full of water and sinking inside a minute. We're going to have to wrap the plug in oilskin and try to hold it in place by other means. And we're going to have a major attempt at getting this water out of the boat or we've had it.'

One man sat with his back to the rowers' bench and pressed with his feet against a piece of wood placed over the hole.

'Hang on in there, Jimmy,' said Robbie Barton, 'you could be there some time. We've got to bail as we've never bailed before.'

More containers were handed out. Only two men were left at the oars to give the boat some leeway. All the rest were pressed into service. Barton began shouting at them as if they were galley slaves of old.

'One, two three, bail! One, two three, bail!'

Bend down, fill up, throw. Bend down, fill up, throw, bend down, fill up, throw, Powerscourt said to himself. It didn't seem to be making much difference.

'One, two, three, bail! One, two three, bail!'

Johnny Fitzgerald had gone back to Estuary House on his own. He made his way to the top floor and peered out into the night through the telescope on the top floor. He could see a few lights at East Portlemouth on the far side of the harbour and some more in the centre of town. But out to sea he could see nothing at all. None of the birds he loved so much were to be seen or heard, only the whisper of the sea. He thought of his friend out there in the English Channel. He remembered some of the adventures they had shared together. Rather like Lady Lucy, Johnny didn't think his friend was really safe on his own during these investigations. He needed someone at his side, somebody to look after him.

After five minutes' bailing, Powerscourt was sure their time was up. The water level didn't seem to be going down at all. The valiant mariner stayed locked in position, his feet anchoring the piece of wood against the hole. Powerscourt didn't think it could stop the flow but it should make it less. Then, just after the point where he was sure his arms were going to break, there was a shout from Nat Gibson.

'Well done, lads,' he cried, it's going down. Keep it up! Keep it up!'

Powerscourt felt he wasn't making his proper contribution to the evening's entertainment. He was growing sluggish. He had lost the rhythm completely. Suddenly he heard voices in his head. It was the twins, Christopher and Juliet, and they were shouting at him. 'Keep it up Papa,' they cried happily, 'keep it up.' Powerscourt smiled and redoubled his efforts.

The clouds lifted suddenly and they could see the *Morning Glory* way over to their right on the Prawle Point side.

'Great God, Robbie,' cried Nat Gibson, 'do you see where he's heading? I did tell him about it on the way out but it can't have sunk in.'

'These are the worst possible conditions for the Salcombe Bar,' said Robbie Barton, hurling yet more water out of his lifeboat. 'An ebb tide and a strong onshore wind. Great God! Would your man hear if we shouted?'

'No, he wouldn't,' said Nat Gibson, 'not a chance.'

Everybody on board the *William and Emma* was watching as they bailed, hypnotized, as the *Morning Glory* sailed towards her doom. She was nearing Limebury Point where the sand bar starts. Inspector Timpson crossed himself and quoted from the poem: 'But such a tide as moving seems asleep,/Too full for sound and foam/

When that which drew from out the boundless deep/
Turns again home.'

'Tell me if I'm wrong, Jimmy,' Lady Lucy smiled at the
young man, 'but I think it worked something like this. Mr
Allen organized everything – the details of how to find
the places, the train times and so on. Mr Harper did the
actual killings, all of them.'

'That's right. Mr Allen hired a car and a driver some of
the time to take him around. A great big car it was, too. He
sent it to Marlow and up to Norfolk so Elias Harper could
get away from that school where he killed the bursar.'

'And why are you all still here? You could have left
Salcombe a long time ago, couldn't you?'

'We could have, but the next Durban boat doesn't leave
until next week. One of the ships had to go in for repairs,
I think, so they lost a sailing.'

'And why did you come to Salcombe in the first place?
Why not hide away in a big city like London or Bristol?'

'I'm not sure you're going to believe this,' said Jimmy,
'but Mr Allen came here once as a child and liked it so
much he decided to come back.'

'Why didn't you go with him, with Mr Allen? Why were
you left here trying to escape disguised as a policeman?'

'He said that if I was with him and he was caught,
the police would assume I was guilty, too, even though
I hadn't committed any crimes. He thought I'd have a
better chance on my own.'

'Tell me, Jimmy, is there a link of some sort between
you and Mr Allen?'

There was a pause. Finally Jimmy said, 'He's my grandfather, Lady Powerscourt. My father died when I was

very young so he's more or less taken his place. I think he brought me along because he liked being with me, one of his own flesh and blood.'

The water level in the *William and Emma* dropped gradually while the men watched the drama by Salcombe Bar. The lifeboat had almost stopped moving now. The cloud had lifted again and the moon shone over the mouth of the Salcombe Estuary. The *Morning Glory* had about fifty yards left before she hit the bar. Several members of the *William and Emma* were praying now, their eyes tightly closed, their lips moving. Usually they were called out here after disaster struck. Now they were looking at disaster unfolding in front of them. Nat Gibson was leaning out over the side to get a better view. He told the crew that the yacht was carrying far too much sail. A long way behind them the grey bulk of HMS *Sprightly* maintained her watch over the proceedings. Then it happened. *Morning Glory* capsized. She keeled over very slowly like a drunken man. There was a tearing, screeching sound as if a mast or some of the rigging had broken free. There was one very long scream. There was no sign of the man aboard.

'What should we do, in heaven's name?' asked Robbie Barton. 'Should we head over there and see if we can find him?'

Nat Gibson was definite. 'No, we shouldn't. We're in no fit state to rescue anybody. It'll be all we can do to rescue ourselves.'

'What would you say are the chances of his being alive?' Inspector Timpson spoke very quietly.

'Very small,' said Nat Gibson. 'Tiny. Many ships have

been lost like that on the Salcombe Bar over the years. There have never been any survivors, never.'

Robbie Barton looked sad as he reorganized his men. No lifeboatman, trained to rescue people from the sea, gives up easily on what he regards as his primary duty. Half, including Powerscourt and the Inspector, were to row. The rest kept bailing. Robbie sent up two great flares to alert HMS *Sprightly* so she might be able to send out a rescue mission to the remains of the *Morning Glory*.

'Twilight and evening bell,' Nat Gibson was pronouncing an epitaph over the missing man, 'And after that the dark!/And may there be no sadness of farewell,/When I embark.'

It took a long time for the *William and Emma* to limp into the harbour. They dropped Powerscourt and the Inspector at the Yacht Club landing stage and staggered off to their own quarters in the centre of the town. Inspector Timpson was assured that the local doctor, who treated everybody rescued by the *William and Emma*, would attend to the wounded shoulder. Powerscourt promised Robbie Barton fifty pounds for the repair of the boat.

Inspector Devereux's prophecy on the train came true, but with only a few minutes to spare. The Chief Constable of Devon, Colonel St John Weston-Westmacott, arrived at the Marine Hotel shortly before ten o'clock, wearing a dinner jacket and a scarlet cummerbund. Inspector Devereux, as the senior officer present, briefed him on the proceedings so far. The Colonel said 'jolly good show' to all and sundry, including the head porter who scarcely deserved it. They were all assembled in the reserve dining room. Jimmy Strauss had gone down to the seafront to await the return of his grandfather.

Very wet and rather pensive, Inspector Timpson and Powerscourt came back, water squelching from their boots. Jimmy Strauss stayed behind at the waterfront, praying for a miracle that never came. The Inspector delivered the news.

'There is a chance that Allen might survive, but I very much doubt it.'

Normally it was Powerscourt who filled in the gaps and answered any remaining questions at the end of his cases. This time it was Lady Lucy who filled the company in on what she had learnt from Jimmy Strauss. Inspector Devereux reported on the further details that had been forwarded by the South African police. Elias Harper had been suspected of murder on no fewer than three occasions but there was never enough evidence for a conviction. Jimmy Strauss would be a very rich young man once the formalities had been carried out. Wilfred Allen had endowed one hospital in Johannesburg already and a school for the poor. The Inspector had also wired to the two other Inspectors, one in Maidenhead and the other in Norfolk, that their crimes had now been solved and they could regard the matter as closed.

'I think you've all done jolly well,' the Chief Constable said again. 'Four murders solved, including the villain who was taken out in a boat and never returned. And to think the centre of the whole affair was here in Salcombe, and that the final action took place on the Salcombe Bar: "For though from out our bourn of Time and Place/The flood may bear me far./I hope to see my Pilot face to face/When I have crossed the bar."'

Three days later the Powerscourts were eating breakfast in Markham Square. The case of the death in the Jesus

Hospital, Powerscourt had told Lady Lucy in the train on the way back, had been one of the most unusual he had ever investigated. Not until the very very end, he said, had we known that we were on the right track. The whole case, so full of conjecture, might have disappeared in a puff of smoke at any moment. This morning Lady Lucy was opening her mail. He checked that her husband wasn't looking as she pulled out a couple of sheets of paper and positioned them carefully behind the teapot. The correspondence came from Salcombe. Before they left she had asked Jimmy Johnston, Sergeant Vaughan's estate agent friend, to send her details of substantial properties in and around the town. Well, here they were, a Georgian rectory in a neighbouring village, and a Victorian fantasy castle high up on the cliffs west of the town, with breath-taking views of the harbour and the estuary. She peered discreetly at the prices. My word, she thought, this place is nearly as expensive as London. But look at the view. Look at the ridiculous battlements and little towers in the Victorian extravaganza. Should she say anything to Francis? Probably not, she said to herself. No point in worrying him before things have been decided.

Francis was muttering into his *Times*. Lady Lucy thought she caught the words 'bloody fools' three times. At first she thought he was talking about the House of Lords. Then she realized he was talking about a cricket match. Slowly and carefully she placed the Salcombe properties back in their envelope.

The next and final piece of correspondence felt stiff inside its expensive envelope. Lady Lucy approved. She had always had a weakness for high-quality writing paper and stationery. Inside this one was an invitation. 'Lady Hermione Devereux', it said on the top line. Then in a slightly larger typeface 'At Home'. Then 'Devereux Hall, Southwick, Northamptonshire'.

Then 'June 27th, 1910, 10 o'clock'. And then, the moment of glory, 'Dancing'. Lady Lucy looked across at her husband. 'What do you know of Devereux Hall, Francis?'

'Huge pile, Lucy, slowly falling down for lack of money. There's a lake there with an island in the middle. Very romantic, I should say, if you like that sort of thing.'

Powerscourt was well aware that his wife did like that sort of thing, as he put it. Come to that, he would have had to admit that he quite liked that sort of thing, too.

'What of it, Lucy? Are they offering guided tours? Charging coach parties to restore the family fortunes?'

'Not so, my love, not so at all. They've invited us to a ball.'

'Great God, Lucy, this must be the first time we've been invited out by one of my police Inspectors. When is this great event?'

'It's at the end of June. It must be round about the longest day of the year.'

'It seems rather a long way to go, just for a couple of dances, Lucy,' said Powerscourt, but his eyes betrayed him.

'Francis, how could you? Of course we'll go.' Lady Lucy sank into a kind of reverie. Beneath her feet she could feel the sprung floor of the ballroom. Around her glided beautiful people bedecked with tiaras and emeralds, their men wearing sashes of the military, medals shining on their chests. The air was filled with the perfume of the flowers. Strauss's 'Emperor' waltz wrapped them in its rhythms, the dancers circling the floor in time with the music.

'Oh, Francis, we must go. We can dance until the dawn and watch the sun come up from the island in the lake. It'll be magnificent, a night to remember in the heart of England!'